Dear Reader,

The *Scarlet* romances I've found for you this month offer very different backgrounds around the world and heroines with a range of intriguing and unusual jobs. I do hope you'll find  g to read as I have!

Kathryn ▓▓▓▓▓▓▓▓▓▓▓▓▓▓▓▓▓▓▓ s a heroine who's an ▓▓▓▓▓▓▓▓▓▓▓▓▓▓▓▓▓ ters in the enthralling ▓▓▓▓▓▓▓▓▓▓▓▓▓▓▓▓ old friends from Kath▓▓▓▓▓▓▓▓▓▓▓▓▓▓▓▓▓▓▓ *let* titles!). *Return to Opal Reach* by Clarissa Garland features an equally glamorous background – the international modelling circuit. But it's an artificial world which Clarissa's heroine rejects in an attempt to find happiness in the Australian Outback. Julie Garratt's heroine in *The Name of the Game* certainly isn't afraid to get her hands dirty: she's a car mechanic! And last but not least we have *Hidden Embers* by Angie Gaynor. Angie's heroine combines two challenging careers (accountancy and running a lodging house) with motherhood!

As always, I've tried to find something to suit everyone this month. Let me know if I've succeeded!

Till next month,

Sally Cooper

SALLY COOPER,
Editor-in-Chief – *Scarlet*

About the Author

Kathryn Bellamy was born in 1953 and educated at Queen Elizabeth's Grammar School in Horncastle, Lincolnshire.

After gaining excellent examination results, she worked in a bank until ill health forced her to resign. Since then, Kathryn has worked for her husband John, a chartered accountant, on a part-time basis, and has been able to spend more time writing fiction, which has always been a much-loved hobby.

Kathryn still lives in Lincoln, and her hobbies include reading, tennis and yoga.

We are delighted to bring you Kathryn's third *Scarlet* novel, featuring characters we know you've come to love and find intriguing from Kathryn's first two *Scarlet* romances, *Game, Set and Match* and *Mixed Doubles*.

KATHRYN BELLAMY

SUMMER OF SECRETS

SCARLET

Enquiries to:
Robinson Publishing Ltd
7 Kensington Church Court
London W8 4SP

First published in the UK by Scarlet, 1998

A copy of the British Library Cataloguing in
Publication data is available from the British Library

ISBN 1–85487–885–9

Printed and bound in the EC

10 9 8 7 6 5 4 3 2 1

CHAPTER 1

Ginny braked the car to an abrupt, skidding halt, then scrambled out and ran towards the brightly lit entrance to the hospital, her heart pounding with dread of what she might discover inside. She pushed open the door, recoiled momentarily as the over-warm, antiseptic smell swept over her, then headed briskly for the reception desk, uncomfortably aware of her high heels clattering too loudly in the hushed atmosphere.

'Excuse me,' she said breathlessly. 'My mother was brought here earlier tonight after a car accident – Mrs Sinclair, Ann Sinclair.'

'Just a moment.'

Ginny waited, containing her impatience as best she could, while the receptionist consulted a list of names before looking up and smiling.

'That's right; she's being settled into her room, but you should be able to talk to her for a few moments if you'd like to wait.'

'So she is conscious?' Ginny expelled a pent-up breath. 'She's not badly hurt?'

'She sustained only minor injuries,' the re-

1

ceptionist assured her, and Ginny sagged with relief. Only now could she admit to herself how frightened she had been at the prospect of losing her only close relative, for she had no siblings and her father had died three years earlier in a sailing accident.

'If you'd like to take a seat over there –' the receptionist pointed with her pen '– someone will come and tell you when you can see your mother.'

'Okay, thanks.' Ginny picked up her bag and turned around, and had to bite back a gasp of dismay as she encountered hostile glares from two almost identical pairs of moss-green eyes. Mother and son, she guessed from the resemblance, as she sat down on a hard-backed chair as far away as possible from the other two occupants of the waiting-area. She stared down at her clasped hands, but was intensely aware of the scrutiny to which she was being subjected.

After what seemed an age, she stole a look from under her lashes: the woman, middle-aged and grey-haired, but nevertheless elegant, had averted her gaze, her face in profile hard and haughty, her mouth thinned to a disapproving line. It was the man at her side who continued to stare at Ginny with . . . contempt, she thought, and she shivered suddenly, despite the oppressive heat. Why would a complete stranger take an instant dislike to her?

She risked another glance, hoping she'd been mistaken, but she hadn't. Her eyes locked briefly, shockingly, onto his, then his mouth, fuller and more sensual than his mother's, quirked into a sneer and he deliberately, insultingly, raked her from top to toe, until Ginny felt her dismay give way to mounting anger.

She sat up straighter in her chair and glared back at the insolent stranger – whose gaze had seemingly settled on her cleavage, she noted furiously, and she refused to give in to the impulse which demanded she cross her arms protectively over her breasts.

She was aware of the incongruity of her appearance, for she had dashed straight to the hospital after returning home from a party, not pausing to change out of her blue mini-dress or to remove her make-up after hearing the news of her mother's accident. But surely her unsuitable attire couldn't be provoking such animosity? She frowned slightly in bewilderment, and told herself they were probably simply anxious, waiting, as was she, for news of a friend or relative . . .

That train of thought led to another, and she wondered unhappily if her mother had been to blame for the car crash, if Ann was responsible for a member of their family being injured, perhaps seriously? They would have heard her announce her name to the receptionist – perhaps they were, not unnaturally at this moment in time, feeling hostile towards anyone named Sinclair?

She opened her mouth to ask if this was the case, then, intimidated by a black frown from the man, closed it again and instead jumped to her feet and moved back to the reception desk.

'May I use your phone?' she asked, deciding to ring Jo, the woman who, together with her husband, Barney, was Ginny's landlady, as well as her boss at the interior design business they owned. But, much more importantly, Jo had become a great friend of Ginny's, almost an older sister. It was Jo who had spoken to the police when they had called at the house, and who had then broken the news to Ginny.

'Ginny!' Jo picked up the phone on the first ring. 'How is she?'

'I still don't know any details, but she doesn't seem to be too bad,' Ginny said cautiously, crossing her fingers superstitiously as she spoke. 'I'm hanging on here until I've seen her, so don't wait up for me,' she said firmly. Jo had offered to accompany her to the hospital, but, after two miscarriages in recent years, she was once again pregnant, and Ginny had insisted she remain comfortably at home.

'Okay,' Jo agreed. 'Drive carefully.'

'Sure. Bye, Jo.' Ginny hung up and turned unwillingly back to the waiting-area, to be met by an even more ferocious scowl than before, if that were possible. She returned the glare, plus the dubious compliment of assessing the man's physical appearance, as he had hers – just to see how he liked being looked over as if he were on offer at a slave auction!

The strong features he had inherited from his mother suited him, she admitted grudgingly; his hair was black and sleek, with just one unruly lock falling over his forehead, his brows were dark and well-defined above a straight nose and that surprisingly sensual mouth, so at odds with the cold, hard arrogance of him. In fact, she decided grudgingly, he would be drop-dead gorgeous – *if* he ever

4

bothered to wipe that supercilious sneer from his face, of course!

He seemed to sense she was watching him, for his eyes flicked suddenly upwards and Ginny forced herself not to flinch away. Instead, she tilted her chin higher and openly continued her appraisal. Although he was now sprawled in a chair similar to her own, she guessed he would top six feet when standing. He had discarded his jacket and the thin shirt he wore emphasized the breadth of shoulder and the hard-packed muscles of his chest.

Ginny bit her lip and glanced at her watch – how much longer had she to wait? she wondered fretfully. She rubbed absently at her temples, for her head had begun to ache – with tiredness and tension, she guessed. Then she caught *him* watching her, and immediately squared her shoulders, reluctant to betray any sign of weakness to this stranger who appeared to have hated her on sight.

She simply wasn't accustomed to provoking such a reaction – especially in men, she thought wryly. Without undue vanity, she knew she had been blessed with rather more than her fair share of good looks, and felt somewhat piqued that this dark stranger could be so contemptuously dismissive of her slender but voluptuous frame, of her large, thickly-lashed blue eyes and the shining fall of honey-gold hair that framed the delicate bone structure of her face.

Saul Lancaster was not as oblivious to Ginny's physical charms as she imagined – he was a healthy, thirty-two-year-old male, and he wasn't blind! But he had known who she was even before she had spoken to the receptionist. Virginia Sinclair – he grimaced at the unsuitability of her name – was obviously her mother's daughter, and Ann Sinclair was trouble with a capital T, always had been.

He hadn't been able to believe his ears when his mother had phoned him at his barracks earlier that evening and asked him to come . . . Correction – he glanced at the ramrod-stiff back and carefully schooled features – his mother never asked for help, never admitted she needed anyone, but he had known she wanted his support. It was hardly surprising that she needed help over this unholy mess his father had created – even more unbelievable than Ann Sinclair's brazen nerve was his own father's stupidity! Saul thought angrily.

Newly arrived back in the country after a gruelling tour of duty in Bosnia, he had hoped to spend the evening relaxing and unwinding. Instead, here he was sitting in a hospital waiting-room . . . He sighed, shifted uncomfortably on the hard chair and glared at Ginny Sinclair, a blonde bombshell like her mother, exuding a potent aura that was part sex-appeal and part innocence. The innocence was a veneer, he knew that, hiding a mercenary, manipulative and calculating character.

All three occupants of the waiting-area lifted their heads, almost in unison, at the sound of approaching footsteps, and Saul uncoiled his athletic form from his chair with an easy grace. Ginny, too, got to her feet, but the white-coated doctor, after a quick, appraising glance at her, turned his attention to

6

the others, and she dispiritedly sat down to resume her vigil.

However, she hadn't much longer to wait: a nurse paused at the reception desk, then smiled at Ginny.

'Miss Sinclair?' she asked, and Ginny nodded, jumping once more to her feet. 'You can come and see your mother for a few minutes now,' she said, and Ginny hurried after her, temporarily forgetting the two hostile strangers.

'How is she?' she asked anxiously. 'How long will she be in hospital?'

'Just a couple of days,' the nurse told her. 'She's cracked several ribs, so she'll be rather uncomfortable for a while, I'm afraid. There's also a slight concussion, plus an assortment of minor cuts and bruises, but nothing for you to worry about,' she finished cheerfully, opening a door and ushering Ginny inside.

'Mum!' Ginny rushed towards the bed, alarmed anew at the sight of her mother, so wan and still against the crisp white pillows and sheets, with the beginnings of a livid bruise on her temple the only colour in her face.

'I'm all right.' Ann Sinclair managed a smile, but her voice was low and tremulous and she clung fiercely to Ginny's hand. 'I'm so glad you're here,' she whispered. 'And . . . I'm sorry, Ginny,' she added, inexplicably, and Ginny frowned.

'Why are you sorry? Mum – the accident – it wasn't your fault, was it?' she asked fearfully. 'No one was . . . badly hurt?' She couldn't say the word 'killed'; the possibility that her mother might have caused someone's death was unthinkable.

'I wasn't driving.' Ann looked away briefly, then turned back to face Ginny. 'I was with Davey; he was driving. He had to swerve to avoid a cyclist and we hit a lamp-post. No one else was injured, but I don't know how badly Davey was hurt; the nurse just fobbed me off when I asked,' she said, rather plaintively, but Ginny barely heard her last words.

'Davey?' she queried, wondering, for the first time, just how her mother had been spending the evening – and with whom.

'David Lancaster,' Ann supplied, her gaze again sliding away from Ginny's. 'He was driving me home, when – '

'Sir David Lancaster?' Ginny interrupted. 'The man Dad worked for? Why were you with him?' she asked slowly, watching her mother with bewilderment that gave way to mounting dismay as she noted Ann's embarrassed confusion and refusal to answer. 'Oh, stupid question, huh?' Ginny grimaced, and Ann nodded slightly.

'A little naïve,' she corrected gently. 'I've been meaning to explain it to you, Ginny, really I have, and I'm so sorry you had to find out like this,' Ann said earnestly. 'I haven't intentionally been hiding the facts from you, but the time never seemed right. I was afraid you might think badly of me,' she faltered. 'I loved your father, Ginny, you know that, but it's been three years, and I –'

'It's okay, I understand,' Ginny broke in quickly, not wanting to hear more, at least not until she'd had time to come to terms with what she had already learned. She supposed news of her mother's involvement with another man shouldn't have surprised her – Ann Sinclair was a very attractive woman, only forty-two, and it was natural that she would want to live as full a life as possible, Ginny reasoned. But . . .

'Mum . . . isn't Sir David married?' she asked uncomfortably, her thoughts on the two people with whom she had shared her vigil.

'Yes,' Ann admitted, after a pause. 'But I haven't done anything to come between them, Ginny. That marriage hasn't been a happy one for many years, if ever. Your father used to tell me about Davey and his women . . .'

'And now you're one of them!' Ginny said, more sharply than she had intended. 'Oh, sorry, sorry,' she said quickly; now was not the time for recriminations.

'Will you see if you can find out how badly he's hurt?' Ann asked tentatively, breaking a silence that was rapidly becoming strained.

'I'll try,' Ginny said, rather dubiously. 'But I doubt the staff will give me any information. Besides, his family is here; at least I think they are,' she said awkwardly, sure now that she knew the identity of the two people who had also waited for news. And it was obvious that they already knew about the role Ann Sinclair played in Sir David's life, she realized miserably.

'I suppose Alice would be informed – she is his next of kin, after all. Although I'm surprised she bothered to turn out at this time of night. Just keeping up appearances, I should imagine; she's very good at that!' Ann said tartly. 'But . . . you said "they" – who else is here?' she asked sharply.

'Her son, at a guess,' Ginny said. 'There's a resemblance, anyhow.'

'Oh, Saul!' Ann grimaced, and didn't meet Ginny's gaze. 'I thought he was still away . . . I forgot Davey said he was coming home – and he'll soon be out for good,' she sighed heavily.

'Out?' Ginny repeated sharply. 'He's been in prison?' she asked, in horror. Ann smiled slightly.

'He's not quite that bad,' she said drily. 'He's an Army officer, but he's decided to leave later this year.'

'Pity,' Ginny muttered; a nice long stint for him in the Falkland Islands or somewhere equally remote sounded a good idea to her.

'Why did you say that – was he rude to you?' Ann asked quickly, and Ginny forced a smile.

'No' She shook her head. 'He never said a word,' she said truthfully. 'Would you like me to collect some things for you from the flat?' She hurriedly changed the subject.

'Yes, please.' Ann gave her a list of items and handed over a key.

'I'll be back tomorrow – or, later today, actually.' She glanced at her watch, amazed to discover it was almost three o'clock. 'And I'll try to find out how Sir David is progressing,' she promised. 'You try and get some rest,' she whispered, dropping a kiss on her mother's cheek, then she turned and hurried from the room as unexpected tears stung her eyes. She dashed them angrily away; why on earth was she crying now, for goodness' sake?

'Delayed shock,' said a deep, male voice from behind her, and Ginny swung round, startled and more than a little angry that *he* of all people should

10

witness her weakness. She lifted her head and met his gaze coolly.

'How is Sir David?' she asked politely. 'My mother is anxious to – '

'I bet she is!' Saul Lancaster laughed bitterly. 'But you can tell her not to worry – her meal-ticket is alive and, if not exactly well, will certainly continue to keep her in the luxury she demands!'

'How dare you talk about my mother like that?' Ginny snapped at him, feeling an almost over-whelming urge to slap his hateful face.

'I dare because it's true, as you well know.' He was totally unmoved by her anger. 'She's a parasite, preferring to live off a man than do an honest day's work. A married man at that,' he added contemp-tuously.

Ginny dug her nails in her palms and counted mentally to ten before asking tightly, 'Tell me, have you ever met my mother?'

'Yes,' he said flatly, his lip curling with disdain at the memory. The one word effectively took the wind out of Ginny's sails; obviously they hadn't got along . . .

Oh, Mum, why did you have to become involved with a married man? she wondered unhappily. Family loyalty dictated she defend her mother, but she felt she was on very shaky ground. How-ever, she squared her shoulders and faced Saul defiantly.

'My father made sure his widow was well pro-vided for – she doesn't need Sir David's money,' she told him hotly. 'And, after all, he's the one cheating on his marriage vows, not her! She was only thirty-

11

nine when my father died and she's a very attractive woman – do you think she should live like a nun for the rest of her life?' she demanded. 'Because I don't, and neither would my father have wanted that,' she finished at last, breathing heavily as she tried to make some impression on the impassive man listening to her. Only, she wasn't even sure that he *was* listening! The expression of cool disdain hadn't altered, and he certainly wasn't about to apologize for his unfounded attack on her mother's character, Ginny realized, and she turned away, too weary and upset to prolong a quarrel with a man so supremely self-confident.

She stalked towards the exit without looking back, but sensed he was following her – or was he simply leaving the hospital, too? She wasn't sure, but her gait became stiff and awkward, and the spot between her shoulderblades itched as she tensed, half expecting a knife in her back! It was with a huge sigh of relief that she paused beside her car and fumbled in her bag for the keys.

'The Porsche is yours?' His voice was hard, bitter, accusatory. Ginny opened her mouth to explain it belonged to Barney Ferris, her boss, and was temporarily on loan to her since he had been banned from driving for three months after several speeding offences. But Saul Lancaster had already jumped to his own conclusions.

'I might have known! Like mother, like daughter! How did you earn that, sweetheart? The same way your mother earns her expensive car and clothes, I suppose? On your back!' he said viciously. Ginny flinched, but said nothing and continued searching frantically for the elusive keys; her only desire was to escape. After what seemed an age, her hand closed over them and she bent quickly to unlock the door.

'Just a minute! I haven't finished with you yet!' Saul snarled, grabbing her arm as she tried to scramble into the haven of the car and swinging her around to face him.

'Let me go!' Ginny struggled futilely in his grasp, but he was too strong for her and pushed her hard against the side of the car, encircling her wrists with a grip of iron. She stared up at him, her heart thumping with fear of the barely restrained violence she sensed in him.

'I don't know what you're talking about,' she faltered. 'I told you, my father left her well provided for —'

'Cut it out!' Saul interrupted harshly. 'Don't give me any more of that rubbish about your mother being a lonely widow, doing no harm to anyone, when you know as well as I that she didn't wait until your father was dead before getting her claws into a richer man! I suppse you'll tell me next that you've never even wondered why an experienced sailor such as your father was fool enough to get caught in a storm and drown?'

As soon as he had spoken the words he wished them unsaid, but it was too late, and he hardened his heart against the anguish in Ginny's eyes. He well remembered how Ann Sinclair could assume just that same expression of injured innocence in an attempt to lay the blame for her own misdeeds on someone else.

For Ginny, it was as if time stood still, as if she

had been standing there with this man towering over her for eternity. There was nothing but his face, set in dark, cruel lines, and his words, dripping like corrosive acid into her numbed mind. Then, as she realized the full implication of what he had said, insinuated, waves of sickness engulfed her and she sagged weakly, would have fallen if not for his continuing manacling of her wrists.

'That's not true – none of it,' she whispered at last, shaking her head in denial. 'I hate you! You're despicable!'

'Not me, sweetheart! Women like you and your mother cause most of the trouble in this world,' he told her, releasing her suddenly and stepping quickly away from her, as if afraid he would become contaminated by her touch.

Ginny couldn't even bear to look at him; all the fight had drained from her and she groped her way into the car and forced her trembling fingers to start up the engine. Somehow she succeeded in finding the correct gear and reversed out of the parking space, speeding off into the night without a backward glance at the man who had so casually and carelessly shattered her peace of mind.

It couldn't be true, she told herself over and over, as the powerful car tore across an almost deserted London. It simply was not true! Mum would never have cheated on Daddy, never! And Ann didn't want or need Sir David's money. Saul Lancaster was wrong about that, wrong about everything! Hateful, arrogant man, appearing out of the blue and flinging his cruel barbs, neither knowing nor caring if his taunts held any truth. Which they didn't,

14

Ginny reiterated fiercely. No doubt he had heard a biased version of events from his own mother and had not bothered to check the veracity of the jealous outpourings of a bitter and spurned woman.

She assured herself again and again that Saul Lancaster was a liar or, at best, mistaken, but his words reverberated around her brain and she felt the devastating loss of her father as keenly as she had on the awful day of his death. More than three years had passed, but right now she felt as if it had just happened; the pain was just as raw and unbearable. Only this time she couldn't try to console herself with the thought that he had not been in pain, nor had he suffered a long illness, but had been happy and fulfilled and had died quickly and suddenly, doing something he loved. That comforting notion had been destroyed forever by Saul Lancaster!

The police car had been following her for quite a distance, siren blaring and lights flashing, before Ginny finally became aware of it. Even then she slowed and veered to the left, thinking she was impeding its progress, but then she groaned as she realised *she* was the target. It was the last straw, and she dropped her head to the steering wheel and burst into tears.

'Crying's not going to help,' said the stern voice of the rather portly police officer who had approached her open window. Ginny blinked furiously to stem the tears and drew a deep breath.

'I'm not crying because you pulled me over,' she told him, indignant that he thought her so feeble. Then words failed her, and she couldn't begin to explain the real source of her distress. 'I've just come from the hospital,' she finally mumbled.

'You'll be going back there, in an ambulance, if you continue driving as you were,' he informed her tartly. 'You were doing over fifty miles an hour in a thirty miles per hour zone, and you went through a red light at the last junction.'

'Oh, God, did I really?' Ginny gasped, appalled; she couldn't even remember seeing any traffic lights . . . She hoped he wouldn't ask her for the car's registration number. Would 'I don't know; it's not my car' be an acceptable answer? she wondered. Somehow she doubted it, and she bit her lip hard to contain the near-hysterical laughter bubbling up inside her. She heard, almost as if he were in the car, Saul Lancaster's voice diagnosing 'delayed shock', as he had earlier, and that sobered her.

'I'm awfully sorry,' she began, scrabbling in her bag for her licence before remembering she had jettisoned most of her usual clutter earlier that evening, putting only the necessities in the smaller clutch bag that matched the shoes she was wearing. 'I'm afraid my licence is at home,' she said, in a small voice, but the police officer had straightened up, his attention no longer on Ginny but on an open-topped sports car that had driven past at speed, then performed a U-turn and begun heading back towards them. Four youths were in the car, the three passengers standing up and yelling while the driver repeatedly honked his horn.

'Leave her alone!' yelled one of the youths, and Ginny grinned before hastily schooling her features.

'I've never seen them before in my life,' she assured the police officer quickly, and he nodded, rather grimly.

16

'Watch your speed in future,' he admonished her, then hurried back to his patrol car to go in pursuit of the youths. Ginny drew several deep breaths, then continued on her way, dutifully keeping an eye on the speedometer.

Finally she reached her destination, and climbed wearily out of the car, glancing up at the windows of the three-storey house in Chelsea which was her home. Well, the top-floor flat was hers, rented from Barney and Jo, who owned the entire building.

Barney was away in Rome, on business for a few days, but because of her pregnancy Jo had elected to remain behind. Ginny noticed the lights blazing from the lower floor, and realized Jo had stayed up after all. She sighed, wanting nothing more than to crawl into bed and escape into sleep, but instead turned and mustered a smile from somewhere as Jo, clad in her dressing-gown, pulled open the front door.

'You ought to be in bed,' Ginny scolded.

'I was, but I couldn't sleep. Were you able to speak to your mother?' Jo asked as she ushered her young friend into the sitting-room, frowning worriedly as she noted Ginny's pallor beneath her make-up, the bruised look to her eyes and signs of recent tears.

'Yes, she's going to be okay.' Ginny sank down tiredly onto the sofa. 'A bit sore, with a couple of cracked ribs and concussion, but she asked me to take her make-up and curling tongs in tomorrow, so she must be feeling all right.' She tried to smile again, but burst into tears instead and sobbed unrestrainedly while Jo tried to comfort her.

'I don't understand,' the older woman said help-

17

lessly, her pleasant features creased with concern and her large brown eyes soft with sympathy. 'If your mother's okay . . .'

'Oh, I'm sorry.' Ginny sat up straighter and sniffed inelegantly, fumbling for a handkerchief until Jo silently handed one over. 'I haven't cried this much since Daddy died,' she muttered, wiping her eyes and struggling for composure. 'Mum is okay, really; it's that horrible man. I hate him,' she said fiercely.

'Who?' Jo was justifiably bewildered. 'The man who caused the accident?' she hazarded a guess.

'No . . . he said dreadful things about Mum, and about Daddy and – oh, Jo, what if it's true?' Her lower lip trembled ominously and she had to wipe away more tears. Jo, with remarkable patience, sat quietly beside her and listened while Ginny, more or less coherently, told her about her discovery of her mother's affair with a married man and, far worse, what the married man's son had implied about Ginny's father committing suicide.

Jo wasn't the least bit surprised to hear about Ann Sinclair – she'd never liked the woman, thinking her shallow and selfish, not a bit like Ginny despite the physical resemblance – but was horrified to hear what else Saul Lancaster had felt it necessary to divulge. Her lips tightened in anger; that had been cruel, even if it were true . . . *especially* if it were true, she amended.

'Was there an inquest into your father's death?' she asked calmly, practical as ever.

'Yes,' Ginny nodded. 'The coroner said it was an accident; a storm blew up out of nowhere and must

18

have taken him unawares,' she remembered, with a slight lessening of pain.

'There you are then,' Jo said robustly. 'This Saul Lancaster doesn't know what he's talking about! Forget him, Ginny, he certainly isn't worth crying over.'

'I'm not crying over him,' Ginny denied quickly. 'It was just the thought that if she was being unfaithful, Daddy might have known . . . been so unhappy . . .' She swallowed back fresh tears. 'If he went off on the boat – oh, not to intentionally commit suicide – but if he was too preoccupied to notice signs of a storm approaching or, worse, if he did notice and didn't really care . . .' She had to stop speaking again, and Jo hugged her tightly.

'There are an awful lot of "ifs" in that, you know,' she said gently. 'That dreadful man ought to be shot! He was probably only repeating malicious gossip he's heard from his own mother – hell hath no fury and all that. How much do you know about the family?'

'Not much, really.' Ginny considered. 'Daddy was chief accountant for Lancaster Electronics, and I met Sir David a couple of times when I called at the office. He seemed quite nice,' she acknowledged, if somewhat grudgingly. 'He always asked how I was getting on at school – you know, the usual stuff grown-ups ask – and he slipped me a fiver once or twice,' she remembered.

'I wouldn't pass that information on to his son!' Jo advised drily, and Ginny smiled slightly.

'Oh, he already thinks I'm a gold-digger – or worse. You should have seen his reaction to my driving a Porsche!' She grimaced at the memory.

'Have you ever met *him* before?' Jo asked.

'No, and I hope I never do again!' Ginny shuddered. 'Men!'

'Talking of men . . .' Jo decided to change the subject. 'You came home alone from the party – what happened to Jamie?'

'Oh.' Ginny grimaced again. Jamie Calvert, her current but probably now ex-boyfriend, was becoming a pain, his initial easy charm and good humour increasingly giving way to bad-tempered sulking as she continued to refuse to sleep with him. 'We had a row.' She shrugged dismissively; the argument with Jamie seemed to have happened long ago, instead of just a few hours since, and certainly no longer seemed important. 'Oh, God, look at the time!' she exclaimed. 'You must go and rest,' she said guiltily, getting to her feet. 'I promised Barney I'd look after you while he's away.'

'I'm fine.' Jo hugged her. 'You're far more tired than I am. Go to bed – and don't even think of coming into work today,' she added.

'Okay, thanks,' Ginny was too tired to argue. 'Goodnight, Jo. And thanks for listening,' she said, kissing her cheek and returning the hug before making her way outside, then turning through the archway at the side of the house and climbing the metal staircase that gave access to her own flat.

Once inside, she pulled off her clothes and let them lie where they fell, pausing only to clean her teeth before falling into bed and pulling the covers over her head.

CHAPTER 2

It was almost noon before Ginny came slowly, reluctantly awake, and she groaned slightly as the events of the night before came flooding back to her. Feeling groggy, and still tired, she sat for a moment on the edge of the bed before putting a call through to the hospital to check on her mother's progress. Ann was recovering well, and Ginny left a message to say she would be visiting later, then, still yawning hugely, she took a long, hot shower; that, together with several cups of strong black coffee, helped her feel capable of facing the day.

Jo had already left for the office, and Ginny drove straight to St John's Wood, to the luxury block of apartments where her mother had moved after being widowed. At the time, Ginny hadn't questioned Ann's motives for sweeping away the past, but now, haunted by Saul Lancaster's cruel taunts, she hesitated in the small hallway and wondered. Wondered, too, how often Sir David Lancaster had been here . . . had stayed overnight . . . maybe he had even bought the place for . . . his mistress.

Oh, stop being so melodramatic, she chastised

herself. The sale proceeds of the family home in Kingston upon Thames would have been more than enough to purchase the flat! The days were gone when titled, wealthy men hid away their paramours in love-nests!

She briskly set about collecting up the clothes and toiletries Ann had requested, but couldn't help noticing signs of a man's presence in the flat. There was a large brown towelling robe hanging next to Ann's smaller pale pink one in the bathroom; a razor and bottle of aftershave in the cabinet; a paperback thriller on the bedside table that she was sure wasn't her mother's taste in reading matter.

Her lips tightened at the sudden vision she had of Ann hurriedly hiding all traces of Sir David's occupancy whenever she, Ginny, was due to visit. Or had she been blind? Had the signs always been there, but she had missed them? And, if that were so, had she also been similarly ignorant of the true state of her parents' marriage? Had they merely put on an act of loving solidarity for her benefit?

Stifling a sigh, Ginny moved into the sitting-room in search of the letters Ann had asked for, together with her writing paper and chequebook. She found them in the small antique writing desk; beneath them was a recent bank statement, and her stomach lurched as the name 'D. Lancaster' seemed to jump off the printed page at her. Knowing it was wrong to pry, but unable to stop herself, she slowly picked up the folded statement and straightened it out, her fingers suddenly cold and trembling.

There it was, in black and white, confirmation of what Saul Lancaster had told her: a standing order credit from his father, a separate item from the pension payment Ann was entitled to receive from Lancaster Electronics. This was a personal payment from Sir David to her mother – for services rendered, presumably, Ginny thought wretchedly.

She felt sick at the discovery, and sat heavily on the sofa, glancing around at the expensive furniture, noting anew the richness of the deep-pile carpet, the luxurious velvet curtains. The room seemed to stifle her, and she jumped to her feet, grabbed up the small suitcase she had packed and hurriedly left the flat. She couldn't go on torturing herself; she had to confront her mother, and the sooner the better, she decided grimly.

She was too cross to bother buying flowers or fruit, as she had intended, and went instead straight to the hospital, marching determinedly along the corridor and walking into her mother's room without knocking. Ann looked up from the armchair in which she was sitting and greeted her with a smile.

'I'm so glad you could get away from work,' she said warmly. 'I'm going mad here, with no one to talk to. Private rooms are all very nice, but a bit lonely . . .' She trailed off, aware there was no answering smile on her daughter's face.

'I've brought everything you asked for.' Ginny dumped the case unceremoniously on the bed. 'Is there anything else I can do for you, Mother?'

'Now I know I'm in trouble,' Ann grimaced. 'You only ever call me "Mother" when you're upset with me. What's wrong, Ginny? Davey, I suppose?' she sighed.

'Yes. I want to know how long it's been going on,' Ginny said tightly. 'And why all the secrecy?'

'I didn't tell you because I was afraid of your reaction – apparently I was right to be.'

'How long?' Ginny repeated.

'Not long,' Ann hedged, wishing she knew if Alice or, even worse, Saul had been trying to cause trouble. Alice's accusations could be shrugged off as the rantings of a jealous woman, but Saul . . . *His* revelations could not be so easily dismissed. 'Davey and I were just friends for a long time before we became lovers. He was good to me, after your father died –'

'Are you sure it was after?' Ginny interrupted, her voice as hard as Ann had ever heard it.

'Yes, of course! You surely don't think . . . ? Ginny, I don't deserve this,' Ann said angrily. 'I resent this . . . interrogation! My private life is my own affair. I –'

' "Affair" being the appropriate word.' Ginny curled her lip scornfully.

'Don't you talk to me in that tone of voice!' Ann half rose from her chair, then subsided with a grimace of pain. 'I've heard more than enough, Ginny,' she warned her daughter. 'I give you credit for being mature enough to choose the men in your life, so kindly afford me the same courtesy,' she said coolly, very much on her dignity.

'The men in my life aren't married! Nor do they pay me!' Ginny wasn't going to back down that easily. 'The fact that Sir David is married is his problem, or his wife's, but how the hell do you justify taking money from him? How can you do

24

that, Mum?' Ginny asked desperately.

'How do you know about that?' Ann asked uncertainly.

'I saw your bank statement,' Ginny said dully.

'I see – so you've been spying on me, Ginny?'
Ann snapped.

'No, it was lying beneath your chequebook,
which you asked me to find. I couldn't help but
notice it. I didn't believe Saul Lancaster when he
accused you of living off his father, but he was
right!'

And that really hurt, she realized, and only hoped
she would never again have to face the blistering
contempt in his eyes. It had been bad enough last
night, when she had truly believed him to be a
malicious liar – it would be intolerable to meet
him again, with the knowledge that he had been
more aware of the true situation than she.

'I do not "live off" Davey.' Ann mustered her
dignity. 'I can live quite comfortably off the pension
and savings your father left me.'

'Then why don't you?' Ginny asked coldly.

'Why should I?' Ann shrugged. 'Davey is a very
wealthy man; he likes me to wear expensive clothes
and jewellery when we go out. This is really none of
your concern, Ginny,' she continued. 'I'm forty-
two and widowed – I don't have to ask your
permission for the way I choose to run my life.
It's easy for you to sit in judgement – you're young,
and have a career. For twenty years my role was that
of wife and mother, then you grew up and went to
college, and my husband died . . .' She stopped
speaking and dabbed at her eyes with a handkerch-

ief, while watching Ginny from beneath her lashes.

'Oh, Mum!' Impulsively Ginny rushed over and dropped to her knees beside her mother's chair. 'I'm sorry,' she whispered. 'I've been so busy with my own life that I hardly ever stop to wonder if you're lonely. And I'm sorry I've been so . . . critical today. But Saul Lancaster made me so angry . . . so frightened . . .'

'Frightened?' Ann smoothed back a stray lock of Ginny's hair in a gesture of reassurance. 'What did he say to frighten you?' she asked gently, feeling she was now in control of the situation.

'He . . . he told me you started your affair while Daddy was still alive,' Ginny mumbled.

'That's simply not true,' Ann said emphatically. 'But, even if it were, why would that frighten you? What else did Saul say?' she asked.

'He . . .' Ginny took a deep breath. 'He suggested Daddy knew about you and Sir David, and that maybe his accident was . . . deliberate,' she said painfully.

'Oh! What a monstrous thing to say!' Ann exclaimed, genuinely shocked. 'You surely didn't believe him, Ginny?'

'I don't know what to think. He seemed so sure of himself,' she said miserably.

'He's wrong about that,' Ann said firmly. 'Now, listen to me carefully – your father loved us both; you know he did. And even if – *if*,' she stressed, 'there had been a problem between him and me, he would never have taken his own life, would never have left you. You must never give it another thought. Promise me you won't?'

26

'Okay.' Ginny nodded finally.

Ann relaxed and began talking of other things until the air of tension in the room lessened perceptibly. Ginny stayed for around an hour, then Ann decided she would like to take a nap, so Ginny took her leave.

She stepped out into the late afternoon sunshine, then her eyes widened in dismay as she caught sight of the unmistakable figure of Saul Lancaster climbing out of a sleek black Jaguar, which he had parked next to Barney's Porsche. He was dressed in Army uniform and seemed even more menacing than he had the night before.

Her first instinct was to flee, to avoid further confrontation, but she was too late – he had already seen her, and she refused to grant him the satisfaction of knowing how he terrified her. Even though she was shaking with trepidation, she determinedly tilted her chin higher and stood her ground as the man she had hoped never to see again walked towards her, his long strides eating up the distance which separated them far too quickly. She wasn't sure what to expect: more insults and hostility, or perhaps he would just ignore her, she thought hopefully. But never in a million years would she have correctly guessed his reaction to seeing her.

Saul hardly recognized her as the vamp from the night before; he knew she was in her early twenties, but with her blonde hair pulled back into a ponytail, her face devoid of make-up, she looked around sixteen in her jeans and T-shirt. She also looked apprehensive, he noted, and bounded quickly up the steps to forestall whatever she might be about to say.

'Ginny, darling!' he exclaimed, loudly enough to be heard by the man watching, and lifted her bodily off her feet.

Ginny, too stunned to protest, looked into the well-remembered thickly lashed dark green eyes.

'Don't say a word,' Saul muttered, then bent his head to kiss her – it seemed as good a way as any of keeping her quiet! He moved into the hospital, still holding her tightly, his body moulded to hers until they were out of sight, whereupon he dropped her unceremoniously to the floor. Ginny stumbled slightly and struggled to maintain her balance.

'Are you nuts?' she hissed, ostentatiously wiping her hand across her bruised mouth. The kiss, if indeed it could be called that, had been hard and punishing, not in the least lover-like.

'Keep your voice down!' Saul took her elbow in an unfriendly grip. 'There's a reporter outside – that little display was for his benefit,' he added, lest she harbour any idea that he might have been over-whelmed by lust at the sight of her. 'You and I need to talk – in private,' he added, as a passing nurse eyed them curiously. 'Excuse me.' Saul bestowed a warm smile and an appreciative glance upon her. 'Is there a coffee-shop on the premises?'

'Yes, down the hall and to your right.' The nurse pointed the way, blushing as he rewarded her with another smile. Ginny put her finger down her throat and feigned nausea.

'Behave yourself,' Saul said sternly, shaking her arm none too gently before pulling her after him in the direction of the coffee-shop. Ginny went, not that she had much choice in the matter, unless she were willing to leave without her arm, she thought crossly, but had to admit to a certain curiosity.

Saul silently pointed to a secluded alcove where they could talk without being overheard, and Ginny went to sit down while he fetched two cups of coffee from the self-service counter.

'How much do I owe you?' she asked, reaching for her purse when he plonked a cup down in front of her. 'I'd hate you to think I'm sponging off you,' she added sweetly.

'Grow up and listen,' Saul advised tersely, taking the seat opposite. 'It's about the guy who stopped to help my father after the accident.'

'What about him?' It was the first Ginny had heard of a Good Samaritan.

'He works on a newspaper – not one of the nationals, but he has contacts with someone working on the *Post*'s gossip column. This guy recognized my father and, although he didn't know the woman with him, he *did* realize she wasn't my mother . . . Are you following this?' he demanded suddenly.

'Sure, but I don't see –'

'You will, when you read the piece in tonight's evening paper – which is likely to be repeated in the *Post* tomorrow morning. There's nothing too blatant – just a couple of question marks about the identity of the "mystery" lady who was in Sir David Lancaster's car at midnight. I think I know how to stop any further speculation, but I need your help.'

'Why on earth should I bother to help you?' she asked, outraged.

'Because if you don't, your mother will find

herself in the middle of a scandal. The whole world will brand her as "the other woman", not just me,' he informed her coolly.

'I don't understand all the fuss – since when have the tabloids been interested in the head of an electronics company?' she asked, perplexed.

'Since he decided to enter politics, of course,' Saul replied, rather impatiently. 'Didn't you know he intends standing for Parliament?'

'No.'

'Well, he is; he's fighting a local by-election in July,' Saul explained.

'Oh. Well, I suppose I can appreciate why he doesn't want any adverse publicity right now,' Ginny said, although she privately felt Sir David Lancaster had brought it all on himself. 'But it's too late to pretend he was just giving an acquaintance a lift home, or something like that – surely the hospital staff realize the situation?'

'They'll keep quiet,' Saul said dismissively. 'I'm sure they know better than to talk out of turn to reporters.'

'Why are you so determined to cover up for him?' Ginny asked curiously. She felt it far more likely that he would use the threat of publicity to force Sir David to end the affair he so obviously disapproved of.

'He *is* my father. And I think he'll be a very good MP, if he's given the chance,' he said. 'But my main concern is for my mother. She's a very proud woman, and –'

'And she hates my mother!' Ginny burst out.

'With good reason, I'd say,' Saul snarled back,

then made an obvious effort to control his temper. 'She's had to live with the knowledge of this affair for some time,' he continued, more quietly. 'And while she was able to convince herself it was a secret from her friends and family she could tolerate it – just. But if this blows up into a public scandal it will destroy her. I'm not exaggerating, Ginny,' he added quickly, as if sensing she was about to interrupt. 'This couldn't have happened at a worse time, with the wedding so close.'

'Wedding?' Ginny frowned, and he sighed with exasperation, running his fingers through his hair, leaving it ever so slightly ruffled, a wayward lock of black hair falling onto his forehead making him seem almost. . . . boyish, Ginny thought. Certainly he suddenly looked human, which was a great improvement, she decided.

'Don't you ever talk to your mother?' he asked irritably.

'Yes, of course,' she said, but rather defensively, having realized in the space of a few hours that she apparently knew very little about her mother's life. 'But she's mentioned nothing about a wedding. Who's getting married?'

'My cousin, Amanda, to Viscount Mallory – you must have read about it in the press?'

'No.' Ginny shook her head, and he sighed again.

'It's going to be a big Society affair – his parents are the Earl and Countess Rosemont, and members of the Royal Family will be present at the ceremony. I personally couldn't care less about the gossip, but it's important for my mother to be able to attend with her head held high and without having to contend with snide comments from the other guests. You can understand that, can't you?' he asked.

'I suppose so.' Ginny shrugged, for it was hard to feel compassion for the granite-faced Lady Lancaster. 'But I don't see what you expect me to do about it.'

'It's quite simple – I want you to come out with me,' he said, matter of factly.

'Excuse me?'

'You heard. I want you to come out with me, very publicly. Amanda and her fiancé are throwing a pre-wedding party tomorrow night, and a lot of young Mallory's aristocratic friends will be there, so the press will be out in force. It shouldn't be too difficult to make sure our presence is duly noted and photographed.'

'I suppose not, but I don't see how that helps . . .'

'Just listen,' Saul advised quietly, but with a distinct edge to his voice which told Ginny he didn't relish being interrupted. 'I've told the *Post* that both you and your mother dined with us yesterday evening to celebrate my return from Bosnia, and that my father was driving your mother home afterwards when the accident occurred.'

'They won't believe that!' Ginny objected. 'He'd have driven me home, too.'

'Not if I'd wanted that pleasure for myself,' Saul said softly, and Ginny stared at him as comprehension slowly dawned.

'That's right.' He nodded, a slight smile tugging at the corners of his mouth. 'What more natural than for me to want my parents to meet my girl-friend and her mother?'

'I was right – you are nuts,' she told him flatly.

'No, I'm not. It will work like a dream. We only need to be seen in public a couple of times to stop the gossip – the party tomorrow night, and possibly the wedding as well. So, what do you say?' he asked calmly, taking her agreement for granted, Ginny thought furiously.

'My God, you've got a nerve!' she snapped at him. 'Last night you and your mother looked at me as if I'd crawled out of the gutter, and now you expect me to do you a favour! I'm to pretend to be your girlfriend until after this wedding and then be dropped like a hot potato, I suppose!'

'You can drop me, if that's what's bothering you,' he said calmly. 'We can stage a public fight – I'll even let you slap my face,' he offered.

'Hmm, it might be worth it, just for the satisfaction of blacking your eye,' Ginny muttered, her own eyes glinting with anticipation. Saul noticed the gleam and grinned slightly.

'So, do we have a deal? Will you go along with my plan?'

'I don't know,' Ginny wavered, lowering her gaze. She ought to tell him to go to hell, after all he had said to her, but, on the other hand, her mother would also benefit from the subterfuge . . .

'Well?' Even when asking a favour, he couldn't mask his impatience – or his dislike, she noted painfully.

'I already have plans for tomorrow night,' she prevaricated, although after the last row with Jamie she thought it doubtful that she would see him again.

'Cancel them.'

'Oh! You really are –' she began, and he put up a hand for silence.

'I had other plans, too,' he told her, rather grimly. 'If I can make the sacrifice, so can you. After all, your mother is the cause of this whole mess!'

'Oh, sure she is! She hijacked your father's car and kidnapped him, didn't she?' Ginny snapped. 'I've only met your father briefly, on a couple of occasions, but he certainly never struck me as being a wimp.'

'He isn't – far from it,' Saul said shortly.

'He built up Lancaster Electronics from nothing, didn't he?' Ginny went on. 'That must have taken a great deal of strength of character, and a lot of determination.'

'So? What's your point?' Saul asked impatiently.

'So, he's hardly the type of man to be pushed around, is he? Yet you continue to blame my mother for his misdeeds, as if she's leading him around by the nose . . .'

'Not his nose – quite a different part of his anatomy!' Saul snorted, and Ginny flushed.

'Do you have to be so crude?' she asked stiffly.

'You can still blush,' Saul noted wonderingly. 'This is getting us nowhere – will you come out with me tomorrow or not?' he asked briskly.

Ginny hesitated, then, 'I suppose so,' she agreed reluctantly. Saul nodded slightly.

'Right. We'd better get our story straight – Amanda is an inquisitive so-and-so and will ask

34

endless questions,' he said resignedly. 'I've been away with the Army for the past four months, so we don't need to explain why she's not heard of you until now. I suggest we say we met at Christmas, shortly before I left for Bosnia, and have kept in touch by letter.'

'Okay.' Ginny nodded.

'I'm thirty-two, I'm leaving the Forces later this year to join a security company here in London – Lennox and Coupland; they supply chauffeur-bodyguards, that sort of thing,' he explained briefly. 'I'm also in the process of buying a house here – I'll give you a copy of the brochure in case Amanda asks you about it,' he continued, and she nodded again. 'Okay, your turn, tell me something about yourself – something that I can repeat to Amanda, of course.' He smiled evilly.

'I'll leave out the sordid details, then.' Ginny smiled sweetly. 'I wouldn't want to shock her. I'm twenty-two, I'm in interior design –'

'Specializing in bedrooms, presumably?' Saul interrupted.

'That's right,' she agreed calmly, then added, 'Sorry to disappoint you, though, my area of expertise is in children's bedrooms, not their fathers'.'

'What a waste,' Saul remarked mockingly. 'Hobbies?'

'Apart from gold-digging? Keep-fit, tennis, swimming . . .'

'Okay, that's enough,' he said abruptly. 'I'd better have your address and phone number,' he said, and while she complied, he scribbled down contact numbers where she could reach him. 'I'll pick you up at eight tomorrow,' he said, checking the address before slipping the piece of paper she'd handed him into his pocket.

'Fine.' Ginny nodded, and got to her feet.

'I'll walk out with you – I doubt that reporter is still hanging around, but he might be waiting for a quote,' he said, falling into step beside her.

A somewhat uneasy silence reigned as they walked, and Ginny began to feel more and more uncomfortable. How could she possibly spend an entire evening with this man? she thought unhappily, and only hoped his cousin was easier to get along with.

'How long will your father be in hospital?' she enquired politely, simply to break the silence – it was quite beyond her to feel any sympathy for someone named Lancaster!

'For about a week,' Saul replied absently, glancing around for a glimpse of the reporter. 'Then he'll be hobbling around on crutches for a while, which should be good for a few votes when he's out canvassing,' he added cynically – and somewhat callously, Ginny thought, suppressing a grin as she stole a sideways glance at him.

We ought to call a truce, she thought next; we're both in the same mess, courtesy of our parents. Talk about the sins of the fathers! Or mothers, in her case, of course.

The burgeoning feeling of empathy lasted all of thirty seconds, destroyed by Saul's glower when he again caught sight of the Porsche.

'I had no idea wallpapering paid so well,' he remarked snidely. Ginny sighed heavily.

'It belongs to Barney Ferris, my boss,' she informed him.

'That doesn't surprise me in the least. You get along well with him, do you?' Saul asked suggestively.

'Yes. Very well. I even live in his house,' Ginny said, knowing he would misconstrue the remark, and his darkening scowl confirmed that he had.

'Won't he have something to say about you coming out with me tomorrow night?'

'He's away on business right now. Besides, he's very . . . accommodating,' she said, as she unlocked the door and slid behind the wheel.

Saul stood back and watched as she drove away, a ferocious frown marring his handsome features. Ginny gave a demure smile and a regal wave in passing, suddenly looking forward to the following evening. She couldn't wait for him to meet Barney – and Jo, of course! It was a pity she and Saul weren't going out for dinner – he could eat humble pie, she thought happily.

Saul watched until the Porsche was out of sight, his thoughts about the Sinclairs, mother and daughter, unprintable. He cursed them both roundly, then turned his thoughts to his father, who was presumably suffering the male menopause or the onset of early senility!

Before seeing Ginny he had been on his way to visit his father, but suddenly he changed his mind and fished in his pocket for his car keys. The mood he was in now, he felt more inclined to break Sir David's second leg than to enquire politely about the first!

* * *

'You're going to do what?' Jo demanded incredulously the next morning, when Ginny outlined her plans for the evening.

'Go out with Saul Lancaster,' Ginny repeated calmly. 'Will it be okay if I wait for him down here? I'd really like you and Barney to meet him,' she said demurely. Too demurely, Jo thought.

'What are you up to?' she asked suspiciously.

'Nothing.' Ginny was all wide-eyed innocence, and Jo snorted her disbelief. But she was in too much of a hurry to get to the hairdresser before Barney's return to question Ginny further.

'Don't forget Barney's flight is due at two-thirty,' she reminded Ginny as she dashed out of the door.

'I won't,' Ginny promised, checking her watch. She also wanted to call at the hospital . . . a dress! She had to have a new dress! And Jamie . . .

She grimaced; she had to cancel their date for the evening. She did that first; unfortunately he was out, so she left a message on his answering machine.

The truth – a bald 'I don't want to see you any more', seemed a trifle harsh, so she merely made her excuses for the evening, explaining briefly about Ann's accident. That done, she mentally crossed one chore off her list and headed for the hospital.

'You're going to do what?' Ann demanded, even more shrilly and incredulously than Jo had, scarcely an hour earlier. Ginny sighed heavily, rubbed her assaulted eardrums, and outlined Saul's plan.

'I don't like it,' Ann said nervously.

'It's not my idea of fun, either,' Ginny retorted, a little annoyed by her mother's ingratitude. 'But it is for your benefit, after all. Unless you want everyone to know about you and Sir David?' she said thoughtfully. 'I suppose it would force his hand,' she added. She felt Sir David Lancaster was currently having his cake and eating it; perhaps it was time he made a choice between the two women in his life and gave a total commitment to just one of them. She said as much to her mother, but Ann quashed that idea immediately.

'I don't want Davey to get a divorce and marry me! He's had a string of mistresses for most of his married life – and that's a hard habit for a man to break,' she said cynically. 'I'm very fond of him, but I wouldn't be his wife for all the tea in China! Alice is more than welcome to continue being Lady Lancaster, especially if he is elected as an MP. All that canvassing for votes and kissing babies! Ugh.' She shuddered visibly, then turned her thoughts back to the more immediate problem. 'You won't let Saul turn you against me, will you?' she asked anxiously. 'God knows what lies Alice has told him about me.'

'He's already made his opinion of both of us perfectly plain,' Ginny said, rather ruefully. 'This isn't going to be a proper date – just a propaganda exercise. Look, I must go now, I have to pick Barney up from the airport,' she said quickly, briefly kissing Ann's cheek before rushing off on her next errand.

'All right, come again soon.' Ann forced a smile, which faded as soon as Ginny was out of sight. This threatened to get out of hand . . . if Saul and Ginny ever sat down for a real heart-to-heart chat . . . After much deliberation, Ann finally picked up the phone and dialled the Lancaster family home in Richmond, something she only ever did when Alice was away.

'Alice? This is Ann Sinclair.'

'Yes?' The one clipped word was as cold as ice.

'Your son and my daughter. It has to be stopped – don't you agree?' There was a short, tense silence broken only by Alice Lancaster's sharp intake of breath.

'The hospital staff have evidently given you the key to the drugs cabinet,' she said frostily. 'My son would never –'

'Saul is taking my daughter out this evening,' Ann interrupted. 'He's covering for David by telling the press we all enjoyed a cosy dinner together on Thursday night. He thinks he can put a stop to any gossip by being seen in public with Ginny.'

'Oh.' Alice paused to weight up the pros and cons of Saul's action. 'If that's all it is, I don't see any problem,' she said finally.

No, you wouldn't, Ann thought, but I do! Ginny had always been a Daddy's girl, and if Saul Lancaster divulged all he knew, Ann was afraid she could lose her daughter, her only child, for ever. But she strove to keep calm; Alice must not guess that she, Ann, had much more at stake in this matter.

'My daughter's an exceptionally pretty girl, as I'm sure Saul has already noticed. And, although he may dislike me, he'll soon discover that Ginny is very sweet-natured – more her father's daughter than mine. And Saul always liked and respected my husband, as I recall,' Ann added pointedly. She forced herself to say nothing more; she mustn't

40

seem too eager, must count on her conviction that Alice would loathe to have her son become involved with the daughter of her husband's mistress. After all, it was almost incestuous!

'I'll certainly keep an eye on the situation, and take steps if necessary,' Alice said finally, and broke the connection without another word.

Ann slowly replaced the receiver and sank back against the stack of pillows. She hadn't felt this vulnerable and frightened since Richard had died, and at least then she'd had Ginny for comfort, but now . . .

It had been madness, becoming involved with David Lancaster, knowing that Saul, if he ever learned of the affair, could ruin everything if he so chose. Perhaps that had been part of the thrill, she thought now, but at the time it had merely seemed a risk worth taking; she'd never dreamed that Ginny might one day become embroiled.

Ah, Ginny. She smiled sadly as she thought of her daughter; she was still so young, still believing in Mr Right and true love that would last for ever. She would never understand Ann's need for excitement, a craving that Richard Sinclair had reluctantly accepted, realizing the occasional fling took nothing away from their own relationship.

Ann sighed as she imagined the horror on Ginny's face, the contempt she would feel for her own mother – she might even believe Saul's assertion that Richard had committed suicide – and she wiped away a tear, then folded her arms protectively across her chest. But the pain she was feeling had nothing at all to do with her injured ribs.

CHAPTER 3

Shortly before eight o'clock, Ginny picked up her beaded clutch bag and checked its contents, then surveyed herself once more in the full-length mirror in her bedroom. The dark lilac silk dress suited her to perfection, its colour making the blue of her eyes seem almost violet, emphasized as they were with toning eyeshadow.

Her make-up was a little heavier than usual, her honey-blonde hair teased and curled into deliberate disarray. She practised pouting vampishly at her reflection as she applied another coat of lipgloss, then grinned happily as she left the flat, making her way, somewhat precariously in her high heels, down the iron steps which clung to the outside of the three-storey house.

She tapped lightly on the kitchen door before letting herself in. Jo turned from her task of preparing a meal for herself and Barney.

'Have you time for –? Wow, you'll knock his eyes out!' she breathed.

'That's the general idea – you don't think it's a little too much, do you?' Ginny asked for reassurance.

'How could it possibly be too much? If there was any less material to that dress, it wouldn't even be a swimsuit!' Jo retorted, then relented when Ginny began to look anxious. 'You look gorgeous,' she told her – truthfully; the dress clung like a second skin, but Ginny had such a glorious figure she could easily carry it off.

'Thanks. You look pretty good yourself,' Ginny remarked, arching one eyebrow. Jo had a satisfied glow about her which had nothing whatsoever to do with her pregnancy but was a direct result of her reunion with her husband. Ginny sometimes envied Jo and Barney their closeness, the deep love they shared which was apparent in every look and gesture. She was determined to one day find that for herself, not to settle for second best as so many people seemed to do. She'd bet her last penny that the Ferris marriage would endure, and neither would ever cheat on the other.

'Oh, shush!' Jo flushed slightly, and gave Ginny a small push in the direction of the sitting-room. 'Come and have a drink with us before Saul arrives.'

Barney was comfortably asprawl in his favourite armchair, a glass of Scotch by his side as he perused the evening paper. He was a huge bear of a man, tall and broad, with a bushy beard and twinkling brown eyes. He glanced up as they entered, then did a visible double-take as he registered Ginny's appearance, which was in complete contrast to the jeans-clad, fresh-faced girl who had collected him from the airport earlier.

'That dress is positively indecent,' he informed

her. 'I hope this guy Lancaster doesn't have a blood pressure problem.'

'He soon will have!' Jo put in tartly. 'It's getting quite chilly – aren't you going to wear a jacket?' she fussed.

'And cover this up?' Ginny's brows rose.

'I take your point; it was a stupid question,' Jo acknowledged, with a sigh. 'Ignore me – I was just being sensible again.'

Barney stood up to pour wine for Ginny and tomato juice for Jo, then resumed his seat.

'Now it's my turn to ask what is probably a stupid question,' he said. 'But aren't I correct in thinking you dislike this Lancaster bloke? That you're only going out with him tonight as some sort of PR exercise?'

'That's right,' Ginny and Jo confirmed simultaneously.

'So, why all the packaging?' he asked.

'It's because I dislike him that I want to bowl him over,' Ginny tried to explain. 'He's in for a shock or two this evening,' she added, rather smugly.

'A heart attack, more likely,' Barney muttered. The doorbell pealed at that moment, and he had no opportunity to question Ginny further.

'That will be him!' Ginny felt a surprising surge of anticipation. 'Will you go and let him in, please, Barney?'

'Why me? Oh, all right,' he agreed amiably, and while he went to answer the summons Ginny dragged Jo back out of the room.

'I don't want him to see you for a minute,' she whispered, and Jo shrugged philosophically and obediently waited out of sight. Ginny's heart was pounding nervously. She wished she had positioned herself better so she would be able to see Saul's face when Barney opened the door to him.

'The stairs to Ginny's flat are through that archway – rather difficult to spot unless you know, I'm afraid,' Barney was explaining. 'But she is here, as it happens, having a quick drink with us, so do come in and join us . . .'

'Now you,' Ginny murmured to Jo, and continued watching through a crack in the door as Saul came into view. He looked immaculate, she noted, in a dark suit and crisp white shirt . . . He also looked rather stunned, she thought gleefully, his eyes widening in surprise when Jo walked towards him.

'I'm Barney Ferris,' Barney introduced himself, and drew Jo possessively to his side. 'And this is my wife, Jo,' he added proudly.

'I'm pleased to meet you.' Jo shook the hand Saul automatically held out to her.

Saul muttered a greeting as he registered two facts: one, Ginny lived in a separate flat, and two, her boss – whose car she drove and with whom she'd said she lived – had a very obviously pregnant wife. Ginny had lied to him, deliberately misled him, and he wondered why. Then he stopped thinking – almost stopped breathing – as his gaze moved to meet Ginny's challenging stare when she stepped into the open doorway.

God, she's a sexy piece, he thought, his body reacting instantly at the sight of her voluptuous beauty.

For a brief moment something flickered hotly in the depths of his dark eyes, but almost at once it was as if a shutter came down, blanking out any emotion he might have felt, Ginny thought, rather crossly. But what had she expected? That he would fall on his knees and beg her forgiveness for misjudging her? Hah! Fat chance!

'Good evening, Ginny,' Saul greeted her coolly.

'Hello,' she responded, rather stiffly, but he had already turned his back on her to resume his conversation with Barney, casually discussing his own recently completed tour of duty in Bosnia and Barney's trip to Rome.

Suddenly the low-cut clinging dress, which showed her curves to perfection, no longer seemed so seductively glamorous as she had believed; now she thought it skimpy and rather too obviously sexy, and she had the uncomfortable feeling that she merely looked . . . well, tarty.

'Are you okay?' Jo asked gently, touching her arm to gain her attention. Ginny looked up and forced a smile as she nodded.

'I'm fine,' she lied.

'He's certainly drop-dead gorgeous – try and enjoy yourself,' Jo urged. Ginny nodded again, glancing over at Saul and Barney, belatedly realizing Barney was relating the tale of her encounter with the police on Thursday night.

'I've been banned for three months for speeding,' Barney was grumbling, for his disqualification still rankled. 'But Little Miss Blue Eyes sheds a few tears and gets away scot-free,' he said disgustedly. 'I told her, I could've sat and cried for a fortnight, but the cops wouldn't have let me off with just a caution.' His complaining was good-natured, Ginny knew that, but she was afraid that Saul did not.

'Nor me,' Saul agreed with Barney, his tone light and pleasant, but the look of disdain he bestowed upon Ginny sent her spirits plummeting. 'But then, you and I don't possess Ginny's powers of persuasion,' he added meaningfully. God, he thinks I bribed the police officer with my body to avoid a speeding ticket, Ginny thought, too miserable to feel angry, and she quickly downed the remainder of her wine before setting the glass down with a decided thump.

'Are you ready to go?' Saul asked coolly. 'Where's your wrap?'

'Oh, I . . .' Ginny suddenly felt the need for an enveloping coat – floor-length, preferably, she thought wretchedly. Jo, sensing her discomfiture, came quickly to her rescue.

'I'm sorry, Ginny, I promised I'd lend you my shawl, didn't I? I won't be a minute.' She hurried from the room, returning moments later with a delicately patterned silk shawl in shades of pink and purple, which complemented Ginny's dress perfectly.

'Thanks, Jo, you're a miracle-worker,' Ginny whispered gratefully, wrapping the shawl protectively around her bare shoulders.

'That's okay. Bye. Have a nice time!' Jo called gaily after them, then exchanged a slight grimace with Barney.

'Why on earth didn't you tell me you weren't living here alone with Ferris?' Saul asked irritably, as he paused to unlock the car.

'You didn't give me a chance!' Ginny began crossly, then had to wait, fuming, while he slammed the passenger door shut and took his time walking around to climb behind the wheel. So much for her expectations of a grovelling apology! 'It's hardly my fault if you go around jumping to conclusions,' she started again, once he was seated beside her, but he merely grunted at that.

The journey, thankfully short, passed in silence, until Saul had parked the car.

'Can you remember the tale we're telling my cousin?' he asked abruptly.

'Of course. We met at Christmas and I've been pining for you ever since!' Ginny said sarcastically.

'Good,' he said mildly, which made her grind her teeth in annoyance. 'Try and look as if you actually want to be with me,' he sighed.

'I'm not that good an actress,' she retorted waspishly, then they both forced a smile as a camera flashed nearby.

The nightclub where the party was being held was one of Ginny's regular haunts, and she began to relax in the familiar surroundings, smiling a greeting to several people she knew while Saul scanned the crowd for a glimpse of his cousin.

'They're over there.' Saul pointed to a noisy group of people gathered in one corner and they began making their way over, his hand warm on her waist as he guided her through the press of people on the dance floor, using his superior height and breadth to force a passage.

'Saul! I'm so glad you could come! How's Uncle David?' A pretty redhead jumped up from her seat as they approached, and reached up to kiss Saul's cheek.

'He's much better – fractious at having to lie in bed, though,' Saul responded.

'I know. At least a broken leg will put a stop to his womanizing for a while!' She giggled. 'I'm not supposed to know about it, but I overheard Mummy talking to Aunt Alice,' she confided. 'Apparently the latest is a real –'

'Shut up, Mandy,' Saul interrupted, but with a smile. 'Ginny will think all Lancaster men can't be trusted,' he added lightly, drawing Ginny forward. 'Mandy, I'd like you to meet Ginny Sinclair – Ginny, this is my cousin Amanda Ashton,' He made the introductions and the two girls exchanged smiles, albeit rather stiffly in Ginny's case, even though she knew the other girl had only been repeating Alice Lancaster's bitter words.

'I love your dress,' Amanda said admiringly, knowing she could never hope to get away with such a skin-tight design.

'And I love what's inside it!'

Ginny turned in surprise at the interruption, and discovered a grinning young man hovering at her shoulder and peering unashamedly at her cleavage.

'Back off, Nige,' Saul told the newcomer, but good-naturedly. 'She's with me. Ginny, this is Mandy's appalling kid brother, Nigel.'

'I am very pleased to meet you!' Nigel Ashton enveloped Ginny's hand in both of his and lavished kisses on the back of her wrist. 'Saul is far too old for you, you know,' he told her solemnly. 'Come and dance with me instead?'

'I don't think so.' Ginny gently disentangled herself; for this evening she would have to remember that so far as these people were concerned she and Saul were an 'item', that she was the girl he had invited home to meet his parents – accompanied by her mother, of course!

Amanda's fiancé, Charles, the Viscount Mallory, was an extremely pleasant young man, not at all the aristocratic fop Ginny had been half expecting, and she enjoyed chatting to him while Saul went to organize a fresh round of drinks. Charles was telling her about the secret honeymoon plans he had made when Saul returned and handed Ginny the glass of wine she had requested.

'Don't tell Mandy,' Charles reminded her, as he moved away to make room for Saul.

'Don't tell Mandy what?' Saul demanded. 'Up to your tricks already, Ginny? A viscount would be quite a catch – even better than your mother's . . . er . . . achievements,' he added snidely.

'You rat!' Her fingers tightened around the stem of her glass and she was tempted to throw the contents in his face – that should ensure they received the publicity he craved!

'We'd better get onto the dance floor – we are here to be seen, after all,' he said briskly.

'Of course.' Ginny got to her feet. 'Would you like me to gaze adoringly into your eyes, too?' she snapped.

'If you like,' he said indifferently, and she gritted her teeth.

'I do *not* like!' she snapped. 'Unless you want to run the risk of having me throw up?'

'Whatever's the matter?' he asked irritably as he guided her on to the dance floor, but he didn't bother to wait for a reply. 'Relax, for God's sake,' he said a moment later, as she resisted his efforts to draw her into his embrace. 'I only want to dance with you!'

As he spoke he ran his fingers lightly down her spine. Ginny instinctively arched away from his touch, only to find her body pressed against his, his arms holding her captive. Saul smiled lazily down into her outraged face and she knew the apparently casual gesture had been a deliberate ploy – which had worked, damn it!

Ginny told herself it was just a dance, nothing more, but the male scent of him filled her nostrils, tantalizing her, making her aware of the muscular strength of him as he moulded her body to his, and she turned her face away, hoping desperately he couldn't feel the betraying pounding of her heart.

He was right to ask what was wrong with her, she thought wildly, physically jumping in alarm when his hand accidentally brushed her bare shoulder, the brief contact sending frissons of pleasurable sensation coursing throughout her entire body. She was sure he must know what was happening to her, and her cheeks burned with mortification.

But Saul was fighting his own battle, and he was wondering if he was more like his father than he had previously thought! If Ann Sinclair has this effect on the old man, I can understand why he risks everything, he thought, drawing the soft, incredibly sexy body even closer, and lightly brushing her collarbone with his mouth.

51

Ginny shivered, despite the heat, and cast her eyes desperately around the dimly lit room, searching for someone or something to distract his attention.

'Saul!' she said urgently.

'Mmm?' he murmured, his breath warm on her cheek, and she jerked her head away.

'There's a man sitting at the bar – he's watching us.' She had noticed him earlier, while talking to Charles Mallory, and had thought nothing of it, but now she was sure his attention was fixed unwaveringly on her and Saul, his eyes briefly meeting hers then sliding abruptly away whenever she glanced in his direction.

'So? Most of the men in this room have been staring at you – don't tell me it's a novelty?' he mocked.

'Not that sort of watching!' Ginny said impatiently. She could differentiate between healthy male appraisal of her face and figure and this probing, intense scrutiny to which she was being subjected. 'He's just sitting at the bar, alone, watching our every move. Do you think he's from the press?'

'Could be.' Saul moved slightly so he could check the occupants of the bar stools. 'What does he look like?'

'Blond, with a beard, around forty – he's sitting about halfway down.'

'I've got him.' Saul let his gaze travel casually past the man, then he looked down at Ginny. 'Don't look so worried,' he chided. 'He's only checking the story I issued to the press. What do you say we really give him something to watch?' Without waiting for a reply, and before she could guess his intention, he bent his head swiftly to hers.

'Saul . . .' He captured her protest with his mouth, effectively silencing her, and, after a moment's brief struggle with herself, Ginny surrendered to the expertise of his touch, luxuriating in the thoroughness with which he leisurely explored her mouth.

She made no demur when his tongue began probing the inner sweetness; instead, she found herself returning the caress, avidly wanting to taste and touch him, as he was her. She gave a small moan and pressed closer; there was no longer even a pretence of dancing. In fact, she was no longer aware of her surroundings, and she wound her arms tightly around his neck, stretching on tiptoe so their bodies were almost welded together from shoulder to hip.

She felt her nipples harden against the wall of his chest, and, with a surge of purely female triumph in her own sexuality, knew his arousal was as great as her own. Such a blatant indication of desire for her body would have repelled her in any other man, but for some inexplicable reason it seemed right and inevitable that she and Saul Lancaster should affect each other so . . .

'What the hell . . . ?' The interruption, when it came, was not from the stranger at the bar but from Jamie Calvert, the man who had until very recently been Ginny's boyfriend. From his reaction, he obviously thought he still was.

He grabbed Ginny's arm and tore her from Saul's embrace, his blue eyes ablaze with fury. Ginny could only stand and gape at him stupidly, too shocked and bereft at the abrupt transition from ecstasy to reality to know what to do or say to defuse the situation.

'Jamie . . .' she faltered.

'You remember my name! How gratifying!' he snarled.

'Who is this, Ginny?' Saul snapped, and she wasn't sure if the coldness in his voice was intended for her or for Jamie. Her, probably, she thought, stealing a look at him, her heart sinking as she noted the grim set to his mouth. It was already hard to believe that same mouth had been hotly demanding on her own, only moments before . . .

'Er, James Calvert . . . Saul Lancaster.' She pulled herself together sufficiently to introduce the two men, although they looked more eager to shake each other by the throat than by the hand, she thought, swallowing nervously.

'I don't want to know his bloody name!' Jamie took Ginny's arm in a painful grasp. 'How's your poor, sick mother?' he sneered.

'Take your hands off her. Now.' Saul spoke quietly, but his very stance was aggressive, Ginny thought, as he squared up to the other man. 'I'd like an answer, please, Ginny,' Saul continued, with what she was sure was deceptive calm. His narrowed eyes were still firmly fixed on Jamie, although he seemed to relax slightly when Jamie obeyed him and released his hold on Ginny's arm.

'He's . . . oh, hell!' Angry and embarrassed, for they were now the centre of attention, she faced up to Saul, not knowing who she was the most angry with – herself, for allowing herself to be talked into this charade, Saul, for putting her in this situation, or Jamie for making a scene. 'I told you I had a date for tonight,' she reminded Saul. 'And you insisted I cancel it. Which I did. So you can just deal with the consequences!' she stormed at him. Then she fled to the sanctuary of the cloakroom, pushing her way through the crowd, which parted easily to let her pass, more interested now in whether a fight would break out between the two angry men.

Ginny locked herself into a cubicle and waited for the trembling to subside. God, what a mess! And she could hardly blame Jamie for being angry, she acknowledged fairly, wishing fruitlessly that she had made more of an effort to speak to him that afternoon instead of leaving a message. She should have told him their relationship was over; well, it certainly was now, she reflected, with grim humour. Even if she'd wanted him, she doubted he would forgive her for that blatant display with Saul.

Her cheeks burned with mortification at the memory of her total abandonment to his kisses, and she placed her fingers over her lips, slightly swollen from the demanding pressure of his mouth. It was just as well they had been interrupted when they had – another few minutes of that assault on her senses and she would have allowed him to make love to her, right there on the dance floor! How was it possible that a man she hardly knew, and certainly didn't like, could arouse her as no other man had ever done before?

'Ginny! Are you in here? I've brought your bag.' Amanda's voice rose above the general hubbub in the cloakroom, and Ginny reluctantly unlocked the door and emerged, a trifle shamefaced.

'It's all right, he's gone,' Amanda told her.

'Who has – Saul?' Ginny asked, and was strangely relieved when Amanda shook her head.

'No, the other guy. Saul, er, escorted him from the premises!' Amanda giggled. 'Who is he? You've not been two-timing Saul, have you? I know he's been out of the country for four months, but he won't stand for that sort of behaviour,' she warned.

'Oh, no, nothing like that. I went out with Jamie for a few weeks before I even met Saul,' Ginny muttered awkwardly. It was the truth, just, but she hated deceiving this girl, whose party she and Saul had hijacked for their own purposes, and where they had just caused a scene.

'Oh, I see. No harm done, then,' Amanda said cheerfully. 'How did you get along with Aunt Alice the other night?' she asked next, and Ginny suppressed a sigh. More lies.

'Well, she seems rather . . . formidable,' she said finally, remembering the glacial stares that had come her way from Lady Lancaster in the hospital waiting-room.

'And some!' Amanda agreed. 'She's always frightened me witless,' she confided. 'Although she's being very nice to me at the moment – my marriage meets with her approval!' She grimaced.

'I can imagine,' Ginny said drily. 'Congratulations, by the way. I was talking to Charles earlier; he seems to be a really special man.'

'He is,' Amanda said dreamily. 'He's so easygoing and laid-back; I always know where I am with him

. . . not like Saul.' She shot a sly look at Ginny. 'You've got your hands full there; it's a pity you rushed off and missed seeing him sort out your ex. Mean, moody and magnificent – that fits Saul to a T, don't you think?'

'Well, two out of three,' Ginny muttered to herself, then she asked nervously, 'Is he very angry?'

'He did look a bit grim when he told me to come and fetch you,' Amanda admitted. 'Perhaps you'd better go and placate him, tell him there's nothing going on between you and that other guy,' she suggested.

'Okay,' Ginny agreed reluctantly. But first she checked her appearance in the mirror, reapplied lipstick that Saul's assault had erased and fluffed out her hair.

She straightened her shoulders and walked, head held high, out of the cloakroom, with Amanda dogging her heels – although Ginny was grateful for that; Saul could hardly rage at her with his cousin hanging onto every word, she reasoned – wrongly, as it happened.

'Get lost, Mandy,' Saul instructed her, taking Ginny's wrist in a firm grip, and, with a sympathetic shrug, Amanda did as she was told.

'I'm sorry; I had no idea Jamie would be here tonight –' Ginny began.

'Obviously,' Saul bit out, not looking at her as he dragged her towards the exit. Ginny struggled to free herself, but to no avail – when she literally dug in her heels he simply put one arm around her waist and lifted her bodily off her feet.

'All right! Cut out the caveman tactics! I'm as anxious to get out of here as you are!' she gasped out, and he dropped her as suddenly as he had picked her up, waiting impatiently while she retrieved Jo's shawl from the attendant.

His face was as black as thunder, dark brows drawn menacingly together in a frown, and the look in his eyes . . . Ginny shivered, and not from the relative coolness of the night air when they emerged on to the pavement. She summoned up her courage to face him – after all, they had surely now received the publicity he wanted? What was his problem? she wondered, beginning to feel as annoyed as he evidently did.

'I don't know why you're so angry,' she said, somewhat aggrieved, then she backed away from the barely restrained fury in him when he rounded on her.

'You don't?' Saul asked incredulously. 'Apparently you enjoy the spectacle of two grown men fighting over you, lady, but I resent like hell being forced into such a distasteful situation! I ought to have let him keep you,' he added contemptuously. 'Although I doubt he wants you now.'

In fact, he remembered suddenly, Calvert had wished him luck 'with the frigid bitch'. Saul had been too angry to register the import of the remark at the time, but now he wondered. Ginny, frigid? Impossible. With those eyes, and that body? And the way in which she had responded to his kisses? Most of his anger drained away, and he had to force himself to concentrate on what she was saying.

'I did tell you I had a date for this evening,' Ginny was reminding him.

'And I assumed you had cancelled it.' Saul ran his fingers irritably through his hair. 'And why the hell couldn't you have been honest with that guy?'

'Honest?' Ginny echoed, her mouth falling open in disbelief. 'What do you call lying to the press, not to mention your own cousin? This whole evening has been a sham – at your instigation, I might add – and you have the gall to stand there and accuse me of not being honest!'

'Keep your voice down!' Saul glanced around, looking for the bearded reporter. The man had followed him and Calvert out of the club earlier, but hopefully that little scene, aggravating though it had been for Saul, had merely added credence to the story that he and Ginny were an item. Suddenly he tensed, and placed a restraining hand on Ginny's arm. 'We're being watched again,' he murmured, which effectively silenced her.

Even more effective was his kiss.

Ginny resisted for a moment, then gave in to the insistent pressure of his mouth, sighing a little as his hands, warm and firm, drew her body closer to his. Saul had convinced himself that the kiss was necessary to provide conclusive proof for the watcher, but he didn't fool himself for long. He wanted this girl, wanted to touch and taste every curve and hollow of her lovely body, wanted her soft skin pressed against his, wanted to hear more of those pleasured sighs from deep in her throat. He temporarily forgot she was Ann Sinclair's daughter, forgot why they were together. At that moment

Ann Sinclair could have single-handedly tried to bring down the government for all he cared. All he could think of was having Ginny, naked and willing, in his bed. It didn't even matter that she was a gold-digger – hell, he had money, lots of it; she could have his credit cards, trust funds, the keys to his Jag . . .

He broke the kiss long enough to murmur, 'I think we should go somewhere more private to finish this, don't you?'

'I . . .' Ginny stared up at him, horrified by the intensity of her desire to say yes! He doesn't even like you, she reminded herself sternly. He hadn't even wanted to take her out for the evening, but now he wanted to use her body as compensation for the inconvenience of changing his plans! Say no, she instructed herself, but no sound emerged. Saul took her silence as acquiescence, and began moving away to head back to his car. The breaking of the contact of their bodies restored some semblance of common sense to Ginny and she held back.

'No,' she said, but the refusal sounded reluctant and unconvincing even to her own ears.

'No?' Saul repeated, in disbelief. His tone of voice went some way to stiffening her resolve.

'No,' she said, more firmly. 'I am not a slut!'

'Did I say that?' he asked, frowning a little, although whether the scowl was one of annoyance at being thwarted or caused by perplexity was difficult for Ginny to judge.

'Not exactly, but you certainly implied it,' she told him haughtily. 'What else would you call a girl who goes to bed with a man she barely knows?'

'Co-operative?' Saul suggested. Ginny glared at him, then she saw the hint of laughter in his eyes and in the curve of his mouth . . . oh, that mouth . . . and her anger dissolved. She gave a reluctant smile.

'Please, Saul, I just want to go home – alone,' she said quietly.

'Are you sure about that?' He gazed at her intently. 'I thought you were a sexy little piece when I saw you at the hospital on Thursday night,' he went on, almost musingly. 'But you really pulled out all the stops tonight, didn't you? And why? To make me want you.' He answered his own question, and Ginny shook her head despairingly. 'Yes,' he insisted. 'Well, you succeeded – doesn't that make you feel good?' he asked, pushing his hands into her hair and forcing her head up to meet his gaze.

'No, it's not what I want . . .'

'Liar. Only your little plan backfired somewhat, didn't it? Because you want me just as much,' he said confidently.

'No . . .' Ginny tried again to protest, but his fingers caressing the nape of her neck were distracting her.

'Yes, you do,' Saul contradicted, a slight smile tugging at the corners of his mouth. 'If that clown Calvert hadn't interrupted us when he did, we'd be in bed together right now,' he said softly, his voice as deep and caressing as his fingers on her skin.

'Then I'm glad Jamie did see us!' Ginny tried to break free; the images his words conjured up were unbearable.

'Stop lying to me, Ginny.' He spoke indulgently, almost as he might to a wilful child, so sure he was right, so sure his will would prevail.

His hands in her hair held her captive and he bent and kissed her again. Ginny summoned up the last of her wavering resolve, her hands balled into fists at her sides as she tried to deny the hot surge of desire spreading through every nerve and pore.

'No!' She tore her mouth free, her breathing ragged. 'Don't! You mustn't do that,' she finished on a whisper.

'Oh, but I'm afraid I must,' Saul contradicted.

'No! I won't be a . . . a brief distraction. You don't even like me, and I certainly don't like you! Now, just let me go home!' She stepped away and hailed a passing cab, which ignored her and sailed on by. Ginny almost stamped her foot in vexation, so desperate was her need to escape him.

'Don't be so melodramatic – I'll drive you home, if that's what you really want,' Saul said, rather curtly. 'I'm not the kind of guy to make a girl find her own way home because she spurns my advances,' he informed her, sounding rather affronted, Ginny thought – perhaps he expected an apology!

She glowered at him, but didn't resist when he placed his hand beneath her elbow and began walking swiftly to where he had parked the Jag.

It was a silent, tension-filled journey back to Chelsea; at least, it was for Ginny, Saul soon had something else to wonder about.

After a couple of routine checks in his rear-view mirror, he became positive the bearded reporter was following them. It didn't add up. He must have the information he needs, Saul thought, frowning. He wondered if his father had already made enemies in political circles, enemies who were determined to find a scandal to finish his career before it had even begun.

Ginny was also absorbed in her own thoughts. Why on earth had she set out to attract him? Instead of dressing to kill, she should have worn a bin-liner, she thought now, when it was far too late. He was right, of course, she *had* wanted him to desire her, so she could laugh in his face when she rejected him; what she had failed to take into account was that the attraction might be mutual . . .

She made as if to scramble out of the car as soon as Saul braked to a halt, but he placed a restraining hand on her arm.

'Careful, we've been followed,' he said quietly.

'Oh, no!' Ginny twisted around to see. 'The reporter? What more does he want?' she demanded.

'Maybe he's a voyeur, and gets his kicks watching us,' Saul said, only half joking. Perhaps the man was waiting to see if he and Ginny spent the night together, wanted a photograph of him leaving the flat in the morning? He frowned, wondering how to resolve that particular dilemma . . .

'I really don't care any more,' Ginny said tiredly. At that moment she couldn't care less what the press might have to say about Sir David's car accident, or his prospects of becoming an MP – anyhow, wasn't a mistress almost a necessity? she wondered cynically. If every MP had to lead a private life that was above reproach, the House of Commons would be empty! Right now she didn't even care if her mother *was* branded 'the other woman' for all the world to read about. 'I've done all the play-acting I intend to,' she informed Saul tartly.

'I'll go and have a word with him, tell him I have to be back at my barracks,' Saul decided, clambering out of the car. 'I'll see you safely inside first,' he added.

'Okay.' Ginny led the way through the arch to the rear of the house and climbed the iron stairs, fumbling in her bag for her keys.

She opened up and switched on the light, but remained in the doorway as she turned to face Saul, unaware of the picture she presented, her blonde hair haloed in the light, her large eyes shadowed with fatigue and a betraying tremor to her mouth giving her a look of vulnerability.

'Are you sure you'll be okay?' Saul asked, frowning slightly.

'I'll be fine,' she assured him. He hesitated, then reached out and ran one finger gently down her cheek before stooping and bestowing a brief kiss on her mouth. He pulled back at once, the brief caress over before she had time to object, a wry smile on his face. His fingers still delicately traced her features, then his thumb brushed her upper lip.

'Goodnight, Ginny; sleep well,' he said finally, then he turned and walked back down the stairs, and was rapidly swallowed up by the darkness.

'Huh! Fat chance,' she muttered. She ran inside and moved over to the window which overlooked the street, standing cautiously to one side as she peered out at the scene below.

She saw Saul stride over to the parked car, but before he reached it the watcher revved up and roared off, evidently unwilling to face his prey-turned-attacker. Ginny let the curtain drop, feeling unaccountably depressed as she heard Saul start up the Jag and then disappear into the night.

CHAPTER 4

On Sunday morning, Alice Lancaster was sitting in her elegant and immaculate drawing-room, sipping her fourth cup of strong black coffee. She was dressed for church, in a navy blue suit adorned by a single strand of pearls, but her thoughts were not of a religious nature as she waited for her son to put in an appearance.

She had been in bed, but not asleep, when he had returned home – late – and had forced herself to remain in her room, not to seem too anxious about the events of the evening. It troubled her that he hadn't bothered to consult her before putting in place his plan to halt any scandal concerning his father and the Sinclair woman, and she wasn't sure that she approved of his action any more than Ann Sinclair. But, unfortunately, the time was long past when she'd had any influence over Saul, she thought, with a small sigh.

'Saul!' she called out when, eventually, she heard his footsteps as he ran lightly down the stairs.

'Yes?' He appeared in the open doorway, dressed in a black tracksuit.

'Coffee?' she enquired first.

'No, thanks; I'm going for a run before breakfast,' he told her.

'About last night – did the party go as expected?' Alice asked casually.

'Mmm, I think so. There were certainly plenty of press photographers around; we'll just have to wait and see what appears in the papers,' he said.

'There'll be no need for you to see the Sinclair girl again, then?' Alice probed.

Saul almost laughed out loud. No need? He had been aching with need all night long . . .

'I shouldn't think so,' he agreed.

'Good.' Alice relaxed slightly. 'I think you've done enough to help your father over this sordid matter,' she said stiffly.

'It was for your benefit, too,' Saul reminded her. 'At least now he'll have to clean up his act; he must realize his private life will come under even more scrutiny if he's elected –' he broke off when the phone rang, and picked up the receiver. 'Lancaster. Yes, she's here.' He held out the phone to his mother. 'It's for you – someone called Dawson.'

'Oh, yes, thank you.' Alice flushed slightly as she took the handset and made no move to talk to the caller. 'What are your plans for today?' she asked Saul.

'A run, then I'll call in at the hospital before heading back to Aldershot,' he told her.

'In that case I won't see you again – I'm going over to the Ashtons for lunch,' she said.

'Okay. Bye, Mother.' It didn't occur to either mother or son to exchange a kiss or a hug, and Saul

67

disappeared to work off his frustrations by running himself into the ground.

Alice waited until she heard the door close behind him before speaking to her caller.

Saul would have been surprised if he could have seen the man: blond, bearded, around forty years old. It was the 'reporter' who had taken such an interest in him and Ginny the night before, who was, in fact, a private detective hired by Alice to check on Ginny Sinclair and, more importantly, to alert Alice if there seemed any likelihood of a relationship developing between the two young people.

Alice Lancaster had lost her husband to the mother; she was damned if she would stand idly by and lose her son to the daughter. Men were such fools, she thought contemptuously; a pretty face and a willing body drove all sense from their heads!

'Yes, Mr Dawson?' she said crisply. 'What have you discovered about the girl?'

Dawson briefly outlined Ginny's background: her job, her flat, the people she spent her time with . . .

'I spoke to several neighbours; she lives alone and there's no steady boyfriend, although there was a fracas at the nightclub involving a jealous young man – your son threw him out,' he told her. Alice winced at that; so, already Saul was making a fool of himself over the chit. 'His name's James Calvert,' Dawson continued. 'I had a word with him and I have his address – I thought he might prove useful.'

'Yes, that's possible,' Alice agreed thoughtfully, storing the information away for the future, but hoping it wouldn't be necessary to involve anyone else in the affair. 'Thank you, Mr Dawson, I think that's enough for the present – I'll contact you again if I require further assistance.' She broke the connection, picked up her gloves and prayer book, put on her hat and left the house to walk the short distance to the church she attended every Sunday.

The newspaper coverage was rather more than Saul or Ginny had hoped for – a photograph of them appeared in the *Post* on Monday, and was picked up by several of the tabloids in the days that followed. It was a picture of them outside the nightclub – a picture of Sir David Lancaster's son and the daughter of the 'mystery lady' who had been with Sir David on Thursday night. The report was what they had wished for, of course; unfortunately, in the photograph they appeared to be welded together . . .

Ginny cringed with embarrassment and was teased mercilessly, especially by Jo. Lady Lancaster also cringed, and promptly revised her opinion of Dawson's usefulness; the situation was in danger of getting out of hand. Sir David laughed, not a bit displeased, and couldn't understand Ann's discomfiture – he thought it was great that their children were getting along so well.

As for Saul . . . it seemed to him as if every soldier under his command had obtained a copy of the picture; dozens littered the barracks and parade ground, dozens more appeared on noticeboards and even in the Officers' Mess. He almost found himself wishing World War Three would break out, just to cause a diversion.

In Sussex, one of Saul's former Army colleagues, Nick Lennox, saw the item while casually perusing the newspaper and simultaneously feeding bread and butter soldiers dipped in boiled egg to his young daughter, Suzy. Nick and Dale 'Coop' Coupland ran the constantly expanding firm of Lennox and Coupland, hiring out bodyguards to the rich and famous. It was this company that Saul was intending to become a part of once his Army days were over.

'Who's that? Saul?' Melissa, Nick's wife, a former Wimbledon Champion, craned her neck to see. 'It must be serious – I didn't think Saul ever took his girlfriends home to meet his parents,' she commented.

'He doesn't usually visit his parents, full stop,' Nick responded.

'No?' Melissa raised an eyebrow.

'No. He's never said very much, but I always gained the impression that his childhood was rather bleak. His father was very busy and his mother rather cold and distant . . . She's certainly a looker,' he added, giving the photograph of Ginny Sinclair rather too much attention, Melissa thought, snatching the paper from under his nose.

'Who is? Saul's mother?' she enquired tartly, and Nick grinned.

'How do you feel about inviting them down soon?' he asked. 'The accountant has finished the books, so Saul can make a final decision on joining the firm. I'll ask Coop to come down as well,' he added. All three had served in the same regiment and had been good friends for a number of years.

70

'That's okay with me,' Melissa agreed. 'Make it this weekend, if possible – I'll soon be busy preparing for Wimbledon,' she reminded him.

Nick grimaced slightly, but said nothing. He knew how much she loved the sport, how much she missed taking part in the major championships – especially Wimbledon. This year she had persuaded her brother, Jack Farrell, also an ex-pro player, to accept a 'wild card' entry into the Mixed Doubles, an event they had won five years earlier, before a car smash had ended Jack's career prematurely.

Now, Nick put his misgivings regarding his wife's career to the back of his mind and reached for the phone, dialling the number of his old barracks in Aldershot.

'Officers' Mess – Major Lancaster, please,' he requested crisply, visualizing the room as he spoke: the panelled walls adorned with pictures of bygone battle scenes in which the regiment had played a part, the polished mahogany tables and huge leather armchairs. Melissa wasn't alone in having fond memories of a lost career, he thought, then he glanced at his beautiful wife and adorable daughter and knew he wouldn't want his life to change in any way at all. Well, maybe a second child, he amended silently.

'Lancaster.'

'Saul? It's Nick – how does it feel to be a celebrity?' he asked, and Saul groaned.

'You should know – you're married to one,' he responded.

'True. Listen, we'd like you to come down this

71

weekend if you can, and bring Virginia, too.'

'Ginny,' Saul corrected automatically, then he continued hastily, 'Thanks, Nick, but I don't think we'll be able to make it.'

'That's a pity; we'd like to meet her, and I thought you, Coop and I could go over the arrangements for you joining the firm – you haven't changed your mind, have you?'

'No, I'm definitely coming out of the Army – in August probably.'

'Yeah, it's no job for a family man . . .' Nick paused expectantly.

'Good God, I'm not getting married!' Saul exclaimed, appalled at the very idea.

'Well, come down if you can . . . hold on –' Nick broke off briefly while Melissa spoke to him, then, 'Saul? Melissa wants to know if you'll need one bedroom or two?'

There was a long pause; Saul's bad humour evaporated suddenly and a slow smile spread over his face. In an instant, he changed his mind about accepting the invitation; of course, the difficult part would be persuading Ginny to agree . . .

'Just the one,' he drawled. 'We'd hate to put Melissa to too much trouble,' he added, and Nick laughed.

'That's very considerate of you,' he said drily. 'Fine, so we'll see you – when? Friday evening or Saturday?'

'Friday night, hopefully. I'll check with Ginny and phone you back,' Saul promised. They chatted for a few minutes longer, then ended the call. Saul stayed by the phone, though, and fished out Ginny's number and dialled – without having any clear idea on how to convince her another public outing was necessary.

'Ginny?' He was startled by the pleasure he felt at hearing her cool, clear tones as she picked up the phone.

'Yes? Who's calling?' she asked, although she had recognized his voice instantly. But she wasn't going to grant him the satisfaction of guessing he hadn't been far fron her thoughts since Saturday evening.

'Saul Lancaster,' he said evenly.

'Oh, hi,' she said vaguely, then decided to stop playing games. 'Actually, I'm glad you called – that reporter, the blond guy, is still hanging around. What shall I do?' she asked, rather tensely.

The constant teasing from her friends and work colleagues was really wearing her down, especially as she couldn't tell them the truth. Also her mother's near-hysteria after seeing the photograph in the paper was driving Ginny nuts, and spotting the bearded reporter sitting in his car parked outside the house had been the last straw. 'I had no idea what I was letting myself in for – I feel like running away,' she confided miserably, and Saul smiled his satisfaction.

'I thought it might be upsetting you. So, if you see that guy again, go and tell him you'll be spending this weekend in the country with me,' he said smoothly.

'Do what?' Ginny exclaimed.

'You heard. I think I told you that I'll be joining a couple of ex-Army friends who run a security company here in London? Well, the senior partner, Nick Lennox, saw the item in the paper —'

'I think the whole world has seen it!' Ginny interrupted bitterly.

'Tell me about it,' Saul sighed. 'At least you don't have six hundred soldiers sniggering behind your back,' he said heavily, and Ginny giggled; perhaps it *was* even worse for him than it was for her, she thought, her own spirits lifting a little at the thought of what he was suffering. Saul smiled slightly at the delightful sound of her laughter, before continuing. 'Anyway, Nick's invited us both down for the weekend . . .'

'Why both of us?' Ginny frowned.

'Why not? He thinks we're an item and he'd like to meet you. Besides, we'll be discussing business, so Nick's wife would welcome your company,' he lied smoothly. 'I think you'll like both of them . . .' He paused, and if Ginny could have seen the wicked glint in his eye she would have run a mile. 'Didn't you tell me you play tennis?'

'Yes, when I can.'

'So does Nick's wife.' He was careful not to mention Melissa by name; even though she had used her maiden name whilst competing, Ginny might make the connection. 'At least, she did until she had a baby a couple of years ago. Perhaps you could give her some tips?' he suggested silkily.

'Well, yes.' Ginny was beginning to come around to the idea. The weather had been hot, London stuffy and unpleasant, and the prospect of a weekend in the country was appealing. It was a pity Saul Lancaster had to be there as part of the deal, but she supposed one couldn't have everything! 'Okay, I'll come,' she agreed, 'but on condition you make no more snide comments about my mother.'

'Agreed,' Saul said promptly. 'I'll pick you up around six on Friday,' he added, and quickly ended the call before she could have second thoughts.

Ginny slowly replaced the receiver and wondered out loud about her sanity, or lack of it. She told Barney and Jo of her plans, but not her mother. Ann was back in her own home in St John's Wood, nursing her cracked ribs and feeling very sorry for herself.

Ginny shopped and ran errands for her, calling in again on Friday lunch-time to ensure her mother had everything she would need until after the weekend. Still she said nothing about seeing Saul – her mother's reaction to the first date and the subsequent pictures in the press had been enough to deter Ginny from ever mentioning Saul's name in her presence again. Besides, she couldn't even explain to herself why she had agreed to spend the weekend with him, so how could she expect anyone else to understand?

'I won't be at home much over the next couple of days,' she prevaricated. 'If you need anything, Jo said you could ring her,' she added, as she dashed out of the door. Barney had allowed her an extended lunch hour, but she had lots to do if she was to be ready when Saul came to collect her.

The heatwave was continuing, and she packed swimwear as well as her tennis clothes, adding one smart dress lest they eat out, plus her jeans and various tops, and was wearing a pink sundress when Saul's Jag pulled up outside the house.

Ginny was overcome with shyness at the sight of him from her bedroom window, and was relieved when she spotted Barney going out to talk to him. She had refused to discuss Saul all week, ignoring all the teasing and inquisitive questions – mainly because she didn't know how to explain what was happening.

She had disliked him on sight, and his behaviour and attitude towards her had been appalling; she could never forgive him for suggesting her father had taken his own life. He was arrogant and aloof, and yet . . . she had never felt so physically attracted to a man, never responded so completely that all other thoughts flew out of her head. Sighing, wondering if she was making a huge mistake, she picked up her suitcase and made her way downstairs.

'I didn't want to mention this to Ginny,' Barney was saying to Saul, 'but that reporter's been hanging around again.'

'Really?' Saul frowned, perplexed by the man's persistence.

'Yes. Ginny seemed to be getting a bit upset by it, so I thought I'd keep it to myself. He's driving a different car – a blue Rover.'

'Right, I'll watch out for him. Do me a favour? If you see him this weekend, tell him she's with me, which is presumably what he wants to know.'

'I'll do that . . . hello, lovey.' Barney turned to greet Ginny as she approached. Saul spun round, discomfited by the surge of pleasure he experienced at the sight of her, and by how much he wanted to pull her into his arms and kiss her until they were both breathless.

She looked enchanting – and a lot less like her mother – with her hair tied back from her face in deference to the heat. Her long, slim legs were tanned and bare, he noted approvingly; he noted, too, that she wasn't wearing a bra . . . Get a grip, Lancaster, he told himself sternly, and muttered a brusque 'hello' as he took her suitcase from her and stowed it into the car.

Those big blue eyes that gave her such a look of innocence were inherited from her mother, and Ann Sinclair couldn't have been much older than Ginny was now when she had begun her deadly games of bewitching men before destroying them. Not me, he decided firmly; forewarned was forearmed – I'm fireproof!

His expression, or rather the lack of one, betrayed nothing of what he was feeling, and Ginny watched him anxiously. After his less than exuberant greeting, she wondered if he had changed his mind about inviting her to meet his friends. If so, surely he could make some excuse for her absence?

'Are you ready to go?' Saul asked her politely.

'Yes, if – if you're sure . . .' She stammered a little. He merely opened the passenger door by way of reply and, after a brief hesitation, Ginny clambered in.

'Have a good time!' Jo leaned out of an upstairs window to shout, and Ginny craned her neck, nodded and waved.

'Bye, Jo, bye, Barney.'

'Bye, lovey. I hope you realize you're depriving me of a chauffeur for the weekend,' Barney grumbled at Saul, for Jo, after one disastrous

77

driving lesson with her husband, had got out when stopped at traffic lights and walked home. It was the only quarrel they had ever had, she'd once confided to Ginny. Ginny had laughed at the time, but, since driving Barney around after his disqualification, she could quite understand Jo's feelings on the subject. Normally the most mild-mannered of men, Barney was intolerable as a passenger, especially when someone else was behind the wheel of his own beloved Porsche.

'Honestly, he talks as if he lives in the middle of the Sahara instead of central London,' she said to Saul. 'He only has to walk fifty yards to get a taxi.' There was no reply, and she turned to steal a look at Saul, and immediately wished she hadn't when he turned his head and they briefly locked glances. Ginny looked away first, lowering her gaze to her hands twisting together nervously in her lap. Saul concentrated on his driving.

'Couldn't you have explained to your friend – Nick? – why we were out together last weekend?' she ventured finally, to break the uncomfortable silence.

'No, he phoned the Officers' Mess and there were too many people around. Besides, the fewer who know the truth, the more likely it is to remain under wraps,' Saul said casually. 'Relax, you'll enjoy yourself. They're a great couple and their little daughter's sweet,' he added, with slightly less conviction. 'Do you like children?'

'Usually I'd say yes to that, but I've changed my mind after the week I've had.' Ginny sighed. 'I painted cartoons all over the brat's bedroom walls and then he decided he wants animals instead!

Luckily, his mother dissuaded him, once Jo pointed out how expensive it would be.' It had been hot, back-breaking work and she stretched, as if still needing to ease her aching muscles.

The movement pushed out her breasts and pulled her dress taut over the firm mounds, Saul noticed. In fact, he was so busy noticing Ginny's breasts that he almost failed to notice the car in front of him braking suddenly; just in time, he slammed his foot on his own brakes and stopped the Jag only inches from the other car's bumper. He fervently hoped Ginny hadn't realized she was disrupting his concentration; he felt it was vital that he retained the upper hand in this relationship.

Whilst they were stationary he reached over to retrieve something from the glove compartment, his hand accidentally brushing Ginny's bare leg as he did so. Oh, God, he thought despairingly, but his desire for her vanished as quickly as it had flared when she shrank from his touch.

'I beg your pardon,' he said icily, as he dropped a brochure onto her lap. 'I was merely reaching for this.' 'This' was the estate agent's details of the house he was buying, and Ginny eagerly picked it up, glad of the distraction. His hand on her leg had sent tremors of excitement coursing through her, an excitement she truly did not want to feel for this man.

'Nick and . . . his wife will expect you to have seen the house,' he added, which instantly put a damper on her interest.

'I'll study it and answer questions on it later,' she said flippantly.

'It's down near the Embankment,' was all Saul said to that.

Ginny carefuly read the details of the mews house: the garage and utility room were on the ground floor, the drawing-room, dining-room and kitchen on the first, with three bedrooms and *en suite* bathrooms above, the master bedroom having views over the river. The price tag caused her to raise her eyebrows, but she had more sense than to comment on that!

'What colour are the kitchen units?' she asked finally.

'What?' Saul frowned.

'Nick's wife – what's her name, by the way? – will expect me to know that,' she explained.

'Oh.' Saul's brow creased with concentration; he hadn't actually seen the house for several months – his solicitor had been dealing with the purchase during his absence. 'Sort of blue – pale blue,' he remembered finally. 'They looked as if they hadn't been painted properly,' he added, and it was Ginny's turn to frown. Then enlightenment dawned.

'You mean they have the "distressed" look?' she queried.

'Distressed? They looked positively suicidal,' Saul drawled, and she giggled. He turned to her and grinned, and Ginny felt a surge of happiness that was almost immediately swamped by an equally overwhelming sense of sadness as she reminded herself that nothing good or lasting could come of this. Maybe, if they had met under different circumstances . . . But they hadn't, and she would do well to keep that in mind.

She bent her head to the house brochure again and soon felt that she could indeed answer questions on its lay-out, the dimensions of the rooms, and recount the whereabouts of every damned cupboard and wardrobe.

As they left central London behind them the traffic cleared, and Saul was able to put his foot down on the accelerator. And as he picked up speed a welcoming breeze blew in through the sunroof and open windows. Ginny sat back, enjoying the cooler air on her face and listening to the Bruce Springsteen tape in the deck, idly watching the passing scenery change from suburbia to motorway, and then to open countryside as they headed for the South Downs.

'Nearly there,' Saul told her, and she sat up, fishing in her bag for a mirror and nervously smoothing back the tendrils of hair which had escaped her ponytail in the wind.

The Lennox house, Nine Elms, was situated on the very edge of the village, a good distance from any other properties, and Ginny gazed admiringly at the large Georgian house as Saul turned into the gravel driveway.

As he braked to a halt a tall, blond, ruggedly handsome man of around thirty-five emerged from the house, carrying a small, golden-haired child. They made a striking picture, the man so broad and muscular and the child, clad in teddy-bear-patterned pyjamas and snuggling close to his side, with one tiny arm curled trustingly around his neck. She obviously adored him, and Ginny smiled sadly, vividly remembering her own father carrying her around long after she was able to walk.

'Saul! Good to see you.' Nick Lennox extended his right hand to Saul, but smiled warmly at Ginny as he did so. She immediately relaxed and felt welcome, and returned the smile happily – something Saul noted sourly.

'Sorry about this,' Nick continued, inclining his head slightly towards his daughter. 'It's a devil of a job geting her to sleep these light evenings.'

'Don't apologize,' Saul said. 'Hi, Suzy,' he greeted her, but she ducked her head shyly into Nick's shoulder and didn't answer. 'Nick, I'd like you to meet Ginny.' Saul drew her forward and she shook hands with him, but left Suzy to lose her shyness in her own time.

'I'm pleased to meet you; we're glad you could make it. Come inside; you must be longing for a cool drink. Mel –' he began, but Saul interrupted him.

'Ginny's quite a keen tennis player,' he said smoothly. 'She's offered to give your wife some tips.' Nick stopped in his tracks and stared at Ginny, plainly astonished. Her smile of agreement faded and she glanced uncertainly at Saul – why the hell was he looking so smug? she wondered.

She soon discovered the reason, for coming towards them was Nick's wife, the familiar face and figure of the 'English Rose', the dark-haired and blue-eyed Melissa Farrell, ex-pro tennis player and former Wimbledon champion . . .

'Oh, God,' Ginny muttered, wishing she was dead. Correction, she wished Saul were dead . . . 'I hate you!' she whispered at him out of the corner of her mouth, before turning to Nick. 'I'm awfully sorry, I didn't know . . . I didn't mean . . .' She floundered. Nick, after throwing a puzzled glance in Saul's direction, took pity on her.

'It's okay,' he assured her quickly. 'There's no harm done.'

They all entered the house and Nick tried to put her at her ease, as did Melissa, not a bit affronted by what had obviously been a genuine misunderstanding, but Ginny was too embarrassed and angry with Saul to act naturally.

A hastily gulped glass of wine calmed her nerves and bolstered her sprits somewhat, and she glanced around her surroundings with interest. The rooms were large, and beautifully decorated and furnished, but it was definitely a home, not a showpiece, as were some of the houses Ginny worked on. Suzy's toys littered the elegant drawing-room, and the little girl clambered happily over the cream sofa without rebuke.

The two men began talking shop, and Melissa took Ginny on a tour of the house, with Ginny again apologizing profusely for her gaffe.

'Forget it – how could you know, if Saul didn't bother to mention it?' Melissa said dismissively. 'I'm quite happy to be known as Mrs Lennox these days,' she added, with a contented smile. 'I'll show you your room; you have plenty of time to freshen up before we eat,' she said, throwing open the door of the guest bedroom, a lovely room in pale pink and grey. 'Your bathroom is through here.' Melissa pushed open another door to the *en suite* facilities. 'Don't worry if you and Saul want to lie in tomorrow,' she said with a grin. 'No one will disturb you.'

Ginny, only just recovered from her initial *faux pas*, stared at the king-size bed in mounting horror, and felt herself begin to blush yet again. The bed seemed to grow even larger as she gazed at it, dominating the room, and she swallowed nervously.

'I'm sorry, but . . .' she whispered.

'What's wrong?' Melissa asked, concerned. Ginny's face had changed colour from red to ashen, and was reddening once more as Melissa stared at her curiously.

'I'm really sorry to be a nuisance, but . . . could I sleep somewhere else?' Ginny managed to ask.

'Somewhere else?' Melissa glanced around the room in puzzlement.

'Yes. Saul and I . . . we're not . . . we don't . . .'

'You're not sleeping with him? Oh, God, I'm sorry!' Melissa exclaimed; now it was her turn to feel embarrassed. 'Honestly – men! I told Nick to ask Saul,' she said crossly.

Oh, yeah? Ginny thought furiously, suddenly sure that this was no honest mix-up.

'You can still use this room,' Melissa decided. 'Saul can have the smaller one at the end of the hall and share a bathroom with Coop when he arrives tomorrow. Have you met Coop yet?' she asked, as anxious to change the subject as Ginny.

'No.' Ginny shook her head. 'I haven't known Saul very long,' she added. Too long, though; definitely too bloody long! she fumed. She had been an idiot to come here, she thought – too late. 'Perhaps it would be better if I return to London,' she said miserably.

'No, don't do that,' Melissa said gently, seeing the

unhappiness in the other girl's eyes. 'Once Coop gets here it will be Army talk morning, noon and night! I'll go nuts if I don't have someone to talk to,' she added, purposely making it seem as if Ginny would be doing her a favour by staying.

'Well, okay, if you're sure,' Ginny said uncertainly.

'Of course I am. We could go shopping in Brighton tomorrow, if you like,' Melissa suggested. 'There are some great antique shops.'

'I'd enjoy that.' Ginny smiled.

'Great. That's settled, then,' Melissa said firmly. 'Do you want to stay here and freshen up, or come and help me put Suzy to bed? For the third time this evening, I might add!'

'I'll come with you.' Ginny decided to stick close to Melissa until Saul had been told of the change in sleeping arrangements! 'Suzy's adorable – how old is she?' she asked, as she followed Melissa out of the room.

'She'll be two next month,' Melissa replied, heading back downstairs to collect Suzy from Nick. The two men were sitting over glasses of Scotch, both comfortably asprawl in huge, squashy leather armchairs.

'And, as you know, he couldn't organize an orgy in a brothel!' Saul was saying disgustedly as they entered the room.

'Behave yourself, Saul!' Melissa rebuked him, rather more sharply than the comment had warranted, Nick thought, and he raised a questioning brow, which his wife ignored.

Melissa picked Suzy up, then glanced back at Saul.

'By the way, Ginny's using the largest guest-room – you're in the smaller room at the end of the hall. Don't forget and blunder into the wrong room, will you?' she enquired sweetly. Saul had the grace to look slightly abashed, and Nick's brow rose even higher, but Melissa, mindful of Ginny listening, shot him a 'I'll tell you later' look, and swept out of the room, with a grateful Ginny at her heels.

She had dreaded a confrontation with Saul once he realized his plans had been thwarted, but she felt sure he wouldn't now abuse Nick and Melissa's hospitality by making a scene. At least, she hoped he wouldn't.

CHAPTER 5

They ate outside on the patio and Ginny began to relax fully, admittedly aided by copious glasses of wine! But Melissa and Nick helped enormously; they were both friendly and easy to talk to, especially Melissa, who was not at all the spoilt prima donna she might have been after her years as a top professional player, with the accompanying celebrity status. Ginny felt her own life and career very ordinary by comparison, but Melissa seemed genuinely interested in Ginny's work.

'I'll take you over to Bellwood – that's where I grew up, now my brother's home – if we have time this weekend,' she said. 'He's been saying it needs decorating throughout. It's a sixteenth-century Tudor building and my sister-in-law's a very modern American, so we can't let *her* loose on it. It might end up looking like a New York penthouse!'

'Melissa!' Nick chided, but with a grin. Melissa merely shrugged, quite unrepentant. Lisa was making Jack unhappy and that was unforgivable – so far as Melissa was concerned, her brother deserved the best.

'Jo Ferris – she's one of my employers – usually views the properties first,' Ginny explained. 'I can give you her number if you're serious about their wanting the work done, but I'd certainly love to see the house,' she said, eagerly and truthfully. Saul, who had been rather silent and withdrawn throughout the meal, narrowed his eyes.

'Fine, I'll talk to Jack about it,' Melissa said. 'Coffee everyone?' She stood up to leave the table, followed shortly by Nick when the phone rang a few seconds later.

Saul leaned across the table to Ginny. 'Don't get too interested in Bellwood – Jack Farrell's married,' he told her softly. 'But then, marriage vows aren't considered too much of an obstacle by you Sinclairs, are they?' he added nastily.

Ginny stared at him, her mood of alcohol-induced gaiety vanishing in an instant. She was about to explain her love of architecture, then mentally shrugged and decided not to bother. There was no point; he wouldn't believe her. Besides, even if his suspicions were correct, she owed him no explanation. And his own behaviour was hardly exemplary, she thought angrily, remembering the supposed mix-up over their sleeping arrangements.

'You're so right,' she agreed, with a false smile. 'We take them about as seriously as your father does! Now, Saul, don't be grouchy, just because your little plan failed,' she added.

'I am not grouchy,' he scowled, his dark brows drawn together, and Ginny almost laughed out loud.

'Yes, you are,' she insisted. 'In fact, you're

sulking,' she told him, and his frown became even more ferocious. 'Why *did* you tell Nick we were sleeping together?' she asked, and he looked at her as if she had lost her wits.

'Why do you think? I want us to finish what we began last Saturday night,' he said simply.

'Well, tough luck. I don't,' she denied flatly.

'Liar,' Saul said softly. He reached across the table and placed his hand over hers, his thumb stroking the inside of her wrist in a lazy, rhythmic motion. Ginny gazed at him coolly, or so she hoped, but the slow, satisfied smile that curved his mouth told her he was well aware of the frantically leaping pulse beneath his touch.

'Liar,' he repeated huskily, and Ginny cast a look of desperation towards the house, hoping to be rescued by Nick or Melissa.

'Don't count on it.' Saul guessed her thoughts. 'Knowing those two, they've probably forgotten all about us and gone to bed – which is where we ought to be,' he added, his voice soft and seductive.

Oh, God, Ginny thought helplessly. She was glad she was already sitting down, for her legs were weak and trembling, her insides fluttering wildly, as if she did indeed have butterflies in her tummy. 'Don't do this, Saul; it's not fair,' she said, as firmly as she could, and snatched her hand away from his. He allowed her to escape, but continued to watch her so intently it unnerved her; she knew he was merely biding his time . . . She picked up her glass and took another great slug of wine, praying Nick and Melissa would return soon.

Ginny would have been relieved to know her

hosts had not actually sneaked off to bed – a siesta that afternoon while Melissa's mother, Rose Farrell, had taken Suzy out had temporarily sated their desire. But, after preparing the coffee, Melissa had waited for Nick to finish his phone call so she could speak to him about the confusion over Saul and Ginny's sleeping arrangements.

'What's Saul playing at?' Melissa frowned, when Nick confirmed Saul had definitely said they would only require one room. 'The poor girl was almost in tears earlier – do you think they had a row on the way here?'

'Could be; there's certainly something wrong. He deliberately let her make a fool of herself over giving you some tips on how to improve your tennis,' Nick told her. 'Come on –' he picked up the coffee tray and headed back towards the patio '– let's get back out there before they murder each other!'

It was still hot, despite the late hour, but a refreshing breeze had sprung up, and it was more pleasant to be outside than in. However, Saul and Ginny were sitting in an almost arctic silence, and Nick and Melissa exchanged rueful glances as they rejoined them.

'That was Coop on the phone,' Nick said, as he sat down. 'He's taking a client to Gatwick airport tomorrow before coming here.'

'He's doing it personally?' Saul queried, surprised. He knew the two partners mostly supervised the workforce, and left the actual 'minding' to the staff – all ex-Army, many from their former regiment.

'We don't usually,' Nick agreed. 'But this particular lady took a shine to Coop,' he explained, with a grin. 'She called in at the office and insisted he look after her during her stay in England. She was prepared to pay over the odds for the privilege, so he agreed. He'll be relieved to be rid of her, though; we've had clients expecting bodyguards to sleep outside their bedroom door before, but this one wanted Coop to sleep inside! He's had to be extremely tactful in how to turn her down without upsetting her,' he added, with another broad grin. He knew the situation wasn't really funny; if a male client had harassed a female member of staff in such a way – not that Lennox and Coupland actually employed any females, other than office staff – the said client would have been told to get lost in no uncertain terms.

'Who is she?' Saul asked, resolving to wind Coop up about it as soon as he saw him.

'An actress – no one's really heard of her, but she's convinced she'll be mobbed wherever she goes if she's not protected. And, as I said, she's prepared to pay for what she wants,' Nick said.

'We have Ace to blame – or I should say to thank, since it's so profitable for us,' Melissa put in. 'He recommended Lennox and Coupland to her.'

'Ace Delaney did?' Saul's brows rose; he knew Nick and Delaney detested each other. 'Why is he putting business your way?' he asked Nick.

'Oh, we looked after his wife a couple of years ago, when she needed help,' Nick explained. 'Ace convinces all his rich showbiz friends they won't be safe in London without a Lennox and Coupland minder, which is great for the firm, but he's single-handedly ruining the tourist trade!' he added drily.

Ginny had listened with mounting excitement – Ace Delaney, the ex-professional American tennis player, had been one of her idols when she was a teenager. His drop-dead gorgeous dark good looks, supposedly inherited from an Apache chief, coupled with his undoubted genius with a tennis racket, had won millions of teenage hearts around the world.

'I had a mad crush on Ace Delaney when he was a player,' she confessed, unaware that Melissa had once felt the same way; had, in fact, had an affair with him before her marriage.

'Join the club,' Melissa said lightly, after a swift glance at an impassive Nick. 'I can introduce you to him, if you like. He and my brother are still great friends, and Ace will be coming over for Wimbledon next month. Of course he's married now, and has mended his ways,' she added, as a reassurance to Nick.

'Huh!' Nick snorted.

'It's true,' Melissa insisted.

'Bad luck, Ginny,' Saul said nastily; in the past few moments he had begun to share Nick's dislike of the American. A short, tense silence followed, which Melissa hastened to fill.

'Yes, well, he and Alexa – that's his wife – have twins, you know,' she babbled. 'Drew and Pippa; they're almost eighteen months old and absolutely gorgeous. They're a real handful, though. I don't know how Alexa copes with two toddlers; I need eyes in the back of my head with just one. Of course, Alexa has a nanny, but even so . . .' She paused for breath and looked imploringly at Nick, trying to telegraph the message that Saul was his friend, so he should help deal with the uncomfortable atmosphere Saul had created.

'Don't you have a nanny for Suzy?' Ginny asked her, and was pleased that her voice sonded cool and unruffled, when what she craved was to scream at Saul or, even better, hit him with something hard.

'No, I don't, although I have considered it quite often.' Melissa smiled her gratitude at the change of subject. 'But when she was tiny I only trusted my mother with her, and we've continued to muddle along. Mum loves taking care of her, and Suzy also spends a lot of time at Bellwood with her cousin. Kit is only six months older, and fortunately they get along well. We often have Kit here when Jack and Lisa want to get away, and it all seems to work quite well,' she finished.

'Suzy is one of my reasons for suggesting Saul join Lennox and Coupland.' Nick took over the conversation after a quick look at Saul, who was still glowering as if someone else, and not he, were responsible for the strained atmosphere. 'I would like to spend more time with my family.' He smiled at Melissa, who grinned back.

'That's what politicians say when they've been caught with their trousers down and have to resign,' she said brightly. Ginny choked on her coffee and didn't dare even look at Saul.

'Excuse me.' Saul stood up and strode into the house. Melissa looked at Nick with a 'what did I say?' expression. Nick shrugged, conveying a 'beats me' reply, before he, too, got to his feet and went after Saul. He had had more than enough of Saul's bad temper – if he wanted to quarrel with Ginny, he could go somewhere else to do it!

If Nick and Melissa felt their evening was going badly, their annoyance was nothing to the blazing anger the normally cold and composed Lady Lancaster felt when the private detective, Dawson, phoned her shortly after eight o clock.

Barney, thinking he was helping the situation, and still under the impression that Dawson was a journalist, had ambled over to the parked Rover soon after it drew up outside.

'If you're hoping to see Miss Sinclair, you're in for a long wait,' he told him cheerfully. 'She's gone away for the weekend with Saul Lancaster.'

'Really?' Dawson was startled, but remained impassive. He was only here because Lady Lancaster had wanted to know more about Ginny Sinclair's private life – he'd bet her Ladyship didn't know about this! 'When will they be back?'

'On Sunday evening, around seven.' Barney repeated what Saul had told him. 'Saul's due back in Aldershot later.'

'I see. Thanks for your help.' Dawson nodded amiably and restarted the car engine.

'Just a sec – which paper do you work for?' Barney asked.

'I'm freelance,' Dawson said blandly, and sketched a brief salute as he drove away.

He didn't go far, just made sure he was out of Barney's sight before pulling in to the kerb and reaching for his mobile phone.

Alice Lancaster, in the middle of hosting a bridge

party, was not best pleased at being interrupted, especially as one of her guests was the Countess Rosemont, soon to be the mother-in-law of Alice's niece, Amanda.

After hearing what Dawson had to tell her, she was almost apoplectic with rage, her guests forgotten. Saul had taken the Sinclair girl away for the weekend! It was intolerable, she seethed, but quickly had her emotions under control, the cool mask in place as she busily pondered what course of action to take.

'That young man you were telling me about – Calvert?' she asked calmly.

'That's right. James Calvert – an actor, or so he claimed,' Dawson said.

'When you spoke to him, did you gain the impression that he's fond of the girl?' She couldn't bring herself to say 'love'. The word wasn't in her vocabulary, not since the stillbirth of her daughter when Saul was two years old.

She knew she had turned away from her husband first, but that had not lessened the hurt when he had so quickly begun to find solace with other women.

She supposed she'd neglected Saul, too, if to a lesser extent, but at least that had made him grow up independent and strong. He had refused point-blank to join his father's company, to be the heir apparent without earning the position on merit, but had chosen his own path. She had been proud of his military career, his rapid promotion, but now . . . This betrayal matched any his father had inflicted on her.

'Calvert was certainly angry at losing her to your

son,' Dawson was saying. 'But whether the damage was to his ego or his heart, I couldn't say.'

'Hmm. An actor, you said?' Alice mused. 'Ask him to come and see me; I think he could prove to be useful.'

'Fine. I'll call him and get back to you,' Dawson agreed, then added, after a slight hesitation, 'He'll probably want money in return for helping you.'

'Doesn't everyone?'

Ginny awoke late on Saturday; she hadn't been able to get to sleep until the early hours of the morning, kept wakeful by both the unfamiliar surroundings and the knowledge of Saul sleeping only yards away.

Actually, he hadn't been sleeping either, but fortunately for her peace of mind she was unaware of that. Frustrated and angry, Saul had tossed and turned in his single bed when he had hoped for far more pleasurable activity in the double bed along the hall! He knew Ginny wanted that as much as he, so why had she insisted they have separate rooms?

He had scowled into the darkness, scowled again as he recalled Nick's blistering words as he took him to task for his behaviour that evening. The fact that Nick had been right didn't help at all.

When Ginny finally ventured downstairs, she followed the sound of voices and the aroma of freshly brewed coffee to the breakfast kitchen. Melissa was there, with Suzy, and an older woman who could only be Melissa's mother, so striking was the resemblance.

Rose Farrell was still an attractive woman, with the same glossy dark hair and incredible navy blue eyes as her daughter. The finely sculpted bone structure was no longer quite so delicate on Rose, however, for, upon reaching her fiftieth birthday, she had decided to throw away her diet books and indulge her love of chocolate, justifying the action by saying running around after her grandchildren kept her fit.

'Oh, hi, Ginny!' Melissa turned to greet her with a smile. 'Did you sleep well?'

'Yes, thank you,' Ginny lied. 'I'm sorry to be so late,' she apologized.

'It doesn't matter. Come and have some breakfast,' Melissa said, and introduced her to Rose. 'Mum's offered to babysit while we go shopping – Suzy gets bored after a while.'

'Shopping!' Suzy announced, with a beaming smile.

'No, poppet, not today. Granny will take you to see the donkeys instead,' she said, by way of a bribe, explaining to Ginny that a donkey sanctuary nearby was one of Suzy's favourite places.

Ginny sat down and helped herself to toast and marmalade while Melissa poured out coffee for them all. Dirty crockery on the table showed that Nick and Saul had already eaten and left, a fact that did wonders for Ginny's appetite. She really didn't feel capable of dealing with Saul just yet. If ever, she amended gloomily to herself.

'Where are the men?' she asked casually.

'They've gone r-i-d-i-n-g.' Melissa spelled out the word and Ginny looked up, bewildered. Then enlightenment dawned when Melissa pointed a finger at Suzy.

'Oh, right,' she grinned.

'Nick often takes her with him, but he figured that wouldn't be much fun for Saul,' Melissa explained later, when they were on their way to Brighton in Melissa's bright blue convertible.

They had a wonderful time, chatting easily as they toured the shops and over lunch, which Ginny insisted on paying for despite Melissa's protests. Ginny was well aware of Melissa's millionaire status, but was determined not to take advantage of her generosity.

However, Melissa promptly retaliated by nipping back to a shop where Ginny had tried on and reluctantly left behind a suede jacket that was too expensive, and buying it for her. When Ginny wanted to return it, Melissa simply tore up the receipt to put an end to the arguement.

Of course, the more she liked Melissa, the worse Ginny felt about the subterfuge, and more than once was on the point of telling her the truth about her relationship – if it could even be called that – with Saul. However Melissa, after receiving a blushing, stammering reply to an innocuous question about how the two had met, tactfully dropped the subject.

A silver Mercedes was parked outside the house next to Saul's Jag when they returned to Nine Elms late in the afternoon.

'Good. Coop's arrived,' Melissa commented, leading the way indoors, laden with bags of shopping.

Ginny hung back a little, guessing Saul and Nick would also be there, and wondering if she could ask

Melissa not to mention the suede jacket. She fully intended repaying her somehow, but could just imagine the sneering contempt on Saul's face if he learned of the purchase.

'He's really nice, come and meet him,' Melissa urged, heading towards the study. 'I bet they're in here, liberating Kuwait all over again,' she added, loudly enough for the men to hear as she opened the door.

Nick looked up from his desk and scowled with mock ferocity at her remark before getting up to pull her into his arms and then kissing her soundly, utterly oblivious to their audience. The display of passion was obviously nothing new to the two men, but Ginny stared down at the carpet in some embarrassment and didn't dare look at Saul. She had caught just one glimpse of him when she entered the room, darkly handsome in black jeans and white shirt, and had then looked quickly away.

'Hi, sweetheart,' Nick murmured, when he finally released Melissa. 'Hello, Ginny.' He smiled warmly at her. 'This is Dale Coupland – Coop to his friends. Coop, this is Saul's girlfriend, Ginny Sinclair.'

'Hello.' Ginny smiled shyly at the third man who stood up to shake her hand. Not as dark or as handsome as Saul, he was attractive, with a friendly smile and warm brown eyes that appraised her face and figure appreciatively, but in no way offensively.

'I hear you're an interior designer – you can come and decorate my flat any time,' he offered, and she grinned, liking him at once. Goodness, they were an attractive lot, these Army officers!

'She's too expensive for you, Coop,' Saul cut in coldly. It might have been a casual remark about her work, but obviously Ginny wasn't the only one to sense the insult, and the temperature in the room seemed to drop perceptibly.

Nick frowned a warning at Saul while Coop hid a smile; if Saul didn't want this gorgeous blonde, well, he would be happy to take her off his hands! In fact, he'd offer to drive her back to London, he decided – to save Saul the journey, of course!

'Where are Mum and Suzy?' Melissa asked, breaking the awkward silence.

'They've gone over to Bellwood,' Nick told her.

'Oh, right. That's my brother's house,' Melissa reminded Ginny. 'Would you like to drive over there after tea? It's only five miles.'

'I'd love to – that's the Tudor house you were telling me about? The house you grew up in?'

'That's the one.' Melissa nodded. 'Let's freshen up first – do you guys want some tea?' she asked.

'No, thanks, we're fine.' Nick held up a glass of Scotch and Melissa raised her eyebrows, then ostentatiously checked her watch before ushering Ginny out of the room.

The Bellwood estate had been in the Farrell family for over three hundred years, although the records showed a brief change of ownership when Jack and Melissa's father, Daniel, had faced bankruptcy over his Lloyd's losses and had reluctantly put the property on the market.

At that time Jack had been a full-time professional player and had declined to buy – the expected sale price of two million pounds had seemed too high a price to pay for sentiment! However, his friend and doubles partner, the mercurial but charismatic Ace Delaney, raised in the slums of LA, had long admired the ancient beauty of the place, the tradition and the history, and had surprised them all by becoming the new owner.

But, typical of Ace, the novelty and expense of playing the role of Lord of the Manor had soon palled and he had been glad to sell the property back to Jack and Melissa after the car crash which had ended Jack's career prematurely.

Melissa told all this to Ginny as they drove the short distance, the love for her childhood home evident in her voice.

'There,' she said proudly, slowing the car as they approached, and Ginny looked eagerly to where she pointed.

'It's beautiful,' she breathed, awed that anyone could call this piece of history 'home'.

The house, with whitewashed timbered walls and diamond-paned windows beneath a gabled roof, nestled in a valley surrounded by wooded hillsides. It seemed to be basking in the late-afternoon sunshine, extending a warm welcome as Melissa drove nearer.

There was a profusion of lawns, still lushly green so early in the summer, flowerbeds containing towering banks of rhododendron bushes in glorious hues of pinks and purple, topiary hedges and even a maze. Plus, of course, a fenced-off tennis court where both Jack and Melissa – Britain's most successful players for decades – had learned the rudiments of the game.

Jack was on the court now, checking on its condition, and he straightened up and came to greet them, a ready smile on his face. At thirty-one, Jack Farrell still had the boyish charm that had captivated legions of tennis fans during his years as a pro. He had dark blond hair, twinkling hazel eyes and an easygoing disposition that had helped him keep the moody, but incredibly talented Ace Delaney focused and motivated during the doubles partnership that had won them all the major trophies of the sport – a partnership that had, as Ace said, lasted longer than most marriages!

Ginny felt she already knew Jack, for since he had stopped competing he had become a regular fixture on TV, presenting tennis coverage from tournaments around the world. His love and enthusiasm for the sport was obvious to his millions of viewers and he had won many awards. In the highly competitive world of professional tennis, which hardly allowed friendships to flourish, everyone liked Jack Farrell, and he never had any difficulty in persuading players to be his guests in the TV studio. There, his warmth and friendliness encouraged them to relax and open up, offering fans rare insights into the personalities behind the public persona.

'The court looks good,' Melissa commented, after the introductions had been made. The Bellwood court had once been the most lovingly tended rectangle of turf outside of London SW19, when they had used it to prepare for the Wimbledon Championships, but it had only been used for fun and fitness in the past couple of years.

'Since you've nagged me into playing again, I figured we'd better give it our best shot,' Jack grumbled, then smiled at Ginny, who was trying not to look starstruck. 'Has she told you we're entering the mixed doubles at Wimbledon this year?'

'No.' Ginny was surprised to hear that.

'We'll probably be out in the first round, but she won't be told.' Jack sighed. Although fully recovered from the injuries sustained in the car crash, he hadn't intended playing competitively again until he was eligible to join the rather more relaxed – and less exhausting – events for the over-35s, or over-the-hills as some of the youngsters derisively called them.

'We'll do okay.' Melissa jutted her chin stubbornly, refusing to admit to the occasional nightmare she had, in which they were indeed beaten soundly and booed off the court . . .

'You haven't played a pro match in almost three years and I . . . hell, I can't even remember,' Jack said, raking his hand through his hair.

'We'll be great,' Melissa insisted. 'The crowd will be rooting for us. We won't be seeded, of course, but I've decided that's to our advantage,' she said brightly.

'How the hell did you figure that out?' Jack demanded; being seeded ensured the top players would only be pitted against those lower in the rankings in the early rounds of a competition.

'Well, with any luck, we'll meet one of the top seeds in the first round, when they'll still be concentrating on their singles matches,' she explained, adding to Ginny that the mixed doubles was the poor relation of the tournament. 'No one takes it too seriously unless they reach the quarters or the semis and can start thinking of winning a Wimbledon title.' Jack still didn't look convinced. 'Oh, come on! It'll be great, just taking part again!' Melissa told him.

'I'd rather sit in the TV studio and watch others battling it out,' he muttered, wishing, not for the first time, that he had refused to go along with her desire to compete again. 'Still, since you're so determined, go and get changed and we'll have a practice,' he said, resigned to the inevitable.

'Sure, in a minute. Where are Mum and Suzy?' she asked.

'Upstairs. Both Kit and Suzy were a bit hot and tired, so Mum took them inside to cool down and rest,' he told her.

'Okay, I'll just go and check on Suzy, then I'll be right out. Come on, Ginny, I'll show you around the house,' she added casually.

'Is that all right?' Ginny looked uncertainly at Jack; it seemed such a cheek, turning up uninvited and poking around a total stranger's home.

'Sure, make yourself at home,' Jack said, with the easygoing friendliness which so infuriated his wife, Lisa. It drove her crazy, the way Jack's family trooped in and out of what had previously been their home but which was now supposed to be *her* domain. Perhaps fortunately for both Lisa and Ginny, the former was spending the day in London.

Melissa led the way into the house. The large

reception hall was two storeys high, the walls and sloping ceiling washed a pale pink and heavily timbered. Ginny glanced around, fascinated, recognizing the many original features, including an enormous open fireplace that would easily accomodate a roasting ox – and probably had in years gone by, she thought.

Several beautiful Persian rugs in hues of pinks and purples covered the ancient oak flooring. Ginny felt she ought to remove her shoes, but instead followed Melissa as she ran lightly up the flight of broad, shallow steps, hollowed in the centre from centuries of use. Ginny dallied a little, trying to absorb the delicate carving of the banisters and also to study the paintings that adorned the walls.

'What a terrific place to grow up in,' Ginny exclaimed, already loving the ancient beauty of the place. It was so obviously well-loved and cared for, and had a homely, welcoming air that made it far superior to similar period houses Ginny had visited – houses that were open to the public but were no longer lived in. It was that difference that made Bellwood so special, she thought, hurrying after Melissa down a long corridor and into a child's bedroom.

It was a large room, with timbered walls and sloping ceiling, the two windows affording wonderful views of the surrounding woodland. I hope Jack employs us to redecorate, Ginny thought wistfully. In fact, I'd love to do this room free of charge, she decided, plans for creating a fairy wonderland already taking shape in her mind.

'Hi, poppet. Have you had fun today?' Melissa

scooped Suzy up and showered her with kisses before turning her attention to the other, slightly older little girl. Kit Farrell was taller than her cousin, as dark as Suzy was fair, with the same thickly lashed navy blue eyes as her aunt and grandmother.

'Hello, Kit, darling.' Melissa hugged her niece, then turned her to face Ginny. 'Kit, say hello to Ginny. She's staying at my house for a couple of days.'

'Hiya!' Kit grinned broadly. She was less reserved than Suzy, who tended to weigh up new people who came into her life with her solemn grey eyes before deciding whether to accept them. Kit simply assumed that everyone she met would be her friend, and treated them accordingly. It broke Jack's heart to see the bewilderment in her eyes when he tried to explain that not all strangers were nice, that when she was away from Bellwood she must always stay close to whichever grown-up was taking care of her.

'Hello, there.' Ginny returned the smile. 'Doesn't she look like you?' she asked Melissa.

It was Rose Farrell who replied, after glancing around nervously, as if she thought Lisa might be listening.

'Yes, she does, but please don't repeat that in front of her mother,' she said. 'She's rather touchy on the subject.'

'She's touchy on every bloody subject!' Melissa muttered.

'Mummy!' Suzy rebuked her. 'Tell Daddy!'

'Melissa!' Rose warned simultaneously, not for

the swear word, but for criticizing Lisa in front of Kit, who was getting sharper by the day and might well innocently repeat remarks she'd overheard to her mother.

'Sorry, sorry; I shouldn't have said that.' Melissa apologized to both her daughter and her mother, then hunkered down to study the drawings Kit and Suzy had been working on prior to her arrival.

'Donkey,' Suzy said proudly, pointing to an unidentifiable splodge of colour on her piece of paper.

'So it is,' Melissa agreed. 'That's very good, poppet,' she said, then studied and praised Kit's effort, which wasn't much better.

'I'm not so sure it's a good idea to take them to the donkey sanctuary – they always clamour to bring one home,' Rose sighed; she'd had a trying day, coping with tears and tantrums in the heat. 'I took some photographs of Neddy today – he seems to be their favourite,' she added.

'Perhaps if I paint a picture of him they won't mind leaving him behind so much,' Ginny suggested, rather shyly.

'Oh, would you? How kind!' Rose brightened and quickly handed over the photos.

Within minutes, Ginny was helping both children with their own efforts while trying to draw a picture of Neddy. She soon realized she would have to make two sketches, one for each child, or there would be trouble at bedtime, as Rose warned darkly. Both children were absorbed in what Ginny was doing, fascinated by the apparent ease with which she immortalized their favourite donkey.

'That's great!' Melissa exclaimed. 'I'd no idea you were so talented,' she added. 'Saul never said you were an artist.'

'I'm working too fast, really.' Ginny ignored the remark about Saul. 'And these crayons aren't exactly what I'd choose to use,' she said, rather apologetically. 'If I can take a couple of the photographs home with me I'll do some better paintings and post them to you,' she offered.

'That would be great. They'd love that – wouldn't you, kids? Say thank you,' Melissa instructed, and they both obeyed quickly. Melissa hovered for a few more moments, then, 'You don't mind if I go and play tennis, do you?'

'No, go ahead,' Ginny said easily.

'We'd have more time to practise if Jack weren't going to Paris for the French Open,' Melissa grumbled, for Jack would be presenting extensive television coverage of the Championships.

'It *is* his job,' Rose pointed out.

'I know, I know,' Melissa agreed, rather impatiently. 'I'll see you all later. Mum – I promised Ginny a conducted tour of the house, so would you mind . . . ?'

'Of course.' Rose knew how eager Melissa was to get out onto the court.

'Great. Thanks.' Melissa quickly disappeared, and a short time later there was the sound of rackets thwacking tennis balls on the court outside.

Rose moved over to the window to watch; from her vantage point it was as if the years had rolled back and her children were teenagers again, both with dreams of fame and fortune.

They had both achieved their goals, but at a cost. Jack's career had been cut short by a car accident that had almost ended his life, and Melissa . . .

Rose sighed heavily, again experiencing the pain of the time when the nineteen-year-old Melissa had been panicked into terminating an unplanned pregnancy. Rose's ex-husband, Daniel, had frequently threatened to bulldoze the court when she neglected her schoolwork to practise, and, despite her success, culminating in a Wimbledon singles title, Rose often wished he had carried out his threat.

A gurgle of joyous laughter from Suzy lifted her spirits, and she turned and smiled at the sight of her two grandchildren romping happily together. Despite Nick's anger and grief over the termination, he and Melissa had eventually been reconciled, and Suzy was the result.

But that other grandchild, who would be six years old now, was not forgotten by Rose, and nor, she knew, by Melissa . . . But regrets were futile; they all had a lot to be grateful for, she thought, moving back to admire the vastly improved – courtesy of Ginny – pictures of Neddy.

CHAPTER 6

Melissa and Jack stayed on the court until the light began to fade, by which time Nick, accompanied by Saul and Coop, had arrived from Nine Elms, bearing pizzas and ice-cream for everyone.

Lisa Farrell, the former Lisa Renwick, also an ex-professional player, returned to Bellwood around the same time, noting resignedly that most of her in-laws were again present, plus a couple of people she had never even met before. Lisa, a tall, rather sulky-looking honey-blonde greeted Ginny coolly, although her attitude warmed a little when Kit showed her the picture of the donkey.

Saul had looked at the picture, too, but made no comment; in fact, his only greeting to her had been a curt nod, and she purposefully sat as far away from him as possible over their meal. They ate, not in the splendour of Bellwood's dining-hall, but in the enormous kitchen, which was a comfortable room, a pleasing mixture of old and new – as was the rest of the house, Ginny had discovered during her tour. It was awesome to think Queen Elizabeth the First had climbed the same stairs, wandered through the same rooms, as Ginny had confided to Rose.

'Her visit probably bankrupted the first owner!' Rose had retorted drily.

'Lisa – are you going to Paris with Jack?' Melissa asked.

'Why?' Lisa responded, rather warily.

'I just wondered if you wanted Kit to stay with us so you and Jack can have a break,' Melissa replied.

'Oh. No, I'm not going; Jack will be too busy,' Lisa said, then took a deep breath. 'I thought I'd take Kit over to San Francisco to visit my parents,' she said, ultra-casual, suddenly pleased that so many outsiders were present. She hadn't yet decided if she would return . . . Jack looked up sharply; this was the first he had heard of a trip to the States, but he kept silent. For now. He had no wish to discuss it in front of the others, or Kit, even if she was half-asleep on his lap. Melissa, however, had no such reservations.

'Again?' she enquired tartly. 'You've only just returned from your last trip.'

'That's not true; we haven't been over since January,' Lisa said defensively. 'My parents see very little of Kit – you don't mind, do you, Jack?' she asked her husband.

He hesitated; he *did* mind, but he could hardly object, he realized fairly. It was true what she said – Joshua and Hannah Renwick saw comparatively little of their only grandchild.

'How long were you thinking of staying?' he asked her.

'Just while you're in Paris,' Lisa lied smoothly.

'You'd like to go and visit Granny and Grandpa, wouldn't you, Kit?' she appealed to her daughter.

'Granny.' Kit pointed to Rose, the grandmother whom she saw almost every day, and beamed happily. Lisa's lips tightened in annoyance.

'Your other granny,' she said shortly.

'Perhaps Ginny's firm can get the redecorating done while you're away,' Melissa suggested sweetly. Too sweetly. Nick shot her a warning glance, which she ignored. 'Mum can oversee things and make the final decisions on colours and patterns – she's always done a great job in the past.'

'Yeah – even when Ace Delaney owned the place,' Lisa shot back, a bitchy reminder that Rose, too, had once had an affair with Ace, and had lived at Bellwood during his tenure, ostensibly as his house-keeper. Rose flushed to match her name.

'Exactly. Ace quite rightly trusted her judge-ment,' Melissa retorted. 'It hasn't been redeco-rated since Jack and I bought it back from him,' she added, a not-so-subtle reminder to her sister-in-law that it had been she, and not Lisa, who had helped Jack raise the purchase price of two million pounds.

'Fine. Do what you want – what do I care?' Lisa snapped, and stood up to take Kit from Jack. 'Bedtime,' she told the protesting little girl firmly. 'Say goodnight to everyone,' she in-structed. Kit did so, reluctantly.

'Suzy has to go to bed, too,' Nick said quickly, in a bid to stop Kit's tears, and that was the signal for them all to leave.

Ginny tried to get a lift in Melissa's car, but Saul

gripped her arm and practically dragged her to where he had parked his Jag.

'You *are* supposed to be with me!' he snapped, when she demurred, which she thought was a bit rich, considering he had ignored her for most of the evening. However, she bit her tongue, too tired to want to quarrel with him.

'Have you definitely decided to join Lennox and Coupland?' she asked politely, instead of bawling him out as he deserved.

'Yes, subject to my accountant checking the books. But I don't anticipate any problems – I've trusted those two guys with my life in the past, so I'm sure I can trust them with my money,' he said, then lapsed into silence.

At Nine Elms, Ginny refused Nick's offer of a drink, and left the two men to their nightcap while she helped Melissa put Suzy to bed.

Then, pleading tiredness, she escaped to her own room, but remained wakeful and on edge until she heard Saul climb the stairs and walk past her room to his own at the end of the hall, without even pausing outside the door or calling out 'good-night', as he did to Melissa. But that was what she wanted, she told herself firmly, punching the pillows and settling down more comfortably.

But it was quite some time before she finally fell asleep.

Sunday dawned hot and sunny again, and they all lazed around the house and garden, drinking coffee and reading the newspapers. Later, Nick set up the barbecue and Ginny began drawing pictures to entertain Suzy. She drew flowers, and then the birds and butterflies that flitted around the garden, then went further afield, drawing the neighbour's tabby cat, followed by the cattle in a nearby field.

Suzy was entranced, and demanded more and more pictures, toddling off into the house and returning with an assortment of stuffed toys that she wanted immortalized on paper. Ginny duly obliged, adding animation to the teddy bears, dolls and a clown, depicting them holding hands and dancing around in a circle.

Ginny was happy to keep the child entertained; she felt she was, in some small way, repaying Nick and Melissa's kindness, and it also prevented her having to deal with Saul. He couldn't do or say anything provocative while Suzy was staying so close to her side. At least, she hoped he couldn't . . .

Saul, nursing a hangover from sitting up late and drinking brandy with Nick and Coop, sat in the shade and watched her with Suzy. She looked about sixteen again this morning, casually dressed, with no make-up and her hair pulled back into a ponytail. Giggling with the child, she looked adorable and innocent – which she certainly was not, he reminded himself firmly.

He picked up a newspaper, but didn't read it, and his eyes narrowed when Coop sat down beside Ginny – somewhat closer than was necessary, he felt. He was unable to hear what was being said, but he knew Coop was turning on the charm – he had seen him at work often enough in the past to recognize his technique.

'Oh, thank you, that would be great!' Ginny exclaimed. Saul sprang to his feet so quickly his chair tipped over and clattered loudly onto the flagstones, alerting the others.

'Uh-oh, trouble,' Nick muttered to Melissa, as Saul strode over to confront Coop and Ginny.

'Serves him right,' she said callously. 'He's been awful to Ginny – I think she'd be much happier with Coop,' she added thoughtfully, and the gleam in her eye made Nick groan.

'What would be great?' Saul demanded, glaring at both Coop and Ginny.

'Oh, Saul, there you are,' Ginny said vaguely, as if she hadn't been constantly aware of his brooding presence. 'As you have to return to Aldershot this evening, Coop's offered to drive me back to London.'

'How kind,' Saul almost snarled. 'But it won't be necessary!' Coop glanced up at him in surprise, then got slowly to his feet and squared up to him.

'Oh, hell!' Nick ground out disgustedly. It had seemed a great idea to invite Saul to join Lennox and Coupland, for the three had worked well together in their Army days. The last thing he had anticipated was the possibility of having to act as a referee for the other two!

'Lunch, everyone!' Melissa called out brightly. 'Sorry it's so late. Coop – will you go and fetch some more ice, please?' she asked, hastily tipping the remaining ice-cubes onto the grass behind her and holding out the now empty container. Coop gave Saul a hard look, then complied with Melissa's request, much to Nick's relief.

115

'I told you last night to try and remember you're supposed to be my girlfriend,' Saul hissed at Ginny.

'I doubt anyone here still believes that fairy tale!' she said scornfully. 'Unless you're a pig to all your girlfriends, of course,' she added, before stalking over to the barbecue.

She was too embarrassed to even look Nick in the eye as he piled her plate with food, but Melissa gave her a kind smile and a reassuring word as she offered a choice of drinks. Ginny merely toyed with her food, citing the heat as the reason for her lack of appetite, and stuck close to Melissa, who began relating outrageous and probably libellous stories of life on the pro circuit until the atmosphere lightened.

'And then there was the time when Al Montoya spent an entire night in a hotel wardrobe because the girl he had picked up was married and her husband turned up unexpectedly! Al could hardly stand up straight, let alone play the following day, but luckily for him his match was against Ace Delaney, and he was in almost as bad a state after a rough night. It was the most pathetic pro match ever played; they both limped around the court like a couple of geriatrics, each hoping the other would default!'

'Are they really that bad?' Ginny appealed to Nick, when she stopped laughing.

'Worse,' he told her. 'But you'll be able to judge for yourself soon.'

'What's that?' Saul looked up sharply.

'I'm giving Ginny tickets for Wimbledon,' Melissa told him calmly. 'She'll have access to the Players' Lounge.'

'I see.' Saul stood up to refill his plate, pausing by Ginny's chair and leaning close to murmur in her ear. 'All those wealthy young men – what an opportunity for you.'

'I know, and I fully intend making the most of it,' Ginny retorted, stung.

'I'm sure you do. Why don't you take your mother along? See if you can find her a rich toy-boy to get her out of my father's life?' he suggested.

'Gladly – if that means *you'll* be out of *my* life!' Ginny gritted out.

She didn't speak to him or even look at him throughout the afternoon, but stretched out on a sun lounger and pretended to be asleep. She was sorely tempted to ask Coop if he would give her a lift back to London, after all, but reluctantly decided against it. She didn't want to risk a repeat of the near showdown that had occurred before lunch.

That still puzzled her – since his plan to force her to share a bed had failed, Saul had hardly spoken two words to her, and she had thought he would be delighted to be spared the chore of having to drive to central London and then head back to Aldershot. Stupid macho pride, she supposed – even though theirs was a make-believe relationship, it would damage his ego if she appeared to favour his friend. Men!

They left after tea, shortly after Coop's departure, and Nick, Melissa and an increasingly tired and grizzly Suzy walked out to the car to wave them off.

'Early bed for you,' Nick told his daughter sternly, mouthing 'And you' at Melissa, who blushed and grinned in delight. Ginny caught the silent exchange and bit her lip as she looked away.

'I wish I had what they have,' she said wistfully, half to herself, as she climbed into the Jag.

Saul heard, assumed she was referring to Nick and Melissa's material possessions, and slammed the door shut with unnecessary force. And as soon as he was behind the wheel he slotted in a cassette, turned up the volume and uttered not one word throughout the journey.

'There's Lancaster's Jag!' Dawson nudged Jamie Calvert as soon as he spotted the car. 'Are you sure you know how to handle this?'

'Of course.' Jamie moved to get out of the car, but Dawson placed a restraining hand on his arm.

'Wait until the girl's inside the house. You don't want her to see you and contradict everything you tell him.'

'He might confront her with it later, anyway,' Jamie pointed out.

'Then it will be your word against hers. But I doubt he'll say anything to her; his pride won't let him,' Dawson said confidently. 'Okay, go now,' he urged, when Ginny disappeared out of sight.

Saul had got out of the car to remove her suitcase and now remained staring after her, his very stance proclaiming him to be an angry and frustrated man! Dawson thought, smiling slightly. He hoped James Calvert could run fast . . .

'What the hell are you doing here?' Saul growled, hardly able to believe his eyes as Jamie strolled casually towards him.

'I'm going to see my girlfriend, of course.' Jamie tried not to quake at the fury in Saul's eyes.

'She dumped you,' Saul said flatly.

'We kissed and made up – I guess she forgot to tell you.' Jamie came to a halt a safe distance from Saul. At least, he hoped it was safe. 'She's in love with me, so why don't you just take your money and shove off?'

'She spent the weekend with me – I guess she forgot to tell you,' Saul mimicked.

'No, she told me.' Jamie shrugged. 'It's no big deal – she's just doing what her mother's brainwashed her into doing,' he said.

'Her mother?' Saul's gaze narrowed.

'Yeah. She's told Ginny to marry money and take her fun on the side . . .'

'Marry!' Saul repeated incredulously. 'Ann Sinclair thinks I'll marry Ginny?'

'If not you, some other rich guy; it doesn't really matter who,' Jamie said carelessly. 'She's in love with me – that's what's important.'

'I don't believe you. You told me Ginny is – and I quote – a "frigid bitch",' Saul reminded him.

Jamie had to think fast, but after a moment he shrugged again and smiled slightly. 'I lied. I thought you'd leave her alone if you thought you were wasting your time. She's not frigid; she can't get enough of it – with me, that is,' he boasted, and Saul wanted to hit him. 'Of course, you're a different matter – she won't sleep with you until you've paid plenty,' he said, gambling that Ginny would have so far been as immune to Saul's charms as she had been to his during the weeks they had gone out together.

'Why do you want her if she has her sights set on marrying someone else?' Saul asked, curbing his temper with difficulty.

'Why should I care who picks up her bills?'

'My God, you deserve each other!' Saul gritted out, turning away in disgust and wrenching open the car door. 'She won't get a penny from me!'

'Are you sure about that?' Jamie taunted. 'She'll drive you so crazy with wanting her that you'll pay her anything,' he told him. He knew, from personal experience, that the more Ginny Sinclair said no, the more men wanted her. 'Why don't you do us both a favour and back off now? I'm an actor, and when I make it big-time Ginny won't need anyone but me.'

Saul didn't reply to that, but gunned the car's engine into life and sped off, so angry he couldn't think straight. Every word James Calvert had uttered had only confirmed his own opinion of Ginny, so why was he fighting it? You're a fool, Lancaster, he berated himself; even having the truth spelled out, a part of you is still blinded by that aura of innocence and unawakened sensuality . . . unawakened? Not according to James Calvert . . . Saul ground his teeth together almost as hard as he ground the car's gears; the harsh sound of the latter reaching Jamie, who turned his head and grinned before loping off to where Dawson waited.

'Mission accomplished,' Jamie said cheerfully, holding out his hand for the money he had been promised. Dawson passed over an envelope containing cash.

'Keep yourself available – Lady Lancaster might need you again,' he said.

120

'Sure, but tell her I want danger money as well next time – I thought he was going to rip my throat out.'

'Don't get greedy,' Dawson warned.

'Okay, okay.' Jamie backed down quickly, well pleased with the remuneration he had received so far. In fact, he would have done it for nothing, just to gain revenge for the ignominy of being thrown out of the nightclub by Saul Lancaster. 'What about Ginny? Shall I call her, to try and find out if he contacts her again?'

'Leave her alone, for now anyway,' Dawson decided, after a pause. 'I'll check back with Lady Lancaster and be in touch.'

'Okay.' Jamie sketched a salute and strolled away, whistling, while Dawson phoned Alice Lancaster.

Saul was unable to leave Aldershot until Wednesday, which was just as well since it gave him a breathing space in which to simmer down and work out his next move.

After a sleepless night on Sunday, following the confrontation with James Calvert, he had finally admitted to himself that he still wanted Ginny Sinclair in his bed, and therefore in his life – temporarily. So, she had a price tag. It galled him, but it would make it all the easier to forget her once he'd had what he wanted from her. After all, he didn't object to paying for good food, wine or a decent car, so, just this once, he would make an exception and buy himself an indecent woman!

When he knocked on the door of Ginny's flat on Wednesday evening, she was just putting the finishing touches to an almost life-size painting of

Neddy, the donkey. She had spent every spare moment on it since the weekend; working stopped her brooding too much, and, besides, she had promised Suzy, and she knew that every day of waiting was an eternity to a child.

She had painted Neddy with a field as background and with the animal peering interestedly over a wooden fence, as in the photograph Rose Farrell had taken. The likeness was a true one, although she had decided to add his name in gold lettering on his red bridle, and hoped Suzy would consider it an improvement.

She frowned a little at the interruption, and almost didn't answer the summons. When she did, she could feel her jaw drop in astonishment, and not just because her visitor was Saul Lancaster, but because he was actually smiling! He was in uniform; the khaki suited his dark good looks and moss-green eyes. Ginny thought inconsequentially of a friend of hers from college, who had systematically worked her way through dozens of Guards officers and refused dates with all other men. Ginny could begin to understand why . . . She pulled her thoughts together, and noted warily that not only was Saul smiling, but he was also bearing gifts . . .

'I owe you an apology,' were his first words, which completely took the wind out of her sails. This must be Saul's twin brother, she thought wildly, before she pulled herself together.

'Just the one?' she enquired tartly, and his smile broadened.

'No,' he admitted. 'May I come in?' he asked politely.

'Er, yes.' She opened the door wider and he stepped inside, his gaze instantly drawn to the painting she had pinned onto the wall.

'Is that for Suzy Lennox?'

'Yes.'

'I'm sure she'll love it,' he said sincerely. 'Won't Kit Farrell's nose be out of joint? Or are you going to paint one for her, as well?'

'No, I've other ideas for Kit,' Ginny replied. 'In fact, I'm driving Jo down to Bellwood tomorrow – Jack Farrell phoned about redecorating the house. That's why I'm rushing to finish this tonight – I thought I'd drop it it in on our way to Bellwood.'

'Don't let me stop you. You can talk and paint at the same time, can't you?' he asked pleasantly.

'I suppose so.' She still eyed him uncertainly.

'I'll put these flowers in water, shall I?' he suggested, and she nodded wordlessly, pointing towards her tiny kitchen with her paintbrush.

His idea of putting flowers in water actually consisted of dumping them in the washing-up bowl and turning on the tap, she noted, with a wry smile. He had also brought a huge box of Belgian chocolates, and he placed those on the coffee table, together with a small oblong box.

'What's that?' Ginny frowned.

'Just a gift; a peace offering. Like I said, I owe you an apology – several in fact.'

'I'm listening,' Ginny said shortly, when he seemed loath to elaborate. She turned away from him and continued painting, glad she only had some easy background detail to add, for her hand wasn't as steady as she would wish it to be.

'I'm sorry I didn't tell you Nick's married to Melissa Farrell – dropping you in it was childish,' he acknowledged. 'And it was unforgivable of me to tell Nick we would share a bedroom; I realize how embarrassing that was for you. I really am sorry,' he said.

'Hmm!' Ginny concentrated on painting a fence while Saul continued trying to mend one. He sat on her sofa, uninvited but unchallenged, and admired the back view she presented to him as she painted. Usually he abhorred the sight of women in leggings, but the clinging Lycra suited Ginny, with her long, slender legs and small, shapely bottom.

'I've treated you badly simply because I despise your mother,' Saul went on, striving to sound both casual and apologetic. 'I had no right to do that . . . let's get that thorny subject out of the way,' he added quickly, noting how her shoulders had tensed at his mention of Ann Sinclair. 'How is your mother?' he asked, ultra-polite. 'Fully recovered from her injuries, I hope?' he lied.

'What? Oh, she's okay,' Ginny mumbled. Actually, her mother was driving her crazy, insisting she never speak to Saul Lancaster again. Ginny wished she had never told her about the weekend away, but unfortunately she'd had no choice after stupidly letting slip she had met Melissa Farrell, and Ann had guessed how the meeting must have come about. It had not occurred to Ginny that Ann might be aware of Saul's friendship with Nick Lennox.

'Now it's your turn,' Saul prompted.

'Huh?' She frowned, then her brow cleared. 'Oh.

124

How are your parents?' she asked, just as politely and insincerely.

'Fine, thank you. My father's out of hospital and will be hobbling about on crutches for a few weeks, but the fracture is mending well,' Saul told her. As if she cared. 'Right, let's forget about the mess our parents have made of their lives and concentrate on us,' he said cheerfully. 'Will you let me take you out to dinner one evening? Or to the theatre – whatever you'd like,' he offered.

'I . . . I don't know.' Ginny shook her head doubtfully. Even when he was being horrible to her, she had found him too physically attractive for her peace of mind – if he continued being pleasant and charming, he would be irresistible. And she wasn't ready for that. But – hadn't she wished they had met as strangers, not burdened by their parents' problems and intrigues? That was what he was suggesting, that they start afresh.

'Well?' Saul prompted, masking his impatience. 'Are you involved with someone else? Have you and what's-his-name – Jamie? – patched things up?'

'Oh, no, I haven't seen him since the night of Amanda's party,' Ginny said absently, her thoughts still on the intoxicating prospect of a new beginning with Saul Lancaster.

Saul's lips tightened at hearing what he thought was a lie, and he almost told her he had spoken to James Calvert on Sunday evening. But he held his tongue. Suddenly it wasn't enough just to bed her; he decided he wanted her to fall in love with him and dump James Calvert, and any others she was stringing along. Only when that happened would he

125

tell her that he had never wanted more from her than the temporary use of her body, and no longer wanted even that . . .

'If you're not with anyone else, why won't you come out with me?' he persisted.

Because I'm afraid you'll try and seduce me, Ginny thought, and knew he probably wouldn't have to try very hard . . .

'It isn't that simple though, is it?' she asked slowly. 'We can't just forget my mother, or yours for that matter,' she added.

'I wasn't thinking of inviting either of them,' Saul drawled, and she turned to grin at him.

'I'll think about it,' she said. Condescending little madam! Saul thought furiously, but he kept his face impassive as he nodded and smiled, as if accepting the reply.

Ginny finished what she was doing and got to her feet, rubbing the small of her back.

'There!' she said, with some satisfaction. 'Do you really think Suzy will like it?' She turned to Saul for his approval.

'I'm sure she will,' he said sincerely. 'Melissa once told me that her first word was "donkey", although Nick insists it was "Daddy",' he grinned.

'She's certainly a daddy's girl, isn't she?' Ginny smiled, a little sadly.

'Were you?' Saul asked softly, seeing the shadows in her eyes.

'Oh yes, he was a wonderful father, although I expect he was too indulgent and spoiled me dreadfully,' she admitted. 'Mum always had to be the disciplinarian – Dad would retreat to the Golf Club or somewhere if I'd misbehaved and needed to be punished. He could never bear to chastise me or see me cry,' she said huskily, then stopped speaking, her throat tight with unshed tears. She took a deep breath and turned back to the painting of Neddy.

'I think I'll leave it hanging here for now; it should be dry by morning.' She hesitated. 'Have you eaten yet? I'm only going to make an omelette and salad, but you're welcome to stay,' she said shyly.

'I'd like that.' Saul smiled at her and her heart flipped over. 'Why don't I go and fetch a bottle of wine?' he suggested, already on his feet and fishing for his car keys.

'There's an off-licence in the next street – just turn right at the newsagents on the corner,' she told him.

'Okay, I won't be long.'

Ginny took advantage of his absence to rush into the bedroom and check her appearance, horrified to see a smudge of paint on her cheek. She washed that off, tidied her hair and applied make-up before returning to the kitchen to prepare the meal, putting aside the roses to arrange later.

Saul noted the make-up as soon as he returned, and, although he thought her prettier without cosmetics, he decided it had to be a point in his favour – unless, of course, she was one of those vain women who couldn't even bear to face the milkman without war-paint, he thought grimly.

'Is something wrong?' Ginny noted the stern expression with some trepidation. Just her luck –

the new, vastly improved Saul Lancaster was about
to revert to form . . .

'No, nothing. I was just thinking about a small
problem with work,' he lied. 'Do you have a cork-
screw?'

'Yes.' Ginny rummaged in a drawer for one and
handed it to him, then reached on tiptoe to the top
shelf for wine glasses.

'Let me.' Saul was close behind her, too close for
comfort; his breath was warm on her cheek and his
body pressed against hers as he leaned above her to
reach the glasses, his fingers casually touching hers
as he did so.

'Thank you.' Ginny's heart was hammering as
she moved away to check on the progress of the oven
chips she had decided to add to their meal, as the
proposed omelette with just a salad had seemed
scarcely an adequate dinner to offer Saul. After
all, salad was considered to be rabbit food by most
men, although why they derided it when rabbits
supposedly had such great sex lives . . .

God, I'm delirious, she thought.

'Why don't you sit down? It will be ready soon,'
she said, rather breathlessly.

Her small dining-area, little more than an alcove
off the sitting-room, was barely large enough to
entertain in comfort. It was perfect when she
actually wanted to enjoy a cosy meal, but definitely
less so when she was as wary of her guest as she was
of Saul. Whether by accident or design, his thigh
continually pressed against hers; his fingers caressed hers whenever he needed more salt or pep-
per, his arm brushed against her breast when he

leaned over to pour her more wine . . . Ginny became so nervous she ate far too little and drank far too much.

'Aren't you hungry?' Saul evidently didn't share her state of nerves and reached across to fork up what she had left on her plate, his upper arm again pressing the softness of her breast. Ginny hastily switched plates with him, and got to her feet.

'Coffee?' she almost squeaked.

'No, thanks,' Saul declined, guessing – correctly – that she wouldn't bother making any just for herself. He didn't want her sobering up . . . 'Thanks, Ginny, that was a terrific meal,' he said sincerely, quite surprised to discover that she could actually cook, even if it was only the basics. He had assumed she was the sort to be eating out every evening – at some man's expense, of course.

'It was no bother. And thank you for the roses; they're lovely. I'll arrange them properly later,' she said, belatedly realizing they were still languishing in the washing-up bowl. 'I do have a nice vase, truly!' she assured him.

'If not, I noticed a couple of empty milk bottles on the doorstep!' Saul grinned at her, then, 'You haven't opened your present,' he said.

'The chocolates? Oh, shall I open them?' she asked, wondering if he was still hungry.

'I wasn't referring to the chocolates.' Saul stood up and retrieved the small oblong box from the coffee table, the third gift, that Ginny had forgotten about until now. 'Open it,' he said, holding it out to her.

Ginny took it from his outstretched hand, slowly

and rather reluctantly, although she couldn't have explained her sudden unease. But she sensed there was a tension about Saul, too . . .

'What is it?' she asked, rather foolishly, as she realized at once.

'Open it and see.' Saul continued to stand over her, and Ginny glanced up at him before tearing off the wrapping, then casting another quick look at him when she saw the gold-printed, world-renowned and extremely exclusive jeweller's name on the box lid.

'I can't accept this.' She held it out to him.

'You don't know what's inside it yet – unless you have X-ray vision,' he said, smiling. Ginny just shook her head.

'It's obviously expensive; please take it back,' she insisted. After a moment, Saul took the box from her, but only to open it and reveal a delicately wrought gold watch, the tiny dial surrounded by a cluster of diamonds and sapphires.

'Don't you like it?' he asked, watching closely for the glint of avarice in her eyes. But she only looked troubled.

'Of course I like it; it's beautiful,' Ginny said truthfully. 'But you can't give it to me,' she added. Her obstinacy puzzled Saul; so far the evening had not exactly progressed according to plan – first there had been her reluctance to accept an invitation to dinner or the theatre, now this.

'What do you suggest I do with it?' he asked, still smiling, but with an effort. When she merely shrugged by way of a reply, he took the watch from its bed of velvet and draped it over his own wrist, then raised a quizzical brow at Ginny. She giggled; the dainty watch looked ridiculous lying across his broad wrist, nestling amongst the sprinkling of dark hairs, and it wasn't even long enough for him to fasten it.

'I had some links taken out so it would fit you – let's see if I guessed correctly,' he suggested, taking her hand in his and placing the watch over her wrist. It fitted perfectly and looked absolutely gorgeous. Ginny bit her lip, sorely tempted.

'Really, I can't take it,' she said awkwardly, wishing he would simply accept her decision. Even more, she wished he would stop holding her hand; she couldn't think straight with his fingers stroking her wrist. 'I'd ruin it – I'm always getting paint on my jewellery,' she added.

'It's just a peace-offering,' Saul said, and instantly felt ashamed of himself for the blatant untruth. But then he remembered the cocksure James Calvert and his blood boiled anew. He strengthened his resolve to get Ginny Sinclair into his bed and then to make her fall in love with him. 'When's your birthday?' he asked, changing tack.

'What? Oh, you're too late for that; it was in March,' she told him. 'Please keep the watch, Saul. If we're still . . . friends at Christmas, I'll accept it as a gift then,' she said.

'Okay,' Saul agreed reluctantly. By now, according to his script, she was supposed to be wearing the watch and nothing else . . . 'Shall I take the flowers and chocolates back, too?' he teased.

'No, I'll accept those as an apology for your appalling behaviour,' Ginny said sternly.

'Yes, ma'am.' Saul sketched a salute and decided to make a strategic withdrawal to review his tactics. Perhaps Calvert had told her of their conversation, he thought suddenly, that would account for her wariness over his new attitude. 'I have to get back to barracks tonight, but I'll call you tomorrow and arrange dinner – okay?'

'Okay,' Ginny agreed, her spirits soaring at the heady prospect of a new beginning with one of the most attractive men she had ever met. If only her mother and his father left them alone, she felt sure they could become . . . friends? Don't be naïve, Ginny, she chided herself. Lovers? A frisson of excitement shook her body as she opened the door for Saul to leave.

'Are you cold?' He turned in the doorway and ran one finger caressingly down her cheek before stooping to kiss her mouth, very briefly, before he broke away and disappeared down the steps and into the night.

Ginny waited for his car to start up, then she closed and locked the door, hugging herself and grinning stupidly with happiness. But it was a happiness tinged with slight unease. She wished he hadn't bought the watch; it was too much, too soon, and it was reminiscent of her mother's relationship with Sir David . . . She shivered again and went to make herself a hot drink to ward off the sudden chill that assailed her.

CHAPTER 7

Ginny told Jo about Saul's visit, and confided her worries, as they drove down to Bellwood on Thursday morning. Jo had already noted the renewed sparkle in Ginny's eyes and the spring in her step, a marked contrast to the withdrawn girl who had barely spoken two words since returning from her weekend with Saul Lancaster. Consequently, she tried to put Ginny's mind at rest regarding the too-expensive gift.

'It seems an extravagant gesture to you and me, but don't forget he's a wealthy man. I don't suppose paying hundreds of pounds for a gift makes much of a dent in his wallet,' she pointed out. 'Perhaps he's always generous to his girlfriends and couldn't understand your refusal to accept it.'

'He certainly seemed surprised,' Ginny conceded. 'But I'm not his girlfriend,' she added quickly.

'Aren't you?'

'Well, he did ask if he could take me out again,' Ginny told her. 'He's phoning me tonight.'

'Will you go out with him?'

'I think so. Provided it's Dr Jekyll who phones and not Mr Hyde,' she added, mentally crossing her fingers that his attitude towards her wouldn't revert to the old hostility and contempt.

They called at Nine Elms first, with flowers as a 'thank you' to Melissa for her hospitality, and to drop off the picture for Suzy. Melissa was alone, taking advantage of Suzy's attendance at the local playgroup to deal with some paperwork concerning her range of tennis clothing and accessories, which had retained its popularity despite her retirement. Melissa had developed a new line, which was soon to be launched, and which she would wear and promote during her brief return to competitive play in the mixed doubles at Wimbledon.

Ginny carefully unrolled the painting and they pinned it on the wall facing Suzy's bed.

'I can frame it later, but I thought she'd like to have it as soon as possible,' Ginny said.

'It's terrific; you've captured him perfectly,' Melissa enthused. 'Suzy will love it – with any luck, she'll be eager to come to bed now! Kit will be green-eyed with envy, though,' she added.

'That's what Saul said,' Ginny replied absently, his image conjured up by Melissa's comment regarding green eyes. No one else had eyes of such a deep moss-green . . .

'Saul? He's seen it? I'm surprised you're even speaking to him,' Melissa commented.

'So am I, actually,' Ginny laughed. 'He called to see me last night and apologized for his recent behaviour,' she told her.

'Good. I'm sure you have Coop to thank for that –

Saul was furious when he thought Coop was muscling in.'

'Yes . . .' Ginny frowned slightly; perhaps that explained Saul's changed attitude. Oh, well, she didn't really care what had prompted it; it was great that he had decided he wanted to be . . . friends. There you go again, Miss Naïve, she chided herself, but her heart was singing with happiness. 'Would you like to see the preliminary sketches I've made for Kit's room?' she asked Melissa, just to change the subject.

Melissa was almost too easy to talk to; Ginny felt she could well find herself confiding too much, which would then no doubt be repeated to Nick, for she couldn't imagine those two had any secrets from each other, and from Nick her comments would reach Saul. Her feelings for Saul Lancaster were too confused, too new, for her to even try and put them into words.

When Melissa said she would love to see her ideas, she fetched her sketchbook from the car and laid out her drawings for inspection. She had drawn Kit's room from memory, and, using its profusion of exposed timbers as the bases for tree trunks and branches, had transformed it into a fairy woodland. Pixies and elves peeked from behind the 'trees', playing hide and seek amongst the foliage.

'That will be beautiful,' Melissa said sincerely, duly admiring the pictures. 'Have you ever thought of going into business for yourself?' she asked thoughtfully, an idea taking shape in her mind. Magazines were constantly asking for interviews with her or Jack, and their children, and Bellwood itself had featured in many articles.

'No, she hasn't,' Jo put in, rather tartly, and Ginny and Melissa exchanged a grin.

'No, I haven't,' Ginny agreed. 'I prefer a regular salary at the end of the month!'

'Talking of which, we ought to be on our way.' Jo pointed to her watch. 'I told Mr Farrell we'd be there before eleven.'

'Oh, Jack's not there – he's taking Lisa and Kit to the airport,' Melissa told her. 'But Mum's at Bellwood to show you around.'

'Still, we'd better be going,' Ginny said. 'Thanks again for the weekend.'

'You're welcome any time. I expect I'll see you soon, but if not we'll get together at Wimbledon. I won't forget your tickets,' Melissa promised.

'That will be great, thank you. I can take time off during Wimbledon fortnight, can't I?' Ginny belatedly asked Jo, who quickly nodded her agreement. She would have agreed, anyway, but did so with more alacrity after Melissa's comment regarding Ginny starting up in competition! She and Barney would hate to lose their most talented artist.

As soon as Jo caught her first glimpse of Bellwood, she was utterly captivated.

'Oh, I want this commission!' she exclaimed. 'In fact, I'll offer to do it at cost.'

'Don't let Barney hear you say that,' Ginny warned. Jo was the creative partner, Barney the businessman.

Rose Farrell took Jo on a tour of the house while Ginny carried indoors pattern books, colour charts and fabric samples. Rose, her eyes red from crying, for she missed Kit dreadfully whenever she was visiting her maternal grandparents in California, was glad to have a project to keep her busy, and promptly agreed to Ginny's ideas for transforming Kit's room.

'It would be lovely if it could be finished for when she comes home,' she said eagerly, and Jo looked enquiringly at Ginny.

'You've almost completed the Morley commission, haven't you? So you could start here . . . next Monday or Tuesday?'

'Yes, no problem,' Ginny confirmed.

'Why don't you come and stay?' Rose suggested. 'Jack's going to Paris tonight, and it's such a big house when one's alone. I'm looking after the place while they're all away and I'd really love the company,' she added.

'You'll make quicker progress if you cut out the daily travelling time,' Jo pointed out, when Ginny didn't immediately respond. Still Ginny hesitated; Saul wouldn't be able to call in here, as he had at her flat last night. 'Ginny?' Jo persisted, puzzled, for it wasn't at all unusual to stay at a client's house while the work was being completed – especially for those outside London. 'Oh!' Enlightened, Jo turned to Rose and grinned. 'How far away is Aldershot?' she asked.

'Aldershot? Oh, Saul Lancaster!' Rose smiled broadly. 'He could probably drive here quicker than into central London,' she said. 'And I certainly wouldn't hang around to play gosseberry,' she assured Ginny, who flushed, and then joined in their laughter.

'Okay, I'd love to stay here, thank you,' she said.

'Good. I'll prepare Melissa's old room for you. She still keeps some of her tennis clothes and rackets there, as they don't have a court at Nine Elms, but she won't mind if you use it,' Rose said happily.

While Jo discussed the work to be done on the rest of the house, Ginny went to Kit's bedroom and began taking accurate measurements of all the walls and alcoves to be painted. Once that was done, she would make miniature paintings to be submitted for Jack or Rose's approval, before settling down to work on the actual room.

She was engrossed in her work, her mind buzzing with ideas and the excitement of transforming the room, when Jack Farrell entered. He didn't register her presence at first, and sat down heavily on the bed, the expression on his face unusually grim and forbidding.

'Jack?' Ginny ventured, then louder. 'Jack?'

'Hmm?' He looked vaguely towards her, then made an obvious effort to pull himself together. 'I'm sorry . . . Ginny,' he finally remembered her name. 'The house is so empty without my daughter . . .' He drew a deep breath. 'She screamed blue murder when she realized I wasn't getting on the plane with them . . .'

'Oh, God, how awful!' Ginny said sympathetically.

'Yeah; I'm sure she's fine now,' he said. 'She'll be bubbling over with enthusiasm for San Francisco when I phone her. Her grandparents spoil her outrageously and she loves riding in the cable cars . . . she'll be fine,' he repeated, as if trying to

138

reassure himself, Ginny thought. Jack took a deep breath and glanced around the room. 'I'll leave you to get on with your work,' he said, getting to his feet and trying to get his mind on all he had to do before the start of the French Open on Monday. 'Ask my mother if you need anything,' he added as he left the room.

He wished he could be certain Lisa would return when she claimed she would, in two weeks' time. She had never really settled at Bellwood; she was a city girl at heart and resented the friendly curiosity of the villagers, people who had known the Farrells all their lives and had a keen interest in them, especially in view of Jack and Melissa's fame.

Jack acknowledged that they could be overly inquisitive at times, but they were loyal, closing ranks against the intrusion of the press, particularly when there had been all the furore over his car accident and then later, when the story of Melissa's abortion had become public knowledge. Not one local had spoken out of turn, or succumbed to cash offers from the tabloids to peddle family gossip. Jack appreciated that; Lisa did not.

Ginny paced the sitting-room of her flat ever more nervously as the evening progressed, watching the phone constantly and even checking that it was working properly. She wished she had asked Saul what time he would ring; even more fervently she hoped it wouldn't be Mr Nasty on the line when – if – he did call.

Finally, at nine-thirty, it rang and she pounced, remembering, too late, the advice in magazines to always let it ring at least ten times before answering so as not to seem too eager.

'Hello?'

'Ginny.' The one word was warm, caressing, and she relaxed immediately; last night hadn't been a fluke. There really was going to be a new beginning . . .

'Yes, I was beginning to think you weren't going to call,' she said, and then bit her lip, realizing she had given him the impression that she had nothing better to do than sit around waiting for him to phone. Saul duly noted the fact, but made no comment.

'I meant to call earlier, but I had something to sort out here. I'm the Duty Officer tonight, and a couple of my squaddies got into a fight with the locals,' he explained, to her relief. 'I'll be on duty tomorrow night, too,' he said regretfully. 'But the good news is that the house sale has been completed and I'm picking up the keys on Saturday. How would you like to come with me and help choose furniture? I have to warn you that it will be a mammoth task – I joined the Army straight from school, and, since I've always lived in barracks, there never seemed any point to buying a place of my own before. I'm afraid I don't own so much as a single cup and saucer,' he said cheerfully.

'I'd love to come with you,' Ginny said truthfully.

'You sure? It's not too much like work, selecting curtains and bedding?' he asked. Just the word 'bedding' set Ginny's pulse racing.

'No, I'll enjoy it. But you won't get it all done in one day,' she added.

'In that case, I'll have to monopolize all your free weekends from now until I leave the Army,' he said.

140

'I think I'll have to sort the master bedroom first – what do you think?' he asked wickedly, his husky tone wreaking havoc with Ginny's composure. Thank God he was on the end of the phone line and not in the room!

'I think you're trying to make me blush.' She tried, and failed, to sound stern.

'Am I succeeding?' Saul teased.

'Yes,' she admitted, and he laughed. 'Have you got all the measurements you need?' she asked, trying to be practical.

'Let's see . . . if memory serves . . . 36–22–34?' he guessed.

'You are awful,' she scolded.

'I know, but am I right?'

'Almost,' she conceded, wishing she did indeed possess a twenty-two-inch waist!

'Which did I guess wrongly?' Saul asked interestedly. 'I'll – Oh, hold on a minute.' He turned away to speak to someone else. 'They've done – *what*?' Ginny heard him bellow and she stifled a laugh, relieved that for once she wasn't on the receiving end of his ire. 'Ginny? Sorry, darling, I have to go,' he said, sounding abstracted. 'I'll see you on Saturday morning, around ten – okay?'

'Okay,' she agreed happily, her heart singing after hearing that casually spoken endearment.

Ginny daydreamed throughout Friday until Jo, ever practical, added a cold dash of reality to the situation.

'Don't you think you ought to tell your mother?' she asked.

'No,' Ginny said promptly, and Jo sighed. 'She'll have hysterics if I tell her I'm going out with Saul again,' Ginny added defensively.

'Aren't you curious to know *why* she gets so upset about you seeing him?'

'It's because . . .' Ginny paused, frowning. 'It's because of her relationship with his father. She's afraid Saul will turn me against her,' she said, but rather uncertainly.

'But that's all out in the open now,' Jo pointed out. 'What else does Saul know that you don't? What is she afraid he might tell you?' she asked softly. Ginny stared at her, her eyes huge with trepidation.

'He was wrong about my father's death!' she said wildly. 'That was an accident, not suicide!'

'I know, I didn't mean that,' Jo soothed her, mentally kicking herself for her tactlessness. 'But don't you think there must be something else? Something that Saul hasn't told you yet, but could if he chose to? Don't you think that's what is worrying your mother?' she asked gently.

'I – I don't know,' Ginny faltered. 'And I don't think I want to know,' she added. She vividly remembered confronting Saul that night at the hospital; she had asked if he had ever met her mother, and the contempt in his eyes when he had said that he had . . .

'I'm not going to see her this evening; I have to wash my hair,' she said mutinously.

'If your phone's out of order, feel free to use ours,' Jo said sweetly. Ginny shot her a filthy look, then she sighed.

'I can't deal with it over the phone. I have to talk to her face to face, so I'll know if . . .' She stopped, aware of being disloyal.

'So you'll know if she's lying?' Jo guessed correctly.

'Mmm,' Ginny admitted reluctantly.

'You'll have plenty of time to wash your hair tomorrow morning,' Jo said pointedly.

'Oh, okay, I'll go this evening.' Ginny sighed her capitulation, knowing Jo was right. 'May I borrow the Porsche?'

'Of course,' Jo smiled broadly.

Ginny phoned first, to check her visit would be convenient – how awful if she arrived unannounced and bumped into Sir David Lancaster!

'Of course! I'd love to see you,' Ann said warmly. 'Come to supper.'

'No, I won't be able to stay long,' Ginny said quickly. Correction, she might not *want* to stay long . . .

As soon as the traffic congestion had eased a little, she drove over to St John's Wood. By the time she arrived Ann was two-thirds of the way down a bottle of wine and pacing nervously, afraid Saul Lancaster might have 'dished the dirt' – although Ginny hadn't seemed upset or angry, just a little cool, she consoled herself.

'Ginny! How pretty you look – is that a new dress?' she enquired brightly. 'Have a drink?' she offered, waving the nearly empty bottle.

'No, thanks, I'm driving,' Ginny reminded her, eyeing her uncertainly. Is she drunk? she wondered uneasily.

143

'Oh, well how about something else? Orange juice?'

'Orange juice would be great,' Ginny said, and Ann bustled about, fetching ice and pouring the last of the wine into her own glass.

'Come and sit down and tell me all your news,' she said, again rather too brightly, Ginny thought, almost brittle, and so tense she seemed about ready to break into little pieces.

'This isn't really a social call,' Ginny told her, and took a deep breath. 'Mum, I know you won't approve, but I'm spending the day with Saul Lancaster tomorrow.'

'Oh? I thought you told me his behaviour last weekend was dreadful? Why put yourself through that again?' Ann asked edgily.

'He's apologized for that,' Ginny said. 'He called to see me on Wednesday and he was really . . . nice,' she finished lamely. Nice? Hardly. Exciting, disturbing, seductive – yes, all of those. But 'nice' was more appropriate for her mother's ears, she decided.

'I'm sure you're not asking for my permission to see him, so why are you here? Has . . . has he told you more lies about me?' Ann asked, wishing she still smoked.

'No. In fact, we've agreed not to discuss your, er, situation with his father,' Ginny told her, which afforded Ann some measure of relief. Unfortunately, she relaxed too soon. 'But I'd like you to tell me why he dislikes you so much,' Ginny continued. 'It's not just because of Sir David, is it? There's something else,' she stated.

'Well, yes, I think you're right,' Ann said, stand-

144

ing up and walking over to the window, keeping her back to her daughter. She had dreaded this moment, and had thought long and hard about how much to divulge. She took a deep breath and turned to face Ginny.

'I've been thinking a lot about Saul's unreasonable attitude and I think I know what's behind it. It was his assertion that your father might have committed suicide that gave me the clue.' She paused, aware of Ginny watching her intently. 'Does the name Bill Taggart mean anything to you?'

'No, I don't think so,' Ginny shook her head. 'Should it?'

'No, not really, you were only about four years old at the time. I just wondered if Saul had mentioned him?'

'No,' Ginny told her.

'Bill was a member of the board of directors at Lancaster Electronics years ago. He – well, developed a crush on me,' Ann said slowly. 'I didn't encourage him, but he kept sending me flowers and suchlike. He was very persistent and it was all rather awkward, since your father worked in his department.' She paused again. 'It caused problems, as you can probably imagine. There were a lot of rumours flying around, most of them unfounded, but the busybodies had a field-day when he walked out on his wife – she was a friend of Alice Lancaster,' she added, and Ginny grimaced.

'Uh-oh!'

'Quite,' Ann agreed drily. 'But that wasn't the worst of it. As I said, Bill was senior to your father back then, and tried to cause trouble for him. But David saw through that, sacked Bill, and promoted your father in his place. So Bill lost his job and his family, since his wife refused to let him see his children.' She took another deep breath. 'Bill killed himself, Ginny,' she said quietly.

'Oh, God!' Ginny said, shocked.

'Yes. His wife – and presumably Alice Lancaster – blamed me. Saul could only have been in his early teens at the time, but I suppose he must have heard the gossip. It was a dreadful time, Ginny, for everyone concerned, but it really wasn't my fault,' she said earnestly.

'I see,' Ginny said neutrally.

'You doubt me?' Ann sat down beside her. 'Well, I remember you coming home from school in tears when a friend wrongly accused you of stealing her boyfriend. And then there was that girl in college who discovered a boy had dated her simply to get to know you. Those girls blamed you when it was the boys at fault,' she said softly.

'Don't remind me.' Ginny shuddered at the memory. She had lost two good girlfriends simply because boys they had liked had preferred her. 'Thanks for telling me, Mum; I didn't mean to dredge up unpleasant memories.'

'Oh, it was a long time, ago.' Ann shrugged, then realized, after a sharp look from Ginny, that she had sounded rather heartless, and hastily changed the subject.

It was only when Ginny was leaving that Ann, despite her reluctance to talk about Saul Lancaster, felt she had to sound a note of caution.

'Ginny – are you falling in love with Saul?' she asked.

'I think I could be,' Ginny admitted.

'Oh, darling, be careful.' Ann was genuinely concerned, and not only for herself.

'Mother!'

'Oh, not that!' Ann said impatiently, then paused to reflect. 'Well, yes, that too,' she amended; the prospect of her sharing a grandchild with David and Alice Lancaster was positively mind-boggling! 'But what I really meant was be wary of Saul's mother. She won't approve of a relationship between you two,' she warned.

'That's her problem.' Ginny airily dismissed Alice Lancaster.

'Hmm, I think you'll find that Alice Lancaster has a habit of involving others in her problems,' Ann said drily. 'Perhaps it would help if I tell David not to visit me any more; that might appease the old battle-axe,' she said, half to herself. She knew there was nothing to be gained by her asking Alice to leave the two youngsters alone – that would only make Alice more determined to break them up. All she could do was ask David to keep an eye on the situation and trust he could foil any of Alice's troublemaking schemes.

'That's for you to decide,' Ginny replied, non-committally. 'Don't stop seeing him on my account.'

'Oh, it's not just you and Saul. All this political business is dreadfully boring, and it will only get worse if he is elected. Perhaps it's time for a change. Actually, I've been thinking over what you said about my getting a job.'

'Really?'

'Yes. You inherited more than your looks from me, you know. I share your artistic talent. Painting has always been just a hobby for me, but maybe it's not too late for me to go to college and make it something more.'

'Of course it's not. I think that's a great idea!' Ginny said warmly, and impulsively reached out to hug her. 'Oh, sorry, do your ribs still hurt?' she asked, hastily releasing her.

'Just a twinge occasionally.' Ann returned the hug; the comfort she derived from Ginny's closeness more than compensated for any temporary physical pain. 'Enjoy your weekend, darling. I'm sorry I've been a cow about your seeing Saul. I've just been so afraid of what he might tell you.'

'Stop worrying. Anyhow, I know the whole story now, don't I?' Ginny asked cheerfully. 'Bye, Mum, I'll call you next week.'

'Bye, darling.' Ann slowly closed the front door and leaned against it. The whole story? She grimaced. All she could do now was to pray Ginny's feelings for Saul were reciprocated – if that were so, he wouldn't say anything to hurt her. Or so she hoped.

On Saturday morning Ginny was too keyed-up and excited to stay cooped up in her flat, and made her way down to the garden to await Saul's arrival, sitting on the bench outside Jo's kitchen window. It was another beautiful day, bright and sunny, but not too hot.

'I bet you haven't eaten any breakfast,' Jo scolded

as she emerged from the house with a tray of coffee and toast.

'No, I haven't.' Ginny smiled as she accepted a cup of coffee but refused the toast.

'No wonder you're so slim,' Jo sighed enviously, before tucking into a piece of toast, lavishly buttered and heaped with marmalade. 'What's on the agenda for today?'

'Shopping,' Ginny told her. Jo choked on a crumb.

'You've found a man who enjoys shopping?' she asked, in tones of awe. 'Now I really am jealous!'

'It's for his new house – he's getting the keys today,' Ginny explained.

'Oh. Still, it's a good sign,' Jo said encouragingly. 'I don't think Barney helped choose any of our furniture. In fact, I . . .' She stopped speaking as she realized she had lost her audience. She didn't need to turn around to guess Saul Lancaster had arrived; the look of mingled excitement and wariness on Ginny's face spoke volumes.

'Good morning.' Saul's deep voice greeted them both, but his gaze was on Ginny, warmly approving of the picture she presented. She was wearing a simple shift dress of soft pink silk, and her newly washed blonde hair framed her face and bounced in glossy waves to her shoulders. Her only make-up was a touch of matching pink lipgloss.

'Hello,' Ginny managed shyly; she thought he looked terrific, in black jeans and a white shirt worn open at the neck and with the sleeves rolled up in deference to the heat. He looked tanned, superbly fit and strong.

'Good morning, Saul. Would you like some coffee?' Jo enquired brightly.

'No, thanks,' he declined, but with a warm smile that made even Jo's heart skip a beat. Wow, she thought. 'I'm in rather a hurry – I had to park on double yellow lines,' he explained, and Ginny got hastily to her feet.

'Where's my breakfast, woman?' Barney bellowed – never at his best first thing in the morning – and wandered out into the garden, blinking blearily in the sunlight. Jo shoved a piece of toast unceremoniously into his mouth by way of reply, and then ignored him. Through a mouthful of crumbs, Barney muttered something uncomplimentary about women who had nothing better to do than sit and gossip while their menfolk starved. Ginny grinned at him as she picked up her bag to accompany Saul.

'Does he often speak to her like that?' Saul asked, taken aback.

'Only when he's feeling very, very brave,' Ginny said solemnly, then she giggled. 'He was only kidding around – he adores her.' She was about to ask if his parents ever teased each other, but luckily thought better of it. Apparently they did not.

'I see,' Saul replied absently, his attention on a rapidly approaching traffic warden. Ginny found herself being bundled into the Jag and driven off at speed.

'Sorry about that – you okay?' Saul grinned at her as she straightened her limbs and tugged her skirt down.

'Fine,' she said breathlessly.

'The traffic's a nightmare this morning, so I thought we'd leave the car at the house and grab a taxi,' he told her.

'Have you already got the keys?'

'Yep. I won't be moving in properly until I leave the Army, but I want to get the basics done today.'

'When do you leave? The Army, I mean?'

'Not until August, I'm glad to say,' he replied absently.

'Oh?' Ginny shot him a puzzled glance, wondering why he was leaving at all if he didn't want to.

'I'll miss the by-election and Amanda's wedding,' Saul explained, correctly interpreting her glance. 'Being in the Forces offers a great excuse to avoid family dos. I simply say I'll be away on exercises or something, and no one's any the wiser,' he added cheerfully.

It was only a short drive to Saul's mews house on the Embankment, and as they approached Ginny recognized it from the estate agent's brochure. Saul locked the Jag away and they entered the house via an internal door leading from the garage.

'Hold on a minute – the burglar alarm is switched on,' he warned her, fishing in his pocket for the key and the piece of paper on which he had jotted the combination. He frowned slightly as he deactivated the alarm. 'I'll never remember that number – when's your birthday?' he asked Ginny. 'March the what?'

'Eighteenth,' she told him, absurdly pleased that he had even remembered the month of her birthday.

'Right. 1803.' He consulted the instructions which the previous owners had left by the control box, and keyed in the new number. 'If you ever receive a phone call in the middle of the night from a drunk demanding to know your birthdate, please don't hang up! It will be me, having forgotten how to turn off the alarm,' he told her.

'Why not use your own birthday?' she asked.

'I'd rather use yours,' Saul told her, with a heart-stopping smile. 'Have a look around, if you're interested,' he suggested.

'Oh, yes, please!' There was nothing Ginny liked better than nosing around other people's properties – she was always the first to arrive with a house-warming gift whenever a friend moved into a new house!

She felt she already knew Saul's from memorizing the details in the brochure, and wandered around happily, her imagination decorating the rooms and filling them with furniture and paintings.

The view of the Thames from the master bed-room was breathtaking, and she allowed herself to daydream a little, thinking how lovely it would be to wake up to such a panorama each morning.

'Bed,' came Saul's husky voice from close behind her. Ginny physically jumped.

'I beg your pardon?' she gasped.

'A bed – the first item on my shopping list,' he explained, his face expressionless, and Ginny flushed.

'Oh. Yes, of course. I was just thinking . . . er . . .' Her mind was a complete blank for several endless seconds, then, 'You ought to put up curtains as soon as possible,' she almost gabbled. 'Empty windows are a dead giveaway to burglars. You'd be asking for trouble, even with an alarm,' she told him.

'Good idea, Sherlock,' Saul said gravely. 'Come on, let's go shopping.'

They took a cab to Knightsbridge, where Saul set about the task as if he were conducting a military campaign. Jo was obviously wrong about him liking to shop, Ginny thought ruefully. She had no time to linger, but was marched from one department to another in quick order.

Only later did she realize he had spent an inordinate length of time choosing a bed! He had enjoyed that, especially her embarrassment when the sales assistant, obviously taking it for granted that they were setting up home together, had asked for her opinion and suggested she remove her shoes to try out various mattresses.

'Yes, come on, darling,' Saul had urged, deadpan. 'We have to be sure it's comfortable.' He lay down and tugged at her hand until she, too, stretched out beside him. 'How was that for you?' he enquired solemnly, making her giggle.

'God, that's enough shopping for one day,' he declared feelingly, when they emerged out into the sunshine. 'How about some lunch?' he suggested.

'Mmm. Why don't we get some sandwiches and eat outdoors?' Ginny said, to his surprise.

'I was going to take you somewhere expensive,' he told her.

'No, it's too nice a day to be in a restaurant,' she told him.

'Okay, sandwiches it is. I'll take you out tonight instead; somewhere intimate, with a tiny dance floor so I have an excuse to hold you close,' he murmured, his arm around her waist drawing her to his side.

'You don't need an excuse for that,' Ginny said breathlessly, then blushed at her own daring.

'I don't? That's good to hear.' A smile tugged at the corners of his mouth and he stopped walking, turned to face her and bent to kiss her, very lightly, on the mouth.

They found a shady spot in the park, a small, grassy mound beneath a large, spreading chestnut tree, and sat down to eat their lunch of smoked salmon sandwiches, a punnet of strawberries and cans of drink.

Saul sprawled on the grass while Ginny sat more primly, too aware of the strong, muscled body lying beside her to eat very much. Saul, with one hunger sated, grew increasingly aware of another as he watched Ginny. He couldn't remember ever wanting a woman as much as he wanted this one; he literally ached with the need to have her. However, he refused to even try and rationalize his determination to win her love as well as her body.

Leisurely, he reached up to touch the softness of her hair, then curled his hand around her neck, tugging gently until she bent her head towards him. Ginny, with his fingers warm and caressing on her skin, had no power to resist, nor any wish to, she readily admitted, if only to herself.

'You taste of sunshine and strawberries,' Saul murmured against her mouth. He shifted his position slightly, raising his body while manoeuvering Ginny until she was half lying across his chest. His arms made her a willing prisoner, his hands on her back both comforting and exciting.

He deepened the kiss, loving the sensation of her soft breasts crushed against his chest, and felt his own desire threaten to spiral out of control when he felt her nipples harden and heard a soft whimper of need from deep in her throat. He was in danger of forgetting which of them was the hunter and which the prey . . .

It was Ginny who broke the kiss, a little frightened by the intensity of her feelings. Her heart was pounding furiously and her hands trembled as she set about gathering up the debris from their lunch.

'Wh – what do you want to do this afternoon?' she asked shakily, and rather stupidly, she realized at once.

'Do you want the truthful answer, or an alternative suggestion as to how we should spend our time?' Saul drawled.

Ginny bit her lip. 'An alternative suggestion,' she said, trying to sound stern, but was afraid she had merely sounded disappointed! Saul evidently thought so, too, and his mouth curved with amusement. He backed off, or at least he appeared to, but only to approach his objective from another direction.

'How about a game of tennis?' he asked.

'Tennis? After watching Jack and Melissa last weekend, I don't think I'll ever have the cheek to pick up a racket again,' she told him.

'They won't be there.' No one would, he thought. 'We could have a swim later, to cool off.'

'That sounds good,' Ginny said.

'Come on, then.' Saul stood up in one lithe movement and held out his hand to her. Ginny took it and he pulled her to her feet, keeping her hand in his as they walked out of the park.

'We'll go back to my house to collect my car and then I'll drive you to your flat to pick up whatever you need,' he said, stepping out to hail a cruising taxi.

He was again unable to find a parking space, and paused briefly outside the house for Ginny to clamber quickly from the car.

'I'll drive around the block,' he said, as impatient drivers behind him sounded their horns.

'Okay, I won't be long,' she promised.

'Ginny – bring a dress for dinner later. Preferably that purple bit of froth you wore for Amanda's party,' Saul called after her. Ginny looked back and smiled.

'You liked that?'

'As my cousin Nigel said – I liked what was inside it!' he drawled, then, 'Okay, okay, I'm going!' he bawled at the irate driver behind him.

Ginny dashed up the steps to her flat, almost tripping as she was too busy searching in her bag for her keys to watch where she was putting her feet.

'Hi, Jo, Barney,' she said, as she spotted them relaxing in the garden. Once inside the flat, she grabbed her overnight case, grinned as she put in the lilac mini-dress, then added clean underwear, her tennis clothes, shoes and a swimsuit. Thinking frantically, she threw in a towel, suntan lotion and her make-up, decided that was all she would need and ran back outside, again almost falling as she negotiated the steps.

'Bye, Jo, Barney,' she said breathlessly. 'I can't stop.'

'That's right, lovey, you keep him waiting. Show him who's the boss,' Barney called out sarcastically, and raised his brows in mock indignation when he received an extremely rude gesture by way of reply. He watched Ginny clamber into Saul's Jag and the car move off at speed, then turned to his wife.

'She was carrying a suitcase.'

'Mmm, I noticed. It's none of our business; she's over twenty-one,' Jo said firmly.

'I thought she didn't even like that guy?'

'I guess she's changed her mind.'

CHAPTER 8

Ginny had assumed they would be going to a sports club nearby, but instead Saul seemed to be heading out of central London.

'Where are we going?'

'My parents' place,' he replied casually.

'What!' Ginny shrieked, so agitated she stamped her foot down on an imaginary brake, such was her desperation to stop the car.

'Relax. They're away for the weekend – Amanda's future in-laws are having a bash at their stately pile in Northumberland,' he told her.

'Weren't you invited? Or did you tell them you couldn't get away from your Army duties?' she guessed, and he turned briefly to smile.

'That's right, I did,' he admitted cheerfully. 'I had better things to do,' he added, and she swallowed nervously, her initial relief at hearing of his parents' absence replaced by trepidation – and a mounting excitement.

Am I ready for this? she wondered, but knew the alternative, which was to ask to be taken home, was definitely not what she wanted. Anyhow, perhaps she was jumping to conclusions, and all he had in mind was tennis and swimming. Believe that and you'll believe those fairies you're going to paint for Kit Farrell are real, she scoffed at herself.

'How good are you?'

'At what?' she yelped, and Saul suppressed a grin, but not quickly enough. 'Stop trying to make me blush,' she scolded.

'I can't resist it, darling. Nor you,' he added, under his breath, and the smouldering look he bestowed upon her left her in no doubt that tennis and swimming were not the only activities on the agenda.

This is crazy. I hardly know him, I don't do things like this, I ought to go home, she thought wildly, but she said nothing.

This is crazy, she's getting under my skin too much. I ought to take her home and forget her, Saul thought, but he, too, said nothing. More to the point, he didn't stop to turn the car around, either, but continued driving.

Ginny sat up straighter and took more notice of her surroundings as Saul indicated his intention to turn into a long, sweeping driveway; she noted, with pleasure, the broad expanse of well-tended lawns bordered with masses of colourful flowering shrubs. The house itself was a large three-storeyed building of red brick, the stone mellowed with age and softened by the tenacious ivy which clung to every crevice on its upward climb, reaching almost to the roof in places.

Saul braked to a halt on the gravel and she clambered slowly out of the car, still looking around her with interest, then she flushed slightly as she became belatedly aware that he was watching her.

'I think I came here once with my father, years ago,' she said. 'He dropped some papers off for your father.'

'I was probably away at school, or already in the Army,' he said. 'Come on inside,' he invited, unlocking the front door and holding it open for her. Ginny hesitated for just a second, then moved into the cool interior.

'Amanda has permanent use of one of the guest-rooms; you should find all you'll need in there,' he said, leading the way up the broad, shallow staircase and throwing open a bedroom door, then standing back to let her precede him.

'I'll see you downstairs in ten minutes,' he said, then closed the door, and Ginny heard him go whistling along the corridor, presumably to go and change.

She didn't immediately put on her tennis dress, but looked around the prettily decorated room, approving the pink and cream decor, and peeking inside the *en suite* bathroom which had a matching colour scheme.

Suddenly remembering his 'ten minutes' dictum, she quickly changed and, emerging rather shyly from the guest-room, made her way slowly down the stairs, giving her curiosity full rein now she no longer had an audience.

Everything was plush, expensive and in the best of taste – and also completely impersonal, she decided, unashamedly peering through an open door into the drawing-room. The furniture looked to be polished to within an inch of its life, there were matching cushions in regimented rows along the two cream velvet sofas in front of the fireplace, and a tidy stack of magazines on a coffee table which was positioned precisely midway between the couches.

There were no photographs that she could see, nor any flowers, despite their profusion in the gardens. It was difficult to imagine a small boy growing up in such surroundings and she felt suddenly sad for Saul, and wondered if he had been happier while away at boarding school.

'Seen enough? Or would you like a guided tour?' The amused drawl from behind her made her blush, and she spun round to face Saul.

'I'm s-sorry,' she stammered, full of confusion, a state provoked more by his appearance than by being caught snooping. White shorts and top accentuated his dark, tanned good looks, and revealed a magnificent physique, she admitted silently to herself, watching him covertly from beneath lowered lashes. The thin sports shirt stretched taut over his strongly muscled torso, emphasizing his broad shoulders and chest, tapering to to lean waist and hips. There was not an ounce of superfluous flesh on his body; he looked like a man in peak condition, and she was suddenly glad she submitted her own body to twice-weekly torture sessions at an aerobics class.

'Come on, this way.' He turned and Ginny followed in his wake, down the hall to a second sitting-room at the side of the house, from where French windows gave access to the terrace. It was very quiet – unnervingly so, Ginny felt.

'Don't your parents need a large staff to keep the house and gardens so immaculate?' she asked.

'My mother has a daily help and we have a gardener who comes in several days a week,' he told her. 'But she doesn't like having people living in, so we're quite alone today!'

Ginny responded to that with a look which should have stopped him in his tracks, but he merely grinned unrepentantly, so she tilted her nose into the air and pushed past him and out on to the terrace.

Patio furniture and huge tubs filled with brightly coloured blooms made it a comfortable suntrap, but Ginny continued on her way down the stone steps and towards the tennis court, noting the swimming pool situated behind a low wall. The water looked cool and inviting, sparkling with the reflection of the sun on its blue-tiled interior.

She waited while Saul unlocked the door of a white-painted pavilion and picked out a racket for his own use from a cupboard, together with a couple of boxes of tennis balls.

'I don't think I'm going to be able to give you much of a game,' she said, suddenly fearful of making an utter fool of herself.

'Ah, well, if tennis is a no-go, we can always think of something else to play,' he said, perfectly straight-faced, yet Ginny eyed him suspiciously before she walked off towards the court. It was a grass court, enclosed by a high wire-mesh fence, and was obviously well-tended, the turf smooth and cropped short, the white lines clearly defined.

Ginny began to feel less jumpy as they started trading shots; he was much further away, at the opposite end of the court, and besides, she found it was impossible to remain mentally tense while expending so much physical energy!

Without conscious thought, she relaxed her muscles as she was forced to run the length and width of the court in an attempt to retrieve the balls Saul effortlessly parried and returned, with interest. She sensed he was holding back on his superior strength of shot, only unleashing the full force of the power at his disposal when male pride dictated he should win the last point of every game.

'Show off!' She glared balefully at him when yet another ball whizzed past her, way out of reach.

'Don't be such a sore loser!' Saul called back, grinning. 'Actually you're not a bad player – for a girl,' he added, with such deliberately blatant condescension that Ginny was able to ignore the remark – just. However, she decided to repeat it to Melissa at the earliest opportuniy!

She gritted her teeth and continued the unequal contest, but was eventually forced to concede defeat. She felt exhausted. Her dress was sticking to her unpleasantly, and she felt sure her face was as red as a beetroot from all her exertion.

'Can we stop?' she called out, rather breathlessly.

'Sure,' Saul agreed readily, and began gathering up the scattered balls while Ginny flopped wearily down onto the grass and struggled to regain her breath.

'Come on, lazy bones.' Saul held out a hand and Ginny let him haul her to her feet, irritably aware that he was still cool and not the least bit tired.

'You okay? You look as if you're about to have a heart attack! And you didn't even win,' he taunted.

'Only because you cheated on line calls,' Ginny replied loftily, and quite untruthfully. 'You men who can't bear to be beaten by a woman really are –' She stopped speaking, alerted by an unholy gleam in his dark eyes. Suddenly she found the strength to turn and run, laughing over her shoulder as he gave chase. Saul caught her easily before she reached the dubious safety of the house and swung her around to face him, his arm curving around her waist.

'Don't you dare kiss me!' Ginny warned as his grip tightened, uncomfortably aware of her sweaty, dishevelled appearance.

'That wasn't on my mind,' he drawled, then in one fluid movement he scooped her off her feet, and the next thing she knew Ginny found herself being tossed into the swimming pool.

Unprepared for the ducking, she had no time to hold her breath and rose to the surface, choking and spluttering. The water seemed icy-cold against her heated body, but she resisted the impulse to swim for the side and instead pretended to be floundering.

'Saul, I can't swim!' she called out piteously, expecting him to jump in and save her. She was sadly disappointed.

'You won't drown – it isn't deep enough,' he said callously, and she stared in disbelief as he began walking towards the terrace, ignoring her plight.

'You . . .' She struck out for the steps at the end of the pool and he turned around, laughing at her. 'Oh!' Too late, she realized she had given the lie to her words. 'How did you know I could swim?' she asked indignantly. 'Or didn't you care if I could or not?'

'If you couldn't, you'd have said so earlier, when I first suggested a swim,' he told her.

'Huh! Well, you might at least help me out,' she complained, pushing her wet hair back from her face. She held out her arm and then, when he bent to take it, quickly grabbed his wrist with both hands and exerted all her strength to try and topple him into the pool, but to no avail.

'Nice try,' Saul acknowledged. 'But I'm wise to you, Ginny Sinclair. Always one step ahead,' he told her complacently as he hauled her, dripping wet and furious, out of the water.

'God, you're so smug!' She tried to hold on to her dignity, which was extremely difficult under the circumstances: the tennis dress, short and skimpy when dry, was now almost transparent and clung like a second skin, and her hair was hanging in rat's-tails around a face devoid of make-up.

'You've only yourself to blame for that ducking – you shouldn't have accused me of cheating,' he said, quite uncontrite. 'I'll get you a towel,' he offered as a peace-offering, but made no effort to move away, and when Ginny looked up at him, she found his eyes burning with an unmistakable message of desire.

'Ginny?' he asked softly, questioningly, and she swallowed, instinctively knowing that one tiny hint of acquiescence from her would unleash the passion she sensed he was only barely holding in check. She gazed back at him, dry-mouthed, unable to simply walk away, which was what she should do, or so the sensible part of her brain screamed at her. Only she didn't feel at all like behaving sensibly . . .

'Ginny?' Saul said again, but he made no attempt to touch her, and they stood, inches apart, the very air around them fraught with sexual tension.

Saul couldn't have said what made him hesitate; she was there for the taking, yet a part of him held back from accepting what she was offering. How can anyone look so sexy and yet so innocent? he wondered. Which was the act, the pretence, and which the real Ginny Sinclair? According to James Calvert, she 'couldn't get enough of it'. He bitterly recalled the younger man's boast, yet Calvert had previously described Ginny as a 'frigid bitch'. Saul no longer knew what to believe, and even as the lustful cynic in him jeered at him for being a fool he turned away from temptation.

'I'll fetch you a towel,' he said abruptly.

'Can't I have a real swim, since I'm already wet?' Ginny asked. 'I put my swimsuit on under my tennis dress,' she added.

'Of course, go ahead. But you'll still need a towel,' Saul replied shortly.

'Okay, thanks.' Puzzled, torn between disappointment and relief, Ginny peeled off her wet tennis dress, socks and shoes and dived back into the pool. Saul caught a glimpse of her slender, superbly toned body, clad in a white swimsuit that was more of a bikini, with a lacy midriff linking the two pieces, before she disappeared beneath the water.

Ginny swam several lengths quickly and then

trod water, enjoying the coolness of it against her skin. She saw Saul had stretched out on one of the sunloungers on the terrace – he appeared to be watching her, but since he had donned a pair of dark glasses she couldn't be sure.

'It's lovely! Aren't you coming in?' she called to him. Saul just shook his head, too aware of his arousal to strip off his clothes! And getting nearer to Ginny would only make matters a lot worse, he thought ruefully. Of course, jumping into cold water should dampen his ardour somewhat, he decided, and, removing only his trainers and socks, he went over and joined her in the pool.

'Good; I was feeling lonely,' Ginny grinned at him, splashing him with cold water and moving rather too near, Saul thought.

'Don't tease,' he warned gruffly.

'I wasn't . . .' Again, there was that look of hurt bewilderment in her lovely eyes and Saul groaned. The cold water wasn't easing his discomfort one iota.

'Don't look at me like that, darling, please.'

'Else what? You'll forget your good intentions?' Ginny knew she was goading him, but couldn't help it.

'Mmm, or, more accurately, I'll remember my bad ones.' He paused, then, 'I brought you here with the intention of seducing you,' he told her frankly.

'Oh.' Ginny looked away, then faced him. 'I think I knew that,' she said softly.

'You still came,' he stated.

'Yes.' They stared at each other for a moment,

then Saul reached out for her hand and she floated towards him, losing her footing in the deeper water. Saul caught her, spanning her waist with his hands as he bent to kiss her. Ginny wrapped her arms around his neck and returned the kiss eagerly, opening her mouth to his questing tongue as desire rose in her, invoking a need such as she had never felt before and which demanded satiation. Now.

'Bed?' Saul suggested huskily, and she nodded wordlessly. He lifted her effortlessly out of the water and then hauled himself up beside her. He grabbed her hand to help her to her feet and then they ran, dripping wet, towards the house.

'Your mother's carpets . . .' Ginny said, looking down in dismay at their wet footprints on the soft, pale grey flooring.

'Sod my mother's carpets!' Saul responded, and continued leading the way upstairs.

His room was cool and only dimly lit, since the curtains were closed against the sun, and Ginny was only vaguely aware of her surroundings. It was a masculine room, with plain cream walls, dark blue curtains and soft furnishings, and heavy mahogany furniture. And a bed. A huge bed.

Saul fetched more towels from his bathroom, using one to dry his hair and draping the other around Ginny's shoulders.

'You're shivering,' he noticed with concern.

'It's cooler in here,' she said, rather defensively.

'It's not that cool . . . are you nervous?' he asked slowly, incredulously.

'A little,' Ginny admitted. 'And . . . I'm not on the Pill or anything,' she added.

'I'll take care of that,' he assured her.

'There's something else . . . I don't think I'm as experienced as you think I am,' she mumbled uncomfortably. Her one encounter, with a boy at college, into which she had entered more out of curiosity than desire, seemed long ago and quite irrelevant. She didn't want to discuss it, but hated more the possibility of disappointing Saul.

'No, I don't think you are,' Saul said, eyeing her thoughtfully. If she were play-acting, she ought to be in Hollywood . . . Any lingering notion he'd harboured of using her and then discarding her vanished without trace. He still wanted to teach her a lesson, but one very different from the original one he'd had in mind, one that would prove very pleasurable to them both. He made a mental note to seek out James Calvert and get the truth from him – by beating it out of him if necessary, he thought grimly.

He reached for Ginny's hands and submitted her to such a hot-eyed scrutiny that she stopped shivering and felt suffused with the heat from his gaze.

'I must look like a drowned rat,' she said, suddenly aware of wet tendrils of hair clinging to her face and neck.

'No, you look like a water nymph,' he said softly, then his eyes gleamed. 'Although I imagine water nymphs are usually naked . . .'

Ginny swallowed, excitement coursing through her veins.

'Then I guess I'm overdressed,' she whispered.

'Is that an invitation?' he asked huskily.

'Yes,' she said, dropping the towel he had given

her and standing before him wearing only the wet, almost transparent white swimsuit. Watching his eyes on her, she smiled tremulously, and reached slowly to undo the halter-neck fastening.

'Let me do that,' Saul said, when her fingers fumbled with the wet clasp. His hands were warm on her shoulders as he turned her around, and Ginny leaned back against his chest as she felt the straps loosen.

Saul slowly pushed the swimsuit down over her breasts and then to her hips, leaving it there while his hands gently caressed her tummy and midriff. Then he moved to cup her breasts and she moaned, arching her back as the soft mounds swelled into his palms.

He bent his head to nuzzle her neck and shoulder while his fingers stroked and teased her nipples into hard peaks. One knee nudged her legs apart and she leaned even more heavily against him. She felt boneless, weightless, every nerve-ending in her body quivering beneath his exquisite touch.

Saul stroked one hand slowly down over her ribs, pausing to circle her navel with his thumb before moving lower. Ginny moaned out loud as he slid one finger inside her, and she heard his answering groan as he encountered the moist heat of her arousal.

'You're ready for me,' he stated throatily, his breath hotly fanning her cheek.

'Yes, oh yes,' Ginny managed to reply, before he spun her around to enclose her in his embrace, his lips seeking hers. Her mouth opened beneath the onslaught, matching the insistent probing of his tongue and pressing even closer.

Without conscious thought she fumbled with his shirt; wet and clinging though it was, it was still an unbearable hindrance. Saul broke the kiss briefly and impatiently tugged the shirt over his head before reaching for her again. Ginny gasped when the mat of hair on his bared chest brushed against her already sensitized breasts.

Saul cupped her buttocks in his hands and pulled her hips closer, leaving her in no doubt as to the state of his own arousal. They tumbled onto the bed, feverishly casting aside the remainder of their clothing before melting together in a close embrace.

Ginny wrapped her arms around Saul, stroking his back and shoulders, loving the strength and firmness of the hard-packed muscles beneath the smooth skin. For a while it was enough just to hold his naked body close as he held hers, but not for long. Instinctively, her legs parted, and he lay between her thighs, kissing her eyes, her cheeks, and even the tip of her nose before capturing her mouth once again.

Ginny moved her lower body against his in blatant invitation. Saul raised his head and gazed down at her; his cheeks were flushed with desire, his breathing as ragged as her own, his dark eyes glittering hotly as they asked an unspoken question.

'Yes,' she whispered. 'Make love to me . . .'

As he eased inside her, beautifully filling the aching void, she closed her eyes in ecstasy, her muscles instinctively opening to accommodate him, then holding him captive deep within her. When he began to move, slowly at first and then with greater urgency, ripples of delicious heat coursed through her veins.

Amazingly, the feelings grew and grew, each thrust sending her spiralling more and more out of control until she was beyond coherent thought. Nothing existed for her but the man she clung to and the miraculous pleasure he was bestowing upon her. Ginny heard someone cry out, vaguely realized it was she who was responsible, and bit down on her lip in an effort to stop.

'Make all the noise you want to, my darling,' Saul whispered against her mouth, then he traced her lips with his tongue, finally dipping it inside to mate with hers. That was Ginny's undoing, and she felt her whole body convulse. She arched her back and cried out, unable even to breathe as wave after wave swept her almost into unconsciousness.

Dimly she heard Saul cry out as he, too, climaxed, and she smiled a purely female smile of triumph as he collapsed on top of her. She closed her eyes and wrapped her arms around him, revelling in the weight of his body on hers. Gradually her heart-beat slowed to its normal pace and she opened her eyes to find Saul watching her intently.

'Now you belong to me,' he told her fiercely, and she nodded, glorying in his possessiveness.

He rolled onto his side, taking her with him, and she lay cradled in his arms, utterly content. She closed her eyes again and snuggled even closer, wanting to capture the moment for ever. Whatever happened in the future, she would always remember this: not just the pleasure, but the wonderful hard strength of his body, the protection of his arms holding her. She felt nothing bad could ever touch her while he was near . . .

Through the open window could be heard the distant sound of a lawn mower; there was a bird singing nearby, and a slight breeze wafted the scent of honeysuckle into the room.

'What's that bird singing outside the window?' she murmured.

Saul listened for a moment.

'A thrush,' he told her. 'Why did you ask?'

'I just wanted to know. I want to remember every detail of this afternoon,' she said dreamily, and his hold on her tightened.

'That almost sounds as if you think we'll never do this again,' he said roughly. Ginny opened her eyes and tilted her head back to look at him.

'I didn't mean that at all,' she assured him. 'Right now I wish we never had to leave this bed,' she said truthfully. Saul relaxed and smiled, and then his mouth took possession of hers, fiercely demanding.

Ginny was amazed by how swiftly their passion reignited. Only moments before she had thought herself sated and sleepy, but now the exquisite ache of desire was uncoiling within her once more and she began caressing him, moved her hips against him in blatant invitation.

He caught her questing hands and twined his fingers in hers, spreading her arms out wide and holding them captive. Ginny tried to move, but couldn't, and when the long, drugging kiss finally ended, she managed to ask breathlessly, 'Why won't you let me touch you?'

'Because you excite me too much,' he told her; the

173

first time, although wonderful, had been too brief for him. 'Later you can touch me as much as you want to, but for now I want to know every inch of you,' he said huskily.

He was as good as his word, Ginny thought bemusedly some time later, before she could no longer think at all. His leisurely exploration of her body had her moaning and writhing mindlessly, and his knowing fingers and tongue set every nerve leaping and quivering with lust. Her breasts were already swollen, the nipples taut with desire, and she thought she might die of pleasure as his heated mouth suckled first one rosy peak then the other, teasing the hardened buds until she cried out.

Finally Saul released his grip on her hands to move down her body, stroking and nibbling at her calves and then her inner thighs. Ginny stopped breathing when his mouth found the core of her femininity, and she tugged feverishly at his shoulders, needing him inside her.

He positioned himself and slid his hard length into her with one fluid movement, and she gave a sigh of pure bliss, pushing against him so he became even more deeply embedded within her. They moved as one, the waves of pleasure more intense than before as he carried her inexorably to a climax more shattering and complete than anything she could ever have imagined.

Slowly, gradually, the spasms subsided and she opened her eyes to discover that he was again watching her closely. She smiled, then pouted when he moved slightly away from her, but she was too exhausted to protest, and, without meaning to, she drifted off to sleep in his arms.

Saul lay propped up one one elbow and watched her, his eyes feasting on every detail of her exquisite face. He didn't want to wake her, but was compelled to touch her, and gently caressed the softness of her cheek with his hand.

Face it, Lancaster, you're hooked, he thought ruefully. His earlier notion of taking her to bed and then leaving her was almost laughable, so impossible would it be. He groaned at the very thought of never seeing her again, never holding her, never hearing her laugh.

He wondered suddenly just how great was her mother's influence. He tried to push the thought aside, but it persisted in nagging away at the back of his mind, so he stopped fighting it and gave it his careful consideration.

He quickly decided, with a huge sense of relief, that Ann Sinclair probably wasn't the driving force in Ginny's life that he had first thought. Ginny had confessed to being a daddy's girl, and Richard Sinclair had been a decent man, honest and loyal – too loyal to his wife, Saul thought grimly.

Also, Ginny had left the parental home, attended college, and now lived alone, earning her own living and standing on her own two feet. He doubted Ann Sinclair had ever done a hard day's work in her entire life! Ann needed men to provide for her; Ginny did not. She was of a different generation, with a different outlook on life, he decided happily. In fact, he now doubted Ginny had an ounce of guile in her lovely body.

He only wished he could make amends for his earlier mistreatment of her; he wanted to shower her with gifts, and would do so, but for the pleasure the giving would afford him, not because he felt Ginny expected it of him in return for her favours. At the thought, he climbed out of bed and retrieved the watch he had bought her from the jacket pocket where it had lain since her refusal to accept it.

Ginny came awake abruptly at the touch of cold metal on her skin, and glanced down to see Saul fastening the gold watch on her wrist.

'What . . . ?'

'Don't argue,' he said firmly. 'There's no point in it sitting in my pocket. Besides, I damaged yours when I tossed you into the swimming pool,' he fibbed.

'You did?'

'Mmm, you took it off before your swim, but I noticed the glass was already beaded with moisture,' he told her.

'It will be okay when it dries out,' she said, trying not to notice how beautiful the watch looked on her wrist.

'Why are you so stubborn?' he asked, exasperated. 'Don't you like it?'

'Yes, but . . .'

'No buts.' He kissed her to stop further argument, and Ginny sighed her capitulation, twining her arms around his neck to pull him closer.

CHAPTER 9

Much later, hunger and thirst forced them reluctantly out of bed, and Saul fetched cold drinks while Ginny showered to rinse the chlorine from the pool out of her hair.

'Do you want to go out for dinner, or shall I send out for something?' Saul asked, sitting on the bed and enjoying watching her as, wearing only a towel, she combed out her hair. He found he was enjoying the domesticity of the situation, and only wished his own house was already fully furnished and ready for occupation. There hadn't been any urgency until now. He wondered idly what it would be like to come home every evening to such a scene, to this woman . . .

'Oh, send out.' Ginny smiled at his reflection in the mirror. She would have liked to cook for him, but was aware that this wasn't her house. In fact . . . 'Are you sure your parents won't be coming back this evening?' she asked anxiously.

'Positive,' he assured her, then grinned. 'You're not worried about meeting them, are you?'

'Well, you must admit it would be rather embarrassing,' she said.

'Mmm, just a bit,' he agreed, with what she thought was remarkable understatement. Then he frowned slightly. 'If they don't like the situation, that's their problem. We're two unattached adults and we'll live our lives as we want, not to suit them.'

'Yes,' Ginny agreed, but rather doubtfully. She recalled her mother saying that Alice Lancaster had a habit of involving others in her problems . . . She didn't think it would be as easy as Saul obviously thought it would be, but she kept her reservations to herself, reluctant to introduce a note of discord into what had been a wonderful day.

The wonderful day continued into the night; despite not going out to dine, Ginny dressed up in the dark lilac dress Saul had requested she wear – not that it actually stayed on very long!

They ate pizza, drank wine and watched a video . . . well, they started watching it, but she couldn't have said later which film was on the screen. Finally, she fell asleep in his arms, exhausted, sexually replete and blissfully happy.

At first, Sunday looked set to be a delightful repeat of Saturday, until a phone call mid-morning set Saul to cursing fluently. The air was blue with expletives as he walked back out onto the terrace, where they had been sitting drinking coffee and idly perusing the newspapers.

'Oh, my God! Your parents are here!' Ginny guessed, scrambling up from the sunlounger and looking wildly around for a hiding place.

'No. Worse than that,' Saul told her glumly, reaching for her hands and holding her close.

'I'm sorry, darling, but I have to go to Cyprus. Today.'

'Cyprus!'

'Yes. Our second battalion is out there. The CO is at a conference and the second in command has been rushed into hospital. I have to fly out and take over,' he explained.

'Oh, I see.' Ginny bit her lip, stupidly close to tears.

'I hope it won't be for long, but if it is, will you fly out for a holiday?' he asked her, and her spirits rose a little. 'I've been there before; I think you'll enjoy the island. I'll find you a good hotel and send tickets. You could bring a friend to keep you company while I'm on duty – I'll be able to fix her up with a date,' he added.

'I'd better bring Claire – she has a thing about Army officers,' Ginny told him.

'Oh, yes? And do you?' he queried.

'I do now.' Ginny reached up to kiss him. 'Just one particular Army officer,' she assured him.

'I'm glad to hear it – I'd hate to have to thump a fellow officer,' he said, wrapping his arms around her, still cursing his bad luck. Why now? he raged inwardly. Thank God he would soon be out of the Army for ever.

He buried his face in the soft fragrance of her hair and smiled wryly as he recalled Nick, barely ten days earlier, telling him the Army was no job for a family man. How he had scoffed at the notion of settling down! He silently swore some more at his misfortune, then reluctantly put her from him. He wanted desperately to make love to her, but refused

179

to yield to the temptation, to take her hurriedly and then leave her.

'Go and get your things; I'll drive you back to Chelsea,' he said.

'I can get a cab if you're in a hurry,' she offered, and he smiled.

'I'm not in that much of a hurry. I want to drive you – okay?'

'Well, if you're sure,' Ginny said doubtfully. 'You won't be listed AWOL or whatever, will you?' she asked anxiously, and he laughed.

'No, nothing that drastic, but I'm afraid I do have to get moving.'

'Okay, I won't be long.' She rushed off and hastily gathered up her belongings from both Saul's room and the guest-room she had used prior to their game of tennis – how long ago that seemed! So much had happened since, she thought happily, pausing to check she had left nothing behind before hurrying back downstairs to where Saul was already waiting. He locked up the house and, five minutes after the phone call, they were on their way.

Luckily, the Sunday-morning traffic was sparse, and Saul made good time, pulling up outside her house just as Barney and Jo were walking back from the newsagent's.

'Hello, lovey.' Barney smiled warmly at Ginny as he opened the car door for her. Then he nodded, rather curtly, at Saul, noticing that he hadn't even turned off the car engine.

Ginny had first worked for Barney and Jo on a casual basis during her college holidays, and they had witnessed her heartbreak over her father's premature death. Consequently, Barney felt almost paternal and protective of her – especially as he considered Ann was too flighty and selfish to be of much help to her only child – and he didn't think Richard Sinclair would have approved of some guy taking his daughter away overnight and then dumping her back home like last week's dirty laundry.

'You had a visitor last night,' he told Ginny, purposely speaking loud enough for Saul to hear. 'It was Jame – Ouch!' He looked reproachfully at Jo, who smiled sweetly.

'Sorry, was that your ankle?'

'James Calvert was here?' Saul asked sharply, wishing he had the time to go and sort him out. 'Ginny?' he said, almost accusingly, she thought.

'I don't know why he would come here . . .' she began, but stopped speaking when Saul grabbed her wrist and stared at him apprehensively.

'If he comes here again, you tell him to get lost,' he said harshly. 'I don't share.'

'I'm not interested in Jamie,' she told him. 'You know I'm not,' she added, hurt that he could even think she would go to bed with one man while still involved with another.

'Okay, I'm sorry.' Saul relaxed, kissed her wrist by way of an apology for gripping it so tightly, then reached over and kissed her mouth. 'God, I wish I could take you with me,' he sighed.

'So do I.' Ginny clung to him for a moment, then reluctantly moved away and clambered out of the car.

'I'll call you as soon as I arrive,' he promised.

'Yes, please do.' Ginny had to blink back tears as

she watched him drive away. Honestly, anyone would think he was going off to war instead of to a holiday island! she chastised herself.

She explained briefly what had happened to Barney and Jo, refused their offer of company and holed up in her flat, drinking endless cups of coffee while her mood veered from the heights to the depths as she alternately relived the happiness of the previous day and night, and contemplated the desolation and loneliness of the weeks ahead.

Eventually, in an effort to take her mind off Saul, she tried to concentrate on all the work to be done at Bellwood, and was packing for a lengthy stay when a knock sounded at the door. She had forgotten all about Jamie's visit the night before, and was surprised to see him standing there, with a rather sheepish expression on his boyishly handsome face.

'Come in.' She held open the door – despite Saul's dictum, she didn't feel it necessary to be rude to him; besides, she was curious.

'Thanks.' Jamie stepped inside, noting at once the half-packed suitcase on the sofa. 'Are you going away?'

'Yes. It's work, though, not a holiday,' she told him.

'Me too. I've finally got my big break, Ginny,' he told her excitedly. 'My agent confirmed it yesterday – I'm off to Hollywood!' he declared dramatically.

'Oh, Jamie, that's wonderful!' Ginny exclaimed. 'I'm really pleased for you. What is it – a blockbuster film?'

'Even better than that. A long-running soap; it's not shown over here, but its ratings are great all over the States. I'm to play an upper-class Englishman, a real cad,' he told her, twirling imaginary moustaches and leering at her. 'My contract is for a year, initially, but I could be there much longer if the viewers like me.'

'I'm sure they will; that's really great news.' She smiled warmly at him.

'Mmm, but talking of behaving like a cad . . .' He shot her a look full of guilt. 'I have a confession to make; my only excuse is that I needed the dosh. And she paid me five hundred quid for just a few minutes' acting . . . I just hope I didn't mess anything up for you,' he said apologetically.

'For me? Who paid you five hundred pounds?' Ginny asked, bewildered.

'Lady Lancaster.'

'How do you know her?'

'She had a private detective spying on you – he contacted me and said she had a job for me.'

'A private detective ! My God . . . Saul's mother paid you – to do what, exactly?' she asked slowly, beginning to feel afraid. Jamie hesitated.

'She paid me to cause trouble for you with Saul Lancaster. I'm sorry, Ginny, but it wasn't just the money – he really hacked me off, chucking me out of the nightclub in front of my friends . . .'

'Never mind all that,' she interrupted. 'When did you speak to him? And what did you say?' she demanded, her voice rising shrilly.

'It was last Sunday evening – you had been away with him for the weekend. Lady Lancaster had found out about it and didn't want a repeat. I told him . . .' He stopped.

'Get *on* with it!' Ginny snapped.

'I told him we were lovers, and that you were only after him for his money . . . I said you would sleep with him if he was . . . er . . . generous,' he finished miserably, uncomfortably aware that he had used far cruder language to Saul Lancaster. Ginny was deathly pale, staring at him in horror, and he felt genuine remorse for what he had done.

'You told him my body was for sale?' she whispered hoarsely.

'More or less – yes, I did.' Jamie nodded. Ginny closed her eyes, fighting down nausea. 'You don't really like him, do you, Ginny?'

'Like him?' she repeated, glancing down at her wrist, at the gold watch embellished with diamonds and sapphires. Now she understood her instinctive feeling of unease when he had first tried to give it to her. My price, she thought dully. 'Like him? No, I don't like him at all,' she told Jamie. 'Thank you for telling me – you've saved me from making a complete fool of myself,' she said, which wasn't true, of course. If only Jamie had confessed twenty-four hours earlier . . .

'I really am sorry – I'll call him and tell him the truth, if that would help,' he offered. Ginny was tempted to accept his help, but only for a second.

'No.' She shook her head. 'Don't worry about it – you only told him what he wanted to hear,' she said bitterly. 'Good luck with Hollywood,' she added brightly, edging towards the door, desperate for him to leave.

'Thanks. Are you sure –?'

'Goodbye, Jamie,' she interrupted. She slammed

184

the door shut, almost before he had stepped over the threshold, then turned and leaned against it, biting her lip so hard in an attempt not to cry that she drew blood. Then her face crumpled and she ran into the bedroom, fell across the bed and lay sobbing as if her heart would break.

'Ginny?' The voice was soft and concerned, the touch on her shoulder gentle and soothing.

'Oh, Jo!' Ginny turned over and the older woman visibly winced at the sight of her ravaged countenance.

'Oh, God, do I look that bad?' Ginny sniffed and tried to smile, but it was a poor effort, and her lower lip trembled as more tears threatened to spill over. She reached for a tissue from the container beside her bed to blow her nose and mop up the tears.

'Whatever's wrong? I heard you crying from downstairs,' Jo said; she had been so worried that she had used the spare set of keys to gain entry – normally she would never intrude on Ginny's privacy.

'I've been such a fool – I really thought he cared, but I should have known better . . .' Ginny glanced down at her wrist, then began tearing feverishly at the fastening of the watch, determined not to wear it – her slave bangle – for one more second!

'Let me do that,' Jo said quickly, afraid the delicate watch might be destroyed. She was quite correct in her thinking; had Ginny been able to remove it quickly, she would have hurled it from the third-floor window or stamped on it, pretending it was Saul's hateful face beneath her foot.

'How much do you think it cost?' Ginny asked

her, when Jo had it safely in her own hands.

'I've no idea – hundreds, maybe thousands of pounds. These stones look very good quality to me, but I'm no expert.'

'Well, at least he thinks I'm a high-class hooker! Let's be grateful for small mercies!' Ginny said bitterly.

'Ginny!'

'Although he made sure he got his money's worth,' Ginny continued wildly. 'Four times yesterday and once this morning!'

'Ginny, don't,' Jo said, distressed.

'It's true. I can't believe how stupid I've been. I knew what he thought of me – after all, he made it perfectly plain from the beginning. When we drove back from Sussex last Sunday he didn't speak to me at all, and I was sure I would never see him again. I should have known something was wrong when he called here on Wednesday evening. Beware Army officers bearing gifts!' she spat.

'But – what's happened?' Jo asked, for she had not heard Jamie's arrival or departure. 'Why do you think he was trying to, well, buy you?' she asked uncomfortably. Ginny repeated what she had learned from Jamie, the telling prompting more tears. Jo almost joined her.

'That's why Saul came back – not because he liked me, but because Jamie told him I was for sale! The one thing Saul was honest about was wanting to get me into bed, he's made that clear all along, and then Jamie told him how to accomplish it!'

'Are you sure that's all he wanted from you? I thought he seemed very smitten – why not call him

186

and discuss it calmly?' Jo urged.

'No. Anyhow, I can't, not even if I wanted to – which I don't. He's on his way to Cyprus . . .' She paused, then grimaced. 'Maybe not, maybe that was a lie, like everything else. He told me yesterday that Army duties always provide a great excuse to avoid certain people or situations. He could have made all that up once he'd had enough of me!'

'Oh, Ginny, I'm so sorry. What are you going to do?'

'I don't know.' Ginny's lower lip trembled anew; the future stretched out endlessly, bleak and lonely. 'I just don't know,' she whispered forlornly.

Saul phoned Ginny as soon as he had settled into his quarters on the base. He had already enquired about reservations at a good hotel nearby and wanted Ginny to come over as soon as possible, for he already missed her like crazy. Such an arrangement was frowned upon by the top brass, but what the hell? He was leaving for good in August, and would be delighted if they decided to dispense with his services even sooner.

Ginny almost didn't pick up the phone when it rang; her mother had already called once and had been unable to successfully hide her relief upon hearing that Ginny never intended seeing Saul again.

However, Ann had sensed there was more to tell than Ginny's vague assertion that they hadn't really got along, and had continued to probe until Ginny's fragile control had snapped and she had slammed down the receiver. Maybe she was being irrational, and grossly unfair, but she partly blamed her mother for what had happened. After all, Saul's own father paid Ann an allowance, and it was Saul's dislike of the mother that had initially caused him to distrust the daughter. Not that any of that excused his behaviour, of course, Ginny thought dully, but she had to admit that there was a twisted kind of logic to Saul's thinking.

'Yes?' she said listlessly, finally tiring of hearing the shrill summons.

'Ginny? I didn't get you out of the bath, did I? I thought you weren't going to answer,' Saul said, too distracted by imagining Ginny in her bath to immediately register her lack of animation.

'I was packing,' she said eventually; just the sound of his voice was making her want to cry again.

'Packing? Oh, of course, you're going to Bellwood,' Saul remembered. 'You'll be able to fly over here to see me, though, won't you?' he asked huskily. 'I'm already missing you dreadfully.'

'Really?' Ginny responded coolly.

'Darling, what's wrong? I had to come out here – you must understand I had no choice in the matter,' he said. 'I didn't want to come!'

'Sure,' she said, still not altogether convinced he actually was in Cyprus.

'Ginny? Is someone with you?' Saul asked, searching for a reason for her monosyllabic replies. She remained silent, and his voice sharpened. 'Is it James Calvert? If so, put him on the line; I want to talk to that young man,' he said grimly.

'He's not here now.'

'But he has been back today? What did he want?'

'He came to tell me he's going to Hollywood; he's got his big chance to succeed and I'm sure he'll become a huge star.' She took a deep, shuddering breath, and then, not sure if she merely wanted to hurt Saul as he had hurt her or whether she needed to salvage some pride, she added casually, 'He's asked me to go with him, and I've decided I will.'

'The hell you will!' Saul blazed.

'Why shouldn't I? He'll be wealthy now, and you know me – I always go to the highest bidder!' Her voice cracked, but Saul was too consumed with his own pain and rage to register her anguish.

'You told me you weren't sleeping with him – was that a lie?' he demanded roughly.

'Of course it was a lie. But over the years I've discovered that my frightened I'm-almost-a-virgin line works well with most men – particularly older men, such as you. You all love to think you're such terrific teachers in bed, don't you?' Tears were coursing down her cheeks, and she felt her heart was breaking. But at least Saul Lancaster no longer believed he meant anything special to her. At this minute that was very cold comfort indeed, but she hoped it would help her in the time ahead. For now, she had to cover the mouthpiece with her hand to muffle the sound of her weeping.

'Goodbye, Ginny.' Saul abruptly broke the connection; the dialling tone hummed monotonously in her ear, but it was an age before she replaced the receiver, suddenly loath to finally sever the link. That was it. Over before it had really begun. A few short weeks ago she had never met Saul Lancaster, so how could it hurt so much? she wondered, sitting huddled in a chair, wrapping her arms around her knees, which were drawn up to her chest in an effort to contain the pain.

While Ginny tried to forget Saul by immersing herself in her work at Bellwood, and Saul was making himself hugely unpopular with the troops in Cyprus by driving them – and himself – mercilessly, Lisa Farrell was in San Francisco trying to decide her future. The decision would have been easier to make if not for Kit, who asked constantly for Jack.

'See Daddy today?' she piped hopefully each morning, and her large blue eyes filled with tears when Lisa explained that no, Daddy was working. Jack phoned every day, of course, but his calls always ended with the child in tears and demanding they go home.

They had been in California for eleven days when Lisa decided to talk over her dilemma with her brother, Hal Renwick. She left Kit with her parents and drove to the tennis academy near Santa Barbara where Hal was a senior coach.

When she arrived, dozens of young hopefuls were out on the courts, practising endlessly, hopes of fame and fortune spurring them on. Lisa felt very old as she watched them for a few moments; she had once been as keen and starry-eyed as they were, but it seemed an awful long time ago.

She wondered idly whether to tell them that life as a pro player was exhausting, often physically painful, and not lucrative except for those few players at the very top. She decided not to; each and every one of them would still hang on to the belief that he or she would reach the number one spot, carrying off trophies and millions of dollars. Instead, she merely asked for her brother's whereabouts and made her way over to his office.

One of Hal's former pupils, Daniella Cortez, was currently at the academy. Ella, at eighteen, was tipped to be a future star on the pro circuit, but her climb up the rankings had been halted earlier in the year when a bout of flu had developed into bronchitis and she had been forced to take an extended break. Consequently she had missed the European clay court season, culminating in the French Open which was now taking place.

Ella's travelling coach was the experienced Katy Oliver, the woman who had guided Melissa Farrell to success, but Katy had stayed in Europe with another young American player, Shanna Douglas, while Ella recuperated and practised at the academy under Hal's tutelage.

Ella and Shanna, in addition to making their mark as singles players, were also shaping up as an excellent doubles team. They made a striking pair. Ella, slim and dark-haired, with soulful brown eyes, and Shanna a buxom blonde. Ella's uncle, Ace Delaney, managed both girls' careers, and sponsorship money for the two beauties was already rolling in – as Ace had predicted it would. Family loyalty was not his only reason for funding Ella's training. In fact, when he had first taken Ella under his wing neither had been aware of the blood tie, for Ace and Ella's mother were only half-brother and sister and had not grown up together.

Today, fully recovered from her illness, Ella was making her way over to Hal's office to discuss the arrangements he had made for her to travel to England for the upcoming grass court season. Hearing voices from inside the room, and tired after a long session on court, she sat down on the bench outside the open window to wait until he was alone.

At first, with her thoughts on her imminent return to the circuit, she didn't register what was being said, but then the words 'divorce' and 'custody' impinged onto her consciousness, together with the realization that Hal's visitor was his sister, Lisa Farrell. Ella barely knew Lisa, and Jack only a little better, but she was well aware of Jack's close friendship with Ace Delaney, his doubles partner for many years.

Ella eavesdropped shamelessly for several more minutes, then, ducking low beneath the window to avoid being spotted by either Hal or Lisa, she sped off to her shared dormitory to phone Ace.

After Ace's marriage to the English girl, Alexa Kane, they, with their twins Pippa and Drew, had moved from his house in LA to a sprawling ranch on the outskirts of Santa Barbara. Ella adored her half-cousins, and spent as much time with them as her constant travelling allowed. Ace, too, she hero-worshipped, but she was a little in awe of Alexa – not that she would ever admit it! Alexa was a millionaire in her own right, accustomed all her life to comfort and luxury, which was in complete contrast to Ella's early years in the slums of LA, brought up mainly by her stepmother and rarely seeing her father. She would be forever grateful to Ace for rescuing her from a life of poverty and fear, from the street gangs and the drugs and crime which were rife.

'Hello?' It was Alexa's cool, clipped British upper-class voice.

'Alexa, hi, it's Ella. Can I speak to Ace? It's kinda urgent,' she said breathlessly.

'I'm not sure if he's around . . . I was lying down,' Alexa said, turning from the phone to ask the housekeeper if she knew of Ace's whereabouts. Lying down? Again? Ella thought, with the impatience of one who had always enjoyed good health. She glanced at her watch; it was only three o'clock. Still, if Ace's reputation for being sexually insatiable was anywhere near being true, she supposed his wife would spend a great deal of her time lying down, for one reason or another! Either pleasing her husband or recuperating . . .

'Hi, honey.' It was Ace's deep drawl. 'Is something wrong?'

'Lisa Farrell's here at the academy, talking to Hal,' she said, glancing over her shoulder to make sure no one was within listening distance. 'She says she's going to divorce Jack and get custody of Kit – she thinks she'll get a better deal if she divorces him here instead of in England.'

'She's probably right – and both her parents are lawyers,' Ace remembered. 'Are you sure about this, honey? I spoke to Jack yesterday and he didn't say anything was wrong. Apart from missing Kit,' he added.

'That's just it – Jack doesn't know. He thinks she's just here for a couple of weeks while he's in Paris. He's expecting them both to return to England next weekend,' she said. 'It's none of my business, but don't you think Jack ought to be warned? I think it's a rotten thing to do,' she finished indignantly.

'So do I, honey. So do I,' Ace said softly; his obsidian eyes glittered and there was a cruel set to his mouth as he considered what he should do. 'Thanks for telling me; I'll deal with it,' he told Ella, and broke the connection.

So forbidding was his expression that even the twins, accustomed to being indulged and pampered by him, steered clear, and Alexa returned to their bedroom to resume resting, although not for the reason Ella had imagined. It was true that Ace was rather demanding sexually, but Alexa adored him and always welcomed his lovemaking.

Never robust, she had never fully recovered from the twins' birth; she loved them both to distraction, but they were exhausting. Her lack of energy was beginning to worry her and Ace, and, although she did her utmost to hide the worst of it from him, he had started to insist that she consult a doctor.

So, without telling Ace, she had already arranged to see someone in San Francisco – not their family doctor, for, if her worst fears were confirmed, she did not want Ace to know the truth. Alexa's own mother had died young, and had been an invalid for some years before that. Alexa could remember her father's barely concealed impatience with his wife, and had later discovered that he had found solace with other women. Alexa was sure she would die if Ace did that . . .

Unaware of Alexa's turmoil, Ace sat in his office after speaking to Ella, pondering what action to take. He considered, and promptly dismissed, the notion of telling Jack what his wife had planned. Jack was too nice, too honest and fair-minded for his own good – he would play it by the book, a tactic which Lisa evidently didn't intend pursuing.

Ace had always felt that Jack had merely drifted into marriage with Lisa Renwick, and thought he probably wouldn't be too heartbroken at the prospect of a divorce. What would hurt him desperately, though, would be the loss of his daughter. A shriek of delighted laughter from his own daughter caused a brief smile to curve Ace's mouth, and he decided that Kit had to be returned to England before Lisa had the opportunity to apply to the courts for her to remain in California. After all, the longer the child remained in San Francisco with her mother, the more likely it was that Lisa would be granted permanent custody.

After a few more moments' deliberation, Ace hit on a solution, and, with a smile that boded ill for Lisa Farrell, he reached for the phone and began dialling . . .

CHAPTER 10

Lisa returned to San Francisco more than a little disgruntled by her brother's attitude. Hal hadn't been at all supportive, quite the reverse – she'd finally had to force him to promise not to phone Jack! So much for family loyalty, she fumed, completely disregarding her own total lack of loyalty to her husband.

Her mood lightened a little when one of her friends from schooldays called and suggested a night out at a nightclub which had only recently opened. After putting Kit to bed, she changed and put on her make-up, and took a cab to meet Kelly. Two of Kelly's colleagues joined them, and Lisa began to enjoy herself, dancing and flirting as if she were already single again.

'Hey, who's that? He looks kinda familiar.' Kelly nudged Lisa. 'And he's gorgeous,' she added, blatantly eyeing up the hunk who had just entered the club and had paused at the entrance to check out the action. 'And he's alone,' she noted, with satisfaction.

Kelly stuck out her chest and stared hard at him,

willing him to look in her direction. Finally he caught her watching him and grinned in acknowledgement before sauntering over towards them. Kelly tried to remember where she had seen him before . . . tall, dark-haired and bearded, brown eyes in a deeply tanned face and wearing just one earring that gave him the look of a pirate . . .

'Hey! I know who he is!' she exclaimed excitedly. 'He's an actor . . . his name is . . . Johnny Dancer!' she said triumphantly. 'Come on, let's go over and say hi,' she urged Lisa.

'He'll think we're groupies,' Lisa objected, hanging back. 'Anyhow, I don't want to meet him; he's a friend of Ace Delaney's – they worked on the same show when Ace decided he wanted to be in showbiz a few years ago.'

'Great. You can introduce me, then,' Kelly said, with rather drunken logic.

'I never met him,' Lisa protested, but Kelly wasn't listening, and had stood directly in Johnny's path.

'Hi, I'm Kelly and this is Lisa.' She smiled brightly.

'Hi.' Johnny returned the smile, but didn't think it necessary to introduce himself. His gaze moved to Lisa and his smile broadened. 'You're Lisa Renwick, the tennis player! I'm certainly pleased to meet you.' He took her hand in his and held onto it.

'That's right. At least, I was. I'm just a housewife and mother these days,' Lisa said, blushing slightly when he refused to relinquish his hold on her hand.

'Hey, don't knock it,' Johnny said quickly. 'Can I buy you a drink?'

'Yes, please,' Kelly put in eagerly. Johnny apparently didn't even hear her.

'No, thanks,' Lisa said simultaneously, rather shortly, and Kelly looked reproachfully at her. Johnny merely looked surprised; 'rejection' was not a word in his vocabulary.

'Sorry to sound rude.' Lisa forced a smile, realizing she had been a little abrupt. 'But any friend of Ace Delaney is no friend of mine!'

'God, he's not my friend!' Johnny said disgustedly. 'We hung around together for a while when we worked on *Country Club*, but he really dropped us all in it. That series was written especially for him, and then he decided he'd had enough, and to hell with his contract and the rest of the cast – he just walked off the set when it suited him. He knew I'd turned down lucrative offers elsewhere to continue with *Country Club*, and never warned me he was pulling the plug. When the show folded I couldn't keep up the payments on my house; even my car had to go. I can assure you, Ace Delaney is no friend of mine!' he finished emphatically.

'That sounds like Ace,' Lisa said, warming to Johnny. 'He doesn't give a damn about anyone but himself. He strolls into our house whenever he feels like it, uninvited and unannounced, and takes my husband off boozing somewhere,' she complained, draining her own glass of vodka. 'Mind you, everyone walks into our house uninvited and unannounced,' she continued grousing. 'We might as well officially open it to the public and charge an admittance fee!'

'You're married to Jack Farrell, aren't you? Ace

told me he and Jack had a lot of wild nights out!'

'Did he?' Lisa said tightly.

'Don't you live in England?' Johnny asked, hastily changing tack.

'Yes,' Lisa said, after a brief hesitation.

'Is your husband here?'

'No, he's in Paris, covering the French Open for British television,' she told him.

'That's convenient,' Johnny murmured, moving closer to Lisa and edging Kelly out. 'Are you sure I can't get you another drink?'

'Well, okay, thanks.' Lisa accepted his offer. She decided she deserved some fun, and had to admit he was rather gorgeous. Kelly wasn't the only girl in the club to be eyeing her jealously, she noted with some satisfaction.

Johnny, second only possibly to Ace Delaney prior to his marriage, was a master at seduction, and he turned on his considerable charm as the evening wore on. He plied Lisa with a potent mixture of booze and compliments, voiced his admiration for her success as a professional tennis player and dropped hints that Jack was in all probability enjoying rather more than just the tennis tournament in Paris.

Consequently Lisa, tipsy, resentful of Jack and turned on by Johnny Dancer, found herself in his hotel room, her clothes littered on the carpet and herself naked on the bed.

'I can't . . . I'm married . . . I've never cheated on Jack,' she stammered, briefly sobering up as she realized the enormity of what she was doing.

'Your marriage is over,' Johnny reminded her,

joining her on the bed and using all of his considerable skill to first comfort and then arouse her, not giving her time or the will to think clearly.

Lisa relaxed beneath his skilful ministrations; her head arched back as his mouth moved down her body, teasing her breasts, then his tongue circled her navel before dipping lower. He moved between her thighs, cupped her buttocks in his hands and raised her hips as his tongue slid deep inside her.

'Oh, God!' Lisa clutched his shoulders, her body convulsing with a mind-shattering climax. She'd not had sex for weeks, childishly depriving herself of pleasure in an attempt to make Jack miserable.

The waves of orgasm slowly receded and she opened her eyes to see Johnny hastily stripping off his own clothes. He lay down on his back and pulled her on top of him, filling her with one hard thrust. Lisa was amazed to find herself quickly spiralling towards another climax, felt Johnny's own release deep within her before she collapsed onto his chest, breathing heavily. Johnny smoothed her hair back from her face and turned her so she was lying by his side.

'If you move to San Francisco permanently, we can do this more often,' he murmured.

'I'm not sure . . .' Lisa didn't even want to think about the future at that moment, but Johnny persisted until she found herself spilling out her resentment of the Farrells.

'Strangers always think Melissa is Kit's mother,' she said bitterly. 'Kit looks just like Melissa did at that age. I sometimes feel as if she's not my daughter at all, just a clone of Melissa!'

'Will Kit be happy here in California if you get custody?' Johnny asked idly.

Lisa hesitated for a moment, then, 'She's only two and a half; she'll settle down and forget Bellwood soon enough,' she said, but she sounded rather doubtful even to her own ears.

'Bellwood?'

'The Farrells have lived there for centuries. Kit loves it, too, but it's only a house!'

'You mentioned her aunt – what about other family?' Johnny asked.

'She's very close to my mother-in-law, who has always looked after her a lot, and Jack's father has a farm a couple of miles from Bellwood – Kit loves going there. Both she and her cousin, Suzy, are crazy about the animals.'

'She'd miss all that, then?' Johnny yawned.

'We do have animals here in California!' Lisa snapped. 'Oh, sorry, I shouldn't be burdening you with my problems.' She sighed. 'The real problem will be taking her away from Jack. She's such a daddy's girl, and never stops asking when she can go home to see him. You should have heard the fuss she made at the airport when she realized Jack wasn't coming here with us. I'm surprised someone didn't call the cops – she sounded like we were murdering her!'

'Poor little kid,' Johnny said – rather reproachfully, she thought. 'Have you thought about letting Jack have custody?' he asked casually. 'From what I've heard about the guy, he's not the sort to turn awkward over visitation rights.'

'Oh, no, he'd be very fair . . .' Lisa said, then

suddenly stopped talking, overwhelmed by guilt. She couldn't, shouldn't be discussing her husband while lying naked in a hotel bedroom with another man. 'I'd better go,' she said quickly, scrambling off the bed and hunting for her clothes. 'My parents will have expected me back hours ago.'

'Sure.' Johnny helped her hunt for her shoes and Lisa gained the distinct impression that he was relieved she was going. But, to her surprise, he pulled her back into his arms for one last kiss before she left.

'Will you come back here tomorrow?' he asked urgently.

'I don't think I should,' she began, not very convincingly, and her resolve quickly weakened when his hands cupped her breasts and teased the nipples into hard peaks.

'Please?' Johnny smiled winsomely, and the last of her resistance melted.

'Okay,' she agreed.

'Around nine – we can have dinner in bed,' he suggested huskily.

'Nine o'clock,' Lisa repeated breathlessly, her heart already pounding with anticipation.' 'Bye, Johnny.' She slipped out of the room and made her way home, already counting the hours until she would see him again.

On Tuesday, Lisa's mood veered between wild excitement and uneasy guilt. At one point she almost decided not to keep her date with Johnny Dancer, but, after convincing herself that she and Jack were practically legally separated, and that she was therefore fully entitled to take a lover, she set off to meet him at the arranged time.

She avoided the main reception area – she was, after all, still something of a celebrity in her home city, and, legal separation notwithstanding, she did not want to be spotted visiting a man's hotel room.

She sped lightly up three flights of stairs and kept her head bowed and her hair hanging across her face as she walked along the corridor. The door to Johnny's room was slightly ajar, and she tapped lightly to announce her arrival before walking in. A tall, black-haired man was standing by the window, looking out at the scene below, and as he turned slowly to face her Lisa's bright words of greeting faded away to nothing.

'You!' she gasped finally, almost fainting with shock and disbelief.

'Yes. Me,' Ace Delaney said mockingly. 'You've really screwed up this time, honey,' he drawled, tossing a video cassette onto the bed.

Lisa stared at it in mounting horror as she realized what it must contain. She remembered – how could she ever have forgotten? – Jack telling her how Ace had secretly filmed himself in bed with Melissa and had later used the tape to try and prevent a reconciliation between Nick and Melissa. Had Johnny done the same? And given the tape to Ace? But why? She'd been set up, obviously, but how . . . ?

'Is that . . . ?' She swallowed, pointing to the cassette. 'Is that . . . me?'

'Yes, you. San Francisco's latest porno star,' he said cheerfully, lest she be in any doubt as to the content of the film. 'It should sell very well,' he mused. 'Johnny's hugely popular, and you used to be something of a celebrity . . .'

'You're not going to make it public!' Lisa sat down abruptly; her legs would no longer support her. She had immediately assumed he would merely show the video to Jack . . . merely? She shuddered, feeling sick, and far too dazed to realize that Ace was bluffing; if she'd been thinking rationally she would have known that he would never inflict such public humiliation on his best friend.

'That depends on you.' Ace leaned against the wall, his arms folded across his chest, the very picture of relaxed confidence, but he was watching her like a hawk. 'If necessary, I'll produce it in court . . .'

'In court?' Lisa's head shot up; this nightmare was getting worse by the second.

'Divorce court. Custody hearing,' Ace said slowly, deliberately. Lisa licked her lips nervously. Only Hal knew about that . . .

'How did you find out that I –?' She stopped, belatedly aware that she would be condemning herself with her own words, stupidly confirming what he had only so far guessed at.

'Find out – what? That you intended taking Jack's kid and probably half his fortune as well? Does it matter how I found out?'

'I . . . I guess not. What do you want?' she asked, already looking defeated, Ace thought, with satisfaction.

'I want you to send Kit back to England. Alexa and I are flying over this weekend, with the twins and the nanny. We'll take care of Kit and deliver her to Bellwood,' he said, matter-of-factly.

'I won't do that! You can't make me give up my daughter!' she said wildly.

'Don't be so melodramatic,' Ace said dismissively. 'I'm doing no such thing. As you so obligingly stated on film, Jack would never stop you having access. In fact, he would be a helluva lot fairer to you than you intended being to him,' he added coldly.

'Maybe not . . . not after he sees . . . that.' She pointed to the tape, grimacing with distaste.

'If you're sensible, he need never see it,' Ace told her. Lisa stared at him, hope flaring even as she wondered what devious game he was playing.

'You . . . you said you'd produce it in court . . .'

'I'll certainly see to it that Jack's lawyer receives a copy – if necessary. But none of that has to happen.' He paused, then, 'Why don't you go home?' he suggested softly.

'To England? After what's happened? How can I?' she asked bitterly. 'Jack won't want me back after what I've done,' she said miserably.

'He needn't know,' Ace said unexpectedly, and Lisa narrowed her eyes at him suspiciously.

'Oh, sure! If I *do* go back, you'll hold this over for me for ever,' she said accusingly.

'No, I won't. All I care about is that you don't take Kit away from her family. She's a Farrell; she belongs at Bellwood with Jack,' he stated flatly. 'As for your marriage . . .' He paused. 'That's for you and Jack to work out – if you both want to. I have no idea whether he even wants you back,' he went on, and Lisa flinched. 'My guess is that he would prefer Kit to have her mother around while she's growing up. Personally, I think she'd be better off with Rose and Melissa as mother-figures, instead of having you bitching at her day and night, but, as I said, that's for you and Jack to decide.'

'I can't face Jack,' Lisa whispered. She couldn't bear to look at Ace, having just realized that he must have watched at least part of the film . . . She shuddered again, almost retching.

'Why not? Because of Johnny Dancer? Forget him,' Ace said impatiently. 'It was a meaningless one-night stand. I've always thought people make too much fuss over such a trivial matter.'

'Well, you would, wouldn't you?' Lisa retorted. Ace glared at her.

'Careful, honey, don't make me angry,' he warned menacingly. 'You're in too much trouble to make snide remarks.' He paused to let that sink in.

'Sorry,' Lisa muttered. Ace nodded, satisfied with her cowed demeanour, her slumped shoulders; it seemed to him she'd already accepted defeat and would do what he told her to do.

'I'd advise you not to tell Jack about Johnny – you'll ease your conscience, sure, but at the cost of making him feel bad. What's the point in that? If there's a chance you can make your marriage work, then keep quiet.'

'I can't go back – not yet anyway.' Lisa folded her arms defensively across her chest. 'Johnny – you set that up, didn't you?' she whispered; it was the only possible answer.

'Yes.' Ace nodded. 'I knew he was short of

money,' he said calmly.

'You . . . paid him?' Lisa felt even more nauseous, used, abused and very, very stupid. She wished
she were with Jack; she needed him. What a fool she
had been . . . She blinked back tears.

'Yes, I paid him,' Ace confirmed.

'How did he know where to . . . pick me up?' She
almost spat the last three words. 'Not through
Kelly?' she asked, for the night out had been
Kelly's idea. But they had been friends since kin-
dergarten . . .

'Kelly who? No, I simply gave Johnny your
parents' phone number. When he rang, you'd
already left for the evening and they told him
where to find you,' he explained. 'That made it
easy for him – his original plan was to pretend to be
a tennis groupie and flatter you into going out with
him.'

'Oh, I made it easy for him!' Lisa agreed bitterly.
'But I still don't understand how you knew I was
considering a divorce.' She frowned. 'The only
person I talked to was Hal,' she said, and despite
her brother's less than supportive attitude she
couldn't believe that he would betray her, and
certainly not to Ace, a man he disliked.

Ace merely shrugged by way of reply, deciding it
was best to keep her guessing. If she ever contemplated something similar in the future, she wouldn't
know who she could trust.

'We're wasting time,' he said abruptly. 'Have you
made your decision yet? Do you want to be a porno
queen? And, believe me, I know how to get the film
distributed throughout the States,' he warned her.

Lisa believed him. 'Alternatively, you can go to court and have the whole world judge your fitness as a wife and mother. Or . . .' He paused again. 'You can phone Jack right now and tell him his daughter's coming home this weekend.'

'I'll . . .' Lisa licked dry lips. 'I'll call Jack.'

'Then do it. Now.' Ace picked up the phone and held it out to her. After a moment, Lisa took it from him and began dialling, after working out the time in France. Jack should be in his hotel, but she wasn't sure if she hoped he would be there or not. He was, and picked up the phone on the first ring. Lisa took a deep breath and forced a brightness into her voice.

'Jack, I've just been talking to Ace.' She shot him a filthy look as she spoke. 'He's flying to England on Friday and I've decided to send Kit with him. She misses you,' she faltered.

'That's great; I miss her, too,' Jack said warmly. 'But what about you? Aren't you coming home?' he asked, sounding as if he genuinely wanted her to return. Lisa bit her lip and had to blink back tears. More than anything she wanted to go back, but she couldn't face him, not yet.

'I thought I'd stay on here for a bit longer. If you don't mind?' she asked, half hoping he would say he did mind . . .

'No, stay for as long as you want to, if you're enjoying yourself,' Jack said finally.

'I am,' she said, with tears rolling down her cheeks. 'I'll get Ace to call you with the flight details, shall I?'

'Sure. I'll be in Paris until late Sunday evening, but Mum's at Bellwood. Ace can take her straight

208

there, or I'm sure Nick will pick her up at the airport if that's more convenient for Ace,' Jack said.

'I'll tell him.' Lisa bit her lip, wanted to say more, but Ace was still in the room, listening to every word. Besides, what could she say?

'Are you all right, love?' The concern in Jack's voice almost caused her to break down.

'Yeah, I'm fine,' she managed. 'I'll talk to you soon,' she added, and quickly broke the connection. She took several deep breaths and glared at Ace. 'Satisfied?'

'We'll collect Kit on our way to the airport.' He ignored her question. 'Have her packed and ready for ten o'clock. And don't even think of "losing" her passport,' he warned, and instantly regretted it, realizing he might just have put the idea into her head! He was confident she was too demoralized to put up a fight, but just in case he nodded towards the cassette still lying on the bed.

'You can keep that, as a reminder of your stupidity and as a warning not to cause trouble in the future. Of course that's only a copy, one of many,' he added.

Lisa looked at the loathsome thing distastefully; she certainly didn't want to take it with her, but she didn't trust Ace not to purposely leave the damned thing there for anyone to find. She stalked over to the bed, picked up the tape as gingerly as she would if it could bite, and stalked out of the room.

Ace let out a pent-up breath. God, he needed a drink! He just hoped he had done the right thing . . .

Kit was delighted to be going home, and was waiting impatiently outside the house soon after breakfast on Friday morning, sitting on top of her suitcase. She jumped up and down with glee when Ace drove up, and immediately began chattering excitedly to the Delaney twins, exerting her authority as the eldest of the trio.

Both Pippa and Drew were dark-haired and dark-eyed, like their father, although Pippa had Alexa's delicate facial bone structure. Although at eighteen months they were still the same height, Drew was the sturdier of the two and his face sometimes sported the notorious Delaney scowl that had intimidated opponents and officials during Ace's years on the circuit.

Lisa silently handed Ace Kit's case and studiously avoided eye contact. Ace hadn't told his wife all the details, but she knew enough to be feeling rather uncomfortable. Of course it was cruel of Lisa to try and deprive Jack of his beloved daughter, but, as a mother herself, Alexa couldn't help but be sympathetic with Lisa's plight.

'This is Coral, our nanny,' Alexa said. 'We'll take good care of Kit, I promise.'

'I know you will.' Lisa nodded.

'Why don't you come with us?' Alexa suggested impulsively. 'You could get a stand-by flight, or we could all wait and reschedule . . .'

'We could not!' Ace said firmly, stowing Kit's luggage in the trunk.

'No . . . I'll follow later, probably in time for Wimbledon,' Lisa said, rather half-heartedly. She had morbidly watched part of the video, late at night, when everyone else was asleep, her finger on the 'off' button lest anyone disturb her unexpectedly. The very thought of Jack ever seeing it made her feel physically ill.

'Kit.' She knelt down and held out her arms to her daughter, holding her close. 'I'll talk to you soon. Daddy won't be at home when you arrive, but ask Granny or Melissa to phone me as soon as you get there – okay?'

Kit nodded, then,

'You come, Mummy,' she urged brightly.

'No, not today.' Lisa forced a smile. Kit's face fell, but only for a moment, and she clambered happily into the car with the twins.

Lisa watched her, recalling the tears and tantrums at Gatwick when they had left Jack behind, and the dreadful bouts of sobbing which had followed for the duration of the flight to California.

I wonder if she'll ask for me as persistently as she's been asking for Jack, she thought bitterly, forcing a smile and a cheery wave as they set off. Ace, damn him to hell, was right – Kit did belong at Bellwood. Now all she had to decide was – did she?

When Ginny learned of Kit's earlier than expected return, she redoubled her efforts in an attempt to finish decorating the child's room before she arrived, glad of the excuse to work until she was exhausted enough to sleep when she finally crawled into bed.

She worked so hard and for such long hours that Rose began to feel guilty for persuading her to live at Bellwood for the duration of the renovation, and remonstrated with her to take things easier, but to no avail. Ginny refused to take time off; what was

211

the point – where would she go? What would she do?

Ginny wasn't the only worker at Bellwood: painters and decorators were busy on the rest of the house, and new soft furnishings were being made at the workshop in London. Jo travelled down every few days to check on the progress and make sure Rose was satisfied with the work.

Jo was delighted with Ginny's work on Kit's room, declaring it the best she had ever done, but was appalled at the rapid deterioration in Ginny's appearance. Each time Jo saw her she seemed to have lost more weight, her tan had faded and the bruises beneath her eyes, denoting lack of sleep, almost matched the vivid blue of her irises.

'Ginny, you must talk to Saul! Please,' she begged.

'Why?' Ginny asked dully, and silently stared her down when she tried to persist. Jo let it drop, but continued to be deeply worried, and talked it over with Barney when she returned to London. Or she tried to. But Barney was incensed by Saul's treatment of Ginny and said so bluntly, and warned Jo not to interfere.

But Jo remembered how Saul had looked at Ginny. Even on that first occasion, the PR exercise of attending Amanda's party as a couple, Saul had certainly not been immune to Ginny's loveliness. There had been a cold disdain, true, she acknowledged reluctantly, but even then he had been unable to take his eyes off her. There had been a definite desire, and last weekend surely there had been much, much more? A reluctance to leave her that

212

spoke of more than mere physical attraction?

'You and your romantic ideas!' Barney scoffed at her. 'It's plain to me the bum just wanted to get her into bed and then skedaddled! It's a pity she ever met Saul Lancaster and she'll be a lot happier without him,' he added firmly. Jo smiled and nodded, but didn't agree. Happier? She doubted it very much.

Jo recalled Barney's words the next time she saw Ginny. Happier – than what, exactly? Right now, Ginny was marginally happier than being suicidal. And that thought set Jo to thinking of Richard Sinclair, Ginny's father. Could Saul have been telling the truth about his death? If Richard Sinclair had committed suicide . . . well, hadn't she read somewhere that the tendency ran in families . . . ?

Deeply worried, she pondered endlessly on what she could do to help, but as she didn't even know how to contact Saul, there was little she could do. Even if contacting Saul *was* the right thing to do!

However, on her next supervisory trip to Bellwood, she arrived just as Melissa was leaving. Jo paused, uncertain, aware she could be making things worse, but Melissa's pleasant smile and friendly greeting prompted her to speak. Besides, how could the situation possibly get worse?

'Can you spare a minute?' Jo asked hesitantly.

'Well, I have to pick Suzy up from playgroup shortly,' Melissa said, glancing at her watch. 'What's on your mind?'

'Ginny. She's so unhappy,' Jo burst out. 'I just wondered . . . well, you and your husband know Saul Lancaster quite well, don't you? Was Saul really sent to Cyprus by the Army?'

'Of course he was,' Melissa said, surprised. 'Surely Ginny knows that? Or does she think he's sneaked off on holiday with someone else?'

'Oh, God, I don't think that's even occurred to her!' Jo said, appalled by the very idea. 'No, she just thought it might have been an excuse not to see her any more,' she explained.

'Really?' Melissa's brows rose. 'I guessed they must have had a row – what was it about?' she asked interestedly.

'I'd rather not go into details,' Jo said uncomfortably; she certainly couldn't tell Melissa that Ginny felt Saul considered her to be little better than a prostitute. 'But I really think they need to talk. Could you or your husband possibly tell Saul she's at Bellwood?'

'Why – where does he think she is?' Melissa asked, intrigued.

'Er, Hollywood. With another man – an exboyfriend,' Jo told her.

'Goodness!'

'There's nothing good about it, I'm afraid,' Jo sighed. 'Oh, dear, I don't want Saul to have the chance to hurt her again. If he really was just stringing her along, well, perhaps you'd better forget I ever mentioned it,' she said hastily.

'I'll talk to Nick; he knows Saul much better than I do. He'll know what to do. He'll sort it out,' she added confidently.

Unfortunately, Nick refused point-blank to interfere. At least, he did to begin with, and continued to say no while Melissa tried her utmost to persuade him, her methods becoming more outrageous and pleasurable as the evening wore on. Her argument, that it was in his interest for the situation to be resolved before Saul joined Lennox and Coupland, particularly in view of Coop's own interest in Ginny, finally won him over although he 'forgot' to admit as much to his sexy, clever wife until much later!

Nick left Melissa to sleep undisturbed and returned to his study downstairs to call Saul. He had to phone Aldershot first, to get the number he needed in Cyprus, and finally got through to Saul in the Officers' Mess.

'Tell me if I'm out of order,' Nick began, 'but I'm calling about Ginny Sinclair.'

'What about her?' Saul asked coldly.

'Is it over between you?'

'As she's in America and I'm stuck here, I'd say it looks that way,' Saul snapped.

'America? She's at Bellwood,' Nick told him, and heard a sharp intake of breath.

'So, she hasn't left yet,' Saul said indifferently. 'Or perhaps James Calvert has found himself a Hollywood babe instead.'

'I haven't a clue what you're rambling about.' Nick sighed, wishing he had stuck to his original guns and refused to interfere. 'So far as I know, she's at Bellwood for the forseeable future – and extremely unhappy,' he added. 'According to Melissa, who heard it from Ginny's boss, Ginny thinks you only said you were going to Cyprus as an excuse to be rid of her.'

'She can't possibly think that!' Saul exclaimed,

but for the first time since that dreadfully cold telephone conversation his first evening in Cyprus, when she had told him she was leaving the country, the pain crushing his heart eased its grip slightly. 'Oh, God,' he groaned. 'I remember telling her that I often use the Army to avoid family dos,' he said slowly. 'But she can't think I wanted to be rid of her! I'll never want that!'

'Never?' Nick questioned slowly. There was a pause, then Saul laughed, a little self-consciously.

'Mmm, never,' he confirmed. 'But . . . it's complicated,' he said, then all at once decided it was worth fighting for; his relationship with Ginny was too important to let anyone else get in the way.

Ann Sinclair was a grasping troublemaker – so what? She was his father's problem, but he could handle her, and Saul certainly couldn't envisage his father committing suicide over anything Ann said or did. His own mother would probably never accept Ginny – again, so what?

'When will you be back in England?' Nick broke into his thoughts.

'Not for a couple of weeks . . . hold on.' Saul hooked the phone onto his shoulder and began rifling his pockets, searching for the flight schedules he had picked up when he had hoped Ginny would be flying out to see him. 'I'm not going to phone her; I have to see her. I'm coming over, even if it's only for an hour,' he decided.

'Is your car at Aldershot?' Nick asked.

'Yeah, I'll get a cab.'

'I'll pick you up at Gatwick, run you over to Bellwood and make sure you catch your return

216

flight,' Nick offered. 'Give me a ring when you know the time.'

'I'll do that, thanks. And thanks for calling,' Saul said gratefully.

'Thank Melissa, not me – I didn't want to interfere!' Nick said drily, and Saul laughed.

'Thanks anyway; I'll see you soon. Oh, and Nick? Don't tell Ginny I'm coming, will you? I want to surprise her.'

'Okay; I'll see you soon. Good luck.'

CHAPTER 11

When Ace and Alexa landed at Heathrow, all three children were truculent and tired. Ace bundled them all into the waiting limo and drove to his father-in-law's house in Belgravia, deciding to take Kit to Bellwood the following day.

After all, Jack was still in Paris, and Rose would just have to wait a little longer to see her grand-daughter – or come and fetch her herself, he thought, as he undressed and fell into bed beside an already sleeping Alexa.

Alexa's father, Philip Kane, idolized the twins, especially Pippa. Drew was too much his father's son, Philip sometimes thought, although he had gradually come around to having the notorious Ace Delaney as his son-in-law. Alexa loved him and was happy; so far, at least, Ace had surprised everyone by proving to be a faithful husband and loving father. The 'I-give-it-six-months' brigade had been sadly disappointed!

Alexa was still exhausted after the flight, and decided to stay in bed, and Philip wanted to spend every moment he could with the twins, so Ace set off alone to Bellwood with Kit on Sunday morning.

The little girl had spoken to Rose on the phone and been told of the work Ginny had done on her bedroom, and she chattered excitedly – and non-stop – to Ace about 'the fairies in my room' throughout the journey.

Although Sunday was supposed to be a day off, Ginny had ignored Rose's protests and resumed working immediately after breakfast. She was really very pleased with the way the room had been transformed; the timbered walls and low, sloping ceiling provided just the right background for the enchanted woodland scenes she had created.

She was too absorbed in her work to hear Ace's arrival, and was perched atop a stepladder, clad in denim shorts and a skimpy T-shirt, painting a portion of the ceiling, when an amused American drawl almost caused her to lose her precarious balance.

'The view around here has certainly improved!' he said. Ginny glanced down into the wicked black eyes of a man she had fantasized about during her teens – she'd even had a poster of him on her bedroom wall – and blushed. The view he was referring to was obviously neither the rolling countryside outside the window nor the scene she was painting.

Flustered, she couldn't think of an even remotely intelligent reply, and instead turned her attention to Kit, who was standing, wide-eyed and momentarily dumbstruck, in the centre of the room, looking around her in open-mouthed delight.

'Do you like it?' Ginny asked casually. Kit could

only nod vigorously to show her approval, then she dashed over to one wall to examine it more closely.

'Don't touch it!' Ginny called out, more sharply than she had intended, and Kit backed off, looking crestfallen. 'You can touch it later, poppet, but right now the paint is still wet,' Ginny explained, carefully climbing off the ladder and going over to the little girl, hunkering down to her level.

'Would you like to help me?' she asked, and Kit's face lit up as she nodded. 'Come over here, then.' Ginny took her hand and led her to a portion of as yet unpainted wall. It would only take her a few minutes to whitewash over Kit's effort before starting work on it herself, she decided.

'What would you like to paint? How about some flowers?' she suggested, and Kit nodded again. 'What colour? Red would be nice, don't you think?' She found Kit a brush and a small amount of paint and she was soon happily occupied.

Ace had watched the exchange silently as he admired the slender blonde beauty – Ginny Somebody, hadn't Rose said? He approved her gentle treatment of Kit, too; in fact, he decided, if Lisa elected to stay in California and go ahead with divorce proceedings, Jack could do a lot worse than keep this girl at Bellwood.

He noticed that she wasn't wearing a ring, and she was really quite gorgeous, he thought, admiring her legs and bottom as she reclimbed the ladder. He didn't feel guilty for checking out her attributes – he was married, he was faithful, but old habits died hard! He would never stray, because that would hurt Alexa, but he had been a rake for too many years to become a saint overnight.

'You handled that well.' He jerked his head towards the happily occupied child. 'Although I'm not too sure her father will appreciate it if she gets into the habit of painting on the walls!'

'Oh, God, I never thought of that,' Ginny said anxiously. 'Do you think I should stop her?'

'No, I was only kidding. She'll lose interest soon enough,' Ace said. He had been studying the artwork, as well as the artist, and was as impressed with the former as he was with the latter. 'My twins will love this,' he continued. 'How would you feel about a trip to California to do similar work on their bedrooms? We have a ranch near Santa Barbara,' he added.

'Do you?' Ginny said, to buy time to think. The offer held some appeal, as well as a certain irony, since she had told Saul she was going to California. Maybe she should go; she'd never been to the States, and she could take the opportunity to see something of the country once she had completed the job. Maybe it was just what she needed – a complete break. 'I'd have to discuss it with my employers,' she told him.

'I hope they pay you well,' Ace commented. 'I'd have thought you'd be better off working for yourself.'

'That's what Melissa said, but it's a bit risky – I don't fancy starving in a garret!'

'You can't play safe all your life.' Ace shrugged. 'I'd pay all your expenses, of course, plus . . . what? Twenty thousand dollars for each room?' he suggested idly, accustomed to signing sponsorship deals worth millions. 'Would that be enough?' he asked. At the mention of the sum Ginny had again almost toppled from her perch, and Ace put out his hand to steady her, placing his palm on her thigh and leaving it there.

'You'd pay me forty thousand dollars to do two rooms?' she gasped; she was rather hazy about the exchange rate, but guessed it was almost more than she currently earned in one year!

'I'm sure you'd be worth it. Think about it,' Ace said lazily. 'There's no rush – we're staying here in England until after Wimbledon. If you decide to come, you can travel back with us . . .'

'Hiya!' Kit piped up suddenly. Ace and Ginny turned as one to see who she was greeting. Ace saw a dark-haired man in khaki glaring at him from the doorway; Ginny, with a sickening lurch, and feeling a confused mixture of longing, hate, anger and sorrow, saw Saul.

Ace still had one hand on Ginny's bare thigh; she wasn't even aware of it, but Saul was. Ace had felt her jump upon seeing the newcomer, could still feel the quivering tension in her body, and purposely didn't remove his hand.

He had never seen the guy before, but guessed, from the uniform, that he was a friend of Nick Lennox. That alone was enough for Ace to enjoy needling him, but added to that was Ace's deep suspicion of any man who willingly signed away his life to the restrictive dictates of the Army! To Ace the word 'discipline' was one even more to be avoided than 'commitment'.

He had always considered Nick to be uptight, and

222

was amazed that Melissa remained happy with him. Here was yet another another stern-faced, glowering member of the British Armed Forces – did they breed them around here? he wondered idly.

After her initial shock, Ginny stared at Saul with undisguised hostility in her lovely eyes. He advanced further into the room, pointedly holding open the door for Ace to leave. Ace grinned, debated whether to stay and cause trouble, then decided not to. Well, not much.

'Don't forget my offer, honey,' he drawled, and patted her cute little backside before sauntering out, taking a protesting Kit with him.

Saul slowly unclenched his fists and waited until Delaney was out of earshot before he moved nearer to Ginny. He was suddenly at a complete loss as to what to say or do in the face of her obvious displeasure.

According to Nick, Ginny was unhappy because of his abrupt departure for Cyprus, yet she was evidently less than pleased to see him. Worse, she had seemed to be quite content in Ace Delaney's company – why had she let the debauched creep touch her? And precisely what 'offer' had he put to her? Just what had been going on before he walked in?

'What do you want? I'm busy,' Ginny said, turning her back on him.

'Sorry to interrupt,' he said sarcastically. 'What offer was he referring to?'

'Not that it's any of your business,' Ginny told him casually, making a great show of cleaning her brush – she didn't trust herself to attempt any painting. 'But he wants me to go back to the States with him – he's willing to pay me forty thousand dollars. What's that in sterling – do you know?' she asked, even more off-handedly.

'It's about . . .' Saul began automatically, then, 'I don't give a damn!' he exploded. 'You're not going!' he stated flatly, knowing, even as he spoke, that he was dealing with this badly – very badly.

'You think not?' Ginny asked, her voice deceptively quiet. She was furious that he evidently thought he now owned her, body and soul. Especially her body, she thought bitterly; she doubted he was overly concerned with her soul! 'If I decide to go, I'll go,' she informed him coolly. 'Your wishes are of no importance whatsoever.'

Saul stared at her, uncertain how to proceed. He fingered the jeweller's box in his pocket, doubting now if she would be pleased with her gift. Knowing he would be short of time in England, he had scoured Cyprus before he left, and had found an exquisite pendant, comprising a Ceylon sapphire on a gold chain.

He had been pleased with his purchase . . . until now. Nothing was going the way he had hoped. Quite the contrary – she wasn't at all pleased to see him, he thought painfully. Nick and Melissa had evidently misunderstood – Ginny's sadness must be due to James Calvert's departure for Hollywood. But why had she been so offhand with him when he had phoned her from Cyprus?

'Nick told me you thought I'd lied to you about having to leave the country – is that correct?' he asked. Ginny merely shrugged, as if it didn't matter to her. 'I flew over this morning and I have to be back this evening – would you like to see my ticket?'

'No.'

'Will you come down from that ladder and talk to me!'

'No.'

'If it's not Cyprus that's bothering you, then what is it? James Calvert? Is that why you're considering Delaney's offer to go to California?'

'No.'

'Ginny, you're driving me crazy!' he said desperately. 'Will you please tell me what's going on? And if you say "no" again, I'll . . .'

'You'll what?' Ginny finally looked up and stared at him, but with an expression of such disdain on her beautiful face Saul wasn't sure whether he wanted to kiss her or throttle her. He sighed heavily, raking his fingers through his hair and looking so bewildered that Ginny almost weakened. Almost. But she couldn't allow him to get near her again, not physically, not emotionally. It hurt too much. Nor could she explain her change in attitude – it was too humiliating to admit to knowing how he had duped her. Strange, really, when it should be Saul who felt the shame of it, not her.

'That tale of going to Hollywood with Calvert – was there ever any truth in it?' he asked abruptly.

'Jamie's already left,' she said carelessly. 'But maybe I have bigger fish to fry here,' she added, giving all her attention to squeezing paint out of a tube onto her palette.

'What does that mean?' Saul demanded tersely.

Ginny concentrated on remaining expressionless,

225

both in voice and features. 'Lisa Farrell isn't coming back for a while,' she said conversationally. Saul felt sick.

'Are you telling me you've set your sights on Jack Farrell?' he asked incredulously. Ginny wanted to weep at the speed with which he accepted her apparent behaviour.

'Maybe,' she shrugged. 'But, as you heard yourself, now Ace Delaney wants me to go to California with him. Of course, he is married,' she said thoughtfully, 'but we Sinclair women don't let a small detail like that spoil our fun, do we?'

'I don't believe this!' Saul burst out angrily, then he paused to reflect. He really did not believe it. 'You're lying to me – I do not believe one word you have just said,' he told her slowly, subjecting her to a piercing, narrow-eyed stare, as if seeking to read her mind, to know her innermost thoughts. Ginny lowered her gaze, seemingly absorbed in the splodge of paint on her palette, mindlessly adding more colours.

'I can't be that wrong about you,' Saul continued softly, and her heart skipped a beat.

'It's a little late to change your opinion of me,' she told him. 'You had me down as a money-grabbing slut the first time you saw me,' she reminded him coldly, and he flinched.

'I can't deny that, I'm afraid. But I changed my mind. You know I did,' he said earnestly.

'I know you pretended you had,' she countered swiftly.

'That was no pretence, Ginny! Just tell me what's gone wrong between us; I'll do anything to put it

226

right,' he said desperately. Ginny's lip curled derisively.

'There's nothing you can do. Except leave me
alone,' she told him bleakly. They stared at each
other in silence.

Ginny truly wished he would just go, before she
gave in to the self-destructive urge to throw herself
into his arms. The effort of masking her emotions
made her look cold-eyed and hard-mouthed – never
had she resembled her mother so much as at this
moment, Saul thought. Perhaps he had just been
fooling himself in thinking she was different, yet
every fibre of his being rejected that notion.

He fingered the jeweller's box and drew it out of
his pocket, never dreaming that that was the worst
possible thing he could do. Ginny saw the box and
her eyes glittered with fury. What was that – the
next instalment of her slave price?

'If that's for me, don't bother!' she spat. 'Save it
for the next poor girl you want in your bed!' She
glared at him with such loathing that Saul's own
temper surfaced.

'Fine. If that's how you feel, then that's precisely
what I will do!' he snarled, turning on his heel and
storming from the room. Ginny's anger and resolve
to resist him crumbled, and she held out her hand
beseechingly.

'Saul . . .' she whispered. He didn't hear.

When Ace deposited Kit, still clutching her paintbrush, with Rose downstairs, he was maliciously
pleased to discover Nick was with her, waiting for
Saul.

227

'Where's Melissa?' he asked casually.

'At home,' Nick replied shortly.

'I think I'll drive over and see her – you don't mind, do you?' Ace asked, knowing that the truthful answer would be a resounding yes. Nick merely shrugged, refusing to rise to the bait. He trusted Melissa completely; unfortunately, he trusted Ace about as far as he could throw him!

Ace sauntered back out to his hired car with a satisfied grin curving his mouth, feeling well pleased with himself. First he'd riled the dark-haired soldier who had eyed the cute blonde so hungrily, and then he'd bugged the hell out of Nick Lennox! America 2. British Army 0.

'Hi, honey.' When he arrived, he greeted Melissa with a kiss on the cheek. 'I've just dropped Kit off at Bellwood and thought I'd call in. Have you got a minute? I need to talk to you about something.'

'Sure, come on in.' Melissa led the way into the drawing-room. 'Alexa and the twins are okay, aren't they?' she asked.

'Terrific, thanks.' His often cruel features softened for a moment. 'Alexa's tired after the trip, but I know she'd love to see you in a day or so.'

'I'll call her,' Melissa promised. 'So, what's on your mind?' she asked curiously.

'This.' Ace took a small folder from his pocket and tossed it over to her.

'Kit's passport?' Melissa looked up questioningly. 'I don't understand – why didn't you leave it at Bellwood?'

'I don't want Lisa to be able to get her hands on it easily. She was intending keeping Kit in California,

228

filing for divorce and custody, all without a word to Jack until the papers were served,' he told her.

'You're joking!' Melissa exclaimed. 'Oh, she is such a bitch these days! I knew things weren't going too well, but . . . Just a minute; you said she *was* intending, past tense. She's changed her mind?'

'With a little persuasion from me,' Ace said modestly. 'I convinced her it would be better if she let Kit travel back with us . . .'

'How?' Melissa asked suspiciously.

'Don't ask; it's better you don't know,' he said, and Melissa grimaced slightly; she almost began to feel sorry for Lisa – Ace was a formidable enemy.

'I've told her I won't mention any of this to Jack,' he continued. 'My guess is she'll come slinking back home before very much longer. But I won't be around to watch her and make sure she doesn't get any more clever ideas in the future. You'll have to do that,' he told her.

'Thanks a lot!' Melissa said bitterly. She glanced down at the passport in her hands. 'Poor Jack; he deserves better,' she said slowly, then she looked up at Ace. 'Don't you think he ought to know?'

'No, I don't,' he said firmly. 'At least, not yet, not while there's still a chance they can patch things up. If it ends in divorce, well, I have some evidence Jack can use against her. But until that happens, you keep your mouth shut,' he told her sternly.

'I can't keep secrets from Jack!' Melissa said. Ace raised one eyebrow and grinned slightly.

'No? I seem to remember we were careful he didn't find out we were sleeping together a few years ago,' he drawled. Melissa blushed.

'That was different,' she mumbled. 'That was my business, not his.'

'Well, I can't stop you telling him, of course, but why make him miserable? Keep it to yourself; that way it will be much easier for them to patch it up. Of course, if Lisa does return and you think she might be pulling another stunt, then give me a call.'

'Okay,' Melissa agreed, albeit unwillingly, then glanced down at the passport. 'But Jack will probably want to take Kit to the States with him later in the year – he'll be going over to New York to cover the US Open,' she reminded him. 'He'll be looking for her passport.

'I know; hopefully it will be sorted out by then, one way or another. By the way, who's the Army guy I saw at Bellwood?' Ace decided to change the subject.

'Oh, a friend of Nick's – Saul Lancaster,' Melissa told him, getting up to put Kit's passport safely away.

'What's with him and the little artist?'

'I don't think even they can answer that,' Melissa said drily. 'But hopefully they've kissed and made up by now,' she added.

'I doubt it!' Ace smirked.

'Why?' Melissa narrowed her eyes at him.

'He looked most put out at seeing me with her; I can't imagine why,' he said, trying to look innocent and failing miserably.

'You were with her? Doing what, exactly?' she asked suspiciously.

'Well, she was perched on a ladder – most precariously, I thought – and I just happened to be

helping her keep her balance when he walked in,'
Ace explained blandly.

'Helping her?' Melissa queried.

'Mmm, I had my hand on her thigh – just to stop
her falling, of course!' he grinned.

'Oh, God,' Melissa sighed.

'I'm ready to go back to the airport,' Saul told Nick
abruptly. Nick took one look at his grim expression
and bit back his objection at being spoken to as if he
were a hired chauffeur.

'Sure,' he said easily instead, kissed Rose and Kit
goodbye and accompanied Saul outside.

Saul sat silently, staring morosely out of the
window as Nick headed back to Gatwick.

'I can understand now why you dislike Ace
Delaney so much,' he said finally. 'He's got the
sort of face I'd never tire of hitting!' he added
viciously. Nick raised one eyebrow at his tone.

'Get to the back of the queue,' he said lightly.
'Anyway, haven't you enough problems right now
without adding Ace Delaney to them?' he asked
mildly. 'I take it you and Ginny didn't resolve
anything?'

'No, we didn't,' Saul said moodily, and lapsed
into another brooding silence.

There was an hour to wait before his return flight
to Cyprus, so Nick bought Saul a Scotch and a beer
for himself, then sat down.

'There's no need for you to hang about,' Saul
said, downing the Scotch in one gulp and beckoning
for a refill.

'It's okay, I've nothing better to do,' Nick said

easily, dismissing, with some difficulty, the thought of Ace alone with Melissa. 'I'm sorry it was a wasted trip.'

'Yeah.' Saul stared down into his glass, as if seeking an answer. Nick, from his own bitter experience, could have told him there was nothing to be gained from getting drunk but a hangover. He refrained from saying so, however, for the knowledge hadn't stopped him drinking when he and Melissa had broken up, and it probably wouldn't stop Saul.

'I really thought she was different, but I should have trusted my first impression and steered clear. She is so like Ann used to be,' Saul mused.

'Ann?'

'Ann Sinclair – Ginny's mother,' Saul said, then hesitated before saying anything further. 'It's a long story.'

'Like I said – I've nothing better to do,' Nick told him, guessing Saul needed to unburden himself. After a moment Saul began talking, slowly at first, getting his thoughts in order.

'I think I told you that Ginny's father, Richard, used to work for Lancaster Electronics?'

'Yes.' Nick nodded.

'He was a decent bloke, and Ann – well, she was just as beautiful as Ginny is now. They are so alike, it's uncanny,' Saul said.

'Did you once have a crush on Ann?' Nick guessed. Saul smiled slightly.

'Sort of. I was just a kid, about thirteen or fourteen. At that time Richard worked under the financial director, a guy called Bill Taggart. No one told me any details, of course, but there was a huge row after an office party, when Ann claimed Bill had raped her. His wife walked out on him, taking the children with her; my father was furious, sacked Bill and promoted Richard in his place.'

'You said she "claimed" he had raped her – do you think she was lying?'

'I know she was,' Saul said flatly. 'Now I do – not at the time, or I'd have said something,' he clarified hastily. 'Back then I thought she was lovely and innocent, and when Bill Taggart hanged himself –'

'Hanged himself?' Nick exclaimed.

'Yes. Everyone thought he'd done it out of guilt and shame, and most people, myself included, thought good riddance to bad rubbish. It was all hushed up; the police weren't involved – Ann had already insisted she didn't want to report it; it was too humiliating, or so she said. Later I realized she was afraid they would quickly discover she was lying. Publicly, and at the inquest, Bill's suicide was attributed to depression over his wife leaving him, and his losing a highly paid job.'

'When did you change your opinion of Ann?' Nick asked.

'Years later, my father asked me to put in an appearance at the staff Christmas party. I arrived late, and heard noises from one of the secretaries' rooms. The party was being held on the top floor and, rather naïvely, I thought maybe someone was pilfering, so I marched into the room and there was Ann Sinclair, spreadeagled across a desk with another member of the board – Gerald Smythe – and she was definitely not being raped!' His mouth

233

twisted with disgust at the memory.

'That doesn't necessarily mean she was lying about the other guy,' Nick pointed out.

'No, I know that,' Saul said impatiently. 'I beat a hasty retreat, more embarrassed than anything else. Later, Ann came looking for me, and, as luck would have it, Richard Sinclair had chosen that moment to ask how I was getting on at Sandhurst. I guess Ann thought I was telling him what I'd seen, and she became hysterical. God knows what everyone else was thinking; luckily they were too drunk to take too much notice. First she tried telling me Gerald Smythe had attacked her. I made it clear what I thought of that, so then she turned really nasty and threatened to accuse me of raping her if I mentioned anything to her husband.'

'Oh, God,' Nick muttered.

'Quite,' Saul said drily. 'I guessed then that she had lied about Bill Taggart, and I confronted her with it. She admitted she had; she said Bill had been a fool who hadn't the sense to conduct an affair discreetly. She repeated her threats to accuse me, and I . . . well, I caved in,' he admitted. 'I was nineteen, and if there was such a thing as DNA testing back then I certainly hadn't heard of it. I knew she'd just had sex, and I thought it would just be my word against hers if she claimed I was responsible – my Army career would have been down the pan, there was also the possibility of jail, and so –' he shrugged '– I just let it go; I figured it was none of my business.'

'It wasn't,' Nick said reasonably.

'I know, but maybe I could have – should have –

cleared Bill Taggart's name . . .' He frowned at what he now thought of as his cowardice.

'Like you said, it would have been your word against hers, especially if this other guy – Smythe? – had backed her story. You never could have proved it,' Nick said calmly. 'I don't see that dredging it all up would have helped Taggart's family much, either. It would all have been extremely unpleasant, and his widow would have had to accept that he had been having an affair.'

'Maybe you're right,' Saul agreed finally. 'I never saw Ann again after that evening, and I tried to forget all about it. Then, a couple of years ago, I heard her husband had been killed in a sailing accident.'

'Suicide?' Nick asked.

'I don't know. At the time I thought it probably was, that the poor guy had finally had enough, but the coroner's verdict was accidental death, so I could have been wrong. I hope I was, for Ginny's sake,' he added quietly.

'Ah, yes, Ginny.' Nick had almost forgotten about her. 'How did you two meet up?' he asked curiously.

'It was about a month ago . . . God is that all?' he muttered, almost to himself; he couldn't imagine a time when Ginny hadn't been part of his life, his thoughts were so full of her. 'My mother phoned, told me Dad had been in a car accident and that his companion was Ann Sinclair. Apparently they had been having an affair for some time.'

'The press report – that first one, hinting at an affair, the one you said was a lie – that was actually the truth?' Nick realized slowly.

'Yes, it was.' Saul nodded. 'I wanted to spare my mother the public humiliation of everyone knowing he was cheating on her, so I came up with the idea of pretending Ginny was my girlfriend, that the five of us had dined together that evening and that my father was merely giving Ann a lift home.' He paused. 'I thought I was being so bloody clever. . . . I should have known Ginny would be trouble; I *did* know,' he clarified. 'When she arrived at the hospital, I knew who she was immediately – she was so like Ann used to be, so incredibly sexy, yet exuding an innocence that makes you want to protect her as well as seduce her . . .' He expelled a deep breath.

'Melissa resembles *her* mother, but they have completely different personalities,' Nick pointed out. 'You don't seem to have given Ginny much of a chance – you were pretty foul to her that weekend at our place,' he recalled.

'I know; sorry about that,' Saul said. 'I shouldn't have involved you and Melissa in my mess, or in my dastardly scheme!' He tried to smile. 'I thought I could take her to bed and then dump her,' he said baldly. Nick raised one eyebrow in amazement, and some distaste.

'If that's your attitude, I'm not surprised she doesn't want to talk to you,' he said coldly.

'That *was* my attitude,' Saul corrected. 'I know I treated her abominably; I couldn't admit it to myself, but I was falling in love with her and fighting it every inch of the way. . . . But we cleared the air, decided to just ignore our parents' triangle, and we were getting along wonderfully well . . .' He paused, remembering the touch and scent of her body, the passion and the laughter, then he shook his head ruefully. 'Then I got the call about Cyprus, and, next I know, she's telling me she's going to Hollywood to be with her actor boyfriend . . .'

'Not in the foreseeable future, she isn't,' Nick told him. 'There's a lot of work still to be done at Bellwood, and I know she's taking a couple of weeks' holiday during Wimbledon fortnight – she's going with Melissa.'

'That's still the plan, is it?' Saul asked, hope stirring; she obviously wasn't in a rush to get to Hollywood . . .

'Yes, I'm sure it is,' Nick assured him.

'She'll be at Bellwood with Jack Farrell – minus his wife.' Saul's optimism didn't last long as he recalled Ginny saying she had bigger fish to fry . . .

'Rose is staying there to look after Kit,' Nick reminded him. 'Besides, Jack isn't the type to use trouble in his marriage as an excuse to have an affair,' he added reassuringly. He paused as a possible reason for Ginny's change of heart occurred to him, then looked across at Saul. 'Maybe she simply doesn't trust you for much the same reason as you don't trust her,' he said slowly.

'What do you mean?' Saul frowned.

'She knows your father cheats on your mother. You've been thinking like mother like daughter; perhaps she's thinking you're a womanizer, just like your father.' He explained his thinking.

'I never considered that,' Saul said slowly. 'She

did once say something to the effect that her mother is a widow and it's my father who's the adulterer . . .'

'It's worth thinking about,' Nick said. 'And something else – Ginny's a lot younger than you, isn't she?'

'About ten years.' Saul nodded.

'So she was little more than a baby when there was all that trouble, the suicide and so on. I don't suppose she knows anything about it, do you?'

'No, I guess she doesn't. Or only Ann's sanitized version of events . . . Ginny knows I despise her mother, but she could assume that's just because of the relationship with my father,' he realized slowly. 'Oh, hell, there's my flight. I'll have to go. Do me a favour?'

'Sure.'

'Keep an eye on things while I'm away. Don't let her go to Hollywood – or anywhere at all with Ace Delaney!'

'What am I supposed to do – kidnap her?' Nick asked ruefully.

'If necessary.' Saul grinned. 'Thanks, Nick.' He strode off towards the departure gate, feeling slightly more cheerful.

CHAPTER 12

Nick pushed Saul's problems to the back of his mind as he drove home; now he was more concerned with the knowledge that Ace Delaney was with Melissa.

He hated the feelings of jealousy and anger he harboured for the American, but had never quite succeeded in dispelling them. When he had first met Melissa, she had been a seventeen-year-old school-girl, smitten with her brother's famous friend and doubles partner, and had barely noticed that he, Nick, even existed!

Of course, that had all changed, but then Delaney had been instrumental in arranging Melissa's abortion. The loss of his first child still caused Nick pain and, although he had eventually forgiven and understood Melissa's hasty act borne of panic, he could never forgive or forget the part Ace had so willingly played.

As if that weren't enough reason to dislike and mistrust Delaney, he had later seduced Melissa and done his damnedest to prevent their reconciliation. Despite four and a half years of blissfully happy marriage, and the birth of their daughter, Nick continued to feel uneasy whenever Ace was around and could never quite forget that the other man had been his wife's first love.

Thankfully Ace was no longer at Nine Elms when Nick returned. He resisted the urge to throw open all the windows in a symbolic act of cleansing his home, and went in search of Melissa.

He found her in the drawing-room, talking to a journalist who had phoned to request an interview. There was always an upsurge in media interest in the former Wimbledon Champion as the tournament approached, and even more so this year since the news of her and Jack's entry into the mixed doubles had been made public.

Nick poured drinks for them both and waited for her to finish the call.

'Thanks.' Melissa smiled as she took her glass from him and curled up beside him on the sofa. 'How did it go with Saul and Ginny?' she wanted to know. Nick grimaced.

'Don't ask.'

'That bad, huh?'

'Afraid so. Has she mentioned anything to you about going to join an ex-boyfriend in Hollywood?'

'No, not a word.' Melissa shook her head. 'Is that what she told Saul?'

'Yes. Maybe she was simply trying to make him jealous.' He paused, then, 'Of course, Ace didn't exactly help matters,' he added.

'Ace?'

'Mmm. Didn't he mention meeting them? He *has* been here, hasn't he?' he persisted, when Melissa didn't reply.

'Yes, he just called to say hi,' Melissa said vaguely. Too vaguely, Nick thought.

'Was that all he wanted?'

'Of course.' Melissa gazed steadily back. She had pondered what, if anything, she should tell Nick, and had decided to keep quiet. She felt Jack's humiliation as if it were her own, and couldn't bear anyone else knowing how Lisa had plotted behind his back, not even Nick.

If Lisa still decided she wanted a divorce, well, then she would tell Nick, but while there was a chance the marriage could be saved the fewer who knew the truth the better. In fact, she wished Ace hadn't told her, although she understood his reasons for doing so – if Lisa managed to get Kit to California again, she would stand a far greater chance of gaining custody, and Melissa was determined to do everything she could to prevent that happening. She was a hundred per cent behind Jack, and pushed aside nagging thoughts of what Lisa must be going through, separated from her child. That last thought reminded her that Kit was again at Bellwood, and she looked across at Nick.

'You've seen Kit? How is she?'

'Fine. Delighted to be back, of course, but impatient to see Jack. She loves her new-look bedroom.'

'Did you take a look?' Melissa asked, and when he shook his head, she continued, 'It really is special; Ginny's very talented. I think she's wasted where she is – she spends most of her time choosing wallpaper for people without the taste to decide for themselves,' she said dismissively. If Jack

241

agreed, she intended using Bellwood for a couple of press interviews scheduled to take place over the next few weeks, and would make sure the photographers took a picture of Ginny's work.

'Is Suzy asleep?' Nick asked suddenly.

'Yes.' Melissa glanced at him and caught the familiar gleam of desire in his grey eyes. As always, her stomach lurched with excitement and anticipation. 'Bed?' she guessed softly.

'Bed,' Nick agreed firmly, taking her hand in his and leading her quickly up the stairs.

Once inside their bedroom, however, he took his time, slowly ridding her of her clothing, kissing each newly exposed part of her body. He loved the way she always responded to his touch, would never tire of hearing her rapid breathing, the soft moans, would always crave the softness of her skin against his, always want, need, the warm welcome as her body opened to accommodate him.

He had desired her every single day of their marriage, but this act was one of possession, born of a primitive need to claim her again as his, to dispel any lingering memory of Ace Delaney.

'Why don't we have another baby?' he murmured, much later, when they were snuggled close together, warm and sated. Melissa tensed a little; much as she loved Suzy, she didn't really want another child – not yet, anyway. She certainly couldn't understand why some women claimed to enjoy pregnancy and childbirth.

'I'm only twenty-six,' she hedged.

'I know.' Nick realized his timing was lousy; she was so busy and preoccupied with her new range of

242

tenniswear, and with her participation in this year's championships.

'I'm not rushing you.' He kissed her forehead. 'I know I get the easy part! Whenever you're ready is fine by me,' he assured her, and Melissa relaxed.

When Nick entered the offices of Lennox and Coupland on Monday morning, Coop, who lived within easy walking distance, was already there, dealing with the mail. He looked up as Nick walked in.

'You have a visitor,' he told him. 'Apparently it's personal, so I showed her into your office and gave her some coffee.'

'Her?'

'Name of Sullivan.'

'Sullivan?' Nick repeated, frowning slightly. 'Thanks,' he said absently, and went immediately to his own office. A dark-haired woman was gazing out of the window, seemingly casual, but she whirled around at the sound of the door opening, her hand to her throat.

They stared at each other in silence for several moments. It was her, Nick thought incredulously: Constance Sullivan! The years rolled away as memories flooded back for both of them. Constance recovered first; she, after all, had known they were about to meet again.

'Hello, Nick,' she said, in the soft Irish lilt that he had once loved so much. 'You haven't changed at all.'

'Nor you,' he responded, with a slight smile. It wasn't strictly true; the once lustrous dark hair had

243

thinned and was threaded with grey, her skin showed signs of the passing years in lines around her mouth and eyes, but those blue, blue eyes were still the same. He'd once described them as sapphire pools, he remembered, with a slight grimace for the lovelorn teenager he had been.

'Thank you, but I know how I look,' Constance said. 'It's not fair, is it? The way men improve with age and women – well, it's just not fair . . .' She paused, and the silence lengthened. She'd had it all planned, every word carefully considered, but now that she was actually facing him she didn't know how to begin.

'Sit down, please.' Nick finally moved forward and pulled out a chair for her. He perched on the edge of his desk and smiled at her. 'How are you, Connie?'

'Well, I'm much better now, but I have been ill,' she told him. 'That's really why I'm here.'

'Oh?'

'Yes. I suppose I should have come before, but I wasn't sure if you'd want me to, and then time passed and I read about your marriage to Melissa Farrell – and there was an article about the business you set up; that's how I knew where to find you,' she explained, rather breathlessly.

'Are you in trouble, Connie?' Nick frowned. 'Do you need my help?'

'Not exactly.' She licked her lips nervously. 'As I said, I've been quite ill, and I needed major surgery . . . I was frightened, and the night before the operation – well, I was thinking all sorts of morbid thoughts, worried I might die.' She laughed self-consciously.

'The thing is, I wrote a letter to . . . my son.'

'Your son?'

'Yes. Michael. I was worried about who would look out for him if I was no longer around, so I wrote him a letter telling him to contact you.'

'Me?'

'He should never have read it,' Connie rushed on. 'I told the nurse he was only to be given it if I didn't recover from the surgery, but there was a mix-up; the letter was passed on to the day staff and a different nurse handed it to Mickey. When I came round from the anaesthetic, he had already read it.' She looked at Nick beseechingly. 'I am sorry.'

'What exactly was in the letter?' Nick asked slowly, although he had an idea he already knew. 'How old is Mickey?'

'Sixteen.'

'He's my son?' It was a statement, not a question.

'Yes,' Connie whispered. She watched anxiously as he stood up and paced the room. 'Are you angry?'

'Angry?' Nick swung round to face her, but couldn't answer the question. So many conflicting emotions were tugging at him, fighting for supremacy. There was some anger, yes, that she had waited until now to tell him he had a son; there was also guilt, for never considering the possibility, for never checking that she was okay. There was curiosity, too, about the boy he had fathered, but mostly there was a dreadful fear of what this might do to Melissa and Suzy. They were his family, the people he loved more than life itself. He wished Connie had kept her secret, but now that he did know he couldn't turn his back on her and her son.

He only hoped Melissa would understand that.

'Nick?' Connie ventured finally. 'I'm sorry, this must be such a shock to you,' she said apologetically. 'But I had to come. I promised Mickey, and if I hadn't come he would have made his own way over here to see you.'

'Is he here in London with you?'

'Yes, we arrived last night. I persuaded him it would be better if I came to see you alone first.'

'God,' Nick muttered. 'I'm scared to meet him. He must think I'm a sod, deserting you both.'

'No, I've explained what the situation was at the time. He understands why I never contacted you before, but I'm afraid he's – well, he's not exactly pleased to discover his father was a British soldier,' she admitted, rather unwillingly, but it had to be said, for she knew Mickey would make his feelings very plain if and when the two met.

'I see,' Nick said, and he did: obviously liaisons between British soldiers and Irish Catholic girls were as frowned upon now as they had been all those years ago. His Army career had almost ended before it had really begun, and Connie . . . she had been in real danger . . .

'You went to live with an aunt in Dublin,' he remembered. 'Have you been there all this time?'

'Yes, but Maura died a couple of years ago, so there would have been no one to take care of Mickey if anything happened to me.'

'Surely he asked about his father long ago?'

'Yes, of course he did. I told him he had died in the Troubles, and that was why we never visited his grandfather in Belfast. My father refused to have anything to do with either of us, so I knew I couldn't ask him to give Mickey a home. Beside, he's old now, and not too well himself. I have no contact with him at all, but an old friend of mine writes occasionally to give me the news. He's never forgiven me or accepted Mickey as his grandson,' she said calmly.

'I'm sorry,' Nick said – rather inadequately, he felt. 'I really messed up your life, didn't I? Did you never marry?'

'No, there was one man, but I was idiot enough to tell him the truth about Mickey. I thought he loved me enough to understand, but I was wrong; he didn't want to marry me once he knew.'

'Oh, God.' Nick felt really wretched. 'What can I do to help, Connie?' he asked. 'If you've been ill . . .' he hesitated, then said bluntly, 'You'll need money. And I owe you that, at the very least. Where are you staying?'

'Oh, we found a small bed and breakfast; it will do – we're not staying very long. And we are not here to cause you trouble, Nick,' she assured him quickly. 'You have a family already, but naturally Mickey is . . . curious.' She settled for that word; it was the kindest emotion her son was feeling for his unknown father.

'And resentful?' Nick correctly guessed another. Connie shrugged.

'I've explained it all as best I can. I'm afraid he's not very fond of me at the moment.' She smiled sadly. 'But this is his first trip to London and he's cheered up a bit since we arrived.'

'Good. I'll show him around, if he'd like me to.

And I really do want to help financially with his future – universtity, or whatever he has planned,' Nick said, rather vaguely. With Suzy not quite two years old, future careers had not been high on his list of priorities.

'We have a flat in Chelsea,' he continued. 'We kept it on after we moved to the country, but we hardly ever use it. It's convenient to stop there after a night on the town, but I can't imagine we'll be needing it for the next few weeks,' he said slowly. Melissa was too busy preparing for Wimbledon and had already said she intended driving in from Nine Elms every day; it was a longer distance but shorter travelling time, and a lot less frustrating. 'Would you like to stay there?' he asked, feeling that offer was a lot more tactful than insisting he pay her hotel bills.

'That would be a help, if you're sure,' Connie said gratefully, for money *was* something of a problem.

'Of course I'm sure. Tell your hotel you're checking out today,' Nick said firmly. 'Go and pack now, and I'll collect you later.' He checked his desk diary. 'Would this afternoon suit you? Around four?'

'That will be fine.' Connie got to her feet and Nick escorted her out, ignoring Coop's questioning glance. He hailed a cab and paid the fare in advance, jotting down the address of her hotel which, as he had suspected, was in a less than salubrious area.

'I'll see you later. And Connie – I'm glad you came,' he said simply.

He walked slowly back inside, not sure if he had just spoken the truth. How the hell was he going to

248

tell Melissa? He had known Connie when Melissa was only nine or ten years old, but he was afraid that fact wouldn't help much. If at all.

'Nick?' Coop began, then followed him into his office, and watched him as he poured himself a liberal amount of Scotch. 'Do you want to tell me what's going on?'

'There's nothing to tell,' Nick shrugged.

'Come off it. I've remembered why her name was vaguely familiar. You once told me about Connie Sullivan – you got mixed up with her on your first tour of duty in Northern Ireland, and the CO bawled you out and threatened to kick your butt back to Aldershot, if not out of the Army.'

'Yes, that was Connie,' Nick said heavily. 'She got caught up in a riot one evening, and I escorted her home. I knew I shouldn't see her again, but, well, I did. We had quite a thing going, until her father found out and played merry hell. And, as you said, someone told the CO and he sent me to join a border patrol. When I returned, Connie had already left Belfast.'

'So why has she turned up now?' Coop asked.

'Can I trust you? Sorry, of course I can,' Nick said quickly. 'I don't know how to explain this to Melissa – I've never even mentioned Connie to her – but, apparently, when her father sent her to Dublin, she was pregnant. I have a sixteen-year-old son.'

'Oh, my God.' Coop reached for the Scotch. 'Melissa will do her nut,' he warned.

'Tell me about it,' Nick said heavily. 'I can't bear to tell her, but I can't deceive her, either,' he said miserably.

'I should keep quiet, for now,' Coop advised. 'At least until you find out what Connie wants from you.'

'I don't think she wants anything,' Nick retorted, rather sharply. 'If she'd wanted money, she'd have contacted me years ago. No, her son has only just found out about me; that's why they have come to London.'

'When are you going to meet him? What on earth will you say to him?'

'God knows.' Nick reached for his own Scotch, then changed his mind and pushed the bottle away; he needed a clear head. 'I'm more concerned with what I'm going to say to Melissa,' he said, and Coop grimaced in sympathy.

'I think you should give them money and get rid of them,' he said. 'That sounds harsh, I know, but you don't want to risk losing Melissa.'

'I won't lose her,' Nick said firmly, feeling sick at the very thought. 'I can't lose her,' he said, half under his breath, but it was more of a prayer than a statement of belief.

'Daddy! Daddy! Daddy!' Kit ran as fast as her little legs would carry her towards her father. Jack scooped her up and lifted her high above his head, making her squeal with delight.

'I've missed you!' he told her, hugging her tightly. 'I should have packed you in my suitcase!'

Damn right you should, Melissa thought grimly, Ace's confidence weighing heavily on her. But, mindful of his warning to say nothing, she plastered a bright smile on her face and asked eagerly for the gossip behind the stories of the French Open.

In the days that followed, Jack was too busy to worry overmuch about the state of his marriage: he was covering the warm-up tournament at the Queen's Club on TV, recording interviews for the forthcoming Wimbledon Championships and, in every spare moment, Melissa was badgering him to practise – she was determined they should do well in the mixed doubles.

Since retiring, three years earlier, she had played only exhibition and charity events, both of which were played for fun and entertainment. This was different, and occasionally she would lie awake at night wondering if she was making a huge mistake. Her last appearance at Wimbledon had been on Centre Court as the Ladies Singles Champion, and she dreaded making an ignominious departure in the first round.

Ace was often at Bellwood, helping her and Jack prepare. And Melissa's ex-coach, Katy Oliver, joined them several times to partner Ace against Jack and Melissa, enabling them to hone their skills as a team.

'I'm supposed to be getting Ella and Shanna into shape for Eastbourne next week,' she had protested, when Melissa asked for her help, but had quickly capitulated. Katy had loved Jack for years, and she supposed she still did, in a slightly different way – thankfully not with the old gut-churning yearning she had harboured for so long.

'Lisa must be crazy, leaving him to his own devices,' she said frankly to Melissa. 'A lot of the young players fancy Jack – they are queueing up to be interviewed by him.'

'That's her problem,' Melissa replied shortly. 'Frankly, as long as she leaves Kit here, I don't care if she never comes back.'

'Does Jack feel the same way?'

'I don't know; I haven't discussed it with him,' Melissa said truthfully. She purposely refrained from mentioning Lisa, lest she inadvertently let slip anything she had gleaned from Ace.

On Thursday, leaving the twins behind in London with their nanny, Alexa accompanied Ace to Bellwood – partly to catch up on news with Rose Farrell, a woman she had come to regard as a second mother, and partly to view Ginny's work. To Ginny's surprise, for she had half expected Ace to have forgotten all about her, he had repeated his offer for her to travel out to their ranch in California.

The work on Kit's room was almost completed now, and Alexa was very impressed. She was not quite so impressed with Ginny's blonde beauty. Ace had never – yet – given her cause to think he might cheat on her, but he had been such a rake before their marriage that she could never quite believe her luck that she was the one he wanted, permanently and exclusively.

Of course, it didn't help that wherever in the world they travelled women continued to throw themselves at him, often elbowing Alexa unceremoniously out of the way. Despite her aura of cool assurance, Alexa's deep insecurities and sense of inadequacy continued to lurk near the surface. She craved constant reassurance, a need Ace didn't fully understand: he loved her, he had married her – what more did she want?

'Alexa's looking rather too thin,' Melissa observed to Ace, waving hello from the court as Alexa walked into the house. Alexa had always been fine-boned and slim, but now she looked positively ill, Melissa thought. She was extremely pale, too, considering she lived in California for most of the year. 'Is she okay?'

'Yeah, she's seen a doctor. He did some tests; she's just anaemic, so he's given her some pills,' Ace replied casually, although he was frowning slightly as he watched his wife. He was more worried about her constant tiredness and lack of energy than he cared to admit.

'The twins must be exhausting for her,' Melissa commented idly, and Ace glared at her.

'We have a housekeeper, two live-in maids and a full-time nanny!' he snapped, annoyed by the implication that his wife was overworked. 'Alexa doesn't have to lift a finger if she doesn't want to.'

'I realize that,' Melissa retorted. 'But, however busy I am with other things, I always want to have time with Suzy, and I'm sure Alexa feels the same. Only she has double the trouble – trust you to father twins!' she added lightly, and his scowl vanished.

'I can't help being extra virile,' he drawled. No, Melissa thought, and that was probably the reason for Alexa's fatigue!

'Are we playing, or chatting?' Jack called irritably, from the other side of the court. Not for the first time, he was cursing himself for allowing Melissa to persuade him into returning to competitive tennis.

He, too, was a past Champion, albeit in doubles, and Melissa was not the only one to fear a humiliating defeat.

'Playing! I'll be there in a minute,' Melissa called back, then she looked at Ace. 'I don't think Lisa's phoned him. Don't you think we should tell Jack what she was planning? Forewarned is forearmed and all that?'

'No, not yet. Let's wait and see what Lisa's next move is. If we tell Jack now, there'll be no going back.'

'Okay,' Melissa agreed reluctantly, and went to join her brother on the far side of the net.

Alexa watched them for a while from the upstairs window as they ran about the court; even in practice they played with a speed and power that was exhausting to watch . . .

She sighed and turned away to inspect more closely the transformation of Kit's room. Ginny was sitting cross-legged on the floor, frowning in concentration as she painted a particularly awkwardly-shaped narrow cranny.

'Goodness, that looks uncomfortable,' Alexa commented. 'Wouldn't you prefer to be painting canvasses?'

'Oh, sure, the Bond Street galleries are queueing up to buy my paintings!' Ginny grinned over her shoulder.

'Oh, well, if –' Alexa stopped speaking and drew a deep breath.

'If what?' Ginny asked, after a moment. Receiving no reply, she glanced back at Alexa, who was slumped on Kit's bed, her face ashen. 'Are you okay?' she asked, concerned.

'No . . . my bag.' Alexa pointed to her handbag, only a couple of yards away. Ginny stood up and quickly passed it to her. 'Could you get me a glass of water?' Alexa gasped.

'Of course.' Ginny ran from the room, almost colliding with Rose, who was bringing coffee for them all. 'I think Alexa's ill,' she explained breathlessly. 'She almost fainted just now.'

'Oh, dear!' Rose exclaimed, then she smiled. 'Alexa, are you pregnant?' she guessed.

'No.' Alexa took a tablet from the bottle in her bag and swallowed it down. 'It was nothing; just the paint fumes in here made me feel a little queasy,' she said weakly. Rose and Ginny exchanged puzzled glances, neither able to detect any such fumes. Ginny always worked with the windows wide open, and besides, there was only a tiny portion of that morning's work which was wet.

'Come and lie down in my room for a while,' Rose said. She helped Alexa to her feet, noting anew how thin and pale she was. Her large gold-green eyes were the only spots of colour in her face, even her lips were bloodless.

'Are you sure you're not pregnant?' Rose asked again, once she had settled Alexa onto her bed.

'Positive.' Alexa closed her eyes, her heart feeling as if it might burst through the confines of her ribcage.

'Shall I fetch Ace?' Rose asked next.

'God, no!' Alexa sat up, too quickly, and sank back against the pillows, gasping for breath. 'No, please don't do that,' she said, more quietly. 'Please don't even tell him that I . . . fainted; he'll only worry and insist that I see another doctor.' She smiled weakly.

'Another doctor?' Rose sat down on the edge of the bed and reached to hold Alexa's hand. It was icy, and Rose automatically began rubbing it gently between her own. 'You've been ill?'

'Not really, just tired. I had some tests, and apparently I'm anaemic. I'm feeling better already with the tablets he prescribed,' she said brightly. Rose didn't believe a word of it. Was Ace playing around? she wondered. And was Alexa on drugs to relieve stress, or taking anti-depressants? One thing she was sure about – the pill Alexa had just swallowed was something more than an iron tablet to aid anaemia!

'I see,' was all she said, loath to interfere, for Alexa could be so prickly at times. But then she saw the glimmer of tears in Alexa's eyes and impulsively reached out to embrace her. 'What's wrong? Can I help?' she asked gently.

'No. No one can.' Alexa took a deep, shuddering breath. 'I think I would like to talk, but only if you promise not to tell anyone,' she said earnestly. 'Not Jack or Melissa, not my father, and especially not Ace.'

'I promise,' Rose agreed readily. Alexa looked at her searchingly, then nodded, as if satisfied she would keep her word. She took a few moments to gather her thoughts – as if she had thought of anything else recently!

'I consulted a doctor in San Francisco, and I've been to see a specialist in London – he confirmed what I'd already been told,' she paused. 'You probably know that my mother had a heart complaint; it appears I've inherited it. Having twins put a strain on my heart that wasn't picked up at the time.'

'How serious is it?' Rose asked quietly; she knew that Alexa's mother had died before her thirtieth birthday.

'It's not life-threatening, but I have to take medication and be careful not to overdo things.' She smiled wryly. 'Of course, that's easier said than done when one's married to a man such as Ace! He lives life at such a fast pace.'

'Alexa, surely that's all the more reason why you should tell him?'

'No,' she said positively. 'I couldn't bear it if he left me at home while he got on with his life. And I'd feel even worse if he gave up the tennis, the travelling, to live a quiet life with me. He'd hate it. He's restless if he stays in one place too long. Eventually he'd resent me. Then he'd be bored with me and he'd feel trapped, and . . . I'd die if he went off with another woman. Of course, I might die anyway,' she said, with black humour.

'Oh, Alexa, don't talk like that.' Rose was deeply distressed by what she was hearing.

'I'm sorry, I shouldn't have said that; it's really not that serious. I told both doctors about my mother's medical history and they assure me that the treatment nowadays is much more effective than that which was available to her twenty years ago. With a bit of luck, I'll still be around when the twins have grown up and have children of their own.'

'I'm sure you will. But you must let me help, even if it's only to talk. And I'm a terrific babysitter,' she added.

'I know, thank you. But I'm lucky enough to have a nanny, and hired help to do the chores. I have a wonderful life, really I do. Ace and the twins . . . they're all . . . wonderful,' she repeated, with a tremulous smile. 'Thanks for listening; I suppose I have been bottling it up inside. I feel a lot better now I've put it into words; it doesn't seem so frightening any more.'

'I'm glad.' Rose regarded her sympathetically. 'Alexa, I understand why you don't want to tell Ace, but what about your father?' she asked tentatively. Rose had once been romantically involved with Alexa's father, Philip Kane, and still had dinner with him once a week. She knew she was going to find it difficult to keep her knowledge to herself. 'If Jack or Melissa were ill, I'd hate it if they kept it from me. I'd want to do all I could for them, and I'm sure your father would feel the same. Please tell him. Or let me do it for you,' she entreated.

'No.' Alexa shook her head vehemently. 'He would tell Ace. He still doesn't totally approve of our marriage, despite being besotted with the twins, and he'd become over-protective and start telling Ace how he should treat me . . . And you know how kindly Ace takes to being told what to do!' she said drily. 'In no time there would be a huge row . . .' She shuddered at the prospect; she could clearly imagine her father yelling at Ace that he was killing her. 'No,' she repeated firmly. 'Daddy would try to keep me here in England and drive Ace away.' She looked Rose squarely in the eyes. 'You promised,' she reminded her sternly.

'I know. I won't tell a soul,' Rose assured her, but with a sinking heart. 'Would you like to stay up here until lunch is ready?' She decided to change the subject, sure Alexa would confide more if she felt the need.

'Yes, I think I will,' Alexa replied.

'Can I bring you anything to eat or drink?' Rose asked as she got to her feet.

'No, thanks, I'm fine,' Alexa declined. Rose hesitated, then stooped to kiss the girl who had so nearly become her step-daughter, then quickly left the room.

She didn't know how on earth she would face Philip Kane – perhaps, with Wimbledon so near, she could quite truthfully claim that looking after Suzy and Kit would be a full-time job that would leave her neither the time nor the energy for socializing? Poor Philip; she knew he already regretted that his only child had married an American and lived abroad for most of the year.

Poor Philip, she thought again. All one wanted, as a parent, was that one's children were healthy and happy . . . She sighed, thinking first of Alexa and then of Jack – just what was going on between him and Lisa? At least Nick and Melissa's marriage was happy and stable – there was no reason to worry about those two!

CHAPTER 13

On the Sunday before the start of Wimbledon fortnight, Bellwood hosted an afternoon party, ostensibly to celebrate Suzy's birthday a few days hence. It was also, in part, a village fête, with everyone invited from miles around. Melissa had also taken the opportunity to invite the press, to display her new range of tenniswear as well as the revamped Bellwood, a venue which was always popular with photographers.

'Will you model some of my clothes tomorrow?' she'd asked Ginny on Saturday. 'I'll be wearing the white, since that's compulsory for Wimbledon, but you'd look great in the blue,' she enthused.

'I'm not a model,' Ginny objected, panicking at the thought of appearing in national publications; the small amount of strictly amateur modelling she had done in college had been quite nerve-racking enough, thank you!

'Nor am I.' Melissa shrugged. 'We'll look terrific – a blonde and a brunette. Please, Ginny?' she asked. Ginny hesitated for a brief moment more, then capitulated. She owed Melissa a favour – well,

more than one, she thought. She was eagerly anticipating spending several days at the All England
Club as Melissa's guest.

'Saul won't be coming, will he?' she asked anxiously on Sunday morning; that possibility was
making her reconsider even attending the party,
let alone modelling skimpy tennis clothes.

'He's still in Cyprus,' Melissa said casually, then
glanced surreptitiously at her watch. Phew! She'd
told the truth – just; his plane wouldn't have taken
off yet.

The decibel level at Bellwood could be heard for
miles around – another good reason for issuing an
open invitation to all their neighbours! Luckily,
most people in the vicinity were at the house
enjoying themselves and unlikely to complain
about the noise.

Fortunately the weather was fine; Rose had
dreaded having dozens of people tramping through
the house to escape rain or cold. Hired caterers had
provided extra chairs and tables, as well as all the
food and drink, plus a huge birthday cake for Suzy.

Melissa had also hired entertainers to keep the
children amused: there was a conjurer, three
clowns, whose slapstick antics had the kids in
hysterics, and a man in a gorilla suit who, as
usual, was soon heartily sick of being fed bananas
by children trying to be kind. And, especially for
Kit and Suzy, they had arranged donkey rides.

Four donkeys from the nearby sanctuary –
'Hopefully the least nervous,' Jack had muttered
darkly – patiently trotted around the stable block.
Nick and Daniel Farrell, Jack and Melissa's father,

supervised the rides and ensured each child received an equal number of turns. Except for Suzy; Nick quite blatantly allowed her to stay at the front of the queue, using the excuse that it was her birthday treat and she could have as many rides as she wished!

Nick watched Suzy's delight indulgently, and thought how easy it was to make her happy – donkey rides, ice-cream and lots of kisses and cuddles. Would she ever become a sullen, uncommunicatave teenager like Mickey?

He'd had several meetings with the boy – it was still hard to think of him as his son – none of which could be described as being successful. Mickey seemed to despise everything Nick stood for; he scorned the idea of further education, and had no career in mind – the only spark of enthusiasm had came when Nick had handed him spending money for his stay in London. He had smiled briefly, mumbled a grudging 'thanks' and disappeared.

Connie's attitude was quite the opposite; she was almost pathetically grateful for his help. He knew it hadn't been easy for her, even prior to her recent illness, trying to cope with an unruly near-adult boy who was chafing against parental restraint, but he often wished she had remained in Dublin!

He was ashamed of the wish. He did feel some responsibility for the boy, and also for Connie's lost chances of marriage but, dammit, it was more than a little late to expect him to become Mickey's father! He could have dealt with it more easily if not for Melissa. A hundred times he had tried to tell her, but couldn't find the words to begin. He excused the delay to himself – she was busy, preoccupied, it was unfair to burden her with his problem when she had so much else on her mind.

Maybe after the party, he had decided, but now it *was* the day of the party, and he still didn't know how to broach the subject . . . Maybe after Wimbledon is over, he thought, knowing how much she was looking forward to it. Yes, I'll definitely tell her after Wimbledon, he decided, then, with a sense of relief tinged with guilt at his own cowardice, turned his attention back to Suzy.

Melissa and Jack gave a joint interview to the press regarding their return to competition, then Jack left Melissa to talk about her range of clothing and accessories. She made sure the photographer took pictures of Ginny's work indoors, then the two girls moved outside to the tennis court. Melissa picked up several rackets and handed one to Ginny.

'I'm not hitting any balls,' Ginny said nervously.

'Relax!' Melissa laughed at her. 'It's just so you look the part.'

The photographer was a man Melissa had worked with before, and he set about putting Ginny at her ease. She quickly stopped feeling self-conscious in front of the camera and began posing happily with Melissa.

When Saul arrived, he spotted the trio on the court and quickly made his way over to them. He had thought long and hard about what could have gone wrong between Ginny and himself; something had obviously upset her in the hours between his dropping her off at her flat on the Sunday morning and his phone call from Cyprus later that same evening.

Had she really chosen to reconcile with James Calvert? Maybe it was just wishful thinking on his part, but his gut feeling told him she hadn't broken off their own burgeoning relationship to follow the younger man to Hollywood. Nor did he believe she was setting her cap at either Jack Farrell or Ace Delaney. She had been too obviously hurt and angry when she'd flung those excuses at him for them to be true. Or so he hoped. He was determined now to coax from her whatever it was that had gone wrong.

However, his conciliatory mood lasted only for the short space of time it took him to reach the tennis court.

'The camera loves you,' the photographer was telling Ginny admiringly. 'Here's my card – if you're interested in setting up a portfolio . . .'

'She's not interested!' Saul snapped. Ginny looked up quickly and his heart sank as he watched the bright vivacity almost visibly drain from her lovely face. Instantly the shutters were down, and she faced him expressionlessly.

Melissa caught the photographer's eye and jerked her head imperceptibly towards the gate; they quickly left the court. Ginny was trying desperately not to remember the last time she had been on a tennis court with Saul Lancaster – and especially she wanted to forget what had happened afterwards.

'I'll sort out my own life, thank you,' she said coldly, and began walking away. Saul followed her and caught her arm.

'I'm sorry, but I did warn you that I'm possessive,' he told her huskily. Ginny stared resolutely at the ground, trying to ignore the frantic beating of her heart. Just the touch of his hand on her arm was affecting her deeply, stirring her senses. Why this man? she wondered despairingly. What cruel fate had decreed she should meet him?

'So you did. But, unfortunately for you, I am not one of your possessions,' she told him, hoping he didn't hear the betraying tremor in her voice. He did, but everything was proceeding so badly – yet again – that he was afraid her emotion was anger.

'A few weeks ago you were mine,' he reminded her.

'Yes, well, we all make mistakes.' She forced a tight little smile. 'Excuse me, I'm going inside to change clothes.' She stalked off, ignoring Saul as he followed behind her.

They walked silently off the court and towards the house. Ginny was beginning to think he intended accompanying her indoors, and even upstairs to her room, and was relieved to see Rose Farrell approaching. Then, with mounting horror and disbelief, she realized Rose was not alone.

'Mum! What are you doing here?' she demanded.

'Mrs Farrell invited me when I phoned to speak to you yesterday. You've been so busy . . .' Ann's voice trailed off, her face a mirror image of Ginny's horrified countenance when she saw Saul Lancaster.

'Hello, Ann. I didn't recognize you standing up,' Saul said snidely. It was the first time he had seen mother and daughter together and the likeness was extraordinary, particularly as Ann had aged very little in the twelve years since he had last seen her. How could he despise the one and be so obsessed with the other? he wondered.

'Don't you speak to her like that!' Ginny rounded on Saul in a fury, although her anger was directed at herself as much as at him. She had been avoiding her mother, not even wanting to talk to her on the phone, unable to stop feeling that Ann was partly responsible for her unhappiness. Perhaps if she had accepted the calls, instead of asking Rose to field them, Ann wouldn't be here now.

'It's all right, Ginny. He has his reasons,' Ann said quietly.

'What reasons?' Ginny demanded, playing devil's advocate. 'He blames you for leading his father astray? What rubbish! The whole world knows Sir David has had dozens of affairs. But, typical male, blame the other woman! Why not try blaming your father for a change?' she asked Saul bitterly. 'Although, God knows, with that hard-faced bitch for a wife it's hardly surprising he goes elsewhere for warmth!' she blazed, then, belatedly realizing she had perhaps gone a little too far – Rose, for one, was looking shocked – Ginny bolted into the house and up the stairs.

Rose looked from Saul to Ann and back again, then she, too, quietly slipped away. Really, she had only invited Ann Sinclair because she had felt sorry for the poor woman, who obviously wanted desperately to talk to Ginny . . . She sighed heavily and went to check on the children. They were hard work, but uncomplicated, she thought a few mo-

266

ments later, after settling a burgeoning quarrel between two of the village children with a couple of ice-creams and leaving them sitting happily together in front of the conjuror.

Ace had taken over on the tennis court, hitting balls with some of the older kids. He was amazingly good with children, considering he had avoided them like the plague until he had become a father. And they all adored him, too. Melissa said it was because he treated them as if they were small adults: he never asked boring questions about stupid school, and was far more likely to offer them a cigarette or a glass of Scotch than give lectures on the perils of booze and drugs.

After Ginny and Rose had left, a heavy silence hung between Ann and Saul. More than a dozen years had passed since their last confrontation, but each remembered it vividly – Saul even more than Ann, who had been rather drunk at the time. But, for them both, it was as if the warm summer's day, alive with the shrieks of happy children, had faded, to be replaced by that Christmas party on a cold, dark winter's evening, the air heavy with cigarette smoke, the sounds those of raucous male laughter, the clink of glasses and music in the background.

'I . . . I know you hate me.' Ann's voice was low, tremulous. 'But please don't tell Ginny what I did. I couldn't bear to lose my daughter,' she whispered. Saul almost laughed at the irony of the last remark; funny, but he couldn't bear to lose Ginny either . . .

'I don't have anything to say to you,' Saul told her coldly. 'And I'm not making any promises about what I might or might not tell Ginny.' He made as if to move past her and Ann put her hand on his sleeve to detain him. Saul looked down at his arm distastefully, much as he would at the touch of a viper, Ann thought, blushing as she hastily removed her hand.

'There's something you ought to know,' she said quickly. 'When I was in the hospital after the car accident, and Ginny told me you were taking her to your cousin's party, well, I panicked. I was so afraid of what you might say to her about me. I certainly didn't want her seeing you again, so I . . . phoned your mother.'

'You did what?' Saul demanded incredulously.

'I phoned your mother,' Ann repeated. 'She was just as appalled at the idea of you and Ginny together. She said she would keep an eye on the situation and deal with it if necessary . . .' She came to a stammering halt as Saul's expression became more grim and forbidding with every word she uttered. 'I'm so sorry,' she finished lamely.

'So far I have kept quiet about your tendency to see men either in jail on false rape charges or hanging from a noose of their own making,' Saul said coldly. 'For Ginny's sake, not yours. But if you get in my way again I'll certainly tell my father – I don't imagine he is so blinded by lust that he would overlook the truth about Bill Taggart.' He paused, then added, 'And, should you consider running to the tabloids with a kiss 'n' tell story when he dumps you, just remember how much dirt I can dish if I choose to.'

'I wouldn't go to the press,' Ann protested. Saul shook his head slightly in disbelief.

'Sure you would – if you thought it would be

more profitable than sleeping with my father!' Saul said contemptuously. 'Just remember what I said.' His eyes bored into hers for a moment, then he turned and walked away. Ann stayed where she was, her eyes brimming with tears. Then she took a deep breath and glanced around uncertainly; Rose had disappeared and she had no idea where she might find Ginny's room.

'You look like you need a stiff drink – I certainly do! Those kids out there are driving me into an early grave!' Ann looked up, startled, and found an attractive man in his fifties smiling warmly at her. 'I'm Daniel Farrell, Jack and Melissa's father,' he introduced himself.

'Oh, I'm pleased to meet you.' Ann took his outstretched hand. 'I'm Ann Sinclair, Ginny's mother. Your wife invited me,' she added.

'My ex-wife,' Daniel corrected, and she brightened a little. 'How about that drink?' he asked.

'That would be lovely, thank you,' she accepted gratefully, and let him guide her into the dining-room.

Ginny changed into jeans and a T-shirt and then crept downstairs as furtively as any burglar, pausing by the landing window to peer out at the line of cars that stretched the length of the driveway, searching for Saul's Jag. It didn't occur to her that he had taken a cab from the airport, and she concluded, with a mixture of relief and disappointment, that he had left.

She wandered outside and sat on the lawn, smiling at the antics of the clowns as they entertained the children. The man in the gorilla suit had joined in, too, chasing after the kids, catching them and throwing them up in the air. Delighted shrieks of laughter rent the air as they ran from him, but they were careful not to run fast enough to avoid being caught, enjoying their thrill of fear. One little tot was genuinely frightened, and hung back a little, then dashed behind Ginny when the gorilla advanced on her, beating his chest.

'Stop it. Go and pick on someone your own size,' Ginny admonished him sternly, after assuring the little girl she was perfectly safe. By way of reply, the gorilla reached down and picked Ginny up off the lawn, slung her over his shoulder and loped off.

'Put me down, you big bully!' Ginny thumped his hairy back with her fists. The children obviously thought this was part of the act and laughed at her predicament. Ginny, while not being particularly amused, wasn't alarmed either – not until he headed for the entrance to the maze.

'Don't go in there! I don't know the way out!' she shrieked. Either his hearing was impaired by being inside the suit, or he chose to ignore her; she wasn't sure which. She continued to struggle to be free, but he simply tightened his hold and didn't set her on her feet until they had reached the centre of the maze.

'You idiot! I told you, I . . . Oh!' Ginny stamped her foot in annoyance when the gorilla removed the face mask. 'Put it back on – it was an improvement,' she told Saul icily. 'I hope you know the way out of here, because I don't.'

'Somebody will find us – eventually,' he told her, with a grin.

'Well, I'm not waiting for them to send out a search party!' She glared at him, suppressing an insane spurt of pleasure that he hadn't left after all. 'The entrance is opposite the dining-room window,' she remembered, jumping up and down to look over the top of the hedge in order to check her bearings. 'So, this should be the way out . . .' she decided. However, 'this' ended in a cul de sac, as did her other attempts to leave, and she became increasingly irritated by Saul, who was lounging comfortably on the deep grass in the centre, quite unconcerned.

'Come and sit down,' he suggested. Ginny glared at him, and sat down as far away from him as possible.

'I'm not apologizing for calling your mother a hard-faced bitch,' she said mulishly.

'I'm not asking you to,' Saul responded mildly, deflating that particular line of argument.

'You look ridiculous in that outfit!' she snapped next.

'Shall I take it off?' he enquired.

'Yes! No! What else are you wearing?' she asked suspiciously, and he grinned broadly.

'I'm fully clothed, so I shouldn't prove to be too much of a temptation if I get rid of this,' he told her, standing up to peel off the rest of the gorilla suit. 'God, it was hot in there. And I never want to see another banana for as long as I live.'

'Which might not be very long at all,' Ginny told him sweetly. 'The only temptation I'm feeling is the urge to hit you! What the hell do you think you're

271

playing at, carrying me in here?' she demanded.

'I'm not playing; I'm deadly serious,' he told her. 'There were too many people around, and I guessed you wouldn't come voluntarily, which is why I borrowed the gorilla suit. Come and sit over here, Ginny.' He patted the grass next to him.

'No.' She folded her arms and glared at him mutinously. Saul sighed.

'Darling, we're staying right here until we straighten things out, so you might as well start talking,' he told her.

'There's nothing to straighten out,' she said.

'We both know that's not true. I want to know who, or what, upset you the day I left for Cyprus.'

'Nothing upset me. I told you what happened – I decided I'd rather go to Hollywood with Jamie than fly to Cyprus to see you, that's all.' She shrugged.

'Don't insult my intelligence,' Saul said calmly. 'You haven't gone to Hollywood – you've been working here.'

'So what? There's no law that says I can't go to the States when I've finished here,' she retorted.

'Yes, there is – Lancaster's law,' he told her, with a slight smile.

'God, you're so arrogant!' Ginny seethed. 'You like to be the one to do the dumping, is that it? I damaged your pride by choosing Jamie over you?'

'Not my pride. My heart,' he said simply.

'Don't.' Ginny turned away. 'That's not fair.'

'Fair? All's fair in love and war . . . and I certainly don't want to fight with you, Ginny.' Saul got to his feet and moved to stand close behind her, too close for her peace of mind, but at least he didn't try to touch her. 'Look me in the eye and tell me you love James Calvert, and I'll go now and leave you alone,' he promised.

Ginny spun round to face him, opened her mouth to utter the lie. But the words dried in her throat as she gazed up into Saul's face. There were lines of tension around his mouth, and his moss-green eyes met hers almost pleadingly, she thought. She lowered her gaze, biting at her lower lip. Saul let out a pent-up breath he hadn't even been aware of holding. God, if she had actually said it . . .

'There's nothing for you here, Saul,' she told him dully. 'You shouldn't have come.'

'Where else would I go?' he asked simply. 'Tell me what went wrong and I'll put it right.'

'It's not that easy. In fact, it's impossible,' she said despairingly.

'Tell me, darling,' he insisted. Ginny wished he would stop calling her darling; she couldn't think straight when he did, especially when he used that deep, warm, husky tone that promised so much. She stayed silent, and Saul made a guess, taking into account Ann's disclosure and Ginny's description of his mother. 'Did my mother contact you? Did she say something to upset you?'

'She hasn't spoken to *me*,' Ginny said, unconsciously adding emphasis to the pronoun. Saul picked up on it immediately.

'So she has spoken to someone about us? Who?' he persisted.

'All right! I give in. I'll tell you.' Ginny turned to him, her eyes blazing with renewed fury and pain. 'Do you remember that reporter, the one we

273

thought was being too persistent?' she asked.

'Yes.' Saul nodded, watching her intently.

'Well, he's not a reporter. He's a private detective, hired by your mother to spy on us or get some dirt on me, whatever he could find. He spoke to Jamie after you threw him out of the nightclub that first evening, and later arranged for him to meet your mother – at her request.'

'Go on,' he urged, when she paused to regain her self-control.

'Your mother paid Jamie five hundred pounds to tell you lies about me. Lies you were very willing to believe!' she added, her voice shaking with emotion. 'He told you my body was for sale, didn't he?' she asked, then hurried on, afraid even now to hear corroboration from his own lips. 'Presumably your mother thought that would deter you from seeing me, but instead it spurred you on, didn't it?' she asked bitterly. 'You had already admitted you wanted to go to bed with me – and then Jamie told you how to get what you wanted! A couple of days later you turned up at my flat, all smiles and charm, bearing expensive gifts . . . my fee!' Her voice cracked on the last two words and she turned away in a vain attempt to hide her tears.

'Ginny!' Saul reached for her, his heart aching for her, all the more because he was responsible for causing her pain, but she twisted away.

'Don't touch me!' she said violently.

'All right, I won't,' he said soothingly, sensing incipient hysteria and backing off a pace.

'At least you're not trying to deny it,' she said, after a tension-filled moment.

274

'No, I'm not. I can't. I wish I could, but you're right – I decided I wanted you, whatever the cost,' he admitted. 'But I changed my mind, Ginny. I didn't just want your body, I wanted your love, too. I realized there was much more than sexual attraction between us – before we made love,' he stressed.

'Huh! Made love?' she repeated scornfully. 'We had sex! I paid for my watch!'

'No, Ginny. We made love,' he insisted. 'By that time I had discounted what James Calvert told me – I figured he'd been trying to make me back off because he wanted you for himself. Then I forgot about him completely; all that mattered was what was happening between you and me. It was so special, darling,' he said huskily.

'Was. Past tense,' Ginny said dully.

'No, I won't accept that,' Saul told her urgently. 'I'm not letting you go. Whatever I have to do, however long it takes, we'll be together.'

'No.' Ginny shook her head, then summoned up all her resolve and faced him squarely. 'Don't you understand? You can never undo what happened. Have you any idea of how I felt when Jamie confessed what he had done and I realized I had been bought? How I still feel?' she demanded, and rushed on before he could answer. 'I'll tell you – I feel sick, dirty; like a hooker hanging around on street corners, for sale to the highest bidder. I can't forget it just because you now claim to have changed your opinion!' she shouted at him.

'I understand,' Saul said quietly, realizing he had to accept defeat, albeit temporarily. He was determined to win her back, but right now didn't even know how to begin. Her pain was too raw, too recent; there was nothing he could think of to say or do that would help. His own pain was a thousand times worse for knowing he was responsible for hers. Oh, he could blame James Calvert, his mother, Ann Sinclair . . . but he had made his own snap judgement, his own decisions, and now he would have to pay the price. Unfortunately, Ginny was paying an even greater price.

He looked at her bowed head, the visible tension in her shoulders as she fought for control, then he sighed and left her alone to regain her composure. He went and picked up the discarded gorilla suit.

'This way.' He touched Ginny lightly on the arm and she followed him mindlessly out of the maze, not even registering the fact that he had known the exit route all the time.

It was a shock to both of them to discover that the party was still in full swing, the sun still shining. They had been so absorbed in each other that anything else had ceased to exist.

'Will you be all right?' Saul asked gently. She was pale and still shaking, but he knew he had to accept, for now, that she wanted nothing to do with him.

'I'll be fine,' She nodded.

'Just one more thing, Ginny,' Saul said quietly. 'When we were together, when I made love to you, did you ever, even for one moment, feel that you were being used? That I didn't care about your own pleasure, only my own? Think about that, please. I'll be in touch,' he added, and quickly walked away before she could tell him not to contact her.

Ginny watched him go; a part of her wanted to

call him back, but the greater part still hurt too much. She wasn't sure she could trust him, either. He had sounded sincere, yet she cringed at the memory of how easily and charmingly he had duped her before – a bunch of flowers, a box of chocolates and a smiling apology – and she had fallen for it hook, line and sinker!

That whole evening had been a charade, so how much of what had happened the following Saturday and Sunday morning was she supposed to believe was not also a farce? Saul driven by nothing other than lust and determination to get his own way? As for his insistence that she accept the watch – what had that really been about? Had he been prompted by conscience? He had got what he wanted from her, so he had felt honour-bound to make the payment? Honour? Huh!

She walked slowly towards the house, deep in thought. She had no desire to rejoin the party and intended going to her room to pack, for she was returning to London that evening to begin a two-week holiday – part of which she would be spending at the Wimbledon Championships as Melissa's guest.

As she passed the open door of the dining-room she heard her mother's laughter, and paused to glance inside. Her lips tightened when she saw Ann sitting close to Daniel Farrell. She obviously isn't aware that he sold Bellwood to avoid bankruptcy, and that although his children are millionaires, courtesy of their careers in tennis, he is no longer wealthy, she thought bitterly. She wouldn't be wasting time on him if she knew that!

Ann, as if sensing the scrutiny to which she was being subjected from the doorway, suddenly looked up and got to her feet, a ready smile on her face which faded once she realized there was no answering smile from her daughter.

'Oh dear, is something wrong?' she faltered.

'My life is in ruins, thanks to you,' Ginny told her coldly. 'If Sir David Lancaster hadn't got you bought and paid for, maybe Saul would never have assumed he could have the same relationship with me!'

'Ginny . . .' Ann said despairingly. Daniel's jaw dropped, and he backed off from Ann, Ginny noted, with savage satisfaction.

'Leave me alone!' Ginny yelled at her, and turned and ran towards the stairs. Let her try and talk her way out of that one! she thought grimly. Ann had ruined things for her with Saul, but maybe now she wouldn't find it so easy to spoil Ginny's friendship with the Farrells.

CHAPTER 14

Ginny was not the only one to be on holiday: Saul, too, had some days' leave owing, and on Monday afternoon he drove from his barracks to his parents' home in Richmond. He used his own keys – for the last time, he had already decided grimly, for he intended removing all his belongings to his new house. And, once he had told his mother a few home truths, he would walk out of this house and never return.

He didn't have much to pack; this house had never really been a home. As a child, he had attended boarding-school from the age of eight, and had spent most of his holidays with his younger cousins at their grandmother's home, a large Victorian house with vast, overgrown gardens and a paddock for their ponies.

After leaving school he had gone straight to the military academy at Sandhurst, and had spent most of the the last thirteen years in various barracks around the world. He had enjoyed his military career – well, most of it; there had been a few uncomfortable or downright terrifying moments,

279

particularly during the Gulf War and in Bosnia, but on the whole it had been an interesting and challenging job.

However, he had no regrets about resigning his commission, particularly now there was Ginny in his life. Well, to be strictly accurate, right now she was in his thoughts and in his heart, but not his life. Not yet. He would win her back. There was no conceit in the thought – he had to win her back, gain her love and her trust. It was as simple and as difficult as that.

But first, unfinished business . . . He threw books, CDs and clothes haphazardly into cardboard boxes, then carried them and his hi-fi equipment down to his car. The daily had already told him that Lady Lancaster was out, having her hair done, so Saul settled down to wait for her return.

He wasn't sure whether to be glad or sorry when his father appeared first, still walking with the aid of crutches. His quarrel was with his mother alone, but he supposed his father might as well hear what had been going on. After all, he was involved, too, although he hadn't had the same malicious intent, and could never have imagined how his affair with Ann Sinclair would cause so much trouble.

'I'm moving my stuff out,' Saul told him, tossing his set of house keys onto a table.

'Keep those. You might want to use the pool or the court while we're out,' Sir David said easily. Saul remembered Ginny, running round the tennis court, then diving into the pool, laughing and happy . . .

'No, thanks, I'll join a gym in town,' he said

shortly. Sir David frowned at his tone, but before he could say anything more, Alice Lancaster swept into the room.

'Saul, how nice! We can all have tea together,' she announced.

'Not for me,' Saul declined, even more curtly. He watched as his mother carefully peeled off her gloves – who else wore gloves in midsummer? he wondered. She placed them neatly beside her handbag, then sat down and faced him with a cool smile on her lips.

'We had no idea you were back from Cyprus. Does this mean you will be able to attend Amanda's wedding after all?' she asked him.

'I doubt it,' Saul replied coldly. 'My invitation included a guest of my choosing, but I don't suppose the girl I have in mind would feel very welcome. And I certainly wouldn't allow her to be insulted or slighted. Not at Mandy's wedding. Not ever. Which is why I'm severing all ties,' he said crisply. Only a slight flickering of Alice's eyelids betrayed any emotion; her face was mask-like, the cool smile a little too firmly in place.

'What's this all about, Saul?' Sir David asked. 'Of course she would be made welcome . . .'

'You may contact me in an emergency,' Saul continued, ignoring his father's interruption. 'But other than that I do not intend returning to this house. And don't expect an invitation to my home,' he added.

'Saul! What the – ?' Sir David turned to his wife. 'Do you know what this is about?' he demanded.

'Yes, I think I do,' she replied calmly. 'The girl he

referred to – I presume he's talking about the daughter of your latest whore,' she told him conversationally. Sir David's head swivelled back to Saul.

'Is that true? Are you seeing Ginny Sinclair?'

'Whenever possible,' Saul told him. 'She's not too happy about my . . . er . . . my family connections,' he added, scowling at his mother.

'Well.' Sir David shifted uncomfortably. 'I, for one, would love to get to know her. And I fail to see why you're turning your back on us.'

'Why don't you tell him, Mother?' Saul suggested. Alice shrugged, stood up and fetched a cigarette from an antique silver box on the coffee table. Her fingers barely shook as she lit it and inhaled deeply.

'James Calvert, presumably,' she said evenly. Saul smiled slightly.

'Got it in one.'

'Pangs of conscience? Or pillow-talk?' she enquired, and Saul balled his hands into fists.

'Who in hell is James Calvert?' Sir David exploded.

'Ginny's ex-boyfriend,' Saul told him, stressing the 'ex' as he glared at Alice. 'Mother contacted him – via a private detective she hired – and paid him to tell me lies about Ginny. He was jealous enough to do just that, but then felt bad about it and told Ginny what he had done. He certainly wanted me out of the way, but he didn't want to hurt her.' The dreadful irony of the situation was that if James Calvert hadn't spoken up, he and Ginny would never have quarrelled!

Sir David stared at Saul, then turned on his wife in a fury.

'You hired a private detective! And paid someone to –?'

'To tell lies, yes. So what? You pay Ann Sinclair to . . . what is it that she does exactly, David?' Alice responded coolly. 'I'm sure her fee is listed somewhere on your tax returns. Social secretary, perhaps? Or personal assistant? Very personal.' Her voice hardened.

'I've had enough. And I've certainly nothing else to say to you – either of you. I'm leaving.' Saul stood up and made for the door.

Alice inclined her head slightly in farewell. Sir David, hampered by the plaster cast on his leg, lumbered after him, calling for him to wait. Had it not been for the broken leg, Saul would have taken no notice, but he couldn't quite bring himself to ignore a cripple, even a temporary one.

'Saul, I had no idea she had done any of that,' Sir David said earnestly.

'I believe you.'

'Has it caused problems for you? With Ginny?'

'Just a few.' Saul's mouth twisted. 'Nothing I can't put right.' I hope, he added, silently and fervently.

'I can accept your decision not to visit us here, but Lennox and Coupland isn't far from my office – we can meet for lunch, can't we?'

'I don't think so,' Saul declined. 'Not while you're involved with Ann Sinclair. And that's not emotional blackmail,' he added quickly. 'It's just the way I feel.'

'I don't understand,' Sir David frowned. 'You're

not a child, you've met other lady-friends of mine in the past.'

'Sure, but Ann's no lady.' Saul clambered into his car and drove off.

Sir David watched him go sadly, then turned and hobbled back inside the house. The only sign of Lady Lancaster's agitation was her smoking an unheard-of second cigarette.

'You've lost him now,' he said roughly, as if she hadn't already guessed that. 'Whatever possessed you to do such a stupid thing?'

'I would have thought that was obvious.' His wife sniffed. 'It's bad enough you making a fool of yourself over the mother, without Saul doing the same with the daughter.'

'If there's a fool around here, it's you,' he told her. 'Stop interfering, Alice,' he warned. 'If you're still hiring that detective to spy on them, call him off. Now.'

'Else what?' she sneered.

'Do as I say! Or face the consequences.'

She tensed. 'Which are?'

'A very public, messy divorce, followed by my subsequent remarriage to Ann Sinclair,' he informed her.

'You wouldn't do that – your political career would be over before it began,' she faltered.

'I'm prepared to take the risk.' He paused. 'Are you?' He didn't wait for a reply, but turned and made his painfully slow progress up the stairs.

Alice stayed where she was, facing the prospect of attending her niece's society wedding alone, as a spurned and soon-to-be divorced woman, and shuddered. Almost worse, she would never be invited to dine at Number 10, Downing Street. Ann Sinclair would go in her place . . .

She picked up her bag and gloves and made her way upstairs, pausing outside David's room – they had not shared a bedroom for many years. Through the closed door she could hear the sound of drawers and cupboards being opened and shut. Frowning slightly, she walked inside.

'You're packing.' She stated the obvious.

'Yes.' David glanced briefly at her. 'I'm going to stay in my flat at the office,' he told her, and she breathed a little easier.

'Not with Ann Sinclair? I don't suppose she is the cooking and ironing type,' she remarked disparagingly. David paused and regarded her with curiosity tempered with sympathy.

'Why do you blame Ann for the state of our marriage? Why have you always blamed the other women? You made it perfectly plain you didn't want me – how did you expect me to react?'

'You've always behaved exactly as I thought you would,' she told him disdainfully. 'But I had hoped for discretion, and a certain . . . fastidiousness on your part.'

'I have been discreet. As for fastidiousness . . .' His lips twitched slightly. 'That is not a quality a man looks for in a mistress.'

'Really?' Alice's nostrils flared. 'Spare me the sordid details, please,' she said frostily.

'That's your trouble, Alice – you always considered sex was sordid. How we ever produced Saul is a mystery.'

'We had two children, David,' she whispered.

'I know. I do remember. It hurt me, too. I also remember you pushing me away after the stillbirth. I buried myself in my work, hoping things would improve, but they didn't, did they? We're both guilty of neglecting Saul's needs, and now we're paying the price. He refuses to take over the business I've spent a lifetime building up, hoping to hand it over to him, and now he wants us out of his life completely. Are you pleased with the results of your meddling?' he demanded.

'No.'

'Then I suggest you consider carefully what your next move is to be. If you want your son back, you'd better be prepared to accept the girl he chooses, whether that's Ginny Sinclair or someone else.' He waited for a reply but none was forthcoming, and he sighed heavily. 'Goodbye, Alice. I'll be in touch,' he said, then limped from the room, struggling with a suitcase.

Alice sought sanctuary in her own bedroom across the hall. From the cushioned window-seat she saw the cab arrive and her husband vanish out of sight.

Moving as stiffly as an old crone, she walked over to her dressing-table, on which stood several silver-framed photographs of Saul: as a baby, a schoolboy, then as an officer cadet at Sandhurst . . . She suddenly wished she had a picture of her stillborn daughter – she had read recently that nowadays bereaved mothers were given photographs, and were even encouraged to hold the tiny bodies. Thirty years ago the so-called experts had deemed it better to dispose of everything as quickly as possible, to pretend it had never happened.

'You'll be able to have another baby, Lady Lancaster,' they had said encouragingly, as if she had failed her driving test . . .

She sighed as she carefully replaced the photographs; it was too late to wonder if things would have been different, better, if that child had lived, or if there had been another. But it hadn't seemed right, not then, to try and replace a dead baby with a substitute. And by the time she had been prepared to risk another pregnancy David had already found solace elsewhere. She had been too proud to fight for him, to beg; it had been easier to maintain a dignified silence and pretend she didn't care.

She thought back, could vividly recall the day she knew she had lost Saul. He was only four years old; he'd fallen off his bicycle, a heavy fall, and he had cut his leg badly. She and his grandmother had been sitting on the terrace and both had stood up to go to him – and Saul had headed unhesitatingly for the comfort and love he knew he would receive from his grandmother. Alice had stood there with her arms held out uselessly, empty . . .

Now she sighed again. Regrets were futile. She had a busy life – golf, bridge, and charity work. If Saul were foolish enough to settle for a tramp like Ginny Sinclair, well, in that case, he could stay away for ever, she thought grimly. She pulled open the drawer of her dressing-table and swept all the photographs inside, then slammed it shut.

Ginny spent Monday morning shopping, buying a huge stuffed donkey for Suzy's birthday, and then had lunch with Jo, who was easing up on her workload in deference to her advancing pregnancy.

Jo, guiltily aware that her interference hadn't helped – and might have actually made matters worse – didn't even mention Saul's name, for which Ginny was grateful. Later, they indulged in strawberries and cream as they watched the Wimbledon coverage on TV.

'You're going there tomorrow, aren't you?' Jo asked, reaching for another strawberry and settling herself more comfortably on the sofa. 'I've only been once, and I spent most of the time queue-ing! It took hours just to get through the gates, by which time I had to queue to use the loo. I saw about ten minutes of tennis before it started pouring with rain!'

'I always went with a group from school,' Ginny said. 'We used to wear our tennis kit and strut about carrying our rackets, hoping people would think we were players!' She grimaced at the memory. 'We were such poseurs.'

'I'm sure you'll enjoy yourself more as Melissa's guest. I'd be cadging tickets myself if not for this.' She patted her enlarged stomach. 'All those muscular professional players. And then there's the men!' She grinned. 'Talking of hunky pro players – have you thought any more about Ace Delaney's offer?'

'Not really; it's for you and Barney to decide,' Ginny replied casually, half hoping her employers would make the decision for her. She had thought about it quite a lot: on the one hand, it might be better for her to get right away from Saul for a

288

while; he was already back in England and she was acutely aware that he would very shortly be living permamently in London, free of the constraints of Army duties. But, on the other hand, a teacherous part of her didn't really want to go so far away . . .

'We won't insist that you go if you don't want to,' Jo told her. 'Of course, as he's prepared to pay over the odds, it goes without saying that there would be a big cash bonus in it for you,' she added. She and Barney had discussed it at some length; they were both loath to lose Ginny's services, which seemed likely if she decided she could earn much more money as a freelance.

'Thanks, I could certainly use it,' Ginny said. Barney had just had his driving licence restored, and she was beginning to feel the loss of having a car at her disposal.

'And we would have no objections if you wanted to stay in California for a holiday after you'd finished the work.' Jo added another carrot. 'Actually,' she continued, talking now as a friend, not an employer, 'I think it would do you good to get away for a while.' She thought Ginny seemed very subdued, and she had heard her footsteps overhead in the early hours, testifying to a sleepless night. 'Mind you, Ace Delaney has a dreadful reputation,' she added thoughtfully, hoping a trip to his ranch wouldn't be a case of out of the frying pan and into the fire.

'Don't worry about that; Melissa says he's a reformed character,' Ginny assured her.

'Really? God, how boring!' Jo exclaimed, and they both laughed.

Despite her unhappiness over Saul, Ginny was genuinely looking forward to attending the Wimbledon Championships, and she eagerly scanned the Order of Play when it was announced late on Monday evening, deciding which matches she would most like to watch. She also checked the weather forecast, and was delighted to hear the outlook was dry and sunny.

As previously arranged, she took the tube to Wimbledon station, where Melissa was waiting for her. Crowds thronged the station, and the streets around the All England Club. Many had been queueing overnight, and some had come well-equipped, with tents and sleeping bags, and portable stoves to provide hot drinks and snacks.

'They're even keener on tennis than I am!' Melissa observed. 'I certainly wouldn't queue all night.'

'I feel like royalty.' Ginny suppressed an urge to wave regally as Melissa drove past the hundreds of fans waiting patiently for the gates to open and swept into the reserved car parking area. There was a buzz of anticipation and excitement that was almost palpable, and Ginny felt her spirits rise.

'Is Nick coming?' she asked casually, ignoring the jeering inner voice that knew she was really asking if Saul would be coming . . .

'No, I think he saw enough tennis matches to last him a lifetime while I was competing.' Melissa grinned. 'He'll probably come and watch Jack and me in the doubles, though. If he can get away from the office – they're really quite short of staff. It will be great when Saul's out of the Army and can take on some of the workload,' she added, with a sideways glance at Ginny. 'How are things between you?'

'Um, rather difficult,' Ginny replied awkwardly. 'I'm sorry not to go into details; you've been really kind . . .'

'What does that have to do with anything? You don't have to confide in me if you don't want to,' Melissa said, somewhat affronted. Really, if she had required payment in return for tickets, she'd have sold them on the black market!

'I'm sorry; it's just that even I don't really know what's happening. I don't know how I feel, and I certainly don't know how Saul feels,' Ginny sighed. 'I thought he . . . cared, but now I know he lied to me just to get me into bed.' She flushed hotly. 'I think I'm going to stick with nice, uncomplicated men in future!' She forced a bright and totally unconvincing smile.

'Yes, but "nice" isn't enough, is it?' Melissa asked. 'Not once you've experienced that special excitement.' She hesitated, not sure if she should interfere. Nick had told her some of what Saul had confided about Ginny's mother, and Melissa was afraid of opening up a can of worms. However, there was such sadness about Ginny . . . She decided to continue, feeling much older than the four years' seniority she had over the younger girl.

'If Saul Lancaster is the one man who makes you feel alive, vibrant, looking forward to each hour you spend with him, well, don't settle for "nice",' she advised. 'I almost did. Hal Renwick wanted to marry me: he was my coach, a good friend, and he loved me, warts and all, at a time when I thought there was no hope for Nick and me. Hal understood my ambition, and he would have been a great help with my career, but . . .' She smiled and shrugged eloquently.

'Yes, but I'm sure Nick never treated you as badly as Saul has me,' Ginny said doubtfully. Melissa arched one eyebrow.

'You'd be surprised; we both did things we're not proud of,' she said quietly, then visibly shook off bad memories. 'Look at Ace Delaney – he's another example. You can't imagine how many people tried to dissuade Alexa from marrying him. Her own father wanted her to marry a business colleague of his, a man she'd dated before she knew Ace . . .'

'A "nice" man?' Ginny guessed, with a slight smile.

'Yep. Ask Alexa if she wishes she had settled for second best, for – what did you call it? – nice and uncomplicated? Substitute boring. Her answer would be a resounding no,' she said confidently.

Belatedly realizing she had interfered after all, she decided to change the subject, hoping she had, if not made matters better, at least not made them worse. 'I promised I'd go and support Ella Cortez,' she said, glancing at her watch. 'Her match is first on Court Two, starting at noon. Do you want to come along, or shall we meet up later?'

'I'll come with you,' Ginny decided, and they made their way to the nearby Court Two. Melissa marched determinedly to the best seats, as if it was her right, which, as a former Champion, it probably was, Ginny thought, tagging along behind and muttering meek 'excuse me's' to the spectators who had already gathered.

Katy Oliver, Melissa's former and Ella's current coach, was already court-side, and she looked up as Melissa and Ginny sat down beside her.

'Hi.' Katy smiled a greeting. 'Glad you could come.'

'I said I would. You two met at Bellwood, didn't you?' Melissa asked, looking from one to the other.

'Sure,' Katy said vaguely, already turning her attention back to the action on court. The two players were still knocking up; Ella's opponenet was a fellow American, although the two had not met in competition before.

'I see Shanna won yesterday,' Melissa commented, referring to Katy's other charge, Shanna Douglas.

'Yeah, I guess they're both doing pretty well,' Katy said, which was praise indeed from her. She didn't believe in over-inflating a player's ego, as Melissa well knew from personal experience. Both Shanna and Ella had reached the quarter-finals at Eastbourne the previous week, and had progressed to the semis in doubles which, considering neither girl had much grass-court experience, augured well for their prospects at Wimbledon.

Many spectators around Court Two recognized Melissa, of course; there was some nudging and pointing, then one woman plucked up the courage to lean across to ask for an autograph. That prompted others to follow suit, and a deluge of programmes were shoved under her nose. Melissa hastily scribbled her name; it was barely legible, but

293

it was definitely Melissa Farrell, not Lennox, Ginny noted interestedly. She wondered idly what Nick thought of that.

'I can't do any more; the players are ready to begin!' Melissa snapped after a few moments, and the spectators settled back into their seats like chastised children, obedient but truculent.

Ginny grimaced slightly and sat as quietly as a mouse as the match got underway, and Katy and Melissa began a low-voiced commentary. Goodness, they take it seriously, Ginny thought, watching Katy, who was jotting down notes in her own unique style of shorthand – a breakdown of points won and lost to aid her in the post mortem which would follow if Ella lost the match. Or even if she won it, but Katy felt she had played a bad game strategically. Ginny also noticed that Katy began using tiny hand movements, as if signalling to Ella.

'Are you coaching her?' she asked, unthinkingly.

'Why didn't you speak a bit louder – I don't think the umpire quite heard you!' Katy snapped sarcastically.

'Sorry. You're not allowed to do that, then?' Ginny realized, and Katy rolled her eyes to heaven.

'Get real,' she muttered.

'Sorry,' Ginny said again, even more humbly.

'Ella's skirt is too short,' Melissa put in quickly, merely to divert Katy.

'God, listen who's talking!' Katy snorted. 'You were always flashing your knickers on court!'

Suddenly there was a stir amongst the crowd, and excited murmurings rippled around the stand as Ace Delaney joined them to check on Ella's progress.

Katy barely spared him a glance, nor he her. They didn't particularly like each other, but each had a healthy respect for the other's abilities. Ace had neither the desire nor the patience to travel with Ella and Shanna, and knew Katy was an excellent coach who could be trusted to bring out the best in them both, and also to guard over them in the often exploitative world of professional sport.

Katy, for her part, was more than happy to leave the business side of the game to Ace; he was brilliant at dealing with sponsors, and both girls already had lucrative deals with manufacturers of clothing, soft drinks and hair and beauty products.

'Hi, honey,' he greeted Melissa affably, and then smiled at Ginny rather absently until he remembered where he had seen her before. 'The twins love Kit's room,' he told her. 'Pippa wants exactly the same as Kit, while Drew wants cowboys and Indians. Think you could do it?'

'Yes, I expect so. Pippa certainly – not so sure about Drew, though,' she added doubtfully.

'We have horses on the ranch – and cowboys, come to that. You can use me as a model for the Indians,' he grinned, and Ginny recalled reading that he was allegedly descended from an Apache chief. 'Would that be okay? I could strip off, find a loincloth . . .'

'Leave her alone,' Melissa interrupted him, seeing Ginny wasn't too sure how to take his banter. 'She has enough man trouble right now, without you adding to it.'

'Really?' Ace suppressed a smile: soldier-boy had struck out, had he? 'Did you talk to your boss about coming over to California?' he asked.

'Yes, she said it's okay, if I want to do it,' she told
him.

'And do you want to?' Ace murmured. Ginny felt
herself blush as he gazed at her. God, he was . . .
macho. But not as exciting or as good-looking as
Saul, she was appalled to find herself thinking. At
that moment she made her decision; she really did
need to get away, to think.

'Yes, I'd love to come,' she said quickly, before
she could change her mind.

'Great. We'll be returning after Wimbledon –
give me your phone number and I'll call you with
the flight details,' he said briskly, handing her a
business card. Ginny scribbled down her address
and phone number, and handed it back. Ace glanced
at it briefly, then slipped it into his pocket. Having
got what he wanted from Ginny, he turned his
attention back to the match.

The discussion between the three ex-professional
players became a bit too technical for Ginny, and
when Ella had clinched the first set, and the players
were towelling down, she got to her feet.

'I think I'll go and have a walk and see what's
happening on the other courts,' she said to Melissa.

'Okay, I'll see you later. Don't lose your pass,' she
warned.

Ginny thoroughly enjoyed her day: the weather
stayed fine and she saw several of her favourite
players in action. And, during tea with Melissa,
she was surprised to discover how many retired
pros made the trip to London for Wimbledon
fortnight – some to participate in the over-35

events, and others, like Jack, now working for the numerous TV companies that covered the Championships.

Even more came simply to enjoy being part of the most prestigious tennis tournament in the world. Ginny was almost tempted to ask people for autographs, but, recalling Melissa's barely concealed impatience earlier, resisted the urge and told herself sternly to stop being so starstruck and gauche.

Melissa wanted to join Jack in his TV round-up of the day's matches, so Ginny made her own way home. As she emerged from the tube she thought she saw Nick Lennox driving by with a teenage boy in his car. I wonder why he's in Chelsea? she thought idly, but promptly forgot about it.

When she arrived home, Barney and Jo had ordered in pizza for dinner, and invited her to join them. She sat with them and chatted until almost midnight. They were both pleased to see her eating, and to hear the enthusiasm in her voice.

'Oh, excuse me.' Ginny stifled a yawn. 'I don't know why I'm so tired – I've been sitting down all day!'

At least she'll sleep tonight, Jo thought. 'Are you going to Wimbledon again tomorrow?' she asked.

'Yes. Melissa and Jack should be playing their first round mixed doubles match tomorrow evening, so I'll hang around to watch that. I hope they win.'

'I bet they will. Melissa Lennox seems to accomplish everything she sets out to,' Jo commented. 'If you ask me, that girl has a charmed life!'

CHAPTER 15

On Wednesday, while Ginny was enjoying herself at Wimbledon, Ann, still deeply distressed by the scene at Bellwood on Sunday afternoon, phoned Sir David and asked him to meet her for lunch.

She was already at the restaurant when he arrived, and he noticed at once that she had downed several large gin and tonics whilst waiting.

'Is something wrong? You sounded upset earlier,' he said. 'I'm sorry I haven't been in touch for the past few days, but it's pretty hectic with the election so near.'

'I know; it's not that.' Ann brushed his excuses aside. 'I think it's time we broke up, Davey,' she said abruptly.

It had been on his mind, too, since the row with Saul, but he was surprised and a little displeased to discover that Ann held the same view.

'Shall we order lunch first?' he suggested, deciding she needed some food to mop up the alcohol she'd consumed.

'Very well.' Ann barely glanced at the menu, ordered a salad and another gin, then waited impatiently for the waiter to stop fussing.

'So. What's the problem?' he asked. Ann's lower lip trembled.

'Ginny hates me,' she quavered. 'She and Saul . . . well, they're obviously violently attracted to each other, but our relationship is causing them problems. It might be too late to help, but I think we should split up.' She stopped and looked at him; he was frowning blackly but said nothing, so she took a huge gulp of gin and continued speaking.

'I've been accepted on a course at art college in the autumn, and, since I'm a little rusty, I've booked myself on a painting holiday in Italy. I'm leaving at the weekend.'

'I see. No discussion; you've just decided, have you?' he asked evenly.

'It's for the best, Davey. Aren't you relieved, really? If you're honest?'

'I'll miss you,' he said, which didn't answer her question. Or perhaps it did.

'I'll miss you, too. But this all started as a bit of fun, and, let's face it, it's stopped being fun, hasn't it?' she asked.

He didn't answer that either, but reached across the table and picked up her hand. 'It's been rather wonderful, though, hasn't it?'

'Yes,' she agreed, with a catch in her throat. 'Would you mind if I skip lunch?' she asked apologetically, feeling there was no point in a long, drawn-out goodbye. 'I'm not hungry, and I have loads to do before I leave for Italy.'

'Very well. Goodbye, Ann. Take care of yourself.' He stood up and kissed her cheek.

'And you.' She returned the kiss. 'Good luck with the election. I hope you win; you'll make a wonderful MP. You're a wonderful man.' She forced a smile and hurried out of the restaurant, tears blurring her vision. Why, oh, why had she played with fire and got involved with him in the first place? she wondered despairingly. She might have known it would end in tears. She knew the answer, of course – excitement. Well, this episode of thrills and glamour might cost her her daughter . . .

Sir David watched her go with a feeling of regret tinged, he had to admit, with relief. Regret because she was good company, bright and fun-loving, and excellent in bed. He wondered idly if Saul had yet discovered if her daughter was the same . . .

Appalled by his own thoughts, he hastily turned to contemplation of the future, specifically the future relationship he might now have with his son. He wondered if it was too soon to tell Saul he had broken up with Ann . . . Yes, it would seem as if he had caved in under pressure, and no one, not his wife, not his son, was going to tell him how to conduct his private life, he thought grimly.

Maybe when Saul was out of the Army – a career Sir David had railed against, but to no avail. Saul had listened with barely concealed indifference to his father raging that he had spent a lifetime building up a successful business to hand over to his only son – and had walked away from it without a backward glance. Face facts: he walked away from his mother and me without a backward glance . . .

Sir David sighed heavily, abandoned his own lunch and returned to his office, stopping off first to buy Ann a diamond necklace as a farewell gift. He couldn't help but notice that the salesgirl was extremely pretty . . .

'I'm sure your wife will love it, sir,' she said, rather archly, he thought.

'Oh, it's not for my wife; my niece is getting married soon,' he said, which was true. 'I say, you wouldn't be free for dinner this evening by any chance . . . ?'

Melissa joined Ginny for tea after she had practised with Jack for their match. Katy and Ace had teamed up to help them prepare, and a large crowd of spectators had gathered to watch, obviously eagerly anticipating the return of the former Champions. Their interest increased both Melissa's excitement and her nervousness.

'This is really stupid,' she said to Ginny, cross with herself. 'I'm almost as scared as I was for my first match here when I was eighteen. That was a mixed doubles too,' she added.

'With Jack?' Ginny asked.

'Yes. I wasn't eligible for the singles that year, and I was really looking forward to the match. But then it was switched form an outside court to Centre at the last moment. God, I was absolutely petrified! I could hardly walk, let alone hit a ball.' She shuddered; she could still remember the awful, stomach-churning fear, the certainty of public humiliation.

'Did you win?' Ginny asked.

'Yes. Well, Jack did. I just sort of went along with things. I managed not to serve too many double

301

faults and he did the rest,' Melissa said. 'That was the start of a long love affair with Centre Court . . . I'd better go and get changed,' she said suddenly. It was far too early, but she felt the need to be in the locker-room, talking to Katy or other players, people who knew what she was feeling, to be soaking up the atmosphere, becoming part of the tournament again instead of just a spectator.

'You'll be okay, won't you?' she asked, belatedly aware that she was leaving Ginny to her own devices.

'Of course. Don't worry about me; I'm having a great time,' Ginny assured her. 'I'll come and watch your match.'

'Good. Nick should be here by then,' Melissa said, rather vaguely, her mind on her tennis.

'Is he bringing Suzy? Or is she too young?'

'I decided she would be too much of a distraction, even with Nick. She'd probably want to join Jack and me on the court and start yelling when Nick wouldn't let her.' She smiled. 'She's with Kit and Mum at Bellwood, so I know she's okay,' she added. 'See you later.' She moved off towards the door, but halted as Ace entered.

'Hi, honey,' he greeted her.

'Hi. I thought you were watching Shanna?'

'I was. She won, in forty minutes,' he said, and didn't sound as pleased as he should that one of his protégées was performing well. 'And you women moan because you don't get equal prize money here!'

'We should get equal prize money,' Melissa insisted. 'The length of the matches is irrelevant.

302

We train and practise as hard as the men, and we generate just as much money for the tournaments. There was never an empty seat when I was competing,' she said, rather arrogantly, but truthfully. 'And women make more sacrifices than the men,' she continued. 'If you were still on the circuit, Alexa and the twins could travel with you – you wouldn't have to give up your career to have a family, in the way women do,' she finished hotly.

Ace regarded her with some sympathy tinged with regret, knowing her outburst had little or nothing to do with the cash rewards of the sport. At the time of her unwanted pregnancy, when Katy Oliver had asked for his help, he'd had no compunction in arranging a termination. Only since the birth of his own children had he realized the enormity of what he had pushed Melissa in to. However, uncomfortable with feelings of guilt, he decided Nick was to blame for creating the problem in the first place!

'Good luck with your match,' was all he said.

'Thanks,' Melissa muttered, already regretting her outburst, and she quickly made her way to the locker-room. She changed and did some warm-up exercises, chatting easily in the familiar suroundings while keeping a watchful eye on the score of the match currently in progress on Court Two, where they were scheduled to play.

Nerves assailed her once more as they made their way out onto court, but the enthusiastic applause warmed her, and her eagerness to compete returned as they began trading shots with their opponents, two Americans who, Jack felt, looked as if they ought to be taking part in the junior event.

Nick arrived just as the match was starting. Melissa beamed happily at him while Jack rolled his eyes in a 'how the hell did she talk me into this?' expression. Nick smiled and sat down, but his thoughts were not on the match. He had called in at the Chelsea flat before coming over to Wimbledon: Connie had been as friendly, apologetic and grateful as usual, Mickey his customary sullen, sneering self.

Nick simply did not know how to deal with the boy – or with Connie, for that matter. He realized now that he should not have allowed them to stay in the flat; they showed no inclination to move and he couldn't quite bring himself to broach the subject. Coop's advice remained the same: pay up and get rid of them. But it wasn't that easy for Nick; he felt consumed with guilt for leaving Connie in such a mess for so many years, and surely he owed the boy more than money? Mickey. His son. He still couldn't feel paternal towards him, could see no Lennox trait or physical resemblance.

He sighed heavily and stared out at the court, seemingly attentive. A rat-a-tat battle of volleying was waging at the net, and finally the American girl whipped the ball down the centre. Jack and Melissa both left it for the other, then stared at each other in amazement. The amateurish mistake should have increased Melissa's nervousness; instead it relaxed her, and she burst out laughing.

How can she not notice the turmoil I'm in? Nick wondered, not for the first time, and with some resentment now creeping into the thought. He knew he should have told her about Connie immediately, but he hadn't, hoping he could sort it out without her knowing.

It would be easier, simpler, if Connie *did* just want money, but she evidently did not. She found her teenage son hard to handle and seemed to believe the sudden introduction of his father into his life would provide the solution to all their problems. She also seemed to be as oblivious to Melissa's existence as Melissa was to hers; she had never mentioned her again since that morning in his office.

Nick sighed again, then clapped along with the other spectators before realizing Melissa had just dropped her serve to trail 1–3. She shot him a look of puzzlement rather than reproach as she moved to take up the net position, and Nick forced himself to concentrate.

'Bloody geriatrics!' the American boy sneered, which so incensed Jack he put renewed effort into his game. Instead of thinking ahead to the TV programme he had to host later, he began leaping about at the net, pouncing on every ball and volleying it away for a winner. They broke the boy to love, and Jack followed that up with four crisp first serves to level the score at 3–3.

Melissa caught his mood of grim determination, and, cheered on by a partisan crowd, they won 6–3, 6–1 in less than an hour. Jack picked Melissa off her feet and hugged her before they advanced to the net to exchange handshakes, both of them grinning broadly. After the insult to his age and experience, Jack had wanted the victory more than any other he could remember, while Melissa's emotion was one of relief that they had justified the granting of a wild card. She felt she could now relax and simply enjoy their remaining matches – hopefully there would be more than one!

Thursday was Suzy's birthday; she had already received many presents at the party on Sunday, but still had more to open. Melissa got down on the floor with her, helping her to rip off the wrapping paper, while Nick watched silently, his heart heavy. He felt guilty because Mickey had never enjoyed such an abundance of gifts, and regret that he had missed the boy's early years, but mostly he was gripped with a sickening dread that the happiness he had taken for granted was about to be shattered, perhaps beyond repair.

'Melissa,' he said urgently.

'Yes?' She looked up with a bright smile, her eyes sparkling with the sharing of Suzy's pleasure. He couldn't bear to dim the light in her eyes, to spoil Suzy's birthday, even if she was too young to realize why it was a special day.

'Nothing, really.' He forced a smile. 'Saul phoned me yesterday – he's free on Saturday and wants to see Ginny. I told him she'd probably be at Wimbledon. I also told him she's going to California with Ace – that didn't go down too well, I'm afraid!'

'You and Saul ought to start an anti-Ace fan club,' Melissa said absently. 'Talking of Ginny . . .' She reached for another parcel. 'This is from Ginny, darling,' she told Suzy, ripping off the tape so Suzy could easily unwrap it. She laughed at the

306

expression on her daughter's face when she clutched the stuffed donkey to her chest. 'Look at his name,' she said, pointing out the gold lettering Ginny had inscribed on his leather bridle. 'Do you know what that says?'

'Neddy!' Suzy said delightedly, guessing correctly. 'Look, Daddy!' Nick smiled and scooped her up in his arms, holding her close and breathing in her sweet, baby scent.

'I have to go.' He handed her abruptly to Melissa and gave her a perfunctory kiss on the cheek before hurrying from the room.

'Okay, bye,' she said, somewhat puzzled. She and Suzy waved goodbye from the window as he drove away, then Melissa turned and surveyed the chaos of presents and torn paper on the carpet. 'I think we'll leave this for Mrs Cooper to clear up, don't you?' she asked Suzy, Mrs Cooper being a villager who came in twice a week to clean the house. 'Shall we go and see Kit and Granny? I expect they'll have more pressies for you,' she told her.

Melissa had intended leaving Suzy at Bellwood for the day, but, since the weather forecast predicted showers over Wimbledon, she decided not to make the trip and stayed at Bellwood.

'Can those two really run faster than you and Jack could at their age, or am I getting old?' Rose asked, late in the afternoon. She loved taking care of her grandchildren, but, oh, dear, they were exhausting!

'Do you really want me to answer that?' Melissa grinned.

'No, I don't suppose I do,' Rose said ruefully. 'Are you going to Wimbledon tomorrow?'

'I thought I would – why? Don't you feel up to having Suzy again?'

'No, it's not that at all. Alexa's bringing the twins over – and their nanny, thank God! I just thought it would be nice if you could be here as well,' she explained.

'Oh, I see. I'll have to check if Jack and I are scheduled to play. Actually, I saw Alexa last week – I thought she looked quite ill.'

'Did you?' Rose flushed. 'Shall we cut Suzy's birthday cake?' she asked brightly.

'Not yet.' Melissa narrowed her eyes at her mother. 'Why are you changing the subject?'

'I'm not,' Rose denied. 'Oh, all right, I am, but please don't ask for details. I promised not to tell anyone.'

'I see,' Melissa said grimly. 'And I won't ask any questions. Perhaps Ace ought to check on his own wife instead of Jac – Oh!' She clapped a hand to her mouth.

'You were going to say Jack's wife, weren't you? What does Ace have to do with Lisa? Not . . . ?' She looked horrified.

'No, he hasn't seduced her, if that's what you mean.' Melissa laughed, then she frowned. 'At least, I don't think he has,' she said slowly. 'He told me he has some evidence Jack can use against her if it comes to divorce . . . he wouldn't, would he?' She looked at Rose uncertainly.

'No, I'm sure he wouldn't,' Rose said, but she didn't sound altogether convinced. 'Oh, dear, what a mess! At least I don't have to worry about you and Nick!' she said happily.

* * *

Friday was another showery day; the covers came off and back on the courts with monotonous regularity, and the locker-rooms, shops, restaurants and souvenir tents were full to bursting. Players milled about, trying to relax while waiting to resume matches.

Melissa chatted to Katy for a while, went along to the TV studio for an impromptu interview, and then mingled with the fans, talking and signing autographs. Finally, bored, and realizing there was no possibility of her mixed doubles going ahead – scheduled last on Centre Court – she decided to leave. She sought Ginny out and offered her a lift home.

'Oh, don't bother; I'll be fine on my own,' Ginny said quickly.

'It's no bother – you live in Chelsea, don't you? Nick and I have a flat there; we kept it on after we moved to Nine Elms. I think – hope – I left a bracelet there the last time we stayed in town overnight. I was going to ask Nick to call in, but I don't want him knowing I might have lost it. He bought it for me when Suzy was born,' she explained.

'In that case, thanks; I'd love a lift home,' Ginny said gratefully – the trains leaving Wimbledon were always packed. 'Actually, I thought I saw Nick the other evening, on the King's Road,' she suddenly remembered.

'Yeah? He was probably just checking on the place,' Melissa said. 'Oh, I almost forgot – Suzy loves her donkey. She slept with it last night.'

Melissa dropped Ginny off at home, then drove

to the flat, praying she would find the bracelet. She couldn't believe she had been careless enough to mislay it, and dreaded having to confess to Nick that she couldn't find it . . .

She unlocked the main entrance door to the building and ran lightly up the stairs to the flat, her thoughts still on the bracelet, remembering how she had awoken from a deep, exhausted slumber after Suzy's birth and found Nick watching her so lovingly. At that moment she had forgotten the pain of labour, the lingering regret of cutting short her career. It had all been worth it just to see that look in Nick's eyes.

Smiling, she unlocked the door to the flat and walked in – just as a young boy walked out of the kitchen, drinking milk from a carton. Her immediate thought was that he was a burglar, and she was too angry to be scared.

'How the hell did you get in here?' she demanded furiously. 'How dare you barge in –?'

'Mam!' the boy called out, and Melissa's jaw dropped. Squatters! was her next thought, and she could hardly believe her eyes when a woman emerged from the bedroom – hers and Nick's bedroom – wearing a dressing-gown.

'Oh, dear.' The woman pulled the material closer around her body. 'Hello, Melissa. My – my name is Connie Sullivan . . .' she stammered.

'I don't give a damn what your name is!' Melissa seethed. 'Get dressed and get the hell out of my flat before I call the police!'

'He hasn't told her,' the boy smirked. Melissa turned on him furiously, but something stopped her reaching for the phone. He was too smug, too confident.

'Nick said we could stay here for a while,' Connie said quietly, glaring at her son. Melissa ignored her.

'Nick hasn't told me what, exactly?' she asked the boy icily. His smile broadened: the rich bitch was about to get her come-uppance!

'He's my father,' he told her, very slowly, enjoying each drawn-out syllable.

'You're lying,' Melissa said contemptuously, then turned and raked the mother with a look of disdain: middle-aged, greying hair . . . what nonsense!

'It's true,' Connie said quietly. 'I knew Nick a long time ago in Belfast. I'm so sorry,' she added, and that was Melissa's undoing. Abuse, gloating, demands, all those she could have dealt with, but this old bag actually dared to look at her with pity in her eyes . . .

Melissa whirled around and ran out of the flat, stumbling down the stairs and out onto the street. She gulped at the fresh air, feeling as starved of oxygen as if she had just completed a marathon.

After a few moments, she steadied herself and returned to her car. She drove unthinkingly, unseeingly, one part of her automatically dealing with the task while her mind tried to absorb the enormity of what she had just heard.

Nick had a son? No! It couldn't be true, just couldn't! The boy didn't resemble Nick, and, anyway, he would have told me, she thought over and over. So why hasn't he mentioned they are staying at the flat? asked an insistent inner voice. Different thoughts, conflicting emotions battled for supremacy: disbelief, anger, pain . . .

Why are you angry if you don't believe? He'd have told me! Nick has a son? Nick has a son!

Then she could hear Nick's voice, asking her to have another child . . .

Always she'd parried the question, denying him what he wanted. Has he been leading a double life? And, if so, for how long? The Sunday papers were always exposing men who ran two households . . . was Nick one of those? A bigamist, even? she thought feverishly.

She was still twenty minutes from home when she realized the significance of the disturbed vision, the tightening band around her temples. She groaned out loud; not a migraine, not now! She had once been plagued with stress-induced attacks, especially after the abortion, when she and Nick had parted . . .

She took one hand off the steering wheel and scrabbled in her bag on the passenger seat, searching fruitlessly for the tablets prescribed to keep an attack at bay. But she had been free of migraine for so long that she no longer kept them always at hand.

She moaned again as a vicious pain stabbed at her temple; she had to get home! Barely able to see, or think, she paused briefly at a crossroads: left lay Nine Elms, to the right, Bellwood – where were her pills? she wondered feverishly.

She let in the clutch, still unable to decide, and instead of turning either left or right did neither, and shot over the crossroads at speed. Too late, she realized she was about to crash into a stone wall and pulled desperately on the wheel, trying to veer away. There was a loud crash, a sickening jolt, and then, thankfully, oblivion.

After Melissa had run from the flat, Connie rounded on her son in a fury.

'That was cruel, Mickey, to spring it on her like that,' she blazed. 'And stupid,' she added, with a sigh. Mickey shrugged, quite unconcerned.

'How was I to know he hadn't told her we were here?' he asked insolently.

'Well, I don't suppose we'll be here for much longer!' Connie snapped, and reached for the phone. She quickly dialled the number of Lennox and Coupland, but neither Nick nor Coop was in the office, and she had no alternative but to simply leave a message, saying it was urgent that Nick call her as soon as possible. She had no other way of reaching him, knowing neither his home number nor that of his mobile; he had told her only to contact him at the office if she needed him.

She felt awful, ashamed now that she had for years been jealous of the younger, prettier, more successful girl who had married Nick. She would never forget the look on Melissa's face when she had learned of their identity.

Mickey listened silently to her frantic phone call, and watched as she made a cup of tea. Or tried to; she was shaking so much she spilled water, tipped over the milk.

'I'll do that for you, Mam. You go back to bed – the doctor said you were to rest.'

'Yes, all right,' she agreed wearily. 'Thank you,

Mickey.' She patted his cheek and returned to the bedroom. Mickey made the tea. He also unplugged the phone.

A passing motorist spotted Melissa's car only a few minutes after the crash. The driver's door had burst open on impact, and Melissa, who had omitted to fasten her seat-belt, had been thrown out onto the road.

He used his mobile phone to call an ambulance and the police, then knelt, rather helplessly, by Melissa's inert form. He knew she shouldn't be moved, but felt useless doing nothing, and eventually took off his jacket and placed it carefully over her.

The ambulance arrived first and he stepped back, relieved to pass over the responsibility. When the police car pulled up a few moments later, he told them what he knew and then left. The police officer recognized her at once; a local man, he knew her father Daniel quite well, and it fell to him to inform her family of the accident.

There was no reply to his knock at Nine Elms, so he drove on to Brook Farm and told Daniel what had happened.

'Oh, my God!' Sick with dread, Daniel drove to Bellwood.

'Daniel!' Rose greeted him warmly. They were good friends now; so much time had passed since the divorce that no bitterness remained, just a shared love and pride in their children and grand-children. 'Oh, God, what's wrong?' She paled at the grim expression on his face.

'Melissa's crashed her car; she's been taken to hospital,' he said, as gently as he could.

'Oh, no! No.' Rose shook her head in denial. 'How . . . how bad?' she whispered.

'I don't know; she was unconscious,' he said unwillingly.

'I must go to her . . . The children,' she remembered distractedly. 'Alexa's here . . . Alexa! Can your nanny stay and look after Kit and Suzy? Melissa's in hospital . . . I have to go,' she said, trying not to cry.

'Of course. Go on, they'll be fine with us,' Alexa urged. 'I'll call Ace; he'll find Jack . . . what about Nick?'

'Try his office, or his mobile . . . the numbers are by the phone,' Rose called, already out of the door. 'Oh, God, Daniel, not again,' she wept, as memories of Jack's awful, almost fatal crash five years before came flooding back. He had lain in a coma, near death, for three long days and nights. 'I can't go through that again. I can't,' she sobbed.

'I know, I know,' he said wretchedly, very close to breaking down himself. 'She'll be all right; I'm sure she will,' he said, trying to convince himself as much as Rose.

Alexa meanwhile had called Ace on his mobile – he was at Wimbledon and immediately went in search of Jack. Nick was harder to locate; he had switched off his mobile before a meeting with a new client, not wanting to be interrupted, and had forgotten to switch it back on again.

He arrived back at Nine Elms to find the house empty, but he assumed Melissa had stayed on at

Wimbledon despite the weather. He decided to have a shower and change his clothes before going over to collect Suzy from her grandmother. Only when he returned downstairs did he play back the messages on the answering machine . . .

Melissa recovered consciousness slowly, painfully; the light seemed harsh, blinding, and she groaned, quickly closing her eyes again and putting her hands to her head.

'You're all right, just a few bruises,' said a soft voice.

'Migraine,' Melissa managed to mumble.

'No, slight concussion,' the nurse corrected. What, as well? Melissa thought.

'Migraine,' she insisted; that much she remembered. The car crash was a blur. 'Pills.'

'Oh.' The nurse went in search of the doctor, who had gone to reassure her family there was nothing seriously wrong. He listened, then looked at Jack, who was more in control than the parents.

'Does she suffer from migraine?' he asked.

'She used to, but she hasn't had an attack for years,' he frowned.

'She's asking for pills – do you know what medication she was prescribed?'

'I can't remember, sorry. Mum?' he asked Rose gently. 'Melissa's migraine tablets – what were they called?'

She looked at him blankly for a moment, then began scrabbling in her capacious bag.

'I think I still have some – I saw them weeks ago and almost threw them away, but I thought that would be tempting fate . . . here!' She handed the out-of-date tablets to the doctor, who gave low-voiced instructions to the nurse.

'We'll keep her here overnight, but there's nothing to worry about. You should all go home.'

'Can't we see her first?' Rose asked.

'Yes, when we've settled her into a room. But just for a moment, and one at a time,' he said.

Rose went first, and Melissa tried not to cry.

'I'm all right, really,' she managed to reassure her, and did the same with her father and Jack.

Nick arrived, white-faced, at the hospital just as the Farrells were leaving.

'She's going to be fine,' Daniel said quickly. 'We've just spoken to her. They're keeping her in for observation, that's all. She can probably go home tomorrow.'

'Oh, thank God,' Nick released a pent-up breath. 'What happened?'

'We don't know,' Daniel replied. 'The police said there was no other car involved; she just ran off the road. Maybe the steering was defective,' he suggested. 'Anyway, she's not badly injured, Nick, but the crash seems to have triggered a migraine.'

'Oh, no.' Nick grimaced in sympathy; he'd witnessed several attacks. 'I thought we'd seen the last of those. Excuse me, I must go and see her.' He smiled briefly and hurried past them.

'Nick – Suzy can stay with me tonight,' Rose called after him.

'Thanks, that would be a great help.' He turned and smiled again before continuing on his way.

He spoke to the doctor first, then quietly entered

Melissa's room. She had heard his voice outside the door and anger shot agonizing needles of pain through her head. But she lay still and pretended to be asleep; she couldn't bear to even look at him, let alone confront him with what she had discovered.

'Melissa?' Nick whispered, but there was no response. He was disappointed not to hear her tell him she would be fine, but was glad she had escaped the pain of the migraine by falling asleep.

He sat and watched her for a long time; Melissa lay, racked with pain, desperate for him to leave, then, as the medication took hold, the stabs of pain receded and she drifted into sleep.

When Melissa next awoke, it was morning. She opened her eyes slowly, cautiously, then tentatively tried moving her head. The worst of the migraine had passed, reduced to a throbbing headache that was at least tolerable. Less easy to bear were the memories of the day before. Nick had a son.

She couldn't eat breakfast, but managed a glass of orange juice and some coffee and was given more painkillers. When the doctor pronounced her fit enough to leave, she phoned her mother and asked her to collect her.

'Jack won't mind if I stay at Bellwood, will he?'

'Of course not, but – ' Rose frowned.

'Please, Mum!' Melissa said desperately.

'I'll be there in thirty minutes,' Rose promised quickly.

When Nick phoned the hospital to ask if he could fetch Melissa home, he was a little surprised to hear that Rose had already collected her. But he assumed she would bring her to Nine Elms and sat down to wait. Only then did he remember the second message on his machine, the one asking him to contact Connie.

He dialled the number of the flat, but heard only a monotonous drone, as if it were disconnected or out of order. Shrugging it off as being unimportant, he replaced the receiver and resumed watching out for Rose's car. After twenty minutes he became seriously worried; surely she hadn't crashed too? He was about to leave the house to go in search of them when the phone rang. He snatched it up.

'Yes?'

'Nick.' It was Rose. 'Melissa's here, at Bellwood. She's okay, but she still has a headache and feels rather sick – you know how she is after a migraine – so I've put her to bed. Daniel's taken Suzy and Kit over to Brook Farm so Melissa can rest here peacefully today.'

'Why didn't you bring her here?' he asked, puzzled.

'I'm afraid she didn't want me to,' Rose said apologetically.

Nick frowned.

'I'm coming over,' he said shortly, and rang off before she could argue.

He drove as fast as he dared along the narrow country roads, gripped by an unnamed fear. He burst into Bellwood without knocking, startling Rose, who was beginning to climb the stairs, carrying a jug of iced water.

'Is that for Melissa?'

319

'Yes, she doesn't want any food . . .' Her voice trailed off as Nick took the water from her and quickly mounted the stairs. She hesitated, then went after him.

When Nick entered the bedroom, Melissa was lying in bed, her eyes closed. She looked deathly pale and the drawn curtains testified that her head still pained her. She didn't stir, assuming it was her mother who had come into the room.

'How are you feeling?' Nick asked quietly. Her eyes flew open and she regarded him coldly.

'Lousy,' she responded.

'I'm sorry.' He put the water down, then sat on the edge of the bed. Melissa turned her face away; she simply didn't feel able to cope with him now.

'Why didn't you come home?' he asked.

'I thought it might not be convenient,' she bit out.

'Why ever wouldn't it be convenient?' Nick asked.

'I thought you might want to use it to house another of your bastards!' she hissed.

'Oh, dear God,' Nick groaned.

Rose, hovering in the doorway, gasped.

'Go away, Nick. Just go away,' Melissa said wearily.

'No, we have to talk about this. I've been trying to find the words to tell you . . .'

'I can't deal with it now,' she said desperately, putting her hands up to her throbbing head.

'Leave her, Nick!' Rose said sharply, when he tried to pull Melissa into his arms, to make her listen and understand. 'She needs to rest; you know she does,' she added, more quietly. Reluctantly, he nodded.

320

'Very well,' he agreed finally. 'Melissa, I'll be back later, to explain what's been happening. I love you and Suzy more than anything in the world, and you're the last person I would ever wish to hurt. Please remember that,' he said earnestly. He waited for a response, but when none was forthcoming got wearily to his feet.

Rose glanced back at Melissa, then followed Nick downstairs.

'Is it true?' she demanded.

'Yes. I have a sixteen-year-old son. I only found out myself recently; I didn't know how to tell Melissa.'

'You should have found a way,' she told him curtly. 'Anything would have been better than this. How could she have found out?'

'I don't know. Unless she went to the flat for some reason,' he said slowly, realizing now why Connie had wanted to speak to him – to warn him.

'He's living in your flat?' Rose asked incredulously. 'Alone?'

'No, his mother's there too,' Nick said unwillingly.

'Oh, Nick, you fool!' she raged. 'Why on earth did you let them move into Melissa's home?'

'They haven't moved in! They're just staying there temporarily while we sort things out,' he said defensively. 'Okay, hindsight's a wonderful thing – it was stupid to let them stay. But I guessed Connie was short of money, and it seemed . . . crass to offer to pay hotel bills. As if I was buying her off.'

'Well, buy her off, or scare her off – do anything, but get this mess sorted out. Quickly,' Rose told him. 'I don't think Melissa will even begin to listen while you have another woman living in her home – a woman who had your child.'

'I'll deal with it today,' he said heavily.

'Now we know the migraine caused the car crash and not the other way around,' Rose realized suddenly. 'She could have been badly injured, even killed!' She stared at him in horror, as if he were a murderer. Nick felt even more wretched, if that were possible.

'Just tell her I love her. Please. I was only trying to do what was best for everyone,' he said, with a rare helplessness.

'I know.' Rose softened slightly. 'Go on, do whatever you have to do to resolve it. Melissa will be all right here with me,' she said. Nick cast a despairing glance upwards, either looking towards heaven for guidance or to where Melissa lay. Rose wasn't sure which.

'I'll be back when I've sorted everything out,' he said finally, and walked slowly out of Bellwood.

CHAPTER 16

The news of Melissa's accident spread quickly.
Connie heard about it on TV and, already per-
turbed by Nick's failure to contact her, became
even more anxious. Finally she decided to try and
locate him again, and only then discovered the
unplugged phone. Mickey! she thought angrily.

'It's not my fault the stupid cow crashed her car,'
he muttered rebelliously, then he slunk off, more
apprehensive than he would admit about facing
Nick.

Connie realized that this meant there could no
longer be even friendship between her and Nick,
and calmly began to pack. She was shocked by his
bleak expression when he finally arrived at lunch-
time.

'I tried to warn you,' she said quickly.

'I know; I got your message, but I couldn't get
through,' he said.

'I'm sorry, but Mickey unplugged the phone,' she
told him.

'Whatever for?' Nick asked in amazement.

'I'm not really sure.' Connie shrugged. 'To cause

trouble between you and Melissa, I suspect. He knew I was trying to contact you – he was here when Melissa came yesterday. I'm afraid he wasn't very kind to her. I heard about the accident – will she be all right?'

'Physically she will, yes,' Nick replied; he didn't dare think beyond that. 'Where is Mickey?' he asked, so grimly Connie was glad her son had disappeared.

'He's gone out; I don't know where. I think he's shocked by what's happened, but full of bravado . . . I've packed up all our things and tidied up. We'll leave this evening; I've already booked our tickets,' she said briskly. Nick nodded, relieved she had made the decision to go.

'It's my fault. I should have been open with Melissa from the beginning,' he said miserably, rubbing his hand tiredly over his face. 'I still want to help you and Mickey,' he continued, 'but I think it's best if we deal through solicitors in future. I'll set up a trust fund for Mickey. Right now, financial help is all I can give him. Maybe later . . .'

'I understand.' Connie nodded.

'I just hope Melissa will,' Nick replied heavily.

Saul heard about Melissa's accident and, after receiving no reply from Nine Elms, phoned the office and spoke to Coop.

'She's fine,' Coop told him, still unaware that her discovery of Connie and Mickey's existence had been a contributory factor. 'Did Nick tell you Ginny Sinclair's going to California with Ace Delaney?' he asked, rather maliciously, since he would be delighted if Saul and Ginny stopped seeing each other. He would never poach from a friend, but being around to pick up the pieces and offer a shoulder to cry on – to Ginny, not Saul – was another matter entirely!

'He told me,' Saul said tersely; he had been tormented by the prospect ever since. To think he had previously considered Nick's loathing of the American bordered on paranoia – now he thought Nick was too easy on the guy! Little less than a week had passed since the party at Bellwood, hardly enough time for her to forgive him, he knew, but he couldn't wait any longer to see her again.

He left Aldershot in the early evening, and once he was only a couple of miles from her flat he phoned her, but promptly disconnected when he heard her voice – he didn't want to give her the opportunity to tell him not to visit, or to go out herself to avoid him.

He stopped briefly to buy flowers, then, remembering her reaction to the last gift he had tried to give her, tossed them onto the back seat of the car. His heart was thumping painfully as he parked and made his way up to the flat, his footsteps ringing loudly on the iron staircase. He rehearsed what to say as he climbed: first an apology, then try to convince her of his sincerity, throw in another apology, then try and explain his initial reaction without destroying what illusions she might have left about her mother, apologize again, grovel if necessary . . . Right, got it . . .

'You're not going to California with Ace Delaney,' was what he said abruptly, when Ginny opened the door. She stared at him, and was about to slam the door shut in his face when he groaned and started smashing his head, hard, against the doorframe. Ginny winced involuntarily.

'Are you drunk?' she asked suspiciously.

'No. Just stupid, arrogant, possessive . . .'

'Well, do continue. You've only just started listing your faults,' she informed him sweetly.

At least she's listening to me, Saul thought hopefully.

'I know; I need the love of a good woman to set me straight,' he told her, with what he hoped was a winsome smile.

'So go and find one,' she told him tartly.

'I have found one. But when I first met her I was too idiotic to realize how wonderful she is,' Saul said earnestly. At least, Ginny thought he was sincere, but how could she be sure? Her belief in her ability to judge men had been severely jolted by the ease with which he had duped her. 'And now she doesn't believe me when I try to tell her how much she means to me,' Saul continued softly.

'Can you blame her?' Ginny asked painfully.

'No. But I'm going to keep pestering her until she agrees to give me another chance,' he promised – or threatened. Ginny was too confused to work out whether she was pleased or daunted by the prospect of his persistence.

'That will probably be a very long time,' she told him.

'She's worth it; I'll wait.' He paused, then grinned. 'While I'm waiting for her to forgive me, how about you and me going out for a drink this evening?'

'You pig!' Ginny tried not to laugh.

'Please?' He smiled again, that slow, heart-stopping smile that was so hard to resist, and Ginny wavered.

'I'll think about it,' she said loftily.

'May I come inside while you're thinking?' He moved forward, as if confident she would let him over the threshold, she noted. Not so easy, she thought grimly.

'No. Wait there,' she told him imperiously, and stepped back and firmly closed the door. She looked at her watch – her own, high street cheapie, not the one he had given her – and wondered just how long he would actually wait.

Telling herself she would need her head examined if she went out with him again, she nevertheless went into her bedroom and rifled the contents of her wardrobe, searching for something he hadn't yet seen her wear. She then took a leisurely shower, all the time convincing herself she should simply leave him on the doorstep . . .

It was a pity it wasn't raining, she thought, with a grin.

Before dressing in a blue dress and matching jacket, she peeked out of the window; his Jag was still parked outside. She smiled slightly and sat down to apply make-up – not that she intended going out with him, of course . . . She was still denying it to herself when she reopened the door, almost an hour after she had closed it in his face. Saul was sitting on the top step of the iron staircase and looked up at her with an exaggerated woebegone expression.

'Are you still here?' Ginny feigned amazement and irritation. Saul noticed her smart outfit and make-up but wisely refrained from comment.

'You might at least have given me a cushion to sit on,' he complained. 'I think I've got piles!' he added morosely, and Ginny stifled a laugh. 'I need a drink – will you join me? Please? I know so few people in London nowadays. It's a lonely life in the Army, defending one's country, often far from home,' he said sorrowfully.

'Oh, very well, just one drink,' she sighed.

'Thank you,' Saul said, so humbly she shot him a look full of suspicion, but he seemed sincere. *Seemed.* He had also seemed sincere in his apologies the evening he'd arrived bearing gifts after his conversation with Jamie Calvert . . . She bit her lip, even more uncertain about what she was doing, allowing him to get near her again, to hurt her again.

She spotted the discarded flowers as soon as she climbed into the car.

'Are those for Melissa?'

'What? Oh, no, they were – are – for you. I was afraid you might chuck them back in my face,' he said.

'Oh.' She looked away. 'Wasn't it awful about Melissa's accident? I phoned Bellwood as soon as I heard, and Rose said she'll be fine after a couple of days rest.'

'Yeah, Coop told me. I tried to call Nick earlier, but there was no reply,' Saul said absently, his attention on waiting for a gap in the traffic. 'Have you enjoyed Wimbledon?' he asked, once he had joined the stream of cars.

'Yes, it's been great,' she enthused. 'The best seats, no queues, star treatment all the way.'

'Good.' Saul smiled at her. 'When are you thinking of going to California?' he asked, ultra-casual.

'I'm not merely thinking of going – I *am* going in ten days' time,' she told him tersely.

'Okay, fine,' Saul capitulated quickly, and returned to the safe topic of the tennis matches she had watched. He had caught snatches of play on TV, but was less of a fan than Ginny.

They both relaxed a little once they were sitting in a pub, still alone, of course, but surrounded by a crowd of laughing, chatting people all intent on enjoying their weekend. They squeezed onto a long, cushioned window-seat, and Ginny was very aware of his thigh pressed against hers, of his arm resting across the back of the bench, not quite touching her shoulders.

Saul sensed she was still wary of him, but her attitude was a huge improvement on the last time they had met, he thought optimistically. It might take a very long time to win her over completely, but he was confident he would eventually have her back. And, when I do, I'll never hurt her again, and I'll never, never let her go, he thought silently, watching every expression on her beautiful face and loving the slight hand gestures she made while she talked. Artist's hands, of course, slender and delicate. He wanted to kiss every single finger, then her wrist, then . . .

'You're not wearing your watch,' he said abruptly.

'Yes, I am.' Ginny deliberately misunderstood

and lifted the arm bearing her old inexpensive watch to show him.

'I was referring to the one I gave you – dare I ask what happened to it?' he asked, forcing a light tone to his voice, belatedly aware that his interruption had caused her to tense up again.

'I imagine Jo still has it,' she told him airily.

'Jo?'

'Mmm, she took it away from me – I think she was afraid I would break it, or chuck it down the nearest drain.'

'Oh.' Saul wished he hadn't asked. Ginny hid a grin at the chastened expression on his handsome face, enjoying the feeling of having the upper hand. She'd better make the most of it, she thought, sure it was only temporary!

'How do you feel about coming over to inspect my house again soon?' Saul asked, rather tentatively, aware that the question held overtones of come-up-and-see-my-etchings.

'Why?' Ginny asked guardedly.

'I'll be living there permanently soon; it's still a house, not a home. It needs a woman's touch . . . '

'Oh, God, don't be so patronizing! You'll be asking me to bake you a cake next,' Ginny said scornfully.

'No, of course I won't,' Saul said quickly. 'What I was trying very clumsily to say . . . to ask you . . . ' He swallowed, wishing his glass wasn't empty, for he needed Dutch courage as never before. He also knew this was far, far too soon, but he had to ask her. He took a deep breath and reached for her hand. 'Ginny, I'm trying to ask you to help me turn it into a home. I don't want to live there, anywhere, without you . . . '

'You don't seriously expect me to live with you?' she demanded incredulously, snatching her hand away.

'Yes. No. Not live with as in co-habit,' he said hastily, cursing himself. 'I mean live with as in marriage. For ever. Babies. Family, the whole bit,' he said desperately. Ginny stared at him in shocked amazement and experienced a moment of pure joy that was quickly followed by doubt.

How do you know he's sincere? jeered the cynical part of her, a part that hadn't even existed until Saul Lancaster entered her life. This could be another ploy, to get you into bed again, or to stop you going to California with the Delaneys, continued the inner voice. I can't trust him, she realized sadly; more to the point, she couldn't, didn't dare, trust her own feelings or instincts. He had fooled her so easily before that she no longer had any faith in her own judgement.

'Of course I won't marry you,' she said coldly, and got hastily to her feet before she could weaken.

'Ginny . . .' Saul reached for her hand again, but she jerked away; she couldn't trust herself to remain strong and knew she had to get away from him.

'No! Don't touch me. I'll get a cab home. And I *am* going to the States with Ace Delaney,' she informed him coolly, before she turned and began pushing her way out of the pub.

She stumbled along the pavement, realized she was about to make an utter fool of herself by breaking down in public, and ducked into a deserted alleyway where she leaned against the wall, dropped her head into her hands and began to sob. She didn't even notice the three men sitting on the ground at the end of the alley, sharing a bottle of whisky. But they noticed her . . .

Saul remained in the pub, oblivious to the laughter and chatter of the crowd around him. She hadn't even asked for time to think it over, just a blunt and very definite no. I should have waited, he thought miserably. I blew it, blurted it out, even made it sound as if all I want is a housekeeper! Or her skill as an interior designer!

Maybe that was it, he thought slowly, as he made his way to the bar for a refill. He hadn't even said he loved her! You idiot, Lancaster, he berated himself; you can't even propose properly! Well, I've never done it before, he excused himself. And what had she meant by that last comment about going to America with Delaney? Did she think he was trying to stop her? I'll have another drink, give her some time to cool down, then go after her, he decided, trying and failing to catch the eye of the harassed barman. It's obviously not my night, he thought ruefully, and changed his mind about the drink and made his way outside.

He fished his car keys out of his pocket and sauntered to where he had parked the Jag. It was then he heard a girl scream, a sound of mingled outrage and fear. Ginny! He spun round and headed for the source of the sound. He almost ran past the entrance to the alleyway, but a glimpse of Ginny's blonde hair just caught his eye in time and he back-tracked quickly.

She had been dragged to the dark end of the alley and was pinned against the wall; two men were holding her arms while another reached inside her jacket. Ginny twisted her face away from his loathsome kiss, drew breath for another scream, then saw Saul approaching, his face a mask of fury.

The men, too intent on their prey, didn't see or hear him until it was too late. With a feral snarl he pulled the third man away from Ginny, taking the other two by surprise. They slackened their grip on her arms, enabling Saul to wrench her from their grasp. He pushed her behind him, placing himself between her and her attackers.

'Get out of here!' he snapped at Ginny, keeping his eyes fixed firmly on the three now very angry, thwarted men. Saul tossed his car keys in her direction without looking at her. 'Go on, get out,' he said roughly. He wasn't afraid for himself, but was terrified of what they would do to her if they managed to overpower him.

Ginny caught and clutched at the keys, and backed off a little, but she didn't leave. She just couldn't; her breath came in quick gasps, her eyes huge as she watched the scene unfolding in front of her.

Saul was intent on the three men, his eyes flickering from one to the other as they edged nearer, trying to guess which would make the first move. He could smell the whiskey fumes and hoped they were drunk enough to have dulled their reflexes; on the other hand, they were full of alcohol-induced bravado and wouldn't be feeling any pain. However, he was confident he could handle the situation . . . until he caught the glimmer of a knife-blade . . .

He swore violently under his breath and concentrated on that greater danger. He feinted towards another man, then pivoted and lunged at the guy wielding the knife, chopping at his wrist; the blow was hard enough to loosen the man's grip and the knife clattered to the ground.

Saul tried to kick the knife out of reach, but another man grabbed him from behind, trying to pin his arms to his chest and make him an easy target for the others to use as a punch bag. Saul swiftly dug his elbow sharply back into the man's ribs, then twisted away, turned and landed a knock-out blow to his jaw.

One down, two to go, he thought grimly, but by that time the third had retrieved his knife and hurled himself at Saul, arm raised to stab him. Saul dodged aside quickly, but not quickly enough, and the blade sliced deeply into his upper arm. He grunted in pain, briefly felt relieved that it was his left arm, and went on to the attack, wanting it over quickly before his injury could seriously slow him down.

The sight of Saul's blood galvanized Ginny into action, and she ran back to the street, which was incongruously bustling with people unaware of the drama being enacted in a darkened alley just a few yards away. She grabbed hold of passers-by, who mostly gave her anxious looks and hurried past.

'Please help!' she begged frantically. 'There's a man with a knife!' she kept saying, and only realized much later that that wasn't the cleverest thing she could have said. Finally, after what seemed an eternity, two heavily built men did stop, and she rushed back to the alley, terrified of what she might find. Two of her attackers were out cold and Saul was advancing menacingly towards the third, who was backing towards the wall at the far end, with no place left to go.

'I'm sorry,' he whimpered.

'No, you're not,' Saul snarled at him, before hitting him, once in the stomach and then a sharp upper cut to the jaw. The man's head snapped back and he fell like a stone. Saul stood over him, his fists still clenched, fury still erupting from deep inside him. 'Now you're sorry!' he gritted to the unconscious form, before stepping away, resisting, with difficulty, the urge to kick the defenceless body at his feet.

'Saul!' Ginny ran towards him. 'You're bleeding!' He glanced down at his arm, which suddenly began to hurt like hell; his shirtsleeve was heavily stained with blood.

'I'm okay,' he assured her, bracing himself against the wall for a moment. 'I told you to leave!' he snapped. 'Don't you know what could have happened – ?' He stopped. Of course she knew. 'Sorry.' He put his right arm around her and held her close, could feel the tremors which shook her body.

'You okay, mate?' asked one of Ginny's helpers.

'Yeah. Fine, thanks,' he said, which was patently untrue, but the two men nodded and left.

'Do we have to call the police?' Ginny asked

335

reluctantly, recoiling at the very thought of the questioning, the probable court case. Why were you in the alley, Miss Sinclair? Were you wearing a short skirt? Make-up? She cringed at the prospect.

'No,' Saul said positively, to her relief. 'I'm an Army officer – I'm not supposed to go around beating up civilians,' he explained.

'They deserved it – the pigs!' She shuddered.

'I know, darling, I know,' he soothed her. Ginny clung to him for a moment, then made a supreme effort to pull herself together.

'I'll drive you to hospital . . .' she began.

'No,' Saul said. 'Same reason – they'll notify the police about a stabbing. It's not that bad – I'll ask the MO to take a look at it when I get back to Aldershot.'

'You can't drive!' Ginny exclaimed. 'You're losing too much blood – you'll pass out at the wheel.'

'I guess you'll have to give me a bed for the night, then.' He grinned at her.

'Oh, you're incorrigible!' she said, exasperated. But she did drive him back to her flat, deciding she could at least try and stem the bleeding. If she couldn't, she would have to drive him back to his barracks; she certainly wasn't going to let him drive himself.

She was vaguely surprised by how calm she felt; she could sense fury and hysterical tears simmering not far below the surface, but for now, at least, that was where they stayed – to be dealt with later, she dimly realized.

Saul realized it too; while she was worrying about him her own emotional reaction was kept at bay, so he meekly went along with what she suggested – besides, he was thoroughly enjoying being fussed over; it made a pleasant change from the cold shoulder, however much he deserved the latter.

'Shh, don't make a noise,' she whispered, as they approached the stairs leading to her flat.

'Why not?' Saul asked, gazing up at the staircase that suddenly seemed very high and steep, the door at the top extremely far away. Quite apart from the stabbing and subsequent loss of blood, Saul had taken quite a few blows, and he would have welcomed Barney's burly strength to help him climb those steps.

'Jo's blood pressure is too high – she was at the antenatal clinic yesterday, and she's not to be upset,' Ginny said firmly. 'Can you manage?' She left him hanging onto the rail while she dashed the last few steps to unlock the door, then returned to help him inside.

Saul collapsed onto the sofa, feeling dizzy and sick. Ginny sped off, running hot water into a basin and finding disinfectant.

'Let me take your shirt off,' she said briskly. Saul managed a grin at that, and she flushed. 'Stop it,' she scolded, and, despite feeling somewhat nauseous herself, she forced herself to concentrate on the bleeding and definitely not on his broad shoulders and muscular torso. She gritted her teeth and gently bathed the wound, revealing a two-inch gash in his upper arm that was still oozing blood.

'It's bled so much, it should at least be clean of infection,' she said hopefully.

'Yes, Nurse.' Saul tried not to wince at the sting

of the disinfectant, and twisted his head to inspect the damage for himself. It felt as if his arm had been almost hacked off at the shoulder.

'I'm sure it needs stitches,' Ginny said worriedly, when she was unable to completely stop the bleeding.

'Just wrap it up as tightly as you can – it will be okay until I get back to barracks,' Saul told her.

'I'll do my best.' Ginny fetched a clean handkerchief and folded it in four, making a thick pad which she placed over the wound before wrapping a bandage around his arm. She sat back on her heels and drew a deep breath, feeling decidedly shaky.

'Thanks, that feels great,' Saul said, untruthfully. 'How about a cup of tea?' he asked, thinking she needed it more than he did.

'Yes, of course. I'm afraid I don't have any brandy or anything,' she said.

'Just as well, since I have to drive back to Aldershot. Tea will be fine,' he assured her, and she hurried into the kitchen.

Saul sat back and closed his eyes, trying to ignore the throbbing pain in his arm. He was bathed in perspiration; not because of his physical pain but because of the raw, gut-wrenching fear he had felt over Ginny's danger. He couldn't forget how very nearly he had stayed in the pub for another drink. If the barman hadn't been too busy to serve him . . .

As Ginny was waiting for the kettle to boil she began to tremble violently, and splashed as much water onto the work surface as into the teapot, clattering cups clumsily onto saucers. She poured out two cups of hot, sweet tea but had to carry them separately into the sitting-room, needing two hands to avoid spilling the contents.

Saul ignored the cup she offered him, realizing that now she was no longer concentrating on helping him, she was suffering shock from the enormity of what had almost happened to her.

'Come here,' he said gently, holding out his uninjured arm. Ginny's lips trembled as she went willingly into the comfort of his arms.

'The pigs! The filthy pigs!' she sobbed, her hands curled into fists.

'I know. But it's okay now; you're safe,' he murmured, smoothing her hair back from her face. Despite the circumstances, he was enjoying having her in his arms, her face pressed against his bare chest, the scent of her hair in his nostrils. 'Don't cry, darling. It's over,' he said, dropping a soft kiss on her tearstained cheek.

'I hate men! I'm going to become a lesbian,' she said vehemently. Saul smiled slightly at that.

'Oh, no, darling, please don't,' he said, and refrained from pointing out that, even if such a conversion were to take place, it wouldn't stop her being desirable to men. 'Drink your tea,' he ordered; her shaking was becoming more pronounced, not less.

Ginny pushed herself away from him and managed to swallow some of the tea. She noticed, for the first time, that her jacket was stained from being pressed against the wall. She felt sick – sick and dirty.

'I need a bath!' she said, shuddering with distaste, and rushed off, afraid she was about to throw up. As she ran water into the tub she began feverishly discarding her clothes, kicking them to one side and deciding to chuck them away. She knew she would never be able to wear them again.

She sank into the hot, scented water and tried to relax. Soon the shivering eased, but she couldn't stop the tears that welled up and trickled down her cheeks.

Saul drank his own tea, then checked the bandage which, so far at least, seemed to have stemmed the bleeding. His mobile was in the car, and he glanced around the room looking for Ginny's phone; he was going to be late back at Aldershot. He grimaced as he remembered they were leaving early in the morning for a ten-day training exercise in the Brecon Beacons. Great; just what he needed!

He spotted the phone and stood up, rather gingerly, but thankfully there was no recurrence of the dizziness that had assailed him earlier. He dialled the number of the Officers' Mess.

'Jeremy? It's Saul. Listen, can you cover for me? I'm still in London.'

'Sure. Is anything wrong?'

'Not really, but I can't leave just yet. I'll be back as soon as I can.'

'Don't forget we're leaving here at ten tomorrow,' Jeremy reminded him.

'I haven't forgotten,' Saul sighed. 'See you.' He replaced the receiver and glanced in the direction of Ginny's closed bedroom door: a tangible barrier. Against him? Was he one of the enemy – a man? He sighed as he guessed that was how she was feeling right now.

He couldn't leave her alone, but he remembered what she had said about not upsetting Jo. Who could he call? He looked down at the pad beside the phone; it was programmed with the ten numbers she used most frequently – all girlfriends, he noted with pleasure and relief. He had heard her mention some of them in passing, but had no idea which one might be best in a crisis. 'Mum' was listed at number six, he noticed, and after a long, deliberating pause he pressed the button. He glanced at his watch: it was almost one in the morning – how bizarre if his father picked up the phone . . .

'Hello?' It was Ann, sounding impatient, finally answering when he had almost given up.

'Ann, it's Saul Lancaster. Sorry, did I wake you?'

'No, I had just left for the airport actually, and dashed back when I heard the phone. What's wrong?'

'Forget it. If you've a flight to catch . . .' he began.

'You didn't just call me for a sociable chat. It must be important – is it Ginny? Is something wrong?'

'Well, yes, there was a bit of trouble tonight. She was assaulted . . . she's okay,' he added quickly at Ann's sharp intake of breath. 'Physically she is, anyway, but she's rather upset and shaken up. I don't think she should be alone but I have to get back to Aldershot.'

'I'll be right over.'

'Your flight . . .'

'Don't be stupid,' Ann said sharply. 'I'm on my way.'

'Fine. Don't hang up just yet,' Saul said quickly. 'This isn't a trick question, but do you have one of my father's shirts I could borrow?'

'A shirt? No, he's taken all his things and moved into the flat at his office. Didn't you know?'

'No, I didn't know that,' Saul said thoughtfully, but he was speaking to himself.

Ann arrived even more quickly than he had expected, courtesy of the late, or rather the early hour. Ginny's bedroom door was still firmly closed, but he sensed she had emerged from her long bath; there were sounds of movement, yet he didn't dare go in. He felt it would be an intrusion. He heard Ann's footsteps on the iron staircase and went to open the door.

'My God, what's been happening here?' she exclaimed, noting his bared chest and bandaged arm. 'Never mind, where's Ginny?' she asked, evidently dismissing Saul's injury as being unimportant.

'She went to have a bath,' Saul told her, and she pushed past him, heading for the bedroom, pausing briefly to cast a glance of horror at the basin full of bloodied water and the stained towel.

'Ginny!' Ann flung open the bedroom door, then stopped and blinked in surprise at the normality of the scene confronting her. Ginny was wrapped in a pink towelling robe, sitting at her dressing-table and blow-drying her hair. She finally felt clean and warm, almost ready to face the world again.

'Mum! What are you doing here?'

'Saul phoned me, said there had been some trouble. What happened? Are you all right?'

'I'm okay. Saul phoned you?' Ginny repeated in amazement. 'God, he must have thought I was in a bad way!'

'Never mind that – what happened?' Ann sat down. 'Can I help?'

'You can take those clothes away and burn them!' Ginny kicked savagely at the bundle on the floor.

'Your lovely new suit!'

'It's horrible! I hate it! I'll never wear it again.' She shuddered.

'What's been going on, Ginny? Did Saul . . . attack you?' she asked slowly, wondering if he had finally gained revenge on Ginny for what she, Ann, had threatened him with a dozen years earlier. 'If so, I'm calling the police!'

'No, no, of course he didn't,' Ginny said quickly. 'He was great, actually. He saved me . . . Three men grabbed me, Mum; they were horrible . . .' She shivered with revulsion.

'Come here,' Ann said gently, and held out her arms. Ginny moved swiftly over to the bed and Ann gathered her close, rocking her as if she were a small child again while Ginny haltingly told her what had happened.

Ann had left the bedroom door ajar and Saul hovered on the threshold, wacthing the two of them silently. The low-voiced conversation between them seemed to be of the all-men-are-bastards variety, and he felt unwanted and unneeded. He wondered if he should just slip quietly away. But he knew he wouldn't see Ginny again before her trip to the States, and he couldn't leave without talking to her. He cleared his throat to gain their attention, then again more loudly. Ann looked up at him impatiently.

'She'll be fine now,' she told him shortly.

'Ginny?' Saul said quietly, ignoring Ann. Ginny wiped her eyes and stood up, clutching her dressing-gown closely around her body. 'I have to go now.'

'Yes, I remember.' She nodded; he'd told her of the forthcoming training exercises while they were in the pub earlier – a lifetime ago it seemed to her.

She managed a weak smile and accompanied him to the door.

'I'm sorry, I never thanked you properly for what you did,' she said. 'I really am grateful. And I hope your arm will soon be better,' she added politely – as if talking to a stranger, Saul thought, someone who had bruised himself slightly while helping her to pick up something she had dropped. His perception was spot-on; unfortunately he didn't follow the thought through to its natural conclusion and realize she simply wasn't capable of dealing with any more emotional issues.

'Ginny, darling, I meant what I said, about marriage . . .' he began urgently.

'No, I don't want to listen.' She shook her head violently.

'Don't you know how special – ?' he tried again. 'No!'

'I love you; I want us to be married. Don't you believe I want you?' he asked, and she paused.

'Yes, I believe you want me. In bed. So did those three pigs who attacked me earlier,' she said distastefully, and he flinched.

344

'Ginny! Please don't bracket me with them. I want more than that, much more. Why won't you believe me?'

'Oh, I believe you. I also believe you would say anything, even propose marriage, to stop me going to the States with Ace Delaney,' she said flatly.

'I see.' Saul tried not to show how hurt he was, and studied her thoughtfully for a moment. She looked pale and strained; perhaps a change of scene would help her recover from the assault. 'Then go to America, with my blessing . . .'

'I don't want your blessing. Nor do I need your permission!' she told him.

'I know,' he said quickly. 'Listen, please. Go — enjoy yourself. And I'll be waiting for you. I'll propose again when you return . . .'

'I still won't believe you,' she interrupted. 'You just don't understand, do you? I *did* believe you, when you came here with your apologies and your flowers and your chocolates and that damned watch! And your lies! All you wanted then was to get me into bed – how can I ever trust a word you say?' she demanded. Saul closed his eyes wearily; there was no answer to that. He was guilty as charged. He opened his eyes and gazed at her, reached out to caress her cheek, but let his hand drop when she visibly flinched away.

'Would I have come rushing to your defence tonight if I didn't care about you?' he asked intently. 'Surely I get some Brownie points for that?' He tried to smile.

Ginny studied him for a moment, then regretfully shook her head.

'Not really, no. You'd have done the same for any woman in trouble, wouldn't you?' she asked thoughtfully.

'I suppose I would, yes,' Saul agreed. 'So I'm not a complete bastard, then?'

'Goodbye, Saul.'

'Goodnight.' He didn't like the finality of that goodbye. 'If you need help while I'm away –' he turned back as it suddenly occurred to him she might be reluctant to venture out alone, especially at night '– call Nick.'

'That won't be necessary. Anyway, I'm sure he'll be too busy looking after Melissa,' she said, and closed the door.

CHAPTER 17

Nick would have loved to have the opportunity of looking after Melissa; unfortunately, he couldn't find her. He had, reluctantly, left her alone all day, knowing that if this migraine followed the pattern of those she had suffered in the past, she would need the whole day to recover physically from the headache and nausea. Consequently, it was early evening before he returned to Bellwood.

'She's not here, Nick,' Rose told him, eyeing him rather coldly. 'She borrowed my car and left about an hour ago.'

'To go where?'

'I have no idea; she didn't want to talk. Too upset, I expect,' she added frostily. Nick ignored that.

'Where's Suzy?' he asked next.

'I imagine she's still over at Brook Farm with her grandfather. Unless Melissa has already picked her up,' she said.

Nick bit back words of recrimination; after all, it was hardly surprising that his mother-in-law was feeling distinctly hostile towards him, but surely she

347

must have realized it would be better to persuade Melissa to stay at Bellwood rather than let her leave in her present fragile state? She was hardly fit to drive, not physically nor emotionally.

He turned away wordlessly and climbed back into his car, using his mobile to phone Daniel Farrell at Brook Farm.

'She was here, yes, to collect Suzy, but she's left,' Daniel told him, and his tone of voice indicated clearly that he had heard Melissa's version of events.

'Didn't you ask her where she was going?' Nick tried to ask evenly.

'No, I did not,' Daniel bit out, and Nick knew he wouldn't tell him even if he knew. 'I'd like an explanation, Nick,' he said sternly.

'After I've found Melissa,' Nick said, matching one curt tone with another, and quickly disconnected.

After a moment's thought, he headed back home; it was after Suzy's bedtime and he hoped to find them both there, but the house was empty and there was no message on the answer machine. Where was she? If she wanted to be alone, to think, why take Suzy? He fought panic as he went to check their passports, and relaxed slightly when he found them; at least she hadn't fled the country, he thought, and tried to take comfort from that. Strangely, Kit's passport was there also, but he shrugged that aside. Where was Melissa?

He sat down and began phoning around, forcing himself to sound casual and relaxed as he asked time and again if Melissa had popped in. The answer was always no, the denials sounding truthful and even puzzled, followed by concerned queries regarding the car accident. Clearly everyone he contacted expected her to be at home recuperating, not out visiting friends.

It was getting late; Suzy would be tired and fretful . . . where the hell was she? Unable to just sit and wait any longer, he picked up his car keys and left. He drove first to Brook Farm and then to Bellwood, figuring that even if she had returned to either parent they probably wouldn't have bothered letting him know.

Jack was arriving at Bellwood, with Kit, just as Nick was leaving, and they almost collided in the driveway. Nick braked and reversed until he was level with Jack.

'Melissa didn't show up at Wimbledon, did she?' It was hardly likely, especially as she had Suzy with her, but he was clutching at straws now.

'No. Isn't she at home resting?' Jack asked, puzzled, for Daniel had obviously kept silent when he had collected Kit.

'No. You're not the only one with a runaway wife,' Nick told him, and put his foot down on the accelerator, spurting gravel beneath his wheels as he drove away. Where could she be?

He was seriously worried, and becoming more so with every minute that passed. He hoped she was staying away to punish him, purposely making him worry, but he feared it was much more than that. He should have explained more that morning; hell, she might even be thinking he had been carrying on an affair all these years.

'I know where Lissa is,' Kit piped up from the back seat.

'You do?' Jack asked, as he unbuckled her from the child's seat and carried her indoors. 'Oh, hi, Mum,' he greeted Rose, who'd come hurrying to greet them; it was way past Kit's bedtime, too. 'What's going on between Nick and Melissa?' he asked.

'Nothing good, I'm afraid,' she said vaguely, pointing meaningfully at Kit, with her too-sharp hearing and unfortunate tendency to remember what she shouldn't. Rose sometimes thought she could spend the rest of her life instilling phrases like 'please' and 'thank you' into her grandchildren, yet just one utterance of a swear word was apparently imprinted in their minds for ever! 'I'll tell you later. Not that I know very much,' she added. 'Come on, darling, supper and then bed,' she said to Kit.

'Just a minute.' Jack stopped her. 'Nick said Melissa's gone missing – is that true?'

'Yes, apparently she's discovered that Nick has another child,' she said quietly. 'I expect that's what caused the migraine.'

'I'm not surprised! My God . . . Kit, darling, you said you knew where Lissa was going. Did she tell you?'

'No. She told Suzy they were going to see the twins. When can I see the twins?' she demanded, but received no answer. Jack and Rose stared at each other in dismay.

'My God, she's gone to Ace,' Jack said slowly.

'No.' Rose shook her head in denial.

'She turned to him before, when she had pro-

350

blems with Nick,' Jack reminded her. 'Can you think of a more effective way of hitting back at Nick?'

'Well, no, but that was before she was married. Before Ace was married,' Rose demurred. 'Oh, dear,' she said, rather helplessly. 'Should we tell Nick, do you think?' she ventured.

'No,' Jack said definitely. 'It's hardly likely to help matters, is it?'

'No, you're right,' she agreed, and sighed heavily. Then she forced a smile for Kit, belatedly hoping she hadn't understood the discussion going on. 'I've got a surprise for your supper,' she told her brightly, taking her hand and leading her off towards the kitchen. 'Have you eaten?' she asked Jack.

'Yes, thanks. I just want to take a shower and then I'll tuck her in and read her a story,' Jack said, heading for the stairs. 'It's okay, I'll get that,' he called to Rose, retracing his steps to answer the phone.

It was Lisa, calling from San Francisco. She had switched on the TV coverage of Wimbledon and heard that Jack and Melissa had withdrawn from the mixed doubles after a car accident. Her heart hammering with dread, she had dialled Bellwood immediately.

'Jack!' She was so relieved to hear his voice. 'Are you okay?'

'I'm fine.'

'What's this about a car smash? You should have called me,' she said reproachfully.

'I've been busy,' he retorted; he'd had a long day.

'If you were that concerned about the family you would be here, and we wouldn't have to phone California every time something happened.'

'Sorry, I didn't mean to snap. I was worried; all I heard was that you had pulled out of the mixed doubles.'

'Yeah, well, it was Melissa who had the prang. She's okay, though,' he added, but rather doubtfully.

'You don't sound too sure,' she said.

'No, well, there's a bit of a problem between her and Nick; she crashed the car because she was upset about something he's done.'

'Really? I thought their marriage was rock-solid.'

'Is anyone's?' Jack shot back, not liking her tone, which smacked more of curiosity than concern.

'Perhaps not,' she conceded. 'Jack, I've been thinking I might come home,' she said, rather tentatively; she had been on tenterhooks, wondering what, if anything, Ace might have told him.

'I thought you were happier in San Francisco,' he hedged, thinking that this was not a good time for her to return. His mother was here, looking after Kit, and now there was a possibility that Melissa and Suzy might be staying for a while – not a state of affairs that would please his wife.

'Not really. It's lovely to spend time with my parents and Hal, but I don't belong here any more,' she said. There was a long pause.

'That isn't a good enough reason to come back,' Jack said, but quite gently.

'I know that. But I miss you. And Kit. Can I

come home?' she asked, in a forlorn-sounding whisper.

'Only if you think you can be happy here. It's not fair to Kit to keep disrupting her life.' Or to me, he thought. 'If you're not coming back to live, I'm going to ask Mum to move in permanently,' he added.

Oh, God, he's got it all worked out, Lisa thought, panicking. 'I know I've behaved badly, but I really do want to come home,' she said earnestly. There was another long pause; Lisa bit her lower lip until she tasted blood.

'Let me know which flight you'll be on and Kit and I'll come to meet you,' Jack said finally, and she expelled a pent-up breath of relief.

'I love you, both of you. Give Kit a kiss from me and tell her I'll see her soon.'

'Sure,' Jack agreed, although he had no intention of doing so, lest she change her mind again and unsettle the child. Kit was happy with her grand-parents, aunt and cousin around, and didn't seem to miss her mother very much. Or was that wishful thinking on his part? Jack wondered as he replaced the receiver. Life had certainly been on a more even keel during Lisa's absence. He might have known it was all too good to last; only the problem wasn't with Lisa but with Nick – just what the hell had been going on there?

Melissa hadn't consciously set out to worry or hurt Nick by disappearing, and didn't examine her reasons for taking Suzy to London, to Ace. She didn't even think of it in that way – of going to Ace, her ex-lover and a man Nick disliked; she had just decided to go and talk to Alexa, despite the fact that they weren't exactly close friends.

'Melissa! Are you all right? No, I can see you're not,' Alexa immediately answered her own question. 'You should be in bed, but come on in. Give Suzy to me,' she urged, and promptly handed her over to Ace. 'Take her upstairs, Nanny's reading to the twins,' she told him. Ace raised his eyebrows but did as she asked, gratefully and quickly passing Suzy over to the nanny. He was fond of Kit Farrell, his goddaughter, but Suzy Lennox's clear grey eyes studied him as warily, and with much the same hostility as those of her father. It was as if she had inherited Nick's dislike and mistrust!

He returned downstairs to catch the end of Melissa's outpouring of jealousy and fury. His black brows shot up once more.

'Mr Whiter-than-white has screwed up?' he asked incredulously.

'Shut up,' his wife advised him tersely, sensing amusement was not far below the surface. 'Unless you can think of something useful to say,' she added sternly. He grimaced and grinned.

'Okay, sorry.' He moved over to Melissa and gave her a quick hug. 'I missed part of it – you say you discovered the woman and her kid living in your flat?'

'Yes,' Melissa sniffed.

'How old is the boy?'

'I don't know – sixteen or seventeen,' she guessed. 'The old bag said she knew Nick a long time ago in Belfast.'

'When he was in the Army?'

'I suppose so.' She shrugged.

'Long before he met you, then?'

'What does that have to do with it?' Melissa demanded crossly. 'He should have told me! How could he let them move into our flat?' she raged, becoming incensed again at the very thought.

'It could be worse,' Ace commented.

'How?' she glowered at him.

'It was obviously only a temporary measure. If he'd intended maintaining a second family in secret, he'd have housed them somewhere you'd never find them,' he pointed out. 'What does he have to say for himself?'

'I don't know; he tried to explain this morning, but I wouldn't listen,' she admitted, then got to her feet. 'Thanks for listening.'

'Where are you going? You ought to be resting,' Alexa said anxiously; Melissa looked so pale, and was far too agitated to be driving around.

'I'm going to face that . . . woman,' Melissa said determinedly. 'I ran away yesterday, but now she and her bastard are going to do some running! Clear back to Belfast!'

'Melissa . . .' Alexa began to protest, but Ace's eyes glinted with approval.

'Good girl. Would you like me to come with you?'

'No, thanks. But . . . can I leave Suzy with you for a while?' She looked at Alexa.

'Of course. She'd better stay overnight. And you, too,' she added. 'Come back here when you've . . . er . . . sorted things out,' she suggested.

'Thanks, I will.' Melissa smiled briefly, then

turned and hurried out, eager for battle. Ace followed her out to her car.

'Are you sure you don't want me to come along?' he asked, intrigued to see this other woman. 'I'm pretty good in a fight.' He grinned at her.

'I know you are,' she agreed drily, recalling the fight he had once had with Nick. Tempted as she was to let him loose on the bag-and-the-bastard – as she now linked them together in her mind – even she wasn't so furiously out of control as to risk it. 'But, no, thanks.' She declined his offer. 'This is my battle,' she said, her chin jutting determinedly.

Ace's grin broadened; even without seeing the opposition, his money was on Melissa!

Melissa arrived at the flat ready to eject the usurpers, using physical force if necessary, but realized as soon as she stepped inside that it was empty. She walked slowly from room to room; everything was neat and tidy, even neater and tidier than usual, she was forced to admit.

There was no visible sign that any cuckoos had lodged here; she even began to wonder if she could have imagined it – if it had all been part of a migraine-induced nightmare. God, that migraine! She'd been free of them for so long, she had almost forgotten how awful they were! She put a hand to her head at the thought; dashing around, consumed with anger, had increased the throbbing, and she went to fetch a glass of cold water, forcing herself to calm down, to breathe evenly and deeply.

Now that there was no battle to be fought, she felt drained of energy and deathly tired. She knew she

needed to rest and wandered into the bedroom . . .
the room the old bag had walked out of wearing only
a dressing-gown . . . her and Nick's bedroom . . . A
sharp stab of pain accompanied the thought and she
winced, then returned quickly to the drawing-room
and curled up on the sofa. She would never sleep in
that bed again. Had Nick . . . ? With that . . . that
mother of his son? She knew him before I did, slept
with him, bore his child . . .

The images she conjured up were unbearable,
and she drank more water, found the painkillers
she had been prescribed and swallowed two, then
lay down and closed her eyes. As soon as the pain
had subsided a little she would leave. She didn't
care if she never saw the place again. Tears pricked
at her eyes as she recalled how happy she and Nick
had been here, both before their marriage and
after, only moving to Nine Elms after Suzy's
birth. Nick wanted more children, she knew
that, yet she had always refused. More tears
threatened and she blinked furiously, turning her
face into the cushion and concentrating on her deep
breathing execises.

Alexa finally persuaded Ace he should phone Jack
and tell him where Melissa had gone. Jack, after
careful deliberation and consultation with both his
parents, phoned Nick on his mobile and passed on
the information.

It was almost midnight when Nick pulled up
outside the block of flats, and he breathed a sigh
of relief when he spotted Rose's car parked a few
yards away. Thank God; she was still here.

He ran up the stairs and let himself into the flat, which was in darkness. Frowning slightly at that discovery, he snapped on the light in the drawing-room and his heart skipped a beat of pleasure and relief when he saw Melissa fast asleep on the sofa. But then his heart pounded with dread when he caught sight of the bottle of painkillers.

'Oh, my God!' He bounded forward and lifted her off the sofa in one movement and began shaking her. 'Melissa!'

'What the . . . ? Get off me!' She pulled herself free and glared at him.

'I'm sorry, I didn't mean to startle you,' Nick said, feeling foolish as well as extremely relieved as he belatedly realized the bottle was almost full. For one appalling moment he had really thought . . .

'Startle me? You damn near frightened me to death!' she said crossly.

'That makes two of us,' Nick muttered, sinking abruptly down into a chair. 'God, Melissa, what are you doing to me?' he groaned. This had been the longest, most worrying night of his entire life – with the possible exception of the night Melissa had spent in labour with Suzy.

'What am I doing to *you*?' she repeated incredulously. 'I'm the one asking the questions, not you!' she yelled, too loudly, and her head began to throb anew. 'Where are the bag-and-the-bastard?' she demanded. 'Where have you hidden them? A cosy little love-nest somewhere?'

'They've returned to Dublin,' Nick told her evenly, deciding it wouldn't be wise to object to her description of Connie and Mickey. 'Sit down,

358

sweetheart, please, and let me explain.'

'I'm listening,' she said, but the accompanying glare, the belligerent stance, with her hands on her hips, warned Nick he was in for a rough time. He recognized the signals; they'd had fights before, but nothing of this magnitude had ever threatened their marriage.

Melissa's expression didn't alter or soften one iota as she listened, but some of the pain and anger abated a little when he said he hadn't known of Mickey's existence until a few weeks previously.

'Coop can attest to that – he was there when Connie turned up at the office. Apparently Lennox and Coupland were mentioned in an article she'd read about you; that's how she knew where to locate me. I hadn't seen her or spoken to her since we were both nineteen –'

'She's the same age as you? Thirty-six? She looks much older,' Melissa cut in. Nick let that pass, too. He figured she was entitled to a few snide comments. 'Why did you bring them here?' she demanded.

'I guessed they were short of cash . . .'

'Well, obviously,' she sniffed, her lip curling.

'Meaning?'

'She wants money from you!' she said impatiently. 'Why else did she turn up?'

'I've already explained that,' Nick said calmly. 'She's been very ill. If she had died there would have been no one to look after Mickey.'

'Oh, right.' Melissa evidently didn't believe a word of it, although whether it was his story or Connie's she was so contemptuous of, Nick wasn't sure. 'So, they were short of money, and you let

359

them stay here until you got the results of a DNA test, is that right?' she enquired.

'DNA test?' Nick frowned, and Melissa's gaze narrowed.

'You did insist on a test, didn't you?' she hissed, so venomously Nick briefly considered lying. But there had already been too much deception, so, rather reluctantly, he decided to tell the truth.

'No, I didn't,' he admitted.

'Oh, wonderful! Some old slag you haven't seen for years turns up on the doorstep and tells you you're the father of her loutish son – who doesn't even look like you – and you believe her? Are you that desperate for a son?'

'What?' Nick blinked; he sure as hell didn't like the direction this conversation – correction, row – was going. 'Of course not. I'm afraid I don't even like the boy. But why should I doubt that he's mine? If Connie had wanted money, she could have been claiming child support instead of struggling alone for the past sixteen years,' he pointed out – quite reasonably, he thought. Melissa evidently didn't agree.

'Oh, isn't she wonderful?' she spat. 'Let's write to the Pope and nominate her for sainthood, shall we? Pregnant and unmarried at nineteen and she struggled all alone . . .' she paused, then screamed at Nick, 'The whole world knows that when *I* was nineteen and pregnant with your child I took the easy way out and killed it!'

'Melissa!' Nick shot out of his chair and tried to pull her into his arms, but she struggled so violently he was afraid she would hurt herself, so he stepped back. 'I never once made any comparison between the two of you,' he told her urgently. 'The similar dilemma you both faced never once crossed my mind,' he said truthfully.

'Huh! You've never forgiven me for having the abortion!' she said wildly. 'It's always there between us.'

'Not true,' Nick said firmly. 'It's you who can't let go of it, not me,' he told her quietly. 'Sure, I was angry and hurt at the time, I'm not going to deny that, but I forgave you a long time ago, and I understood why you felt you had no other choice. I never stopped loving you.'

'I don't believe you. You're always going on about having more children – well, now you have another one! *If* she's telling the truth. But you're so willing to believe her, aren't you? You've finally got the son you wanted!'

'Don't you dare imply I have ever felt disappointed that our child is a daughter,' Nick warned. He was prepared to take criticism of his recent behaviour as a husband, but not as a father. 'I was there when Suzy was born, and I have loved her and looked after her every day of her life. Now, you listen to me. If it makes you happy –'

'Happy?' she interrupted scornfully.

'If it makes you less angry,' he amended, 'I'll insist on a paternity test – all right? And if I am Mickey's father, then I'll pay my dues. Not because I love him, or because I love Connie, but because I despise men who walk away from their families. I do *not* run away from my responsibilities. I am not asking you to adopt him, or even speak to him, just to accept that I have to make financial provision for him. Is that clear?' he demanded.

Melissa stared at him, then shrugged slightly and walked away from him. She went and stared out of the window for a few moments, collecting her thoughts. Nick watched her warily, and tensed when she swung around to confront him, wondering what was coming next.

'Did you love her?' she asked, quite calmly.

'You were only nine years old when –'

'Did you love her?' she asked again, sharply this time, and he sighed.

'I was in love with her, yes,' he admitted. 'But it wasn't real love or I'd have fought for her, instead of caving in to my CO's demands. He made it clear to me that my career was on the line, and that was more important to me than Connie.' He paused. 'I had to fight for you – remember?' he asked softly. 'Your father thought I was too old for you and your brother thought I would distract you from your tennis . . . they didn't deter me, nor did your career, which took you to a different country almost every week. Nor . . .' He hesitated briefly, then continued, 'Nor did the abortion. I still loved you and wanted to marry you,' he finished quietly.

Melissa digested all that in silence for several minutes.

'If you'd known she was pregnant . . . would you have married her?' she asked painfully.

'I wouldn't have wanted to marry her, but I suppose I might have felt compelled to offer,' he admitted reluctantly. 'But it would have been a huge

362

mistake. And as soon as I had met you I'd have realized you were the one for me.'

'If you'd married her, you might never have met me,' Melissa said slowly.

'Of course I would.' Nick smiled slightly. 'How could I possibly have gone through life without meeting and loving you?' he asked simply.

Melissa bit her lower lip.

'Sweetheart, I am so sorry I didn't tell you as soon as Connie came to see me. I was . . .' He hesitated. 'I told myself it wouldn't be fair, that you were too busy, too happy about taking part in Wimbledon again for me to trouble you with my problem, but the real reason I didn't pluck up courage to tell you was that I was terrified of losing you,' he confessed. 'I was going out of my mind this evening, wondering where you had gone, if you would come back. Don't leave me,' he pleaded.

It seemed to him that an eternity passed before Melissa walked over to him and into his open arms. He held her close, unspeaking, and Melissa rested her cheek against his chest, her arms wrapped around his waist.

'Let's leave any more talking until tomorrow and get some rest,' Nick suggested finally. 'I think we both need it.'

'Yes,' Melissa was drooping with exhaustion. 'But not here. I'm not sleeping in that bed ever again,' she said mulishly. 'The old bag slept in it.'

'Yes, but not with me.' Nick sighed. 'I'm sorry; I suppose I should have simply paid her hotel bills, but she needed peace and quiet. She's still recovering from a hysterectomy.'

'Oh, I bet that spoiled the reunion!' Melissa said tartly. Nick's arms tightened almost painfully around her.

'Stop it. I love you – only you. I'm desperately sorry that you're upset, and I understand that, but you must believe that there is nothing going on between Connie and me. There was no reunion, just talk about Mickey's future. You do accept that I have to help the boy?'

'I suppose so. *If* he's your son,' Melissa said stubbornly.

'If,' Nick agreed, knowing he would have to insult Connie by insisting on a DNA test. He didn't like it, but he'd do it. 'Now, can we get some rest? You don't really want to wake Suzy now to drive home, do you?' he asked, naturally assuming Suzy was asleep in the bedroom.

'She's not here – I left her with Alexa,' Melissa told him.

'I see,' Nick said thoughtfully. 'You really did come here to do battle, didn't you? What had you in mind – chucking them both bodily out into the street?' he asked curiously. Now that the worst was over, he was almost enjoying his wife's jealousy. Almost.

'If necessary, yes,' she said firmly. Nick smiled at her lovingly.

'I adore you, Mrs Lennox. And I'm glad you're on my side – most of the time.'

'I'm on your side *all* the time,' Melissa corrected. 'You wouldn't be the man you are if you'd turned the bag-and-the-bastard away,' she told him, finally conceding that he might have acted properly. There

364

had been much less venom in that 'bag-and-the-bastard', but Nick wondered how many years would pass before she deigned to use their names. So long as those years were spent with him, he didn't really care, he decided.

'Can we get some rest, please?' he asked again. 'I'll turn the mattress over,' he offered. 'Or we can squeeze into the spare,' he suggested hopefully.

Melissa considered that briefly, but found she didn't want to use a bed the lout had slept in, either. 'No,' she said, and pointed to the sofa, which folded down into a double bed in case of extra guests. 'This will do for tonight,' she said, stifling a yawn. 'Tomorrow I'm buying new beds. I wonder how much it would cost to fumigate the place?' she mused. Nick raised his eyes skywards, but made no objection, too relieved he wasn't being kicked out to sleep in his car!

While he fetched pillows and duvets from the bedroom Melissa made a brief call to her parents, just to reassure them that she was fine, and with Nick. Fortunately for Nick, she was too exhausted for it to occur to her that the bedding might be equally contaminated by the bag-and-the-bastard, and she undressed quickly and fell asleep almost immediately.

Nick lay on his side, watching her, fighting his own need for sleep. He felt as if a huge burden had been lifted from his shoulders. Sure, he was probably in for a lot more earache on the subject, he decided ruefully, but he could cope with that.

He bent his head and gently kissed her, careful

not to wake her, then he lay back and felt his body and mind slowly relaxing into slumber. The bag-and-the-bastard; he knew he shouldn't find it funny, but he did, and a broad grin curved his mouth as he finally fell asleep.

CHAPTER 18

Ginny awoke slowly, reluctantly, unwilling to face the day, but it was a few moments before she remembered the events of the night before and she sat up, fighting waves of nausea. She could almost feel the rough groping . . . ugh! Retching, she scrambled out of bed and ran to the bathroom, hanging onto the wash basin and splashing cold water onto her face. Illogically, it wasn't just the violence inflicted on her that upset her; she had been deeply affected by Saul's fury, the sickening thud of his fists on human flesh . . .

'Ginny? Are you all right?' Ann hovered anxiously in the doorway.

'Oh, Mum, I'd forgotten you were here,' Ginny said, the tone of her voice indicating that she wasn't exactly thrilled by her presence.

Ann sighed heavily. She had passed what remained of the night on Ginny's sofa, kept awake by both physical discomfort and pangs of conscience. Confession time, she decided unhappily.

'I've made some toast and coffee. Come and have some breakfast; I want to talk to you.'

'Now?' Ginny asked reluctantly.

'Yes,' Ann said firmly. Ginny slowly followed her back into the kitchen and poured herself a glass of orange juice from the fridge.

'Did I hear Saul correctly last night when he was leaving? He's asked you to marry him?'

'Yes, I suppose so,' Ginny said listlessly.

'You suppose so? Aren't you sure?' Ann's eyebrows rose.

'No, I'm not. He's such a good liar. I don't know if he meant it,' Ginny said bitterly.

'But if he did mean it? Would you accept?' Ann asked. Ginny daydreamed happily for a moment, then reluctantly shook her head.

'I can't trust him,' she said sadly.

'But you love him?' Ann persisted.

'I . . . yes!' Ginny burst out. 'And I shouldn't; that's why I'm going to California, to get away from him. You don't know how he's treated me,' she said miserably.

'I might not know the exact details, but I imagine he's treated you as he would me,' Ann said calmly. 'He's let his dislike of me colour his judgement, or I should say he *did* let his dislike of me obscure his judgement. Unless I'm very much mistaken, he has quickly realized that you are not at all like me. You see, Ginny, Saul Lancaster has very good reasons for being, well, wary.'

'What reasons?' Ginny almost sneered; nothing excused his treating her as if she were a whore.

'This is very difficult for me,' Ann said haltingly, 'so please remember that I'm telling you only so you can view Saul's behaviour in a different light. I

368

think your future happiness lies with him, Ginny, so don't let past mistakes – mine or, more recently, his – get in the way of that. Or your hurt pride,' she added, then fell silent.

'What are you trying to tell me?' Ginny asked, almost fearfully; she had a feeling she didn't want to hear it.

'You remember I mentioned a man called Bill Taggart?' Ann said hesitantly.

'Yes, you told me he committed suicide, and you thought Saul might blame you for it. But it wasn't your fault,' Ginny said slowly.

'Yes, well, I'm afraid I was to blame . . . I didn't tell you the whole truth about that, Ginny.'

'Go on,' Ginny urged, when she stopped speaking. Ann drew a deep breath.

'Bill and I were having an affair,' she said quickly. 'We were . . . caught . . . and I panicked, claimed Bill had attacked me –'

'You . . .' Ginny frowned down at her coffee cup. 'You cheated on Daddy,' she said finally, to Ann's amazement, but to Ginny that somehow seemed more important than the death, years before, of a man she had never met.

'Well, yes, I did,' Ann admitted. 'I loved your father, Ginny, but I craved excitement occasionally. I couldn't help myself,' she added, and Ginny glared at her.

'You hurt Daddy and drove a man to suicide just because you craved excitement!' Ginny's voice rose. 'And Saul knew about this, did he?'

'Not at the time, no. No one did. Well, maybe Alice Lancaster guessed – as I told you before, she and Bill's wife were good friends.' Ann paused, wished she still smoked, then took a gulp of strong coffee instead. 'Years after Bill died,' she continued shakily, 'Saul caught me . . . with another man,' she confessed in a whisper. Ginny's eyes were wide with disbelief – and contempt, Ann thought, near to tears. 'It was at a party. Later, I saw him talking to your father and, well, I went a little crazy, I think. I told Saul that if he didn't keep his mouth shut about what he'd seen, I would –' She stopped and licked her parched lips.

'Go on,' Ginny said tersely.

'I threatened to claim he had raped me. I wouldn't have done it,' she went on quickly, 'but Saul obviously believed I would – poor boy, he must have been terrified. He was barely out of school . . .'

'So that's why he hates you so much,' Ginny whispered. 'It's nothing to do with your affair with his father.'

'That's finished now,' Ann said quickly, but Ginny was no longer listening to her. It was hardly surprising that Saul had been prepared to believe the worst, especially after Jamie had confirmed his suspicions. She sighed and frowned, feeling he should have instinctively known she wasn't a money-grabbing trollop, despite his opinion of her mother. That opinion, admittedly, was based on fact, but she still felt that while what she had just learned explained his attitude, it didn't excuse it.

'Ginny? Please don't hate me,' Ann pleaded miserably. 'I never wanted you to know all this; I've only told you now to help you and Saul.'

Ginny just looked at her. Does she expect me to

thank her? she thought incredulously.

Ann waited in vain for a response, then sighed and got slowly to her feet. 'I expect you'd like me to leave.' She waited again for a reply, but none was forthcoming. 'I'm going to Italy, if I can reschedule my flight. When are you leaving for California?'

'Next Tuesday,' Ginny replied.

'Then I won't see you until you return. I hope you enjoy yourself,' she paused. 'And I hope we can be friends again,' she added softly. Ginny shrugged slightly; Ann hesitated, then kissed her cheek before walking slowly from the flat.

Ginny was still sitting over cold coffee and toast when the phone rang half an hour later. It was Saul, already in Wales, keeping an entire platoon waiting in an Army truck while he nipped into a call box.

'Ginny. I had to phone – how are you?'

'Okay,' she said listlessly, then, 'How's the arm?'

'A bit stiff; I've a couple of stitches in it now. Listen, darling, I know you need time, and I'll wait for as long as it takes. I meant what I said last night; I love you and I want to marry you, more than anything else. Will you think about that, please? And will you let me know when you're coming back from the States?'

'I . . . I'm not sure,' she said hesitantly.

'Please,' he said urgently. 'Let me meet your flight.'

'I don't know. Maybe,' she said, and hung up. She really didn't want to speak to him, didn't know what to say, or even how she felt about him.

Saul had to be content with that 'maybe'. He was clinging desperately to the memory of the Saturday

371

they had spent together – at his parents' house, of all places. He had spent that day and night falling deeply and irrevocably in love, and he was almost sure it had been the same for her. She had been passionate and responsive in bed, but inexperienced, untutored, obviously not in the habit of indulging in casual sex. He hoped.

When Nick and Melissa called at Eaton Square to collect Suzy, Ace didn't even try to suppress a smirk.

'I thought I was the reprobate around here,' he said mockingly to Nick. 'At least I haven't left a trail of illegitimate brats in my wake!'

'None you know of, Delaney,' Nick retorted grimly, adding 'yet,' which wiped the smile off Ace's face.

Melissa drove her mother's car back to Bellwood, with Nick following behind in his Jag.

'Are you all right?' Rose asked Melissa anxiously, glancing over to where Nick was waiting in his car.

'Yes, I think so.' Melissa hugged her. 'We'll see you soon. Thanks for looking after me, and for the loan of the car.'

'You're welcome.' Rose returned the hug. 'By the way – Lisa's coming home.'

'Is she, now?' Melissa said thoughtfully, then she walked over and climbed into Nick's car, and told him the news.

'That's good. Isn't it?' he asked, sensing her doubt.

'I'm not sure. She might just want Kit,' Melissa said slowly.

'That reminds me – did you know we've got Kit's passport at our place? You're looking shifty,' he added accusingly.

'Mmm, Ace left it with me. Lisa was intending getting a divorce and filing for custody in California, so Ace asked me to hang onto Kit's passport. Please don't say anything to Jack, though; Ace reckoned it was better if he didn't know – not while there was a chance they could patch things up. I'll have to play it by ear once she arrives.'

'Why didn't you mention this before?' Nick asked.

'Oh, you're the only allowed to have secrets, are you?' Melissa snapped, then she grinned. 'Sorry, couldn't resist that. I didn't tell you because . . . it was demeaning for Jack,' she explained slowly.

'I understand.' Nick nodded, remembering the day Ace had called at Nine Elms and Melissa had been vague about the reason for his visit . . . He smiled and shook his head slightly – would he ever totally conquer his jealousy of her past relationship with Ace?

When they arrived at Nine Elms, Melissa clambered slowly out of the car and looked around her appreciatively, feeling as if she had just returned after a long absence.

'It's good to be home.' She smiled at Nick, and he held her tightly.

Later, Melissa decided to remove Kit's passport from its present somewhat obvious hiding place; she couldn't quite banish an absurd – she hoped – picture of Lisa creeping around the house searching for it. She took it upstairs to her bedroom, removed the top tray of her jewellery box to hide it underneath . . . and gasped. There lay the bracelet she had feared she had lost – the one Nick had given her on the day of Suzy's birth; the one she had hoped to find at the flat.

'Something wrong?' Nick came up behind her, resting his hands lightly on her shoulder.

'No.' She tilted her head back to look at him. 'This is why I went to the flat – I thought I'd lost it.'

'And I thought I'd lost you.' Nick bent and dropped a kiss on the nape of her neck. 'Have you forgiven me?'

'For what? For being careless when you slept with another woman seventeen years ago? For facing up to your responsibilities?' Melissa smiled slightly. 'Yes, I forgive you,' she said, pulling his head down to hers for a long, healing kiss. 'But I'm still buying new beds for the flat,' she added firmly.

Lisa decided against telling Jack her time of arrival, and took a cab from Heathrow early on Monday evening. She hadn't taken the earliest available flight, hoping Ace would have left England before she returned.

The drive seemed to take for ever; she was keyed-up, excited and very, very nervous of meeting Jack – as if it were their first date.

'Are you sure this is the place?' The cab driver queried, guessing from her American accent that she was a tourist. Bellwood looked like a top-class hotel but there was no signboard proclaiming it to be so.

'I'm sure. I live here,' she told him, and hoped

desperately that was still true.

'Yeah? Great place to live,' he enthused. 'I wouldn't like the job of cleaning all those window panes, though!' He grinned. Lisa smiled and handed him a huge tip on top of the fare.

She left her suitcases on the drive and approached the front door timidly, even wondered if she ought to knock . . . Summoning up all her courage, she squared her shoulders and walked inside. The first person she saw was her mother-in-law.

'Lisa!' Rose recovered from her surprise quickly and moved to kiss her cheek. 'We'd have met you at the airport if you'd called. Jack's upstairs putting Kit to bed. I'm so glad you're back. I really must get home; I have to . . .' Her mind went blank; she just knew she ought to leave. 'But first I must get over to Nine Elms and help Melissa with Suzy,' she was inspired to say. 'She's still not feeling on top form after the car accident,' she explained, rather breathlessly.

'Tell her I'll call her tomorrow.' Lisa forced a smile, hoping she would still be here then.

Her heart was pounding painfully as she slowly mounted the stairs; she was deathly afraid of what might happen in the next few minutes. What if Ace had told Jack what she had done? Or what if Jack had simply decided he and Kit were happier without her? She couldn't really blame him if he had; she'd been irritable with both of them for months . . .

She paused outside Kit's open bedroom door, didn't even notice the fairy woodland scene Ginny had created, took a deep breath and walked in. Kit was asleep, looking utterly adorable, with her thick black lashes fanning her creamy cheeks, a fluffy white rabbit clutched firmly in her little hands.

Jack had closed the book he had been reading and was waiting for a few minutes to be sure she had settled for the night before he left her. He hadn't registered Lisa's presence. She was glad of the respite and just gazed at him, wanting to smooth back a lock of dark blond hair that had flopped forward onto his forehead. What an idiot I've been, she thought wretchedly; what girl could possibly have a better husband or father for her child?

Finally Jack rose from his chair beside the bed and caught sight of his wife. A flash of pleasure lit his hazel eyes, then his expression became guarded.

'I don't want to wake her,' Lisa said softly. Jack nodded and walked towards her. Lisa backed out of the room, holding his gaze. 'I'm so sorry,' she began, tears welling.

'Shush, don't cry.' Jack put his arms around her and she leaned against him.

'I've been such a bitch. I didn't even know why I was behaving badly, but I worked it out on the flight.' She paused and wiped her cheeks. 'I think I've been jealous and resentful of Melissa – this is her home, she grew up here. The villagers love her and they're so proud of her – I'm still "the American girl Jack Farrell married". Melissa was the Wimbledon Champion and a much better player than I ever was. I never beat her, not even at the start of her career, when I'd already been on the tour for a couple of years. She broke my brother's heart and married Nick, and they are so crazy about each other . . . but then, when you said they were having trouble, I suddenly stopped resenting her . . . Am I making sense?' she asked, hiccuping.

'Sort of. I suppose there are a lot of Farrells around here. But you're one, too,' he told her. 'I know you're a city girl at heart – would you be happier if we moved to London?' he asked.

'Your family has lived here for centuries,' she said.

'So?' Jack asked simply. Lisa wondered why she wasn't jumping at his offer.

'But you love it here. So does Kit,' she said slowly. 'You don't want to sell up, do you?'

'Well, no, but I guess Melissa would probably buy me out,' he said, a little wary of bringing his sister back into the conversation. 'The place would still be in the family. But it is only a house; I'm more concerned with having a home for the three of us.'

'Really?' Lisa's lower lip trembled. 'I want to come back; I've wanted to for weeks. I was too stubborn . . .' Or feeling too guilty . . . She took a deep breath. 'Jack, I have to tell you . . .' she began.

'No,' he said roughly, his arms tightening around her. 'If you had a fling with another man in San Francisco I don't want to know about it!' Lisa stared up at him, at the misery in his face, and knew Ace had been right. What was the point in easing her conscience if it only served to hurt Jack?

'No, nothing like that,' she denied quickly. 'It wasn't important; it can wait. Jack . . . ?' Suddenly weak with lust and longing, she leaned against him. 'Can we go to bed? Please?' she asked huskily. Jack finally relaxed and nuzzled her neck.

'That's the nicest thing you've said to me for

months!' he said fervently, then took her hand in his. And, laughing and eager as teenagers, they raced towards their bedroom.

Ginny travelled to California with the Delaneys the following day. Their ranch was unbelievable, with land stretching beyond the horizon and the house itself reminding Ginny of something out of an American soap opera.

As Ace had told her, there were real horses and cowboys for her to use as models for the paintings Drew wanted in his room. She took many photographs, but laughingly declined offers from the ranch-hands to pose for her. Goodness, they were a friendly bunch!

She enjoyed herself enormously, but thoughts of Saul intruded often, especially late at night when she was alone. During the day she was too busy to give serious consideration to a marriage proposal that might or might not have been sincere, but at night she tossed and turned, wondering what would happen when she returned to England.

She began to wonder just how long she would be away; the twins constantly wanted to 'help' her with her work, which put a brake on her progress, and Ace and Alexa were terrific hosts, too, treating her as a guest rather than an employee. She met many of their friends, including some Hollywood hunks from Ace's acting days. He wasn't actually doing her a good turn by introducing her to them – he thought of it more as a bad turn to Saul Lancaster!

Ginny didn't realize his motives, of course, but his plotting was to no avail. She would find herself thinking, 'Gosh, he's dishy, but . . .' or 'He's really nice, but . . .' She constantly recalled her conversation with Melissa, regarding 'nice' men, and how that would never be enough, not once she had met the one special man who made her feel truly alive, unbearably excited.

She thought often about her mother's confession – that and, to a lesser extent, Jamie's admission of deliberately misleading Saul made her understand the reasons behind Saul's hostility and mistrust, but . . . That damned word again! But. He had thought she was for sale. She still cringed whenever she thought of that. He claimed to have changed his opinion of her, of course, and perhaps he had.

He had certainly warned her about his bad intentions that Saturday at his parents' house, and had backed away at first, admitting that he had taken her there solely to seduce her. She acknowledged, if only to herself, that she was in love with Saul Lancaster, but . . . God, that had to be the vilest word in the English language! That and the phrase 'if only'. If only they had met as strangers. If only her mother hadn't been his father's mistress . . .

The weeks sped by and she was no nearer a decision about Saul. Perhaps he wouldn't propose again, she thought, and found she didn't like that idea one bit. Had she rebuffed him once too often? He could have been badly injured or even killed saving her from that attack, and her thanks had been somewhat grudging . . .

'Stay for as long as you like,' Ace told her when her work was completed. 'You've not seen much of

San Francisco yet, have you? Raul will gladly show you around!' He grinned, Raul being the ranch foreman, who was smitten with Ginny's blonde English beauty.

'Oh, stop teasing,' Ginny replied, blushing. 'He's very nice, but . . .' Oh, God, here I go again, she thought despairingly. 'Sorry, what did you say?' she asked apologetically, belatedly aware she had been daydreaming about Saul again instead of listening to Ace.

'I said, perhaps you would like to stay and keep Alexa company while I go to New York – it's the US Open at the end of the month,' he explained.

'Isn't she going with you?' Ginny asked, surprised.

'I'm only going for a couple of days this year, just to do a bit of business,' Ace said quickly, glancing over to his wife. Anaemic? Hah! He had been rather slow on the uptake, and cursed himself for that, but he had finally figured it must be something more serious. He'd practically had to beat the information from the doctor, but now he knew the truth and intended she should have the restful life she needed.

It hurt that she hadn't confided in him, but he understood her reasons. His own pre-marriage reputation as a womanizer and her own deep insecurities made her fear rejection. However, she was much better and the medication was helping her heart do its work, but he had decided a trip to New York – which was always hot and humid this time of year – was out of the question. He had some sponsors to see regarding Ella and Shanna, and he wanted to discuss their future plans with their coach, Katy Oliver, but, as he had told Ginny, he need only be away a couple of days.

'I'll talk to my boss and ask how long I can stay,' Ginny said, and phoned Jo the very next day.

'The work you did at Bellwood has been featured in several magazines,' Jo told her excitedly, 'and we've been inundated with enquries, But you stay on in California for a while if you want to,' she added quickly, anxious to be accommodating, for she and Barney would hate to lose her.

'I won't stay long; I'm feeling a bit homesick,' Ginny confessed, then, ultra-casual, asked, 'Have you seen or heard from Saul Lancaster? He'll be living in Chelsea now.'

'He hasn't called here,' Jo said slowly. Homesick? Lovesick, more like! she thought. 'His father won the by-election, though. And there was a spread in the gossip columns about his cousin's wedding.'

'Oh, right,' Ginny said uninterestedly. Life in London was evidently moving along just fine without her . . . Saul's life, too? How long could she expect him to wait?

'How long do you expect him to wait?' Melissa demanded, a couple of days later. She was calling from her home in the Napa Valley: she, Nick and Suzy were taking a break now that Saul had joined Lennox and Coupland – Lennox, Coupland and Lancaster now.

Melissa was feeling a bit miffed with Ginny. She had gone to a lot of trouble to get her work into the public eye and now she was sulking – or skulking – on Ace's ranch! And Nick and Coop were sick of

381

Saul mooning around the office. Nick had even offered to postpone their holiday so Saul could go out to California himself, but Saul had refused to do that, saying he had told Ginny he would be waiting for her to contact him when she returned.

'God, talk about a Mexican stand-off!' Melissa had exclaimed, and had decided to talk to Ginny, especially after Alexa had confided that Ginny was apparently as miserable with the situation as Saul.

'Don't you think you've punished him enough for one mistake? A big one, I admit, but still a mistake,' Melissa continued.

'I'm not staying here to punish him,' Ginny objected.

'Are you sure about that?' Melissa queried. God, if she could forgive Nick the bag-and-the-bastard, surely Ginny could forgive Saul? Especially as Ginny's ex-boyfriend and her good-time trollop of a mother were largely responsible for the misunderstanding? She said as much, though rather more tactfully, then decided she had interfered enough. 'Just trust your gut instinct,' she advised finally.

Twenty-four hours later, Ginny boarded a plane for Heathrow. She had phoned Jo, and Barney was picking her up from the airport. She had considered asking Saul, but had decided not to – mainly from vanity! The trip to California had been her first long-haul flight and she had arrived feeling – and looking – exhausted and washed out. She didn't want Saul to see her until she had rested, taken a long bath and was armoured with make-up.

The plane landed at seven-thirty a.m. UK time, and she noticed immediately a distinct chill in the air as she disembarked, She realized the eventful summer was coming to an end.

As she waited to collect her luggage she scanned the crowd for a glimpse of Barney's huge frame, then her heart skipped a beat when she spotted Saul! He had seen her, too, and smiled at her . . . politely? Yes. Not warmly, eagerly, but . . . politely, she decided with a slight pang, and gave him a cool smile in return.

'Let me take those.' Saul relieved her of her suitcases. 'Barney asked me to come in his place – he had to take Jo to the hospital late last evening,' he explained.

'Oh?' Ginny said vaguely, forgetting for a moment that Jo was due to give birth. Barney had asked him to come? Was that the only reason he was here?

'I gave him my mobile phone number; he'll ring when he has any news,' Saul continued as he began striding purposefully towards the exit.

Ginny trailed after him, hopelessly disappointed that he didn't seem pleased to see her. She'd thought, imagined – several times, actually, in great detail! – that when they met again he would sweep her into his arms and propose. He *had* said he would propose again . . .

Actually, Saul was having to fight the urge to pull her into his arms and ask, no, demand that she marry him, but he was fearful of rejection. After all, she had asked Barney to meet her, not him; she hadn't even told him she was returning to England. He stowed her bags in the car and opened the door for her.

'You're looking well,' he remarked casually. 'Had a good time?'

'Yes, thank you. How are you enjoying your new job?' she asked, just as casually.

'Fine; it feels good to be in one place.' He smiled briefly, and they set off back towards central London. The conversation became even more stilted as he drove.

'Has your arm fully healed?' Ginny asked him politely.

'Yes, no problem. How about you – any nightmares?' he asked.

'Not any more. I was jumping at shadows for a while, but I'm okay now. Being away from London helped a lot.'

'Good.' Saul nodded.

'Did you go to your cousin's wedding?' Ginny ventured, after a long silence.

'Er, no, I didn't.'

'Oh.' Another long pause. 'Jo told me your father won the by-election.'

'Yes, I think he'll do a good job.' *If* he can avoid scandal, he thought silently.

'I'm sure he will,' Ginny agreed, then she lapsed into silence.

Saul glanced at her profile; he was weighing up every word he uttered, afraid he would start demanding to know if she had been involved with another man in California – he had been haunted by the knowledge that she couldn't have been very far away from young James Calvert in Hollywood. He knew his own temper and possessive streak too well

– *and* Ginny's likely response if he started insisting she never leave him again.

They both jumped slightly when his mobile rang. Saul snatched it up.

'Yes? Oh, great! Yes, she's with me now. It's Barney,' he said briefly to Ginny as he passed the handset over.

'Barney? How's Jo?' she asked excitedly.

'Wonderful! We have a son,' he announced, sounding as triumphant as if *he* had spent the last twelve hours in labour instead of Jo. 'Almost nine pounds,' he added proudly. Ginny winced in sympathy for Jo and automatically crossed her legs.

'Congratulations! Is Jo okay?'

'Yes. She's really happy – over the moon. She's fast asleep now, poor love, but it was all worth it,' he said. Easy for you to say, Ginny thought, but she knew Jo would agree.

'Have you decided on a name yet?' she asked, for that particular argument had still been raging when she had left for California.

'Yes. Sam,' he told her. 'And we'd like you to be his godmother, Ginny.'

'Really? Oh, yes, please! When can I come and see him?' she asked eagerly.

'Now, if you're not too wiped out from the flight. As I said, Jo's asleep, but Sam's awake – he's much more alert than the other babies,' he added. Ginny grinned at that and shook her head slightly. The Ferris baby was obviously going to be a genius!

'I'll see you soon. Bye.' She turned to Saul. 'Can you drop me off at the hospital?'

'Of course,' Saul said easily. Drop her off? As in,

leave her there and go on his not-so-merry way alone? Not likely!

Ginny made no comment when Saul cut the engine and got out of the car to accompany her inside the hospital. They followed the arrows pointing the way to the maternity wing and found the waiting-room. Barney was fast asleep, his broad frame half off the rather small chair and his head tilted sideways against the adjoining seat.

'Should we wake him?' Ginny whispered. 'He looks so peaceful, but he's going to have an awful crick in his neck.'

'Leave him,' Saul advised. 'I imagine he's been up all night. As for the crick in his neck – I expect he'll be too happy to even notice.'

'You're probably right,' she agreed. 'Let's find the nursery,' she suggested, eager to see her godson. A nurse directed them to the glass-fronted room, and they peered at the tiny swaddled bundle, able only to see a red, screwed-up little face and tiny fists.

'Hello, Sam,' Ginny said softly. 'Welcome to the world.'

Saul, after a brief glance at the baby, turned to watch Ginny; a slight, tender smile was curving her lips, a soft light of love and awe shone in her beautiful eyes. He slipped his arm around her waist and moved closer. His heart began to pound heavily as she fitted snugly against his side.

'This is where it all started for us,' he said. 'Well, not this exact hospital, of course.'

'I remember,' Ginny said, rather shortly. Saul cursed himself for his stupidity in reminding her of what a bastard he had been to her in the beginning.

'At least we're here for a good reason this time,' he went on quickly.

'The best,' Ginny agreed.

'Not quite the best,' he paused, and summoned up all his courage. 'It would be even better if I'd spent the night pacing up and down in the waiting-room instead of Barney.'

'Like hell you will,' Ginny retorted. 'You'll be in the delivery-room with me, holding my —' She stopped and blushed as a delighted smile spread over Saul's face.

'I love you so much, Ginny,' he said fervently, and she gazed up into the intensity of his dark green eyes.

'I know you do,' she whispered, and all her doubts had vanished. There was no other man for her.

Saul slowly bent his head and kissed her mouth, oh, so gently and sweetly. His hands moved to cup her face in his palms, touching her skin delicately, almost reverently.

'Please don't leave me again,' he said hoarsely, before deepening the kiss.

Ginny clung to him, thrilling to his touch, then his arms went around her and he gathered her close. She felt loved, protected, but so excited she trembled with desire. Saul never wanted to stop kissing her, but broke away to ask one very important question. However, Ginny spoke first.

'I know what my mother did to you, all those years ago. I haven't spoken to her since she told me.'

'Don't cut her out of your life,' Saul said, and

387

realized he meant it. 'After all, I can never thank her enough for giving birth to you,' he smiled.

'What about your parents?' Ginny asked anxiously. Saul shrugged.

'They can be happy for us, or not; it makes no difference to me. As far as I'm concerned we'll make our own family – just you, me, and a couple of those.' He nodded towards the row of cribs, as if choosing sandwiches from a snack bar, Ginny thought, and she laughed delightedly.

Saul smiled down at her. 'I love to hear you laugh, to watch you smile. I know I hurt you badly, but I promise I'll spend the rest of my life making you happy,' he said earnestly.

'I know that.' Ginny smiled up at him and his hold tightened.

'I have missed you so much; I can't bear another day without you. Will you marry me, Ginny? Please?' he asked huskily. She nodded happily.

'Yes, and I'm sorry I went away; I needed to think, but I love you . . .' Any further words were smothered by his kiss, and she surrendered herself to the flood of desire that swept over her, pressing so close to him that their bodies were almost one.

'If you keep that up, you'll be back here yourselves in nine months' time!' laughed the nurse who had directed them to the nursery.

Both Ginny and Saul heard her cheery comment, but neither was willing to break the kiss to make a reply. However, they shared the same thought: I hope she's right.

THE EXCITING NEW NAME
IN WOMEN'S FICTION!

PLEASE HELP ME TO HELP YOU!

Dear *Scarlet* Reader,

As Editor of *Scarlet* Books I want to make sure that the books I offer you every month are up to the high standards *Scarlet* readers expect. And to do that I need to know a little more about you and your reading likes and dislikes. So please spare a few minutes to fill in the short questionnaire on the following pages and send it to me.

     Looking forward to hearing from you,

Sally Cooper

Editor-in-Chief, *Scarlet*

QUESTIONNAIRE

Please tick the appropriate boxes to indicate your answers

1 Where did you get this Scarlet title?
Bought in supermarket ☐
Bought at my local bookstore ☐ Bought at chain bookstore ☐
Bought at book exchange or used bookstore ☐
Borrowed from a friend ☐
Other (please indicate) _____

2 Did you enjoy reading it?
A lot ☐   A little ☐   Not at all ☐

3 What did you particularly like about this book?
Believable characters ☐   Easy to read ☐
Good value for money ☐   Enjoyable locations ☐
Interesting story ☐   Modern setting ☐
Other _____

4 What did you particularly dislike about this book?
_____

5 Would you buy another Scarlet book?
Yes ☐   No ☐

6 What other kinds of book do you enjoy reading?
Horror ☐   Puzzle books ☐   Historical fiction ☐
General fiction ☐   Crime/Detective ☐   Cookery ☐
Other (please indicate) _____

7 Which magazines do you enjoy reading?
  1. _____
  2. _____
  3. _____

And now a little about you –
8 How old are you?
Under 25 ☐   25–34 ☐   35–44 ☐
45–54 ☐   55–64 ☐   over 65 ☐

cont.

9 What is your marital status?
   Single ☐   Married/living with partner ☐
   Widowed ☐   Separated/divorced ☐

10 What is your current occupation?
   Employed full-time ☐   Employed part-time ☐
   Student ☐   Housewife full-time ☐
   Unemployed ☐   Retired ☐

11 Do you have children? If so, how many and how old are they?
   _____
   _____

12 What is your annual household income?
   under $15,000 ☐ or £10,000 ☐
   $15–25,000 ☐ or £10–20,000 ☐
   $25–35,000 ☐ or £20–30,000 ☐
   $35–50,000 ☐ or £30–40,000 ☐
   over $50,000 ☐ or £40,000 ☐

Miss/Mrs/Ms _____

Address _____
   _____
   _____

Thank you for completing this questionnaire. Now tear it out – put it in an envelope and send it, before 31 August 1998, to:

Sally Cooper, Editor-in-Chief

USA/Can. address
SCARLET c/o London Bridge
85 River Rock Drive
Suite 202
Buffalo
NY 14207
USA

UK address/No stamp required
SCARLET
FREEPOST LON 3335
LONDON W8 4BR
Please use block capitals for address

SUSEC/3/98

Forthcoming *Scarlet* titles:

NO SWEETER CONFLICT Megan Paul
When she's sent to interview her 'cousin' Jacob Trevelyn, Florence tries to act with journalistic detachment, and at first succeeds. Until the fact that there's no blood tie between them – *and* her memories of their shared past – start getting in the way!

DANCE UNTIL MORNING Jan McDaniel
Claire Woolrich is used to a wealthy lifestyle . . . drop-out Wheeler Scully isn't at all impressed! They are forced to spend the night together, but surely Claire doesn't need to worry about making a lasting impression on this unsuitable man?

DARK DESIRE Maxine Barry
Dedicated to building up her career, Electra Stapleton has no time for romance. She is particularly wary of handsome stranger Haldane Fox. But Haldane is on a mission which will have an everlasting effect on Electra . . .

LOVERS DON'T LIE Chrissie Loveday
Simon Andrews might be very different from the student she originally fell in love with, but Jenna finds him even more irresistible second-time-around. Trouble is, Simon's now married with a child – isn't he? And with a secret in her past she *must* hide, Jenna *can't* give in to her desires.

JOIN THE CLUB!

Why not join the *Scarlet* Reader's Club – you can have four exciting new reads delivered to your door every month for only £9.99, plus TWO FREE BOOKS WITH YOUR FIRST MONTH'S ORDER!

Fill in the form below and tick your two free books from those listed:

1. *Never Say Never* by Tina Leonard □
2. *The Sins of Sarah* by Anne Styles □
3. *Wicked in Silk* by Andrea Young □
4. *Wild Lady* by Liz Fielding □
5. *Starstruck* by Lianne Conway □
6. *This Time Forever* by Vickie Moore □
7. *It Takes Two* by Tina Leonard □
8. *The Mistress* by Angela Drake □
9. *Come Home Forever* by Jan McDaniel □
10. *Deception* by Sophie Weston □
11. *Fire and Ice* by Maxine Barry □
12. *Caribbean Flame* by Maxine Barry □

ORDER FORM

SEND NO MONEY NOW. Just complete and send to SCARLET READERS' CLUB, FREEPOST, LON 3335, Salisbury SP5 5YW

Yes, I want to join the **SCARLET READERS' CLUB*** and have the convenience of 4 exciting new novels delivered directly to my door every month! Please send me my first shipment now for the unbelievable price of £9.99, plus my TWO special offer books absolutely free. I understand that I will be invoiced for this shipment and FOUR further *Scarlet* titles at £9.99 (including postage and packing) every month unless I cancel my order in writing. I am over 18.

Signed ....

Name (IN BLOCK CAPITALS) ....

Address (IN BLOCK CAPITALS) ....

....

Town .... Post Code ....

As a result of this offer your name and address may be passed on to other carefully selected companies. If you do not wish this, please tick this box□.

*Please note this offer applies to UK only.